Days of
AIR and
DARKNESS

By Katharine Kerr

Her novels of Deverry and the Westlands

DAGGERSPELL
DARKSPELL
THE BRISTLING WOOD
THE DRAGON REVENANT
A TIME OF EXILE
A TIME OF OMENS
DAYS OF BLOOD AND FIRE
DAYS OF AIR AND DARKNESS

Her works of science fiction

POLAR CITY BLUES
RESURRECTION

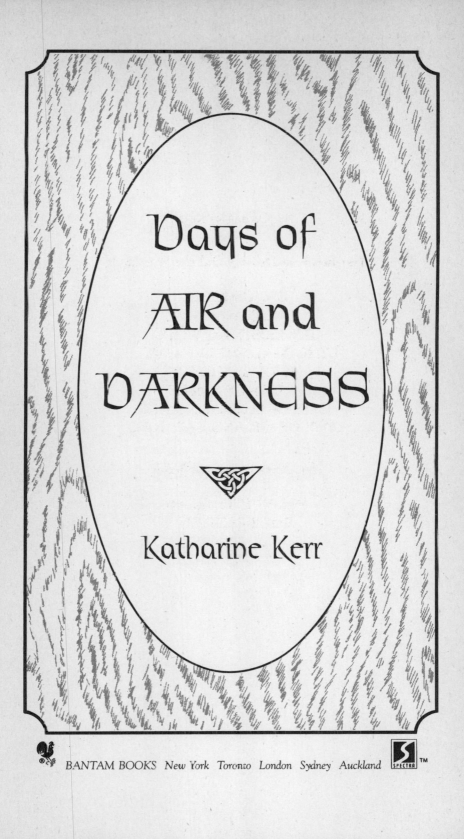

Days of
AIR and
DARKNESS

Katharine Kerr

BANTAM BOOKS *New York Toronto London Sydney Auckland*

DAYS OF AIR AND DARKNESS

A Bantam Spectra Book / August 1994

SPECTRA and the portrayal of a boxed "s" are trademarks of
Bantam Books, a division of
Bantam Doubleday Dell Publishing Group, Inc.

BOOK DESIGN BY ELLEN CIPRIANO

MAPS ON PAGES XIV–XV DESIGNED BY COMPASS PROJECTIONS

Library of Congress Cataloging-in-Publication Data
Kerr, Katharine.
Days of air and darkness / Katharine Kerr.
p.   cm.
ISBN 0-553-37289-0
1. Women—Fiction.   I. Title.
PS3561.E642D37   1994
813'.54—dc20   94-7032
                                                              CIP

Published simultaneously in the United States and Canada

PRINTED IN THE UNITED STATES OF AMERICA

BVG 0 9 8 7 6 5 4 3 2 1

For my aunt,
Beatrice Regina McClellan

ACKNOWLEDGMENTS

"Round up the usual suspects . . ."
Many thanks to Alis Rasmussen, Mark
Kreighbaum, Elizabeth Pomada, and Howard
Kerr, for invaluable advice and support.

CONTENTS

A Note on
the Pronunciation of
Deverry Words

The language spoken in Deverry, which we might well call Neo-Gaulish, is a member of the P-Celtic family. Although closely related to Welsh, Cornish, and Breton, it is by no means identical to any of these actual languages and should never be taken as such.

Vowels are divided by Deverry scribes into two classes: noble and common. Nobles have two pronunciations; commons, one.

A as in *father* when long; a shorter version of the same sound, as in *far*, when short.

O as in *bone* when long; as in *pot* when short.

W as the *oo* in *spook* when long; as in *roof* when short.

Y as the *i* in *machine* when long; as the *e* in *butter* when short.

E as in *pen*.

I as in *pin*.

U as in *pun*.

Vowels are generally long in stressed syllables; short in unstressed. Y is the primary exception to this rule. When it appears as the last letter of a word, it is always long whether that syllable is stressed or not.

Diphthongs generally have one consistent pronunciation.

AE as the *a* in *mane*.

AI as in *aisle*.

AU as the *ow* in *how*.

EO as a combination of *eh* and *oh*.

EW as in Welsh, a combination of *eh* and *oo*.

IE as in *pier*.

OE as the *oy* in *boy*.

UI as the North Welsh *wy*, a combination of *oo* and *ee*. Note that OI is never a diphthong, but is two distinct sounds, as in *carnoic* (KAR-noh-ik).

Consonants are mostly the same as in English, with these exceptions:

C is always hard as in *cat*.

G is always hard as in *get*.

DD is the voiced *th* as in *thin* or *breath*, but the voicing is more pronounced than in English. It is opposed to TH, the unvoiced sound as in *th* or *breathe*. (This is the sound that the Greeks called the Celtic tau.)

R is heavily rolled.

RH is a voiceless R, approximately pronounced as if it were spelled *hr* in Deverry proper. In Eldidd, the sound is fast becoming indistinguishable from R.

DW, GW, and TW are single sounds, as in *Gwendolen* or *twit*.

Y is never a consonant.

I before a vowel at the beginning of a word is consonantal, as it is in the plural ending *-ion*, pronounced *yawn*.

Doubled consonants are both sounded clearly, unlike in English. Note, however, that DD is a *single letter*, not a doubled consonant.

Accent is generally on the penultimate syllable, but compound words and place names are often an exception to this rule.

•   •   •

I have used this system of transcription for the Bardekian, Dwarvish, and Elvish alphabets as well as the Deverrian, which is, of course, based upon the Greek rather than the Roman model. As faithful readers of this series know, my decision to use this simple approach rather than the full scholarly apparatus developed at the University of Aberwyn has been roundly attacked of late in the academic press. Such readers will be glad to hear that the lawsuit against those attackers, in particular a certain Elvish professor of Elvish, filed on my behalf by my publishers, is proceeding nicely through the courts in Aberwyn, where in due time it will reach the gwerbret's malover and be resolved, once and for all, and in our favor, or so I may hope.

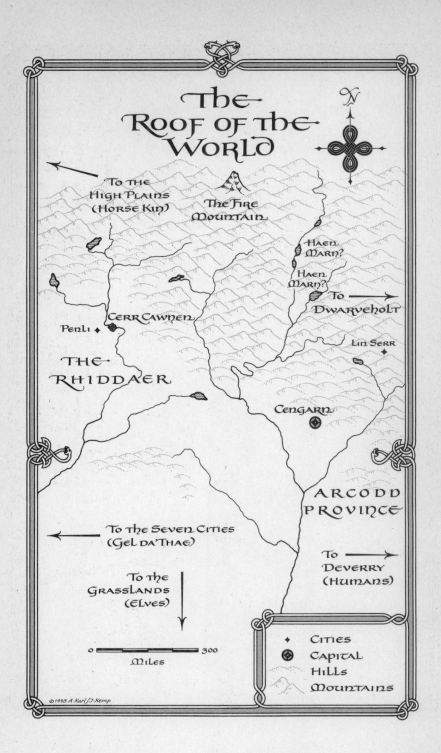

The
ROOF OF THE
WORLD

N

To the
High Plains
(Horse Kin)

The Fire
Mountain

Haen
Marn?

Haen
Marn?

To
Dwarveholt

Cerr Cawnen

Penli ◆

Lin Serr ◆

THE
RHIDDAER

Cengarn

ARCODD
PROVINCE

To the Seven Cities
(Gel da'Thae)

To
Deverry
(Humans)

To the
Grasslands
(Elves)

0 ━━━━━━━ 300
Miles

◆ Cities
◉ Capital
Hills
Mountains

© 1993 A. Karl / J. Kemp

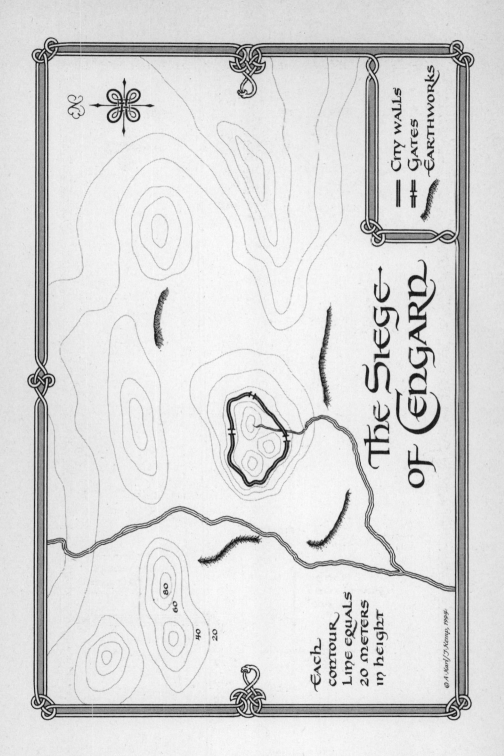

The Siege of Engard

Each contour Line equals 20 meters in height

© A. Karl / J. S. Kemp, 1994

City walls
Gates
Earthworks

80
60
40
20

PROLOGUE
The Northlands, 1116

ALBUS

The opposite of Rubeus in all things, thus generally an omen for good. Yet when it falls into the House of Lead, pertaining to matters of war, it does signify days of air and darkness, and an evil upon the land.

—The Omenbook of Gwarn,
Loremaster

Under a starry night two men and a dragon camped by a river. Though the wind blew warm, the men had built a fire for light, and the great wyrm lay her head as close to it as she dared. The rest of her glittering body and folded wings stretched away into shadow. Well over twenty feet long, not counting the tail curled round her haunches, the greenish-black dragon kept raising her head to look about her and sniff the summer wind. On the opposite side of the fire sat a young man of the Mountain People, though he was tall for one of them at five-and-a-half feet. He had high dwarven cheekbones and a flat nose, narrow eyes, shadowed under heavy dwarven brows, and his hair was a brown close to black, as was his close-cropped beard. Every time the dragon went on guard, he would start up, then mutter a curse under his breath and sit again.

"Rori?" he said finally. "What be troubling the beast?"

Rhodry Maelwaedd stopped his restless pacing and walked back into the pool of firelight. He was well over six-feet-tall but built straight from shoulder to hip, and his raven-dark hair and cornflower blue eyes marked him for an Eldidd man, even though that province lay hundreds of miles to the south, all the way across the far-flung kingdom of Deverry. Weather-beaten, grizzled, Rhodry was still a handsome man, and he looked human enough—at first glance, anyway.

"I don't know," he said. "It's a pity you never learned the Elvish tongue, Enj. It's the only thing she speaks."

"And where would I have come across elves, all the way up here? Well, before I met you, anyway."

"True spoken." Rhodry turned to the dragon and began speaking in the language of his father's people. "What's wrong? Do you smell trouble on the wind?"

"What? No, not yet, anyway." The dragon's voice rumbled and growled like a turning millstone. "But I like to keep a bit of a guard."

"Sensible enough, and my thanks."

She rippled her long wings, then rested her head on her coppery-green paws, though she kept an eye open to watch him. On the third finger of his right hand, Rhodry wore a silver ring, a flat band inscribed on the outside with a design of roses and on the inside, with her true name.

"Naught's wrong." Rhodry sat down on the ground a few feet from Enj and spoke in the rough patois of Deverrian and the mountain tongue that they both could understand. "She's just troubled, like we are."

"It's been a miserable bad day, truly."

Rhodry laughed, a high mad chortle of a berserker's howl that made Enj wince and the dragon raise her head to hiss like a thousand cats.

"You must admit, Enj old lad, that you've a fine gift for understatement. You've lost home and kin both, and I've lost a woman I loved with all my heart and soul, and what do you call it? A miserable bad day. Well, truly, it was that, I suppose."

"My apologies, then!" Enj snarled like the dragon. "But ye gods, what do you expect me to do? Orate like one of your wretched bards?"

Rhodry wiped his grin away.

"I'm sorry. Forgive me."

The two men stared at each other for a long moment; then Enj held out his hand. Rhodry shook it. His mouth set hard against mourning, Enj returned to watching flames dance along logs.

Rhodry's heavy sword belt lay beside him on the ground. He

3

pulled a dagger free of its sheath and began fiddling with it, polishing the narrow blade on his sleeve, holding it up to catch the light. When he flicked it with a thumbnail, the blade rang like silver, though it was as hard as steel. The dragon's coppery eye followed every glint.

Their camp lay in a broad valley where a river flowed through scattered pines and high grass. All round rose the mountains of the Roof of the World, in those days untrod and unsettled by either dwarf or man. Framing the valley, hills climbed, dark with trees, while beyond them rose the high peaks, their perpetual snow gleaming a faint silver in the light from the overarching stars. Down from the foothills, the night wind brought them the sound of wolves howling on the hunt. Arzosah raised her massive head to listen.

"They're moving away from us," she remarked. "I do wish you'd sheathe that knife, Rori. It's driving me daft, watching you play with it."

He smiled and closed one broad hand round its hilt.

"You know," she went on, "if you need someone to hate, you could blame Evandar. I do."

"For what? The vanishing of Haen Marn?"

"Nah, nah, nah. What do I care about your stupid island? It wasn't my home. I blame him for the troubling of me."

"I should have known." Rhodry translated this exchange for the puzzled Enj, then turned back to her. "Well, if he hadn't given me this little ring, you'd be all nice and snug, sure enough, lolling round in your fire mountain and chewing on a cow bone or two."

"Don't mock! It's bad enough you've enslaved me. Don't mock me, too."

"Watch your courtesies when you speak to me."

She whined, rolling an enormous copper eye to the stars. He held up his hand to catch the firelight on the ring.

"My apologies," she said. "You're a harsh man, Rhodry Dragonmaster."

"I intend to stay that way and stay alive."

She whined again, flopping her head onto her paws. He glanced at Enj to find him utterly expressionless.

4

"We should turn in," Rhodry said. "Think you can sleep?"

"Not without dreaming. Let's let the fire burn awhile."

"Very well." He looked at the dragon, who was quietly snarling to herself. "Still thinking of Evandar?"

"Yes. If ever I find him again, I'm going to eat him. Munch crunch gobble gone."

"A fine sentiment, but I'm afraid you can't really eat him. He doesn't have a real body, not one made out of meat, I mean, like you and me."

"Just like him! The final cheat of all!"

"A spiteful beast, isn't she?"

The voice came out of the dark beyond the fire. His dagger in hand, Rhodry scrambled to his feet as a figure strolled toward them. A silver glow like moonlight hung in the air round him so that they could see him clearly, a tall fellow, slender, dressed in a long green tunic and buckskin trousers. His hair was the bright yellow of daffodils, his lips were the red of sour cherries, and his eyes were an unnatural turquoise blue, bright as gemstones. Yet the strangest thing of all were his ears, long and delicately pointed, furled tight like a fern in spring.

"Evandar!" Rhodry hissed.

The dragon slapped her tail upon the ground with a dull boom like an avalanche. He could hear her scuffling to her feet behind him.

"The very one." Evandar made him a bow, then raised one hand to point a long and slender finger at the dragon. "Arzosah Sothy Lorezohaz! Remember that I know your name."

She snarled, opening her mouth wide, but she held her place. Enj crouched by the fire and stared at their visitor.

"What brings you here?" With a nod Enj's way to include him, Rhodry spoke in the Deverrian patois.

"A warning for you," Evandar said in the same. "Are you heading south?"

"We are. Cengarn's under siege. Did you know that?"

"Of course. I know everything that's worth knowing about this war, Rhodry Maelwaedd."

5

"Oh, do you now? Then where's the relieving army? We'll be looking to join up with it."

"Go to Lin Serr first. Garin and his troop of axmen haven't left yet."

"What? I'd have thought them long gone."

"There's an obstacle in their way." Evandar flashed him a grin. "A small army's tramping round the countryside. Horsekin."

Enj winced and swore.

"The filthy bastards!" Rhodry said, half-laughing. "I want a chance at killing me a few."

"You'll get it," Evandar said. "But stay on guard while you're flying south, because there's some peculiar birds who soar between worlds, and I think me one of them means you harm."

"Shape-changers!"

Evandar smiled, briefly.

"It's the raven I'd watch out for. A bird of ill omen, always, but particularly ill-omened is the raven I have in mind. You're wearing some sort of talisman of hiding, aren't you?"

"I am."

"I thought so. No doubt your enemies are having a fair bit of trouble scrying you out, and so they'll have to come look for you in the flesh. Be careful, very careful. The raven woman's as dangerous as they come."

"We'll keep alert, then, and my thanks. Answer me somewhat, will you?"

"Probably not, but you can ask. I only set riddles. I don't answer them for naught."

The dragon swung her head his way and growled. Oho! Rhodry thought.

"All right, then," Rhodry said aloud. "Why would you come to warn me? I don't recall ever doing anything for you, and yet you've helped me a good many times now."

"I don't know. It's a riddle I've set for myself, a riddle as new and shiny as a gold coin, and here I never meant to do such a thing." Evandar tilted his head a little to one side, suddenly solemn, and yet it seemed that he was acting the role of a man thinking rather than

6

truly thinking something through. "I suppose there's only one thing the answer could be."

"And that is?"

Evandar laid a hand along the side of Rhodry's face, then kissed him full on the mouth. His hand felt oddly cool, more like silk than flesh, but the kiss was warm enough. Rhodry could neither move nor think till Evandar released him.

"That could be it, indeed." Evandar took one step back and vanished, suddenly and utterly gone, without so much as the flicker of a shadow.

Rhodry raised his hand and touched the dagger to his mouth, stood there narrow-eyed and speechless while Enj goggled and Arzosah made the long rumbling noise that did her for a laugh. Rhodry turned on her with a snarl.

"Oh, stop your cackling, Wyrm! Why didn't you tell me you could speak the language of men?"

"You never asked, Dragonmaster." She stopped rumbling, but he suspected her of doing whatever it was dragons did when they smirked. "So. Evandar isn't real flesh and blood, is he? I never would have guessed it."

"I said hold your tongue!" Rhodry flung his hand up to make the ring flash. She whined and crouched like a kicked dog. "Oh, my apologies. I shouldn't be taking it out on you."

"A harsh man, but a just one." She relaxed with a toss of her massive head. "I could be enslaved by worse."

There remained Enj. It took Rhodry a long moment to make himself look his friend in the face.

"That wretched wyrm," Enj said, "pretending she couldn't understand a word I said, making you babble back and forth like an ambassador!"

Rhodry let out his breath in a sigh. The matter, he knew, would stay closed between them from now on. He sat down again and leaned back against his bedroll.

"And what or who is this Evandar fellow?" Enj said.

"I'm not truly sure. He has the ears and eyes of a full-blooded elf, but I've been told by sorcerers that he's naught of the sort.

7

Riddles, indeed!" Rhodry spat into the fire. "They say he's some kind of spirit who's never been born, and that he lives in some kind of magical country that lies beyond the world, not that it's floating in the air or suchlike—just 'beyond,' they say. None of it makes a bit of sense to me, curse them all! But Evandar's got dweomer, all right, the way other men have blood running in their veins."

The dragon clacked her fangs in a sound that, he suspected, did duty as a snicker.

"Indeed?" Enj considered for a long while. "Do you think he'd know where Haen Marn's gone off to?"

"I've no idea, but I suspect that if anyone does, it'd be him. Maybe I'll get a chance to ask him." Rhodry shot the dragon a murderous glance. "And no smart remarks from you."

Arzosah curled her paw and contemplated her claws, but he could have sworn she was smiling.

After a few hours' troubled sleep, they woke at dawn. Arzosah clambered to her feet and stretched her wings, throwing huge shadows over the entire campsite, then folded them back and waddled down to the river to drink, which took a while because she lapped water like a cat rather than sucking like a cow. The men sat by the ash of their dead fire and shared stale flatbread and a strip of venison jerky.

"How long till we reach Lin Serr?" Enj said.

"On her back? No more than three days, more likely a pair."

"There's some food left, but not much. If we could wait a day, I could catch us more."

"Truly, I've never seen a man as good as you at foraging in the wild country. But time's short."

Enj nodded, glancing away upriver, where once the magical lake and island of Haen Marn had sat upon the countryside like a bowl on a table. By its dweomer it had vanished, taking itself away from marauders and the dangers of war—how or where, they didn't know. With it, though, had gone Enj's kin and clan, his home and his entire life, leaving behind only a long stretch of empty grass, green in the bright sun.

"I was just thinking," Enj said in a shaking voice, "that it may be that the isle will return, with the danger gone off south."

"Think it likely?"

Enj shrugged. His eyes were brimming tears.

"Tell me somewhat," Rhodry went on. "Have you ever marched to war?"

Enj shook his head no.

"I thought as much. Here, why don't you let me take what food we have, and you stay here to hunt and wait. I've seen you in wild country, and I know that you can live here for years if you have to. If the war ends soon, I'll come back. If Haen Marn returns, you come south and find me."

"Will you think me a coward if I stay, Rori?"

"Never, my friend. Never that."

Enj started to speak, then wept, covering his face with his hands. Rhodry got up and strolled down to the river to join Arzosah.

"The small creature's sniveling again," she remarked.

"He's no warrior. Let him weep. If my soul weren't dead, I'd weep, too."

"Your soul is dead?" She swung her massive head round fast to look at him. Water drops gleamed among the scales on her chin.

"Just a way of speaking."

"Never ever say such a horrid thing again! It curdles my blood, just hearing the words. Don't you realize that such can happen to men, and that it's the most unclean thing of all under the sky?" She shuddered with a swishing of wings. "Horrible!"

"Well, my apologies. I feel like my heart's died, then, if that suits you better."

"It does. A dead heart is sad, but not horrible. Rather common, actually. Males do kill their own hearts over losing the females they love." She sighed in a long rustle of wings. "Was this Angmar the only woman you've ever loved?"

"Do you care?"

"I do. We females like knowing these things."

"Well, then, no, she wasn't the only one. I loved someone named Jill when I was very young, but she left me."

"And that's sad, too. Was it for another man?"

"It wasn't, but for the dweomer."

"Ah! Naught to be done about that! When it calls, you follow."

"So she told me."

"You sound bitter still."

Rhodry shrugged and watched the river flow. He could see the rippling reflection of her massive head, watching him.

"I've lost a mate," she said at last. "My heart didn't die, me being female and all, but his loss wounds me still. For your Angmar's sake as well as his, I'll eat the first Horsekin we slay."

It was, Rhodry supposed, an honor of sorts.

"Then I thank you. Ah, well, I shouldn't be surprised that I've lost her—Angmar, I mean. It's better she's gone, for her sake."

"Well, if the wretched Horsekin had found Haen Marn—"

"Just so. No doubt my one true love sent them. She's the jealous sort, truly, which is why I've lost every woman I've ever loved. If I'd dared to go on spurning her, she would have sent Angmar to the Otherlands. She's a great queen, you know, and she could have done it easily. I've been marked for her love from the beginning of my life, no doubt about that, and I've lost all her rivals."

"And just what are you talking about?" The dragon swung her head round to glare at him. "What great queen?"

"The one woman I've ever loved who's truly loved me in return." Rhodry flung one hand in the air in salute. "My lady, Death. Oh, we've had a long fine affair of it, Death and I, and always have I served her well, sending her many a pretty gift from battle. Some day she'll take pity on me, like she takes pity on all men, and let me sleep in her cold, cold arms. I tell you, Wyrm, I begin to long for her more and more."

Arzosah stared at him, her huge and alien eyes unreadable. At length he laughed, but it was just a normal sort of chuckle.

"If you've drunk enough," he said, "it's time to fly south."

"I suppose you're going to put those nasty ropes round me again."

"I am. But not as many this time, because Enj will be staying here."

"Well, that's one thing to the good, then. He'd get so beastly sick, and I was always afraid he was going to soil my scales with one of his ends or the other. Are you sure I can't just eat him and put him out of his misery?"

"Very sure. Now come along."

As Rhodry started to walk back to the camp, dweomer touched him as tangibly as a cold hand, then let go and vanished. He suddenly felt as if someone were watching or trying to watch him before this disembodied gaze swept on and disappeared. He swore aloud.

"What is it?" Arzosah snapped. "You've turned white."

"Let's get out of here. Someone's looking for us, just like Evandar said, and I don't much like it."

"I don't suppose any creature in its right mind would. Here! I just thought of somewhat. You've got that lovely talisman round your neck, so how did Evandar find us? Unless, of course—" she paused for a clack of fangs—"unless love guided him."

"Hold your black and ugly tongue, Wyrm, or I'll order you into that river!"

Rhodry turned on his heel and strode back to camp, with her padding after in a rumble of laughter.

Every morning at dawn, Jill would leave her chamber in the broch of the gwerbret's dun. She'd trudge up the five floors worth of circling staircase and climb through the trapdoor onto the flat roof of the main tower, which had become an arsenal of sorts. All round the edge stood little pyramids of stones, ready for a last desperate defense, and bound sheaves of arrows, wrapped in oiled hides to keep off the rain. While she caught her breath, she would look out and consider their situation. Like an island from a shallow sea, the three hills of the city of Cengarn rose from its besiegers, who spread out on all sides and camped just beyond bowshot from the town walls.

Cengarn lay in a beautiful situation for defense. To the north, across a narrow valley, lay broken ground lower than the city itself, and beyond that strip rose hills that would have taken two armies to secure against a counterforce. Even though the invaders had to place

11

men on the north ground to complete their line, those troops were exposed and vulnerable. To the east, the broken ground became a long ridge, where white tents decked out with red banners stood— Jill suspected that the important leaders of the Horsekin sheltered there.

To the south and west the land fell away, leaving the city perched on the top of cliffs. At the western edge of town, where the dun itself stood, any climb up would require ropes and stakes, while to the south, the road ran steep and narrow. Below the cliffs in those directions stretched a wide plain, where the bulk of the army camped, comfortable but vulnerable to attack when the relieving army finally arrived. To protect their men on the plain, the Horsekin were digging ditches and piling up earthworks, or rather, their human slaves were doing the digging and piling. Since they depended on their heavy cavalry and needed to ensure free movement for their own horsemen, they would never be able to make a solid ring all the way round the camp. Rather, they'd placed earthworks as baffles more than walls to protect vulnerable points.

Inside the city walls seethed potential chaos. Crammed into every valley among the three hills, lining every street, crowding every open space, townsfolk and refugees from the farms roundabout huddled amidst cattle and sheep, dray horses and chickens. They'd been living that way for weeks now, and the gwerbret's town marshals had recruited some of the men from their lord's warband to help keep order. Fights were breaking out over food and water, though for now at least the town ran no danger of starving, and over space, a scarcity indeed. Filth, human and animal, was piling up, swept or carried down to line the inside of the walls. In a pinch, it could become another weapon, hurled by basket or catapult. Even up at the dun, which stood behind its own walls on the highest hill, the stench rose thick. From long practice, Jill could ignore it, but the threat of plague was another knife at the city's throat.

She herself felt none too strong these days, nor did she look it. Her hair, cropped off like a lad's, was perfectly white, and her face was thin, too thin, really, so that her blue eyes seemed enormous, dominating her face the way a child's do. Overall, she was shockingly gaunt, not that such was so unusual for a woman who was over seventy. What worried her was the shaking fever she carried in her blood, an unwelcome memento from a long-ago sojourn in tropical lands. Even though she was the greatest master of dweomer that the kingdom had ever seen, she could cure herself with neither magic nor the medicines known in those days. All she had to fight it was her strength of will.

Every day, before she began her magical work, she would try to scry out Rhodry. Normally, since she'd known him so long and so well, she would have seen his image simply by turning her mind his way; her vision would have appeared on any convenient dappled thing—the clouds in the sky, sunlight dancing on a bucket of water, trees tossing in a wind—with barely an effort on her part. These days, though, she could only summon a haze as thick and gray as smoke where an image should have been. Although she couldn't know, she could guess that he wore some powerful talisman, whose bound spirit worked to hide him. On the morning that Rhodry took leave of Enj, though, her scrying just happened to coincide with Rhodry's thinking about her, and for the briefest of moments she caught a glimpse of him.

"At least he's alive," she said aloud. "And I'll thank the gods for that."

It was, of course, perfectly natural to fear for a fighting man at the beginning of a war, but Jill had a further concern. Some months past, she'd received in a hideous flash of ill-knowing a glimpse of bitter Wyrd hanging over him as if upon dark wings. The omen had come in such a rush of certainty, like a brand burned into her mind, that she knew the vision for a true one. Yet even if he'd been close by, there was nothing she could say to him, no warning she could deliver. Mentioning such an evil omen to a man might well bring it about, just by planting the thought in his mind that he was doomed. She could only try to protect him as best she might when the event came upon him.

At the moment, she could spare little time for worrying about the man she once had loved and still considered a friend. Her real work was guarding the city by reinforcing a peculiar sort of battlement round it. In the brightening dawn, servants were hurrying round the ward far below on their various errands, and from their barracks the warband strolled out, yawning and stretching, occasionally looking up her way, but the dun had seen enough dweomer by now to put up with her standing on the tops of towers and doing odd things. She walked into the center of the circular roof and focused her mind on the blue light of the etheric.

It seemed that the bright sunlight round her faded and a different light rose, dim and silvery, though through it she could clearly see the physical world. In this bluish flux, she raised her arms high and called upon the power of the Holy Light that stands behind all the shadowy figures and personified forces that men call gods. Its visible symbol came to her in a glowing spear that pierced her from head to foot. For a moment, she stood motionless, paying it homage, then stretched her arms out shoulder high, bringing the light with them to form a shaft across her chest. As she stood within the cross, the light swelled, strengthening her, then slowly faded of its own will.

When it was gone, she lowered her arms, then visualized a sword of light in her right hand. Once the image lived apart from her will, she circled the roof, walking deosil, and used the sword to draw a huge ring of golden light in the sky. As the ring settled to earth, it sheeted out, forming a burning wall round the entire town of Cengarn. Three times round she went, until the wall lived on the etheric of its own will. At each ordinal point, she put a seal in the shape of a five-pointed star made of blue fire. After the sigils of the kings of the elements blazed at the four directions, she spread the light until it was not a ring but an enormous sphere of gold, roofing over the dun and the town both and extending down under them as well. Two last seals at zenith and nadir, and Cengarn hung in the many-layered worlds like a bubble in glass.

At the end of the working, she withdrew the force from the image of the sword, dissolving it, then stamped three times on the roof. Sunlight brightened round her, and she could hear the sounds of the dun, shut out earlier by sheer concentration. The portion of the sphere above the earth, however, remained visible—that is, visible to someone with dweomer sight. Such sight could never penetrate the glowing shell, and everyone inside the sphere would be safe from prying eyes as well as from spirits sent by their enemies.

Before she left, she made one last attempt to find Rhodry. This time, nothing—not one scrap of vision, not the slightest sense of place. With a shake of her head, she went down to the noise and bustle of the great hall, where men talked in low voices of matters of war.

Rhodry was at that moment flying south from the Roof of the World on dragonback, which is not the smoothest sort of traveling in the world. Each wing beat thrust Arzosah forward in a rolling motion, at times close to a jump, especially when she was gaining height. Sitting on her neck or shoulder felt like standing on the prow of a small boat heading out from shore against the waves. After some days of practice, though, Rhodry had found his balance. Rather than trying to straddle her neck like a horse, he knelt and sat forward, steadied by his knees, resting as much on his own heels as her flesh so that he could roll with her wing beats. Bracing himself against them was futile. At times, he would let go the ropes, first with one hand, then with both, to see how secure he really was.

What he needed to learn next, he realized, was fighting from dragonback. He carried a curved elvish hunting bow which might serve him in battle, though he wanted to fight close in as well as from an archer's distance. A spear would do splendidly, he decided. He could brace himself between two scales and thrust with a long spear as his Deverrian ancestors were said to have done back in the Dawntime, before they'd left their original homeland, that mysterious country called Gallia, now lost to their descendants forever.

By leaning well forward and screaming at the top of his lungs, Rhodry could talk to Arzosah in fits and starts.

"Have you seen any traces of Horsekin?"

"What do you mean, traces? You can see the road they took as well as I."

He sighed. He was learning that she could be very literal minded.

"I mean, have you seen any Horsekin? Now, I mean. Ones we can fight."

"Oh. No."

"Well, keep an eye open, will you?"

"Of course, I— Here! What's this?"

She flung up her head and sniffed the wind, then with a curve of her wings beat backwards to slow and steady herself in midflight.

"Horsekin?" Rhodry said.

"Dweomer! I smell it strong!"

Rhodry swung his head round, scanning for enemies. He, too, could feel a sensation for which smell seemed as apt a metaphor as any, a tingling in the air that transmitted itself to the skin of his face and hands. For the briefest of moments, the sky ahead of them seemed to swirl as if a wisp of smoke were blowing by. With a flap of wings and a harsh cry, an enormous raven materialized dead ahead of them, as suddenly as if it had come through an invisible door.

For a moment, as it hovered, beating its wings to keep its place, the giant bird stared straight at him. Behind the round, gold eyes, Rhodry could see the human soul of the shape-changer—he was sure of it, irrational though it was—and feel the malice therein. All at once, he recognized her. The memory rose in his mind like a piece of flotsam, long drowned, that a storm wave catches and brings up into the sun for one brief moment, only to let it sink again. But he remembered remembering and knew that somehow, against all reason, he recognized this tormented soul and knew it to be female.

The raven shrieked and dodged. Arzosah flicked her head to one side and snapped, the huge jaws closing with a clack like a wagon gate, but the raven let herself fall away, fluttering helplessly as she spiraled down. With a roar, Arzosah dropped after. The raven twisted in midair and vanished. A lone feather twirled down to the grasslands below. Arzosah flapped once, turned, and settled on the ground nearby.

"Where did she go?" Rhodry slammed a frustrated fist into his palm. "We almost had her."

"Off to Evandar's country, most like. This creature has dweomer, Master, power such as I've never smelt before."

When the dragon stretched out her neck, Rhodry slid down to the ground, then paused.

"How can you smell dweomer?"

"It's like the air after a storm when lightning's struck, all clean and tingling, but a danger smell, too."

"Huh. Interesting. I think I smelt it myself, there for a moment."

"That's your elven blood. All of the People know magic in their hearts."

Rhodry retrieved the black feather, like a real feather in every respect save one, that it stretched a good three feet long. His memory taunted him. How could he recognize such a powerful creature without putting a name or time to their meeting? With a shake of his head, he ran the feather through his fingers, felt it turn cold, seem to run like water, tingle in his hands. He yelped and dropped it. On the grass lay a long strand of a woman's raven-black hair, glistening with blue highlights in the sunlight.

"Ah," Arzosah said. "She's turned herself back, wherever she is."

Rhodry mouthed an oath.

"Do you want to hear a strange thing, Master?"

"By all means. It seems to be the day for them."

Arzosah rumbled in her version of laughter.

"So it is, so it is. But when she dropped into our world and looked at you, I could have sworn she recognized you."

Borne on its inner wave, the memory rose again, and this time, the image of a face came with it. Impossible! he thought. It could never be her, never! And yet in a wordless way, he knew perfectly well that it was, that he had met again an enemy from many years past, when he and Jill were young. It had happened, in fact, during their very first year of riding the long road together. And a strange affair that was, he thought, as soaked with evil magic as a battlefield is with blood, strange then and stranger to look back on now, when I know a thing or two more than I did then.

17

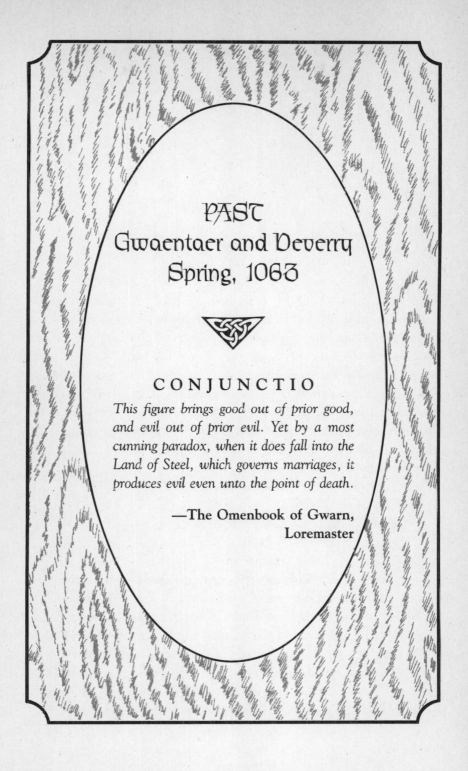

PAST
Gwaentaer and Deverry
Spring, 1063

CONJUNCTIO

This figure brings good out of prior good, and evil out of prior evil. Yet by a most cunning paradox, when it does fall into the Land of Steel, which governs marriages, it produces evil even unto the point of death.

—The Omenbook of Gwarn,
Loremaster

1

THE TAVERN CATERED, IT seemed, to shabby young men, laughing and talking among themselves—craftsmen's apprentices from the look of them. Jill propped one foot up on a bench and settled her back against the curved stone wall. Since she and her man both carried the silver dagger, the mark of a notoriously poor band of wandering mercenaries, the other customers seemed willing to ignore them, but she preferred to take no chances. Besides, even though she wore men's clothing and had her blond hair cropped off like a lad's, she was very beautiful back in those days, and men had seen through her ruse before.

"What's so wrong?" Rhodry whispered.

"They're all thieves."

"Ye gods! Do you mean we're drinking in a—"

"Shush, you dolt!"

"My apologies, but why are we—"

"Not so loud! What other tavern in Caenmetyn is going to serve a pair of silver daggers? It's a fancy sort of town, my love."

Rhodry studied the crowd and scowled. Even in a black mood, when Rhodry was young (and he was barely one-and-twenty that year), his elven blood was obvious to those who knew how to look; his face, handsome all through his life, was so finely drawn in those days, with a full mouth and deep-set eyes, that it would have seemed girlish if it weren't for the nicks and scars from old fighting.

20

"Which way shall we ride tomorrow?" he said at last. "I've got to find a hire soon."

"True enough, because we're blasted low on coin. You should be able to find a caravan leaving here, though."

"Ah, by the black hairy ass of the Lord of Hell! I'd rather find some lord with a feud going and ride a war. I'm as sick as I can be of playing nursemaid to stinking merchants and their stinking mules! I'm a warrior born and bred, not a wretched horseherder!"

"How can you be sick of it? You've only ever guarded one caravan in your life."

When he scowled again, she let the subject drop.

Oddly enough, about an hour later, someone offered Rhodry a very different type of hire. Jill was keeping a watch on the door when she saw a man slip into the tavern room. All muffled in a gray cloak, with the hood up against the chill of a spring night, he was stout, on the tallish side. When he approached the table, the hood slipped, giving Jill a glimpse of blue eyes and a face handsome in a weak sort of way.

"I heard there was a silver dagger in town." He spoke with a rolling Cerrmor accent. "I might have a hire for you, lad."

"Indeed?" Rhodry gestured at the bench on the opposite side of the table. "Sit down, good sir."

He took the seat, then studied them both for a moment, his eyes flicking to Jill, as if her standing while he sat made him nervous. Since he was wearing striped brigga and an expensive linen shirt under the cloak, she figured he might be a prosperous craftsman, perhaps a man who made incense for the temples, judging by the scent that lingered around him. All at once, Jill's gray gnome popped into manifestation on the table. He had his skinny arms crossed over his narrow chest, and his long-nosed face was set in a disapproving glare for the stranger, who of course saw nothing. The stranger leaned forward in a waft of Bardek cinnamon.

"I have an enemy, you see," he whispered. "He's insulted me, mocked me, dared me to stop him, and he knows blasted well that I've got no skill with a blade. I'll pay very high for proof of his death."

21

"Oh, indeed?" Rhodry's dark blue eyes flashed with rage. "I'm no paid murderer. If you want to challenge him to an honor duel and formally choose me for your champion, I might take you up on it, but only if this fellow can fight and fight well."

Biting his lip hard, the stranger glanced round. The gnome stuck out its tongue at him, then disappeared.

"An honor duel's impossible. He, uh, well, won't respond to my challenge."

"Then I'm not your man."

"Ah, but they always say that silver daggers have their price. Two gold pieces."

Jill nearly choked on her ale. Two gold pieces would buy a prosperous farm and its livestock as well.

"I wouldn't do it for a thousand," Rhodry snapped. "But at that price, doubtless you'll find someone else to do your murdering for you."

The fellow rose and dashed for the door, as if the dolt had just realized that he'd said too much to a perfect stranger. Jill noticed one of the thieves, a slender fellow with a shock of mousy-brown hair, slip out after him, only to return in a few minutes. He sat down companionably across from Rhodry without so much as a by-your-leave.

"You were right to turn him down, Silver Dagger. I just talked to the idiot, and he let it slip that this enemy of his is a noble lord." The thief rolled his eyes heavenward. "As if anyone would touch a job like that! If one of the noble-born got himself done in, wouldn't the town be crawling with the gwerbret's marshals, poking their stinking noses into every corner and wondering how the likes of us made our living? You silver daggers can just ride on again, but us guildsmen have to live here, you know."

"True spoken," Jill broke in. "Here, did he say where this noble lord lived?"

"Not to put a name to it, but I got the feeling, just from a few things he said, like, that it was somewhere to the south."

After the thief took himself off again, Jill sat down next to Rhodry on the unsteady bench.

22

"Thinking of riding south, my love?"

"I am. It gripes my soul, thinking of one of the noble-born murdered by some base-born coward. Wonder if we can find our plump little killer again?"

But although they searched the town before they rode out, they never saw or smelled him.

The late afternoon sun, flecked with dust motes, streamed in the windows of the great hall. At the far side of the round room, a couple of members of the warband were wagering on the dice, while others sipped ale and talked about very little. Tieryn Dwaen of Bringerun lounged back in his carved chair, put his feet up on the honor table, and watched the first flies of spring as he sipped a tankard of ale. His guest, Lord Cadlew of Marcbyr, sat at his right and fussed over a dog from the pack lying round their feet. A fine, sleek greyhound of the breed known as gwertroedd, this dog was new since Cadlew's last visit, or at least, the last one when he'd had time to pay attention to something as mundane as a dog.

"Do you want him?" Dwaen said. "He's yours if you do."

"Splendidly generous of you, but not necessary."

"Go ahead, take him. He's the last thing my father ever bought, and for all that he's a splendid hunter, I'd just as soon have him out of my sight."

Cadlew looked up with a troubled toss of his blond head.

"Well, in that case I'll take him with me when I ride home. My thanks, Dwaen."

Dwaen shrugged and signaled the page, Laryn, to come pour more ale. The boy was the son of one of his vassals sent to the tieryn for his training, and raising him was now Dwaen's responsibility. Even though it was over a month since he'd inherited, Dwaen still found it terrifying that he was the tieryn, responsible for the de-mesne and the lives of everyone on it.

"You know," Cadlew said, and very slowly and carefully, "I've been wanting to talk to you about the death. I can't help thinking you were a bit of a fool."

"Fine friend you are. Did you ride all this way just to twit me?"

"Nah, nah, nah, my friend, and I call you that truly. I came to give you a warning. Lord Beryn offered you twice the gold of your father's blood price. I don't see why you didn't take the lwdd and be done with it."

"Because I wanted my father's murderer hanged. It should be obvious."

"But young Madryc was the only son Beryn had. He won't forget this."

"Neither will I. Da was the only father I happened to have, too."

With a sigh, Cadlew drank his ale in silence. Although he felt his wound of rage opening, Dwaen could forgive his friend's lack of understanding. Doubtless every lord in Gwaentaer was wondering why he'd pushed the law to its limit and insisted that the gwerbret hang Madryc. Most would have taken the twelve gold pieces and got their satisfaction in knowing that Beryn had impoverished himself and his clan to raise them.

"It's the principle of the thing," Dwaen said, choosing his words carefully. "It's a wrong thing to take gold for blood when a man murders in malice. If it'd been an oath-sworn blood feud or suchlike, no doubt I would have felt different, but that drunken young cub deserved death."

"But it would have been better if you'd killed him yourself instead of running to the laws like a woman. Beryn would have understood that."

"And why should I add one murder to another when we've got a gwerbret not forty miles north of here?"

"Ye gods, Dwaen, you talk like a cursed priest!"

"If I'd had brothers, I would have been a priest, and you know it as well as I do."

In a few minutes, what kin Dwaen did have left came down from the women's hall; his mother, Slaecca, and his sister, Ylaena, with their servingwomen trailing after. Her hair coiffed in the black headscarf of a widow, Slaecca was pale, her face drawn, as if she were on the edge of a grave illness, every moment slow and measured to mete out her shreds of strength. Ylaena, pretty, slender, and sixteen, looked bewildered, as she had ever since the murder.

"Here, Mother, sit at my right, will you?" Dwaen rose to greet the dowager. "Cado, if you'll oblige by sitting with my sister?"

Cadlew was so eager to oblige that it occurred to Dwaen that it was time he found his sister a husband. Although he glanced his mother's way to see if she'd noticed the young lord's reaction, she was staring absently out into space.

"Oh, now here, Mam, Da wouldn't have wanted you to fill your life with misery just because he's gone to the Otherlands."

"I know, but I'm just so worried."

"What? What about?"

"Dwaen, Dwaen, don't put me off! I can't believe that a man like Beryn is going to let this thing lie."

"Well now, it'd be a grave thing for him to break the gwerbret's decree of justice, and he knows it. Besides, he's got his own sense of honor. If he kills me, there'll be no one left to carry on the blood feud, and I doubt me if he'd do a loathsome thing like killing a man who had no hope of vengeance."

Slaecca merely sighed, as if in disbelief, and went back to staring across the hall.

On the morrow, Dwaen and Cadlew took the gwertrae out to hunt rabbits in a stretch of wild meadowland some few miles from the dun. They had no sooner ridden into the grass when the dog raised a sleeping hare. With one sharp bark, it took off after its prey. Although the brown hare raced and dodged, leaping high and twisting off at sharp angles, the gwertrae ran so low to the ground and fast that it easily turned the hare in a big circle and drove it back to the hunters. With a whoop of laughter, Cadlew spurred his horse to meet it and bent over to spear the hare off the ground with one easy stroke. All morning, they coursed back and forth until the leather sack at Cadlew's saddle-peak bulged bloody from their kills.

The chase took them far from the farmlands of the demesne to the edge of the primeval oak forest, dark and silent, which once had covered the whole southern border of the Gwaentaer plateau, but which in Dwaen's time existed only in patchy remnants. At a stream they dismounted, watered the horses and the dog, then sat down in the grass to eat the bread and smoked meat they'd brought with them. Cadlew cut the head off one of the hares and tossed it to the gwertrae, who stretched out with its hind legs straight behind and gnawed away.

"Oh, a thousand thanks for this splendid gift," Cadlew said. "I think I'll name him Glas."

"If you like, tomorrow we can take the big hounds and ride into the forest. We could do with some venison at the dun."

"And when have I ever turned down a chance to hunt?"

Thinking of the morrow's sport, Dwaen idly looked into the forest. Something was moving—a trace of motion, darting between two trees among bracken and fern. Even though the oaks themselves were just starting into full leaf, the shrubs and suchlike among them were thick enough. Puzzled, he rose for a better look. Cadlew followed his gaze, then with a shout threw himself at Dwaen's legs and knocked him to the ground just as an arrow sped out of the cover. It whistled over them by several feet, but if Dwaen had been standing, he would have been skewered. Growling, the gwertrae sprang up and barked, lunging forward at the hidden enemy. Another arrow sang and hit it full in the chest. With a whimper, Glas fell, writhed, and pawed at the air, then lay still. Another arrow hit the grass and struck quivering not two feet from Dwaen's head. He felt a cold, rigid calm: they were going to die. With neither mail nor shield, it mattered not if they lay there like tourney targets or tried to charge; it was death either way. Oh, great Bel, he prayed, come to meet us on the misty road!

"Shall we charge?" Cadlew whispered.

"Might as well die like men."

Cadlew rolled free, grabbed a spear, and jumped to his feet with a war cry. As he did the same, Dwaen could almost feel the bite of the arrow bringing his Wyrd. But the enemy never loosed his bow again. When they took a couple of cautious steps forward, he saw nothing moving among the trees but a bird on a branch.

"Well," Dwaen said, "I think me I've just been given a message."

"Beryn?"

"Who else? I wager that if I'd been alone, I'd be dead by now, but no doubt he didn't want to murder you with me. He's got naught against you and your clan."

"If he tries to kill you again, he'll have to kill me first, but I'd rather it was in open battle."

"It might come to that."

Cadlew picked up the dead gwertrae and slung it over his saddle, but since Dwaen didn't want his womenfolk alarmed, they asked a farmer to bury it for them rather than taking it back to the dun.

All that afternoon, even though he managed to make polite conversation with his guest and his family, Dwaen brooded. Lord Beryn's lands were only about ten miles to the west, close enough for him to haunt the edges of the demesne in hope of catching his enemy unaware. Yet he couldn't imagine Beryn using a bow instead of a sword, and besides, how had the old bastard known exactly when and where he'd gone to hunt? Not that he and Cadlew had made any secret of their plan—the question was how Beryn had heard of it, a question that was answered the very same night, when he went up to bed.

Theoretically, now that he'd inherited, Dwaen should have been using his father's formal suite on the floor just above the great hall, but since he had no desire to move his mother out of her bed, he kept to his spare, small chamber on the third floor of the broch. When he came in that night, carrying a lantern himself rather than bothering a page, he saw a lump under the blankets on the narrow bed. He threw the covers back and found a dead rat, mangled, stabbed over and over to a blood-soaked mess, and stuffed into a neck wound was the tail feather of a raven.

With an involuntary yell, Dwaen jumped back, the lantern shaking and bobbing to throw wild shadows on the walls.

"Dwaen?" Cadlew's voice came muffled through the door. "Are you all right?"

"Not truly. Come in, will you?"

27

When Cadlew saw the rat, he swore under his breath, then took the poker from the hearth and flipped the foul thing onto the floor.

"Beryn's got a man in this dun," Cadlew said.

"Obviously, unless that peddler who was here this afternoon was actually a spy."

"Who would have let him come upstairs? Here, on the morrow, I'll send a message home and tell them that I'm staying at your side."

"You've never been more welcome."

Dwaen gathered up his blankets and went to share Cadlew's chamber, but he lay awake for a long time after his friend was snoring. Although he'd realized that Beryn would hate him for demanding justice, he'd never thought the lord would seek such a coward's revenge. But he's got no choice, he thought, because if he challenges me openly, the gwerbret will intervene. A traitor in his own dun! The thought sickened him, that one of his own men could be bribed against him. It might only be a servant, of course, but still, he was forced to realize that from now on, he could trust no one.

The round, thatched farmhouse sat behind a low earthen wall about a hundred yards from the road. Out in the dusty yard, a man was throwing a bucket of slop to a pair of skinny gray hogs. When Jill and Rhodry led their horses up to the gate, he lowered the bucket and looked them over narrow-eyed.

"Good morrow," Rhodry said. "Would your wife happen to have any extra bread to sell to a traveler?"

"She wouldn't." He paused to spit on the ground. "Silver dagger."

"Well, then, could we pay you to let us water our horses in your trough?"

"There's plenty of streams in the forest down the road. But here, that forest is our lord's hunting preserve. Don't you silver daggers go poaching in it."

"And who is your lord?"

"Tieryn Dwaen of Bringerun, but he's too good a man to have any truck with the likes of you."

At that, the farmer picked up his bucket and turned back to his hogs. As they rode off, Rhodry was swearing under his breath.

About a mile farther on, the forest sprang up abruptly at the edge of cleared land, a dark, cool stand of ancient oaks, thick with underbrush along the road. In the warmth of a spring day, Jill found it pleasant, riding through the dappled shade and listening to the birdsong and all the rustling, scrabbling music of the lives of wild things—the chatter of a squirrel here, the creak of branches there, the occasional scratching in the bracken that indicated some small animal was beating a retreat as the horses passed by. That she would be riding through this splendor with her Rhodry at her side seemed to her the most glorious thing in the world.

"Shall we stop and eat soon?" Jill said. "We've got cheese, even if that whoreson piss-pot bastard wouldn't sell us any bread. I hear water running nearby."

Sure enough, the road took a twist and brought them to the deep, broad Belaver, which paralleled the road. At the bank, they found a grassy clearing that sported a tall stone, carved with writing. Since Rhodry knew how to read, he told Jill that it served notice that no one could hunt without permission of the tieryn at Bringerun. After they watered their horses, they ate their cheese and apples standing up, stretching after the long morning's ride, and idly watched the river flowing past, dappled with sun like gold coins. All at once, Jill felt uneasy. She walked away from the river and stood listening by the road, but she heard nothing. That was the trouble: the normal forest noise had stopped.

"Rhodry? We'd best be on our way."

"Why?"

"Don't you hear how quiet it is? That means there's men prowling round, and I'll wager they're the tieryn's gamekeepers. We'd best stay on the public road if we don't want trouble."

They mounted and rode out, but as they let the horses amble down the road, Jill realized that she was still listening for something, hunting horns, barking dogs, some normal noise that should accompany gamekeepers on their rounds, but she never heard any. In about a mile, the birdsong picked up again.

As they rounded a bend, they met another party of riders ambling toward them. Two women led the way, a pretty lass in a rich blue dress, and an older person in gray who seemed to be her servingwoman from the deferential manner in which she spoke. Behind them on a pony rode a page carrying a big basket, and bringing up the rear, a swordsman on a warhorse, their escort. Since he was wearing no mail, they could see the blazon, a stag leaping over a fallen tree, embroidered on the yokes of his shirt. Jill and Rhodry pulled off the road to let the lady past, a courtesy which she acknowledged with a sunny smile and a wave of her gloved hand.

"My lady?" Rhodry called out. "May I ask whom we have the honor of seeing?"

"Lady Ylaena of Bringerun." The page answered for the lady, as was his place. "Sister to Tieryn Dwaen."

Rhodry bowed from the saddle with such a bright smile that Jill felt a stab of jealousy. She would never have pretty dresses and soft, pale skin like Ylaena's. On the other hand, she could knock Rhodry all over a stable-yard if he ever tried to betray her, an advantage that the lady would lack in dealing with her eventual husband. Once the noble party had ridden by, they returned to the road.

"No doubt they're meeting that hunting party we heard," Rhodry remarked.

But his words caught Jill like an omen. Although she tried to talk herself out of it, she felt trouble round them like a cold wind. They'd ridden no more than half a mile when she surrendered.

"Rhoddo, we've got to turn back. That lady's in danger. I know it sounds daft, but I know it as well as I know the sky's blue. If we meet them, and I'm wrong, we can make up some tale about having lost a bit of gear in the road or suchlike."

Jill could hear her voice shaking, and it was that fear that convinced Rhodry. As they turned back, she was wishing that they could dismount and put on their mail, but she somehow knew that there was no time. Suddenly, they heard a woman scream, and then a shout and the clash of metal on metal. With a howl of unearthly laughter, Rhodry drew his sword and kicked his horse to a gallop. Sword in hand, Jill raced after him.

As they charged up to the clearing by the river, Jill saw a welter of horses and ill-armored men: two attacking the stag rider, who was already bleeding as he swung his sword and yelled; two more grabbing the reins of the ladies' horses, and one last beating the helpless page about the head. Rhodry charged straight into the melee and killed a man from behind, then swung on another. Jill galloped past and cut at the man struggling with the reins of Ylaena's terrified palfrey. When she sliced him across the back, he screamed and dropped the reins.

"Ride!" Jill shouted at the lady.

When Jill shifted her weight in the saddle, her battle-trained horse swung round to the rescue of the servingwoman, whose screams echoed above Rhodry's berserker's laugh. Jill ducked her enemy's clumsy blow and slashed him across the throat.

"My apologies," Jill said. "You poor bastard."

For the briefest of moments, he stayed upright, staring at her in disbelief, then fell dead over his horse's neck. Jill's stomach churned; for all that she was good with the blade she carried, she hated killing. She had no need of sending another man to the Otherlands that day, however, because the rest of the bandits were already racing down the road to the north.

"Let them go!" Rhodry called out. "We can't leave the women."

When Jill turned back, she found him dismounted and pulling the stag rider down from his saddle. Although the servingwoman clung to her saddle-peak and sobbed, Ylaena dismounted and ran to the page.

"Get down, Larro. Let me see what that man did to you."

Shaking too hard even to weep, the lad swung down and threw himself into her arms. Jill dismounted and joined Rhodry, kneeling beside the stag rider. His face slashed with bloody cuts, he tried to speak, then died in Rhodry's arms.

"Ah, horseshit." Rhodry laid him down gently. "I didn't think they had brigands in this part of the kingdom."

"Not brigands," Ylaena said from behind them. "My brother would never allow such a thing, not if he had to call in every alliance he had to chase them from his lands."

They rose, Rhodry hastily wiping his bloodstained hands on his brigga.

"I owe you my life, silver daggers. Will you escort us back to my dun? I'll see that you're well paid for it."

"My lady will have our protection for the honor of the thing." Rhodry made her a bow. "But we'd best hurry. Those cowards might realize that there's only two of us and come back."

Between them, Jill and Rhodry got the dead men tied over their saddles. When they rode out, the lady, her servingwoman, and the page each led one of the extra horses to leave Jill and Rhodry free in case of attack, her at the head of the line, him in the dangerous rear guard. As they trotted down the road, Jill turned constantly in her saddle and peered into the trees, but apparently the attackers were the cowards Rhodry had called them, because their terrified procession came free of the forest without any more trouble. Out on the open road among the settled farms, they were safe. With a sharp sigh of relief, Jill sheathed her sword, then fell back to ride beside Ylaena.

"I'll take the reins of that horse, my lady. You shouldn't have to lead it like a caravan guard."

"My thanks." Ylaena handed them over. "You know, I think it's the strangest thing of all that another lass would save my life, but you have my heartfelt thanks."

Tieryn Dwaen stood by the hearth in his great hall and shook with rage. Rhodry had never seen a man as furious as this slender, dark-haired young lord, whose right hand clenched and unclenched on his sword hilt for the entire time that it took for Ylaena to tell the tale, sitting in her brother's chair with Lord Cadlew behind her. When she was done, the tieryn turned to the silver daggers.

"And how can I ever repay you for this? I never dreamt they'd dare harm my womenfolk, the bastards!"

"They, Your Grace?" Rhodry said. "Who?"

"Someone's been trying to murder me. It's just that I never would have thought in a thousand years that Beryn would take his vengeance out on my sister."

Ylaena covered her face with both hands and wept, while Cadlew patted her shoulder.

"Dwaen," he growled, "I want blood for this."

"So do I. Lots of it."

"They weren't going to kill me." Ylaena struggled with her voice to steady it. "I heard them yelling. 'Don't harm the ladies,' they said. They were just going to take us somewhere."

"And what would they have done then?" Cadlew snarled. "When you ride to war, Dwaen, me and my warband will ride with you."

"If it comes to war. I intend to let the gwerbret settle this by law if ever I can."

Cadlew muttered some inaudible frustration.

In the great hall, every man in the warband and every servant in the dun stood round, straining to hear. Dwaen yelled at them all to get out, then asked Cadlew to escort Ylaena up to the women's hall. He himself took Jill and Rhodry to the table of honor and insisted on pouring them mead with his own hands.

"My lord?" Rhodry said. "I was just up in Ebonlyn, and someone tried to hire me to murder a noble-born man. I'm beginning to wonder if the man was you."

"Mayhap it was. Let me tell you my tale."

While Dwaen told him of the previous attempt on his life and Beryn's probable motive, Rhodry grew more and more baffled.

"By the pink asses of the gods, Your Grace, why doesn't he just challenge you to an honor duel? You could have the matter settled before the gwerbret even heard of it."

"I've spent many an hour wondering the same thing. Rats in my bed? It sounds like old tales of witchcraft and suchlike. I can't believe Lord Beryn would stoop so low."

Lallyc, the captain of the tieryn's warband, trotted over and knelt at his lord's side.

"Your Grace? None of the men recognize those two dead'uns, and here we spent plenty of time with Beryn's men before the murder."

"Well, I never thought Beryn would send men from his own warband." Dwaen gave him a black-humored grin. "He might as well hire a herald to proclaim his intent as do that. But I can't think of another man in the world who'd want me dead. Unless, Captain, I'm just being vain?"

"Not in the least, my lord," Lallyc said with a firm nod. "I've never known you to harm anyone. Why, you wouldn't even cheat in a horse race. Besides, if anyone else felt injured, they'd know they could come sit by our gates and starve in safety. I can't see you breaking the holy laws by driving them away."

"True enough. Well, looks like I've got a hire for you, silver daggers."

When Cadlew returned, the two lords worked out what struck Rhodry as a sensible plan. If Dwaen rode to the gwerbret in Ebonlyn, he would be vulnerable out on the road, because his rank only allowed him to bring an honor guard of fifteen men into the gwerbret's presence, fewer than Beryn kept in his warband. If Cadlew accompanied him, however, the young lord could bring ten men of his own, and since it seemed clear that Beryn had no intention of murdering Cadlew if he could help it, having him along would doubtless be the best protection Dwaen could have. They could also bring the two silver daggers in addition to the honor guard, because Jill and Rhodry qualified as witnesses.

"I'll take Laryn, too," Dwaen said. "But I don't want to risk bringing Ylaena in to give evidence."

"Your Grace?" Rhodry put in. "But will she be safe here as long as there's a traitor in the dun?"

"She won't, and that's true enough. Ah, by the hells! To think that I got into this stinking mess out of regard for the laws and naught more!"

34

As she considered Dwaen's peculiar story, Jill grew more and more sure that the traitor had to be a servant, not a rider, because members of the warband had no business being anywhere near the tieryn's chambers. A servant seen near his bedroom, however, would be taken for granted. All afternoon, she wandered round the dun and introduced herself to the various servitors, the head groom, the blacksmith, the pigkeeper, and finally, the cook, each of whom told her they thanked the gods daily for giving them places in the dun of a lord who was, for a change, so generous and just. Jill found it very hard to believe that any of them would ever betray their master.

Jill left the kitchen hut to find a battle brewing. A pair of kitchen maids were standing by the well, their buckets forgotten beside them while they took turns sneering at a blond lass who had her hands set on her hips and her mouth twisted in sheer rage.

"You've got a man in the village," said one of the mockers.

"And what business is it of yours?"

"None, I'm sure, but you'd best be careful, you with one bastard already."

"You're naught but a slut, Vyna," the other mocker joined in, and she was a severe sort with squinty eyes at that. "I don't see how you can carry on like that, with never a thought for the consequences."

"Don't you call me a slut." Vyna's voice was dangerously level.

"I will!" said Squinty Eyes. "Slut! Slut! Slut! Leaving your baby behind you!"

Scarlet with rage, Vyna charged, grabbed her hair with one hand, and slapped her across the mouth with the other. Shrieking, the third lass joined in, all of them pulling each other's hair and scrabbling with their nails at each other's faces. Jill ran forward and intervened just as the cook came waddling and yelling out of the kitchen. While the cook bellowed for peace, Jill grabbed the pair of lasses and knocked them apart so hard that they cowered back by the wall. Vyna stood sobbing, her dress torn, the tears running down her face.

"My thanks, Silver Dagger," the cook said. "As for you two, get on with your work. You've tormented the lass enough, and I'm sick to my guts of hearing it."

Jill caught Vyna's arm and led her to a private spot among the various huts and storage sheds. Sniveling, the lass wiped her face on her apron and stammered out thanks.

"Most welcome. I hate seeing two against one in a fight."

"They've been on me and on me ever since I came here. Don't they know how much it ached my heart to give up my baby? I miss him every day, but I had no choice."

"Where did you leave him? With your kin?"

"I didn't. My Mam wouldn't take me in." Vyna stared down at the ground, and her voice dropped. "But I was lucky, I suppose. I used to work in another dun, and the lady gave me the coin to put my baby in fosterage to a farmer's wife she knew."

"I see. It wasn't Cadlew's dun, was it?"

"It wasn't. What made you think so?"

"Oh, just an idle wondering. He and the tieryn seem such close friends."

"They are, but they'd never notice the likes of me. Here, my thanks again, but I've got to get back to my work."

She turned and ran across the ward, dodging among the huts as if to hide from Jill and the world as well.

Jill went upstairs to the women's hall, which filled half of the second floor of the broch, a spacious sunny room with two Bardek carpets on the polished wood floor and a profusion of chairs and cushions scattered about. Ylaena and the dowager Slaecca sat together near a window, sewing on an embroidered coverlet that draped both their knees—part of Ylaena's dowry, Jill assumed. Jill bowed to the dowager and knelt beside her chair.

"Now you're not to trouble your heart, my lady. Lady Ylaena can tell you that I don't carry a sword just for the pretty scabbard, so no one's going to harm you."

Slaecca whispered out a thanks so faint that her daughter leaned forward and squeezed her hand for reassurance.

"Come now, Mam, Lord Cadlew's promised me that he'll guard our Dwaen, too. I'll just wager the gwerbret puts a stop to all of this as soon as he finds out."

"I'll pray so," Slaecca said. "Oh, by the Goddess! I don't want things coming to a war."

At dinner that night, Dwaen found out how seriously Rhodry took his post as bodyguard when a page brought them each a tankard of ale. Just as the tieryn went to drink, the silver dagger grabbed his wrist and snatched the tankard.

"Allow me, Your Grace." Rhodry took a cautious sip, thought about it for a moment, tried another, waited, then finally handed the ale back. "If His Grace would oblige, he'd best not have so much as a drink of water from the well without me or his captain trying it first."

"Ye gods, I think I'd rather die than have another man poisoned in my stead."

"His Grace is honorable, but we've sworn to die protecting you in battle, so why not at table, too?"

Dwaen forced out a sickly smile. He felt like a badger in a trap, waiting for the hunter to appear and spear him through the wickerwork. Rhodry, fortunately, proved good company, whether talking about his life on the long road or passing along bits of gossip about the noble-born. Dwaen began to wonder about this silver dagger, a courtly man by every phrase he used or graceful bow he made, but a dishonored outcast all the same. Jill puzzled him just as much. It was extremely odd to think of a woman charging right into the fight on the road, odder the more because as the women settled themselves at table, Jill was talking with his mother about some typical female matter. While he waited for Rhodry to sample the meat and bread on his plate, he overheard a bit of it: one of the kitchen lasses apparently had a bastard out in fosterage, and

Jill and Slaecca were predictably (to his mind at least) distressed for the lass.

"How awful to leave your baby behind!" Slaecca said. "Jill, later you might ask Cook for me just where Vyna was in service before. The poor lass."

"My lady, I already did, and it's rather interesting. Cook seems to know an awful lot about the countryside round here."

Just then, Rhodry handed the tieryn his plate back.

"Well, my mouth's not burning yet, Your Grace."

"Good. I'm wretchedly hungry."

At the end of the meal, Slaecca spoke to one of the serving lasses, who trotted off only to return in a few minutes with another servant, a blond woman, heavy breasted yet lithe. If she's the one with the bastard, Dwaen thought, it's no wonder.

"Now here," the dowager was saying. "How old is your baby?"

"Just a year, my lady."

"Well, it would be hard for you to tend both your work and him, but when he's two years old, you may fetch him and bring him to live with you. Let me think on it: mayhap we can find him fosterage closer to us, so you can visit him more often."

The lass broke out sobbing and stammered her thanks through a flood of tears. Dwaen noticed Jill watching with an odd expression, a crafty sort of curiosity, as the lass rose with an awkward curtsy and fled the great hall. Yet she assumed a small sentimental smile when she noticed the tieryn leaning forward to speak.

"Now here, Mam, that was kind of you."

"Well, the poor child!" Slaecca said. "She looks naught but sixteen, and it was probably some handsome lout of a rider, pressing her with compliments and little gifts from the day she entered service."

"And the compliments stopped," Jill remarked, "as soon as her belly began to swell."

Dwaen had no doubt of that. In a few minutes, the women rose to go upstairs and leave the men to their drinking. Dwaen and Rhodry settled in over flagons of mead and seriously discussed the possible identity of the traitor in the dun.

"It has to be someone good with a bow," Dwaen said.

"Well, more like he's just running messages out. If this Lord Beryn hates you so much, he's probably salting men round the countryside."

One at a time, the tieryn considered the men in his warband and his noble-born servitors, even though the very wondering ached his heart. That one of his own men, someone who'd pledged his life to him in return for his shelter, would turn against him was worse than a physical blow. Although he wanted to believe the traitor a servant, there he was at a decided disadvantage, because he barely knew one servant from another.

"We'll have to question your chamberlain, Your Grace," Rhodry said at last. "Can he be trusted?"

"By the gods, I always thought so! Brocyl served my father for twenty long years."

"Then there's no reason for him to turn against you now."

"So one wants to believe, silver dagger. I'll talk to him in the morning; I see he's left the hall already tonight, and he's getting on in years." Dwaen drained the last drops in his goblet and got up. "I want to talk to my sister. I suppose you'd best come with me, much as I hate feeling like I've got a nursemaid."

"I can always wait outside the women's hall, but I'd best be along on the stairs, Your Grace."

Yet when Ylaena opened the door, she automatically ushered Rhodry in with her brother. Slaecca was sitting in a cushioned chair near the hearth, while Jill sat on a footstool at the lady's side. The tight lines round his mother's mouth spoke of tears hastily stifled.

"Ylaena, my sweet, there's somewhat I've got to settle before I ride to the gwerbret, just in case I don't come back."

Ylaena drew herself up straight with a flash of worried eyes.

"It's time we discussed your betrothal. What would you say to Lord Cadlew?"

His sister's smile was as bright and sharp as a flash of sun dancing on water, but it faded as she cast a nervous glance her mother's way.

"Do you have somewhat against him, Mother?" Dwaen said.

"Naught, except his rank. He's an ordinary lord, for all that his lands are rich enough." Absently she looked away into the fire. "These are no times for joy, Dwaen, but if your sister can find a little in her betrothal, I won't say her nay."

"My thanks." Ylaena turned to her with her eyes spilling tears. "And my thanks to you, brother."

Dwaen realized then that she and his mother had doubtless discussed possible suitors for many a long hour already. He was about to try to make some jest to lighten the mood of things when someone knocked with a timid little rap on the door. Jill was up so fast that it seemed she'd been waiting for this and ran to open it. Outside stood the kitchen lass who had the bastard.

"Oh, His Grace is here!" The lass looked genuinely terrified. "I'll come back."

"Don't run now." Jill grabbed her wrist and hauled her inside. "Come along, Vyna. I swear that no one will harm you, even if I have to fight them off myself. Come tell our lady whatever it was you wanted to say."

Trembling, on the edge of tears, Vyna walked over and knelt at Slaecca's side, bringing with her the scent of roasted meat and soapy water.

"Come now, child," the dowager said. "Is it somewhat about your baby?"

Vyna wept with a shaking of her whole body.

"My lady, I'm so sorry. I'm so frightened, but I can't lie anymore. I never thought they'd try to hurt the Lady Ylaena, truly I didn't." She began to sob, the words bursting in little spurts. "They said they'd kill my baby. Don't let them kill my baby. I didn't want to. Don't let them kill my baby. I swear it, they made me do all those things. I can't do it anymore, you're too good and kind, but please, by the Goddess herself, don't let them kill my baby."

Dwaen felt that he'd turned into an oak and put down roots. So this was their terrible traitor! Jill knelt down next to her and put an arm round her shoulders.

"You met a man places and gave him information, didn't you? Who was he?"

"I don't know. One of Lord Beryn's riders. He came to the dun just as I got kicked out of it. I met him in town or down by the river. Everyone thought I had another man. You heard them, Jill, you heard them call me a slut."

"Of course. What do you think made me wonder about you? Now here, when do you meet him again?"

"On the morrow, but I won't go. Oh, Goddess, Goddess, Goddess, don't let them kill my baby."

"No one's going to harm him, because if his grace gives me permission, I'm riding tonight to fetch him."

"His grace will give you an escort of twenty men to make sure you bring him home safely," Dwaen said. "I'd go myself, except I doubt that your Rhodry will let me."

"His grace is ever so correct." Rhodry bowed in his direction. "Not at night, Your Grace, when it's easy for accidents to happen."

The farm where Vyna's son was in fosterage was twelve miles away on the edge of Lord Beryn's lands. As the warband alternately trotted and walked their horses down the dark road, Jill was praying that the baby would still be there. It was possible that Beryn's men had taken the child hostage just to make sure that its mother stayed under their control. Of course, it was also possible that they had no intention of ever harming the baby but had merely counted on a young and ignorant lass believing that they would. Finally, after a long three hours and a last few minutes of confusion at a dark and unmarked crossroads, the warband found the farm. As they rode up, dogs began barking hysterically inside the earthen wall that surrounded the steading. When Lallyc pounded on the gate and shouted in the tieryn's name, a crack of light appeared around a shuttered window. In a bit, an old man came out with a tin lantern in his hand. Lallyc leaned down from his saddle.

"Do you have a baby here in fosterage for a lass named Vyna?"

"We do, sir, we do at that. What's all this?"

"We've come to fetch him to his mother in the tieryn's name.

Do you recognize the blazons on my shirt? You do? Splendid. Now go get the child, and wrap him in a blanket or suchlike, too."

At the head of the line, Jill waited beside the captain. She could hear the old man shouting inside the farmhouse, and a woman yelling in anger. Finally, a youngish woman with a dirty, torn cloak thrown over her nightdress ran out to the gate.

"Who are you?" she snarled. "How do I know you won't hurt the child?"

"I'm the tieryn's captain, and I'm here to keep the child from getting hurt. Now fetch him out or we'll knock this gate down to come get him."

"Here, lass," Jill said, and much more gently, "the tieryn sent a woman along to carry the baby home. Would he have done that if he were going to have it killed or suchlike?"

The woman raised the lantern and stared into Jill's face; then she nodded agreement.

"He's a sweet baby. I'll miss him."

Jill supposed that the sweetness of babies was an acquired taste. On the long ride home, she found the squirming, wailing bundle a nuisance and little else, even though one of the men led her horse to give her both hands free for the job. She tried singing to him, bouncing him, even kissing him, but the baby, torn out of his warm cradle into a cold night and the arms of a stranger, wept the whole way home until the poor little thing was hoarse and whimpering. By the time that she could finally hand him over to his jubilant mother, she was praying to the Goddess that she'd never conceive.

Before she went to bed, Jill joined the tieryn and Rhodry at the table of honor for a well-earned flagon of mulled ale.

"No trouble on the road, I take it?" Dwaen said.

"None, Your Grace. It gladdens my heart that you'll forgive poor Vyna."

"She seems as much a victim as any of us. While you were gone, she described this fellow that she's been meeting. The cook always sent her on errands into town, you see, because she was the oldest of the three kitchen lasses, so she could get a word with him when she needed to."

"We've got to get our hands on him," Rhodry put in. "But if his grace sends the warband into town, the bastard will probably flee."

"And the whole town will know what's been happening, too," Dwaen said with a pronounced gloom. "I hate to think of my subjects gossiping about me night and day."

"I'm sure they do that already, Your Grace." Jill helped herself to some of Rhodry's ale while she thought. "Here, it's still cold, this early in the spring. I can wear some of Vyna's clothes and muffle myself up in her cloak. Then when he follows me, Rhodry can pounce on him."

"Excellent, but I'll send Lallyc in, too. We can't have you getting hurt, lass."

At noon on the morrow, Jill went to Vyna's tiny room, which she shared with the other two kitchen maids, in the servants' quarters over one of the stables. Next to Vyna's straw mattress was the bottom of an ale barrel, sawed down and filled with straw for a rough cradle for the baby. While Jill changed into Vyna's clothes, the kitchen lass sat the baby on her lap and cooed to him.

"What's his name?" Jill said.

"Bellgyn, Mam's pretty little Bello. Oh, you just can't know how glad I am to have him here and safe."

"Um, well. My heart's pleased for you, anyway. Can I ask who his father was? Some good-looking young rider?"

Her face dead pale, Vyna busied herself with arranging Bellgyn's little shirt.

"My apologies. It's no affair of mine, and I don't need to press on an old bruise."

"Bruise? I suppose it is."

"Didn't it ache your heart to love a man and then have him refuse to claim you?"

Vyna shook her head in a hard shudder.

"There was never any way he would have married me. I always knew that. All this time, I've been carrying the secret in my heart, and it hurts like poison. It was Lord Madryc, Beryn's son."

"So that's why his noble mother was so kind."

She nodded, her eyes brimming tears.

"Did you love him?"

"I hated him and every inch of his twisted guts, but how could I say him nay? He always stank of ale, and he'd grab me so hard that I truly thought he'd kill me some night in his pleasure. When I heard he'd been hanged, I laughed and laughed and laughed."

"Ah. He sounds a man much like his father. I can't say I honor this stinking Beryn, if he'd be ready to kill his own grandson to drive home a threat."

"That's not true. His lordship would never know who sired my baby. Madryc never would have admitted the thing, not to his father. I swear, the old man has twice the honor of his rotten ugly son, and he might have beaten him black-and-blue. Her ladyship made me promise never to tell the lord. That was the price of the coins she gave me. You should have seen her, Jill, mincing and practically holding her noble nose, and all because her precious little son had blasted well raped me. Ah, ye gods, I hated him, always stinking of sweat and ale."

Picking up her mood, the baby began to whine and fuss. Jill finished her dressing and left them alone.

Although Jill rode behind Rhodry for most of the way to town, when they came in sight of the walls she dismounted and walked on alone, getting a good head start in case Vyna's mysterious contact should be waiting at the town gates. Following the kitchen lass's instructions, Jill went past the market square, turned down the street by the saddlemaker's, and saw at last the tavern with the wooden sign of an ox hanging over the door. At the doorway, she paused, peering into the dim smoky room, which smelled of sour ale and roast meat. Near the hearth, the man Vyna had described was watching a couple of merchants play at dice. A blond, with the high cheekbones and narrow eyes of a southern man, he glanced her way and smiled.

Jill looked over her shoulder as if she were afraid of something, then beckoned him to follow her. As he set his tankard down, she left the doorway and walked round back, to find no sign of Rhodry and Lallyc. In her heart she cursed them both and wished she were wearing her sword. When the fellow came up, Jill let out a little squeak and pretended to have a stone in her shoe. She knelt down, letting the hood fall around her face, and mimed getting it out.

"Here," he said. "Is someone following you?"

Jill shook her head no.

"You're not Vyna! What is this?"

"She sent me instead." Jill got up slowly. "Cook wouldn't let her leave the dun."

"I don't believe a word of that, lass."

When he stepped forward to grab her, Jill charged, taking him so off guard that she got a good punch in his stomach before he could defend himself. With a grunt, he staggered back, then recovered and swung openhanded at her face. Hampered by the long dresses, Jill dodged barely in time.

"You little bitch! What is this?"

When he lunged again, she dodged sideways, then tripped over the hem of her dress and nearly fell. He grabbed her by the shoulders and hauled her up, yelped as she raised a knee and got him hard between the legs, but hung on grimly and tried to pin her back against a wall. A shout—Rhodry's voice—the man let go and spun round to run for it. Jill slammed her fist into his kidneys, kicked him in the back of the knee, and shoved him to the ground just as Lallyc and Rhodry raced up.

"You bastards! What took you so blasted long?"

"A crowd on the streets." Lallyc knelt down and disarmed their prey.

By then, the noise had attracted a smallish crowd of its own.

"Naught to worry about, lads," Rhodry called out. "This stinking swine was trying to rape this poor innocent lass. We'll just take him along to the tieryn."

Dwaen and half the dun were waiting by the honor hearth in the great hall. Although Vyna identified their prisoner as the man who met her regularly, nobody in the warband recognized him for a member of Lord Beryn's troop. The tieryn questioned him, Rhodry mocked him, and Lallyc got in a few barbs of his own, but the prisoner never said a word, not even his name, merely smiled with faint contempt during the entire session. Finally, Lallyc glared at the man and rolled up a sleeve with exaggerated care.

"There's more than one way to get a man to talk, Your Grace."

"Not in my dun!" Dwaen snapped. "I know what you're planning, and you can just put it out of your mind."

"His grace is an honorable man," Rhodry broke in, "but his life is at stake. Lallyc and me can just work him over someplace where you don't have to watch."

"You won't! I won't have a helpless man tortured. It's against the will of the gods, and that's an end to it."

The prisoner looked at the lord with eyes poisoned by contempt.

"We'll take you along to the gwerbret." Dwaen seemed unaware of the look. "If you refuse to give evidence in the malover, then the laws state you can be put to death, and so we'll see how long you keep your lips laced. Lallyc, get one of the men to shut him in a shed. Keep him under guard, and make sure he's got food and water —decent food and water, mind."

Later that afternoon, Lord Cadlew returned with ten men from his warband. As the two lords, with Rhodry in attendance, sat drinking in the great hall, Dwaen noticed Ylaena, halfway up the spiral staircase and hanging over the rail like a child trying to see what the grown-ups are doing down below. Apparently Cadlew noticed her, too, because he blushed for no discernable reason.

"There's somewhat we'd best settle before we ride," Dwaen said. "Do you want to marry my sister? She wants to marry you."

Cadlew's grip tightened on his tankard.

"I realize she's far above me in rank, and never would I let such a thing come between us, Your Grace."

"Don't be a stuffy bastard. I have every intention of seeing you two betrothed if it pleases you both."

"Oh." Cadlew considered the ale in his tankard for a long moment, then got up, slowly and deliberately. "Perhaps I'd best speak formally to your mother."

"It seems advisable, truly."

Cadlew looked his way, started to speak, then merely grinned. He dashed for the staircase, though Ylaena was gone, doubtless back to the women's hall to wait for her suitor there as the formality of the thing demanded. Dwaen watched him running up after her till he ducked out of sight onto the landing above, then turned to Rhodry.

"Well, there. If Beryn does manage to dispose of me, Cadlew will inherit through Ylaena, and Beryn will regret the day he ever made an enemy out of my friend."

"I believe it, Your Grace. From what I've seen of Lord Cadlew, he'd get you a splendid revenge, but I'd just as soon he didn't have to. I've been thinking about the precautions we should take once we reach the gwerbret's dun. I haven't forgotten that fellow in Caenmetyn who tried to hire me to kill you."

"For all we know, Beryn's planning on attacking us on the road. If he's got one of his men watching the dun from a distance, he'll know when we're riding out and lay another ambush in the forest. That reminds me—where's Jill?"

"Up in the women's hall, Your Grace. She told me earlier that the local gossip was truly interesting, whatever she means by that."

Like Dwaen, Jill had been wondering if Beryn was going to try another ambush, but the combined warbands, followed by six packhorses laden with gifts of food for the gwerbret's hall, reached Caenmetyn without incident. Although Gwerbret Coryc's provincial demesne was a poor one by gwerbretal standards, his dun walls rose imposingly enough round a huge central broch surrounded by four squat half-brochs and a cobbled ward. While Dwaen, with Cadlew and Rhodry along for witnesses, went to the great hall to lay his formal complaint, Jill helped the servants haul all their gear up to the tieryn's chambers in the main tower. While they worked, she made friends with one of the manservants and got him to introduce her to the various servitors, particularly to the head groom, a stocky fellow, mostly bald, named Riderrc.

It was easy for her to use her horse, a beautiful golden gelding of the breed known as Western Hunter, to get a friendly conversation going. While they discussed Sunrise in particular and horses in general, she could ask casual questions about the various important officials in the dun, particularly the chamberlain, the most important of all.

"He's a decent enough lord, I suppose." Riderrc sucked his teeth in a meditative way. "Fussy about every blasted detail, but no one bribes him for a favor, I tell you."

"Amazing! Many a chamberlain's got rich selling access to his gwerbret."

"Our Tallyc would choke rather than take lying silver."

"Interesting. Well, I'd best be getting back upstairs."

But Jill went to the kitchen hut, which was as big as a small house. In the thick smoke, two cooks were frantically yelling at a squad of kitchen maids, while the chamberlain himself supervised the carving of a whole hog, and serving lasses and pages dashed around filling baskets with bread and bowls with stewed cabbage. In that madhouse, a would-be poisoner could slip all manner of things into the food and drink, but on the other hand, it would be near impossible to ensure that only Dwaen and his retinue ate the tainted servings. Jill hoped, at least, that the murderer would draw the line at poisoning the gwerbret, his entire household, and several hundred riders just to finish off one man. For a few minutes, she hesitated, wondering if she should tell Rhodry where she was going, then realized that she wouldn't be able to get him alone to tell him privately. With a glance at the lowering sun, she trotted off to the main gates, pausing only to identify herself to the guards so they'd let her back in, and headed out into the town.

It took her some time to find the thieves' tavern again, curiously uncrowded for the dinner hour. She got herself a tankard of dark ale and stood chatting with the tavernman while she jingled a couple of coppers in one closed hand.

"Do you remember the night that me and my man were in here? We were sitting right over there, and this fellow in a long gray cloak came in."

"Remember it I do. I thought he was a strange one to be coming into a place like this."

"Just so. You don't happen to know who he is, do you?"

"I don't, but he must have been a master craftsman, all right. There was fine wool in that cloak of his."

"Or maybe a scribe or suchlike? He had soft hands, and he smelled like temple incense."

"So he did." The tavernman spat into the straw to help his concentration. "Never seen him before or since, so he can't live here in town. I've lived in Caenmetyn all my fifty years, I have, and I know everyone in it."

When Jill returned to the gwerbret's palace, she snagged a page and sent him up to the women's hall with a message. Before they'd left Dwaen's dun, she'd asked Ylaena to write her a note to the gwerbret's lady, Ganydda, giving Jill a formal introduction. The lad returned quickly enough and escorted her up to the reception chamber, littered with a profusion of heavy furniture and silver oddments. At each long window hung a curtain of Bardek brocade in the gwerbretal colors of green, silver, and yellow. Ganydda, a slender woman with graying hair, startled-looking blue eyes, and prominent teeth, greeted her kindly and had a servant lass bring a cushion so that Jill could sit near her feet.

"The lady Ylaena speaks highly of you, Jill."

"My thanks, my lady, though doubtless she flatters me unduly."

"How well spoken you are! You must forgive an old woman's curiosity, but whatever possessed a pretty lass like you to ride off with a silver dagger? He's awfully handsome, of course, but honestly, my dear! It must have been quite a scandal."

"Not truly a scandal, my lady, because you see, my father was a silver dagger, too. I had no position or anything to lose."

"Really? How fascinating! You must tell me all about it."

Although Jill normally parried such questions, that night she chattered about true love in general and Rhodry in particular until

49

she could see she'd won the lady's confidence—although she avoided telling her why Rhodry was riding the long road. At that point, she could work the talk round to Tieryn Dwaen's current troubles.

"My heart absolutely goes out to Slaecca, losing her husband to that drunken little—well, in a drunken little brawl," Ganydda said. "And now to have her son threatened is really too much to bear. I pray that things won't come to open war."

"It must be sad for Lord Beryn's wife, too, the poor lady, seeing her husband put himself in danger after losing her only son."

"Well, perhaps it would distress her." Ice formed in Ganydda's voice. "One must always think the best thoughts one can about people, mustn't one? But then, there's no doubt that Mallona's had a hard enough life. My dear Jill, wait until you see Beryn puffing and snorting at my husband's court, and he's a good bit older than her, you know."

"Truly? Lady Slaecca never mentioned that."

"She's so charitable, isn't she? But he is, and I've often wondered why she only had that one pregnancy, if you take my meaning."

Jill smiled and arched one eyebrow.

"Oh dear, what if worst comes to worst?" Ganydda went on with a certain relish. "I wonder what poor dear Mallona will do. I can't see her fitting into the temple life, I just simply can't."

"Doesn't she have a brother to go back to, my lady? The Lady Ylaena mentioned one."

"Um, well, a brother of a sort. Let me see, what did happen to him? He was the youngest son of a poor clan, you see, and so he ended up living just like a commoner, and his mother was so upset. He received a small inheritance from an uncle, and he became a merchant—can you imagine it—some said he was actually running a brothel down in Cerrmor, but I never believed it for a minute. People will say the nastiest things sometimes."

"But what about all her other brothers, then?"

"Well, you see, when this Graelyn—I believe that was his name —betrayed the honor of his blood, Mallona was the only one who

50

spoke on his side, and she and her kin no longer speak, for all that it's been ten years now. I think her father arranged the match with Beryn as revenge of a sort, although I shouldn't say that. I mean, he might have thought it a perfectly good match. After all, you can't tell one old man that another doesn't have much life left, if you take my meaning."

When Jill managed to make her escape from the lady's side, she headed upstairs to Tieryn Dwaen's chamber. On her way, she met a serving lass carrying a tray with a silver flagon and goblets upon it.

"Here, Silver Dagger," she called out. "You're with the tieryn's party, aren't you?"

"I am. Shall I save you a few steps and carry that up?"

"Would you? Some fellow from his grace's retinue handed it to me and said to deliver it, but with all these guests, I've got so much work to do."

"Of course you do. Rude of him."

Dwaen, Cadlew, and Rhodry were all sitting in the reception chamber of the suite, the two lords in chairs, Rhodry on the floor by the door. When she brought the mead in, Cadlew rose with a small bow and took the tray from her.

"Splendid idea, Jill. We found a water jug in one bedchamber, but that won't do a man any good."

"Well, my lord, I'm afraid you don't dare drink this mead. I've got the feeling it's been poisoned."

Her feeling was confirmed when Rhodry dipped the corner of a rag in the mead, tasted a scant drop of it, and immediately washed his mouth out with the aforementioned water.

"Crude," he remarked. "Cursed crude. No one in their right mind would have drunk more than one sip of this."

"Ah, by the great hairy balls of the Lord of Hell!" Dwaen was decidedly pale. "Why would someone go to all this trouble to poison the stuff, then?"

"Why did they put that rat in your bed, Your Grace? To make you squirm, to drag it out and make you wonder when they'll finally kill you." Rhodry glanced at Jill. "Think I should go berate the chamberlain?"

"It won't do any good, and spreading the news around might do harm. You could go down to the great hall and find out how easy it is for someone to get into the broch."

Rhodry did just that, but he came back with the discouraging news that it was remarkably easy, even at night, for any well-dressed man who was generous with his small coins. Merchants and travelers did it all the time, mostly to gawk at the dun and maybe to get a glimpse of the gwerbret or his wife. At times, even, after a particularly lavish feast, the gwerbret summoned the town poor into the ward to be given the leftovers. Jill and Rhodry both agreed that the only way they were going to keep strangers away from the tieryn was to raise a general alarm and have the gwerbret put the dun on full alert, a plan that Dwaen outright forbade, much to Cadlew's annoyance and Jill's relief. Rousing the dun would give her whole game away.

Since it would be several days before Lord Beryn would arrive at court to answer the formal charges, Rhodry resigned himself to keeping a close watch over the tieryn and hoping for the best. As the tedious time crawled by, he grew annoyed with Jill for leaving the whole job to him. It seemed that the only time he ever saw her was at meals; she was always off talking to the servants, gossiping with the women in the dun, or wandering around town where, for all he knew, she might well be in danger. By the end of the third day, he was ready to shake her. They finally got a few minutes alone after dinner.

"Just where were you this afternoon?" Rhodry snapped.

"Talking with the head of the merchant guild. It took me all day to bribe my way in to see him."

"What did you want to do that for?"

"And then I went to the temple of Nudd to talk to the priests. Every merchant who comes through town stops to pray there."

"So what? What do merchants have to do with anything?"

"Lots, my sweet love. I think me you're going to be surprised."

"I don't want to be surprised, blast you. I want to know right now what you're up to."

"All right. Here come his grace and Lord Cadlew now. Let's see if they'll ask the gwerbret a favor for me. I want to speak to our prisoner again."

Since his own curiosity was running high, Dwaen was willing to do just that, and Coryc himself was more than willing to grant Jill's boon for the same reason. With four of the gwerbret's men along for a guard, they all trooped out to the gaol, a long, squarish stone shed, half of which served as a general dungeon for beggars, drunkards, and suspected thieves, and half as private cells for more unusual men. Inside one of these tiny rooms was their prisoner, sitting on a heap of fetid straw. When a guard opened the door, he rose, setting defiant hands on his hips.

"If you persist in refusing information," Gwerbret Coryc said, "I'll have you hanged."

Stubbled and dirty, the prisoner ducked his head in a submissive nod. Several days of bad food and living with the results of same had erased his contemptuous confidence.

"This shouldn't take long, Your Grace." Jill stepped forward. "Would you have the guard see if he's been flogged recently?"

Although the prisoner fought and squirmed, a pair of guards pinned him and pulled his shirt up with little trouble. In the torchlight, they could all see the fresh pink scars, about ten of them, crisscrossing his back.

"Very well," Jill said. "Now, lad, I've got just one question for you. Who's Lady Mallona's lover?"

Although for a brief moment Rhodry thought she'd gone daft, the prisoner yelped like a kicked dog, and all the color left his face.

"So." Jill favored him with a smile. "I thought she had one, truly. Was it you? You're good-looking when you're clean."

"It wasn't, by every god of my people. I wouldn't have a thing to do with her when—" He broke off with a foul oath.

"So, she was sniffing round you, was she? It's no wonder you refuse to talk. One word, and you start giving everything away. Very well, then, hold your tongue a while longer. I'll nose him out sooner or later."

With a nod to the guard to lock the prisoner up again, Coryc led the rest of them out into the ward.

"All right, Silver Dagger, you've got some game afoot, and you can blasted well let the rest of us know what it is."

"Your Grace," Jill said, "I'll beg you a boon. If I'm right, this crime is truly scandalous. So I don't want to make any charge or raise anybody's suspicions until we're assembled in a proper court of law. Of course, I'll tell you if you order me to, but I truly do think we should wait until your malover. Your wife will tell you that I'm trustworthy."

"She already has, actually. Very well. Your request's both fair and honorable." The gwerbret looked round with an apologetic smile, since he doubtless knew perfectly well that everyone there was burning with curiosity. "After all, Lord Beryn should arrive on the morrow."

Lord Beryn did indeed arrive, during the noon meal. As Dwaen's bodyguard, Rhodry was sitting next to the tieryn at the gwerbret's table when from out in the ward came the clatter and bustle of armed men dismounting. The enormous hall fell silent as everyone, noble-born and commoner alike, turned to stare at the door. With ten of his men behind him, Lord Beryn strode in, a tall man, raw-boned and grizzled, with sweeping gray mustaches and narrow dark eyes that darted this way and that. Rhodry figured that he was about fifty winters old. He gestured to his men to wait, then strode across the great hall and knelt, with a profound grunt, at the gwerbret's side.

"Now what's all this, Your Grace? I've been wading through rivers of evil gossip, saying that I'm trying to kill Tieryn Dwaen of Dun Ebonlyn. It's cursed well not true."

"True or not, the matter's serious enough to warrant an inquiry." Coryc rose to tower over him. "If both parties agree, we'll convene the malover immediately. The priests are here and waiting."

"Indeed?" Beryn swung his head and glared at Dwaen. "Listen, you little coward, I've got every reason in the world to kill you, but if

I was going to, I'd call you out to a duel like a man—if you had the guts to face me."

Rhodry grabbed Dwaen's arm and forced him to sit back down.

"Lord Beryn, I call for silence!" Coryc snapped. "Tieryn Dwaen, there's be no dueling in my hall."

With a doglike growl, Beryn settled back on his heels.

"My lord," Coryc went on, "the tieryn has reliable witnesses. We are going to hear these witnesses in proper order, in my chamber of justice, with the priests of Bel there as well. Am I understood?"

"You are, Your Grace." Beryn's voice began to shake. "Didn't I accept Your Grace's judgment on my son? Didn't I stand in your ward and watch without lifting a finger when—"

"Don't vex yourself, Beryn." Coryc turned and made an ambiguous gesture with one hand. "All the witnesses present? Good. Then come along, come along. I want this grievous affair settled and done."

The gwerbret's chamber of justice was a big half-round of a room, hung with banners in his colors. In the curve of the wall stood two tables, one for his grace and his scribes, one for the priests and theirs. The witnesses stood on the gwerbret's right, the accused and his supporters on his left. The rest of the hall was packed with spectators—officials, riders, servants, even a few townfolk, a quiet but jostling crowd that spilled out through the double doors into the corridor beyond. As Dwaen and Cadlew laid their deposition concerning the archer and the dead dog, the rat in the bed, Vyna's tale, and the capture of the prisoner, the crowd stopped moving and seemed to crouch on the floor, straining to hear every word. Beryn's color turned from sun-bitten tan to red and back again. Finally, Rhodry was called forward to tell of the attack on Lady Ylaena. He'd barely finished when Beryn broke, charging forward to stand before the gwerbret.

"Your Grace, never would I order such a cowardly thing! How could you believe it of me, attacking a woman!"

"His lordship forgets himself again. As of yet, I believe naught, one way or another."

Beryn started to speak, but just then two guards appeared, shoving their way through the crowd and dragging the prisoner along with them.

"You!" Beryn snarled. "You little bastard! What by every god are you doing here?"

"My lord!" Coryc snapped. "Do you know this man?"

"I do. His name's Petyn, and I had him flogged and kicked out of my warband not long ago. He was stealing from me."

Although everyone in the crowd gasped, Coryc turned to look at Jill, who was smiling to herself as she stood out of the way near the wall.

"All right, Silver Dagger," the gwerbret said. "It's time for you to spill everything you know."

"So it is, Your Grace." Jill came forward and made a reasonable curtsy, seeing as she was wearing a pair of brigga. "Petyn, let's start with you. There you were, publicly shamed, turned out of the warband without a copper to your name. I'll wager you rode south. Where did you meet the man who hired you?"

Petyn shook his head in a stubborn no.

"I know what he looks like," Jill went on. "A stout fellow, with a high voice, and he's a merchant pretending to be a scribe. He deals in perfumes and incenses, actually. He was a friend of Lady Mallona's brother, and he was kind enough to bring her news every now and then, until Graelyn died last year. That's the brother's name, Your Grace—Graelyn. But this incense seller was a rich man, and I'll wager he offered Petyn plenty, especially since he had him round up four other lads for the hire."

"Here!" Lord Beryn's voice rose to a squeak. "Are you talking about Bavydd? He used to stay in my dun with us, just every now and then."

"So that was his name, was it? He gave a different one to the priests of Nudd here in town, but I figured it was a false one. Come on, Petyn. Are you really going to hang for a man who wouldn't lift a finger to help you?"

"I'll hang no matter what I do, you little bitch! Why should I say anything? You seem to know the lot already."

"What is this?" Coryc slammed one hand down on the table. "Jill, are you saying that this merchant is behind these murder attempts?"

"Not exactly, Your Grace. I don't think for a minute that he wanted to kill the tieryn. He wanted to push Beryn and Dwaen into open war and let them kill each other. Or maybe he was hoping you'd believe it was all Beryn's fault, and you'd hang him for breaking your ban on the blood feud. Then he, Bavydd I mean, could marry the Lady Mallona and take her away."

"I see." Dwaen's voice was more a sigh. "Beryn, I owe you both an apology and some restitution for this."

"No doubt," the gwerbret said. "But that will be a separate matter. Jill, I take it you're laying a formal charge of attempted murder, as well as adultery, against this Bavydd, a merchant of Cerrmor."

"I'm not, my lord. He was just a tool."

Everyone was staring at Jill now, from the priests of Bel to the lowliest servant in the crowd. Rhodry had never heard such a crush of people keep such a silence.

"Well, you see, Your Grace," Jill went on, "they could have run off together any time and been safe in Cerrmor, under another gwerbret's jurisdiction, before her husband could track her down. Bavydd's wealthy. He could pay Lord Beryn three times his wife's marriage-price when the matter came to court, and I'll bet his lordship would have taken the money, too, and not pressed the matter, because everyone tells me he didn't much fancy her anymore. So why this elaborate plot? Your Grace, it had to be someone who hates Tieryn Dwaen, and there's only one person under great Bel's light that it could be."

Involuntarily, the gwerbret glanced at Beryn, but Jill shook her head in a mournful no.

"Your Grace, you've all been looking for a man, haven't you? Women hate just as bitterly and as well. Your Grace, everyone tells me that Lady Mallona doted on her son, and he wasn't just her only son, he was her only child. She must have hated Dwaen for having him hanged and brooded on it till she went mad. And then there's the serving lass. Who else could have got Vyna a place in Dwaen's dun, all under the cover of kindness? And who else would have known that Vyna had a child they could hold hostage? Who else would have hated the Lady Ylaena, too? The women in your dun told me that Mallona was awfully taken with Lord Cadlew, and it's also common knowledge that he spurned her cold. Ylaena was her rival. Mallona would have enjoyed her revenge, all right, if that pack of brigands had got Ylaena alone somewhere. But how could Mallona hire the men and give them orders? Send a messenger along the roads to announce she had a hire for murderers? Invite them into her husband's hall? That's where Bavydd came in."

All at once, Rhodry remembered Lord Beryn and looked his way to find the lord kneeling on the floor. It seemed that Beryn had shrunk into himself, turned old and gray and somehow smaller. With a drunken gesture, Beryn raised his head and keened like a man over his dead.

"Your lordship has my sympathy," Jill said. "Truly he does. But I don't see why he should suffer for someone else's crimes."

"No more do I," Coryc said. "I want the lady brought here for questioning. Indeed, with his lordship's permission, I'll summon an honor guard and ride to fetch her myself."

Like a warrior stabbed on the battlefield but determined to stand until he dies, Beryn staggered to his feet. By law, he had the right to ride home and defend his lady with his life from these charges, and Rhodry stepped forward, half without thinking, his hand on the hilt of his sword. Beryn saw the gesture and began to laugh, a ghastly sobbing mirth.

"Stay your hand, Silver Dagger. Your milksop lord's safe from me. I only ask one boon, Your Grace. Don't make me watch her hang. I loved her once."

"Done."

Coryc began to speak further, but the crowd broke, first into whispers, then into an excited gabble that grew louder and louder as the people swirled about. Coryc hesitated, then yelled at the guards to clear the hall and be done with it. In the confusion, Beryn gathered his sworn men round him like a dressing for a wound and swept away; when Dwaen tried to follow to apologize further, Rhodry and Cadlew held him back. The gwerbret was so thickly surrounded by clamoring priests that he never did bother to formally adjourn the malover.

Once the chamber was reasonably clear, Rhodry looked around for Jill, but he found her gone. Blast her! he thought. What's she up to now? Since Dwaen was quite obviously safe, he left his hire and went after her. As he was walking down the stairs, he smelled something, a familiar scent—a hint of cinnamon and musk, exactly that which had hung round the man who'd tried to hire him for murder. Rhodry threw up his head like a hunting dog and raced down the spiral at a dangerous pace. For a moment, at the foot of the stairs, he caught the scent again, but the great hall was packed with gossiping people. By the time he made his way to the door out, he could find neither scent nor sight of the man who, he could assume, had to have been Bavydd of Cerrmor.

After a short search, Jill discovered Lord Beryn and his men out by the stables. Silent and miserable, they were unsaddling their horses, and when she approached, they all stared at her in angry bewilderment, as if they couldn't decide whether she was the cause of their lord's trouble or his savior from it. Beryn himself, however, raised one hand and flapped it in dispirited greeting.

"My lord, I know I've brought you great grief, but I've come now to bring you a little solace. May I speak?"

"Why not, Silver Dagger? I can't think of one wretched thing you could do to hurt me any worse."

"You've lost your only son, and I know it's a grievous thing to think your clan will die when you do. But I've come to tell you that your son sired a son before he died. It's the child we spoke about in the malover, Vyna's babe. The child's a bastard, of course, but he could be legitimized."

Beryn wrenched himself half round, then began to shake, like a spear stuck in the ground with a smack that then quivers itself still. At last, he turned to her again.

"I remember when the lass was sent away. Didn't take any notice at the time. Some woman's matter, I thought. Why didn't my lady tell me about the child?"

"Would she have told you anything that would have pleased you?"

"Ye gods." For a long moment he was silent. "The little bitch."

"Here, my lord, how could the poor lass have turned your son away?"

"Not the lass, you wretched imbecile of a silver dagger! My wife." He began to pace round and round in a tight circle. "Is the babe healthy?"

"He is, my lord. His name's Bellgyn."

Round and round, and always he stared at the dirt beneath his feet. Jill made him an unnoticed bow and slipped away.

On the morrow, as soon as the dun came awake, the gwerbret summoned the two lords and their retinues to the table of honor in the great hall. Coryc rose, carefully impassive, and gave Beryn a nod of greeting.

"I have a formal announcement to make, my lord," Coryc said quietly. "I intend to ride to your dun to question your lady on this matter of justice. If his lordship wishes to ride to her defense, then he has my guarantee of safe conduct out of my city and on my roads."

Beryn snorted profoundly.

"When you ride, Your Grace, I want to join your hunt for this piss-poor bastard merchant." Beryn jerked his thumb in Rhodry's direction. "This silver dagger tells me that he's sure Bavydd was in town last night. I'll bet he's fleeing south right now. A boon, Your Grace. If we catch him, let me have him."

Coryc hesitated, looking Dwaen's way as if the tieryn were his own conscience, there to testify about Bel's laws.

"It's not for me to say what his grace may or may not do," Dwaen said. "My father's death was more than I could bear in silence, but this time I'll no longer push my rights before the law. Whatever you want done with the merchant, Your Grace, do."

"Then your boon is granted, Lord Beryn," Coryc said. "And we'd best get ready to ride."

All that day, the warbands pushed their horses hard and arrived at Dun Ebonlyn in early afternoon, where they stopped to eat and to tell Lady Ylaena the news. As the men were filling in, Jill saw Lord Beryn turn his men out of line and stop beside the gates. When she pointed him out to Dwaen, the tieryn rode over and made Beryn a small bow from the saddle.

"His lordship is welcome in my dun," Dwaen said, "if he can bring himself to enter it."

Slouched in his saddle, Beryn considered the offer. In the strong afternoon light, he looked exhausted, his eyes bloodshot, his cheeks slashed with deep wrinkles from a life out in the sun and wind. Finally, Beryn sighed.

"His Grace is most generous," Beryn said. "My men and me can eat out in your ward. I've no desire to distress your lady mother and sister with my presence at your table."

"As his lordship desires, but I'll have food from my stores brought out to you."

"My thanks. That much I'll accept from you."

The two men looked at each for a moment, neither smiling nor scowling.

"I have a small matter to lay before you," Beryn went on. "Your silver dagger here tells me that kin of mine is sheltering in your dun."

"Vyna's baby, Your Grace," Jill put in. "Madryc sired the lad."

Dwaen caught his breath in a little whistle of surprise.

"I'll want to claim the lad," Beryn said, "formally and legally, once we settle this other matter. He's the only blasted kin I've got left."

"Never would I stand in your way, my lord, provided the lass agrees."

Beryn scowled, started to speak, then merely shrugged and rode on inside.

Beryn's men found a place to sit in the curve of the inner wall. Servants hurried out, bringing bread and cold meat for the men and the best oats for their horses. Beryn sat down on the cobbles in the midst of his warband and bellowed for ale. Jill hurried to the kitchen hut, where she found Vyna piling bread into a basket. On her back, the baby slept in a cloth sling.

"Cook?" Jill called out. "Lord Beryn's men need ale."

"Men always need ale," the cook said. "Pages! Where are you, lads? Run and get a small barrel."

In the resulting confusion, Jill could draw Vyna to one side.

"I've got some important news. Lord Beryn knows about your baby. He wants to claim him and raise him as his heir."

Vyna froze.

"Can you bring yourself to give him up?" Jill went on. "You know that Dwaen would never let the lord take him against your will."

Vyna laid the basket down and wiped her eyes on her sleeve.

"He'd have everything in life this way," Jill said. "Even a title, and you'd have a chance to find a man of your own."

Vyna turned and walked blindly out of the kitchen hut, the baby swaying and bobbing on her back. Jill ran after her, catching up to her near the well just as Lord Beryn himself came hurrying over with a chunk of bread in his hand. Her head high, Vyna refused to curtsy; she stood her ground and let the lord look her over.

"I do remember you, truly," Beryn said. "And that's the baby, is he?"

"He is, my lord," Vyna said. "My child."

Beryn had a thoughtful bite of bread and went on considering her. He towered over her, a strong man still, gray hair or not, his narrow eyes utterly cold and not a trace of a smile on his face, but Vyna stared back at him with her mouth set like a warrior's.

"You'll swear the child is my son's?" Beryn said.

"He's mine first, my lord, but your son had somewhat to do with getting him."

"A strong-minded lass, aren't you?"

"I've had to be, my lord."

Beryn finished most of his bread, then threw the crust away.

"Well, you'll be better off in a dun than you've been in the kitchen," he said. "After we've attended to this other matter, I'll ride here and fetch you and the lad."

"Me, my lord?"

"Well, think, woman! What am I going to do with a babe in arms? I'd only have to find him a nurse anyway. Might as well be you."

Lord Beryn turned on his heel and walked back to his men. Vyna covered her face with her hands and sobbed aloud.

"Hush, hush," Jill said, patting her shoulder. "There, see? No one's even going to take him away from you. But I don't envy you, shut up in that dun with his lordship there."

"I'd put up with the Lord of Hell if I had to for my baby. He's better than that, I suppose." With one last sob, she wiped her face on her sleeve. "I'm more afraid of what everyone's going to say about me than I am of him."

"I doubt me if you've got much to worry about. Lord Beryn would take it as an insult if anyone mocked the mother of his heir, and I'll wager no one insults his lordship lightly."

Once the men had eaten, they changed horses, then rode out fast, determined to reach Beryn's dun by sundown. A few miles down the road, they met a single rider, coming fast on a gray gelding. With a yell, Lord Beryn pulled out of line and galloped to meet him with the rest of his escort streaming after. A river of men and horses surrounded the rider and swept the noble lords into the eddy as well. Rhodry, of course, stayed close to Dwaen.

"It gladdens my heart to see you, my lord," the rider said to Beryn. "I was riding to Caenmetyn with a message for you."

"Indeed?" Beryn leaned forward in his saddle. "Then spit it out, lad."

"Somewhat's wrong with your lady. After you left, she was all upset, like, but well, we figured that she would be, with you gone off like that to face—well, trouble and suchlike." He gave the gwerbret a nervous sidelong glance. "But anyway, in the middle of the night, that merchant comes to the gates on a foundered horse. Bavydd. Do you remember him, my lord?"

"Very well indeed. Go on."

"And he says he has news from Caenmetyn, and so of course we let him in. We all thought it was good of him to ride so fast with the news for your lady. So anyway, Bavydd stays for a bit, and Lady Mallona tells us not to worry, because the malover's gone in your favor. And so we cheered the merchant and then all went to bed. In the morning, the gatekeeper tells us that Bavydd rode out not long after we left the great hall, on a horse your lady gave him, to make up for his, like. But now the Lady Mallona's shut up in her chamber, and none of her women can get her to answer the door. So we thought about climbing up and going in through the window, but we couldn't do that, not into your lady's chamber, so we thought we'd better get you a message and ask what to do."

Beryn looked Rhodry's way with expressionless eyes. Rhodry merely shrugged, supposing, as the lord doubtless did, that the lady had chosen to cheat the gwerbret's justice and die on her own terms. Beryn turned back to the rider.

"Well, here I am. Let's ride and get back there."

Behind its low walls, Beryn's dun was a straggly, untidy place, a low squat broch, a dirt ward crammed with stables and storage sheds. When the warband streamed in through the gates, it filled the ward and turned it to a riot of confused servants and dismounting riders. Shouting his name, Beryn's fort-guard mobbed their lord, then told him the same story all over again, while the chamberlain bowed to the gwerbret and apologized repeatedly for the humble lodgings. At a whispered order from Dwaen, Rhodry stuck close to Lord Beryn, who barely seemed to notice he was there.

"Should we get a couple of axes and break down the door, my lord?" a rider said. "Take a while, but we'll get it in the end."

"My lord?" Rhodry stepped forward. "I'm good at climbing. If you'll give me permission to enter your lady's chamber, I can go up the broch and come in through the window easy enough."

"My thanks, Silver Dagger," Beryn said. "Come round here. I'll show you which window it is."

As they hurried around the broch, Beryn's narrow eyes showed no more than a flicker of distaste for the discovery that inevitably waited for them. He pointed out a window on the second floor of the rough stone broch, then ran inside to wait in front of the lady's door. Rhodry took off his spurs and sword belt, handed them to Jill, then jumped to a windowsill and started up from there. Since little ledges and flat flints stuck out all over the wall, the rough stone was easy climbing. At the window, he found the shutters closed, but he pushed them open with one hand and clambered inside.

The dimly lit chamber reeked with the sickly odor of vomit and some sweetish drug. On the canopied bed lay a figure, huddled up, clasping its stomach with both hands. Rhodry strode over and pulled the blanket back to find a stout man, naked, his skin bluish, his broad face contorted and blue from his last agony. He lay in a pool of vomit and urine, and his bloodshot eyes stared up sightless at the embroidered blazons on Lord Beryn's bed. Rhodry stepped back fast.

"Gods preserve us! She's a ruthless little bitch!"

He ran to the door and unbarred it to let Lord Beryn and the gwerbret in. At the sight of the corpse in his bed, Beryn swore aloud. He began to shake, a tremor of rage that left him speechless and scarlet-faced. Behind him came Coryc with Dwaen and Lord Cadlew, with Jill trailing behind. Coryc's careful mask of sympathy shattered at the sight.

"Bavydd!" Coryc said. "It has to be! Oh, by the hells, then where's Lady Mallona?"

"Your Grace, if I may speak?" Jill broke in. "I'll wager she's wearing Bavydd's clothes and riding one of her husband's horses. It must have been her that the servants saw leave the dun last night."

"And she's heading south for Cerrmor," Beryn snarled. "I'll wager on *that*."

"Cerrmor?" the gwerbret said. "Why would she do that?"

"Where else can she go?" Beryn spoke so quietly that it was frightening. "Her wretched brother had a wife and children there, and Bavydd must have kin. I know my wife, Your Grace. She could fool the gods themselves when she gets to lying. But she'll never reach Cerrmor. I swear it by the Lord of Hell himself. She'll never reach it alive."

Yelling for fresh horses, Beryn ran down the stairs. Although the gwerbret hurried after him, Dwaen hesitated, motioning to Jill and Rhodry to wait with him.

"Think we'll catch her?" the tieryn said.

"Who knows, my lord?" Rhodry said. "She's got a day's start on us, but only one horse. Huh. I'll wager she can steal others. I wouldn't put anything past her."

"Not after this." Dwaen shuddered. "She must have been driven mad, the poor woman. Maybe she started hating her merchant, seeing him as the man who'd led her into these crimes or suchlike. The source of her dishonor, that kind of thing."

"His Grace is much too kind," Jill broke in. "I'll wager she wanted to save her own skin and naught more. But she hasn't ridden south."

The men turned to stare at her. Rhodry was struck by how odd she looked, pale, yes, as might be expected, but cold sweat beaded her forehead, and her eyes stared across the room as if she were seeing someone standing there. When Rhodry glanced, he could see no one.

"Jill, what do you mean?" Dwaen said. "How do you know?"

She shook her head, on the verge of trembling.

"I don't know how I know, Your Grace, but I do know. We can ride south all we want, but we won't find her."

In the end, Jill was proved right, but they did take a prize of sorts. The gwerbret left Tieryn Dwaen and Lord Cadlew behind to keep order at the dun, then rode out with Lord Beryn and a token escort from his personal warband. Rhodry went with them to bring back a report for the tieryn. In the blue twilight, they trotted fast down a dirt road and headed for the forest preserve where Beryn had his hunting lodge. By the time they reached the forest edge, night had fallen, forcing Beryn to slow the line of march. Their only road was a winding track between old oaks.

"I trust his lordship knows the trail," Coryc shouted.

"Like a gamekeeper," Beryn called back. "It's not far now."

In a bit, a faint glow appeared in the darkness ahead. Cursing under his breath, Beryn broke into a jog and headed straight for it. Rhodry kicked his tired horse and caught up just as they burst out into a clearing, where stood a long wooden building, half-house, half-shed. The glow came from its unshuttered windows, a pleasant firelight burning against the night's chill. Out in front, three men were yelling at each other as they frantically tried to saddle their horses; they'd been warned by the unmistakable clatter of riders coming their way. Screaming a war cry, Beryn drew his sword with a flourish and charged. Sword in hand, Rhodry followed, but at the sight of the gwerbret and his men pouring into the clearing, the three fell to their knees and cried surrender.

"Where's Mallona?" Beryn yelled. "Where's my wife?"

"Not here, my lord. I swear it! We were waiting for Bavydd to bring her."

The lords and their men dismounted and surrounded their prey.

Rhodry ducked into the house and took a good look round. Bedrolls and other gear lay strewn on the uneven wood floor; hunting spears hung on the wall by the rough hearth. Judging from the garbage strewn about, the pack had been waiting here for some days. Only one unusual thing caught his eye, a little silver chain lying on a bench near the door. When he picked it up, he found hanging from it not a pendant or silver bauble, but a raven's feather. Reflexively, he slipped it into his pocket, then trotted back out and found the three men spilling everything they knew in the hope of a quick death, not a slow one.

Jill's theories had been as accurate as they needed to be. Petyn had hired the fellows in a town to the south, where they were hanging round a tavern in hopes of getting work as caravan guards. He'd taken them to the hunting lodge, where Bavydd had turned up, scattering coins and bringing good provisions to buy loyalty. At first, they'd had their doubts about the job, until Bavydd made it clear they weren't really going to murder Dwaen, just make it look like they were going to.

"But then he told us to take that lady on the road," one of the men burst out. "I didn't like that." He shot his fellows a venomous glance. "Bastards, all of you, and Petyn was the worst."

"Oh, bastards, are we?" snarled the other. "You were quick enough to take that fat merchant's coin, lad."

"That's enough," Coryc said. "What did the merchant tell you to do to the lady after you'd taken her?"

"Whatever we wanted to," the lad said. "I didn't like that, Your Grace, I swear it. We were to bring her here, have our sport with her, and talk like we were Beryn's men. Then we were supposed to put her back on her horse and let her go."

"It's a cursed good thing Tieryn Dwaen isn't here right now," Coryc remarked to no one in particular.

All three of the captured men were staring at Rhodry.

"Oh, I recognize you well enough." Rhodry turned to the gwerbret. "These are the lads, all right, who killed Dwaen's rider, the one who was escorting Ylaena and her servingwoman."

"Very well, Silver Dagger. They'll pay for that, too. My Lord Beryn? Let's get our three rats on their horses and get back to your dun."

Before they rode out, Beryn found a torch in the lodge and lit it at the hearth, then had one of the gwerbret's men put out the fire. Everyone followed the bobbing point of light from the torch at the head of the line as they picked their way back through the forest and across the meadow. By the time they reached the dun, it was close to midnight.

Beryn's great hall, such as it was, was crammed with men, sitting on straw, standing and leaning against the wall, while frantic servants rushed back and forth with ale and bread. The noble-born found what stools and benches as they could and moved them round the battered-planks-over-trestles that served Beryn as a table of honor. Beryn sat slouched in the only chair, one foot braced against the table, and drank steadily, looking across the room with eyes so dark it was doubtful that he was seeing the farther wall.

"Now, here," Coryc said at last. "It'll be futile to take tired men on tired horses out on the south road tomorrow. I want to see your lady brought to justice as much as you do, but by the hells, we don't even know if she went straight south. If she keeps her wits about her, she'll ride a roundabout road to throw us off the track."

Beryn grunted and stared into his tankard of ale.

"Wits are the one thing she's never lacked," Dwaen put in. "I wonder if we'll ever get her back."

"I'll send messengers to Cerrmor tomorrow," Coryc said. "The gwerbret there will relay them to the city council, and out of courtesy to him, they'll find her."

"If she's even going to Cerrmor," Jill muttered.

The noble-born ignored her and went on squabbling for some time, until Dwaen found his common sense.

"Now here, Your Grace, we've got a pair of silver daggers, and they're famous for tracking men who need to be tracked. Why not a woman?"

"True spoken." Coryc turned to Rhodry. "I'll put a bounty on her. There'll be fifty silver pieces for you if you bring her back to my justice."

"His Grace is most generous," Rhodry said, "but there's somewhat about being a bounty hunter that rubs me wrong."

"Don't be a dolt, Rhodry," Jill snapped. "That's enough coin to buy you a remount if you lose your horse in a scrap someday."

"True enough. Well and good, Your Grace, we'll take your hire —if, of course, Tieryn Dwaen will release me."

"Gladly. I don't suppose my life's in danger anymore."

Beryn got up, the tankard in his hand.

"Not from me. That rotten young cub of mine was too much like his mother, anyway."

Beryn hurled the tankard against the wall, then ran from the room. They heard the door slam behind him.

"The poor old bastard," Cadlew remarked with a sigh. "I'm blasted glad now I never screwed his wife."

"You're the very soul of honor," Dwaen said. "But you should be glad for more reasons than one. If she'd got tired of you, she might have served you some cursed strange mead." All the men laughed in a small spasm of nerves.

Noble-born and commoners alike, the men found themselves what places they could to sleep that night. A little hunting out in the ward brought Rhodry and Jill a storage shed, festooned with the few remaining strings of last year's onions, with enough room near the door for them to spread out their blankets. Exhausted as he was, Rhodry sat awake, watching the dapples of candlelight on the rough walls.

"What's wrong?" Jill said.

"I just keep thinking of poor old Bavydd. He wasn't a pretty sight."

"He wasn't, but well, we've both seen worse."

"Just so, but this was a particularly vile sort of death. I mean, there he was, poisoned by a woman."

"Is that what makes it so vile, that his killer was a woman?"

"Of course. Ye gods, she must be a fiend from hell!"

"I don't know. I mean, truly, she broke every law of the gods and the king both, but I almost feel sorry for her."

"Have you gone daft?"

"Well, here she was, trapped in this dun with a man like Beryn." Jill sat up, shoving the blankets back. "Everything I've heard about her said she's got more wits than most people, and a strong will, too, and some of the women said that when she was young she was so merry, always laughing and singing. She would have been a perfect wife for a great lord, running his big household and angling to get him favors at court and suchlike. But she ends up moldering here, and all because she defended her brother from their father's wrath."

"A lot of women end up in country duns. They make the best of it without taking lovers and studying poisons."

"True enough. I suppose you're right."

Yet she sounded doubtful still. He would have said more, but she slipped her arms around his neck and kissed him. He could forget all his worries in the feel of her body, pressed close to his.

Yet in the morning, the worries about the bounty hunt ahead of them came back with the rising sun. After they dressed, they opened the door against the reek of onions. Jill pulled on her boots, then merely sat on the floor, looking out at nothing in particular.

"Somewhat's troubling you," Rhodry said.

"It is. Where did she get that poison?"

Rhodry had to admit that it was an interesting point. When he'd been growing up in Aberwyn's court, he'd been taught a bit about poisons in sheer self-defense—highly placed men were always in danger of intrigues—but he'd never seen or heard of anything like the drug that had killed Bavydd.

"Well, they say you can buy some cursed strange things on the Cerrmor docks," Rhodry said. "Imports from Bardek. Bavydd probably brought it to her."

"If he brought it, how come he was stupid enough to drink it?"

"Good point. Unless it was tasteless. The best poisons always are."

"Maybe. I mean, it must have been that. But I'd like to make sure, and for that, we'll need its name."

"Well, I can tell you the one Bavydd used in the gwerbret's palace—just a raw dose of belladonna."

"Bavydd? Oh, of course, it must have been him who gave that serving lass the mead. So if he had the belladonna, he must have brought her the other poison, too."

"He just never dreamt she'd use it on him."

It made perfect sense, yet they exchanged an uneasy glance. With a toss of his head, Rhodry rose, catching the doorjamb in one hand and staring out across the ward, where the gwerbret's men were beginning to ready their horses.

"Jill? Do you think there's sorcery mixed up in this somehow?"

"I do, but I couldn't tell you why."

A cold stripe of fear ran down his back. Just the summer before, dweomer had swept into his life like a storm-wave, bringing Jill with it, leaving her behind like some long-buried treasure brought up from the sea. Yet he was always aware that sorcery threatened to sweep her away again. He kept remembering a man named Aderyn, who had magical powers beyond what Rhodry had ever believed possible, telling him that Jill was marked for the dweomer herself. He refused to believe it. She loved him, she belonged to him, and that's all there was to that. But when he turned to look at her, sitting on their dirty blankets amid sacks of moldy flour, he found her staring off into one of those private spaces that only she could see.

"Let's ride," he snapped. "Mallona has, I'll wager, and she's getting farther away all the time."

"No doubt." Jill scrambled up. "Which way shall we go?"

"I was hoping you could tell me that."

As soon as the words were out of his mouth, he regretted them. There it was again: dweomer. As if she knew what he was thinking, she smiled in a wry sort of way.

"Well, let's go south for a little ways. That's what I would do if I were her. Lay a false trail toward Cerrmor, and then go somewhere else."

"Sounds reasonable. Oh. Ye gods, I nearly forgot." He reached into his brigga pocket and pulled the by now ill-used feather on its chain. "What do you think about this? I found it in Beryn's lodge."

Jill took the chain and considered it with the same look she'd give maggoty meat.

"I've seen one of these before, when I was still traveling with my Da," she said at last. "They'd hanged the woman who was wearing it. I don't know why. Da wouldn't let me look at the corpse for more than a moment, and he wouldn't let me ask the townfolk, either."

She started to toss it away, then reconsidered, kneeling down to put it in a saddlebag.

"You should give that to the gwerbret," Rhodry said.

"Well, sooner or later. But I want to show it to someone else first. I'm starting to get another idea. You know, I heard some rather strange things about Lady Mallona when I was up in the women's hall of Coryc's dun."

"Obviously. Ye gods, I'll never forget the look on poor old Cadlew's face."

"Not just that, dolt. There were rumors that Mallona studied the Old Lore. Lady Ganydda swore she didn't believe it, but she was awfully eager to repeat it. She was supposed to have been fond of a strange old woman near her brother's dun when she was a child—"

"And of course the poor old woman was a witch." Rhodry finished this all-too-familiar bit of gossip for her. "Any old woman who lives alone is always supposed to be a witch."

"True spoken, but consider this. Mallona had that lover for a couple of years, and she only had the one child by Beryn. Now, whether that was Beryn's trouble, who knows, but if that lover was a cold stick, she wouldn't have bothered with him, and she wasn't interested in Cadlew for fine conversation. Why doesn't she have a couple of bastard children to palm off as her husband's?"

"They always say the Old Lore can remove that kind of nuisance from a woman's life, don't they?"

"Just that." Jill thought for a moment. "Lord Beryn's cook told me that every now and then, the lady had weak spells, when she'd take to her bed for days and look terrible ill."

"Ye gods! I never realized that the servants in a dun know about every blasted thing their masters do."

"Oh, doubtless the cooks and suchlike in Aberwyn could tell plenty of fine tales about you, Rhodry Maelwaedd."

Rhodry had the unpleasant feeling that he was blushing.

The hunt should have been easy. A woman traveling alone was such an unusual thing in those days that anyone she passed should have noticed and remembered her. A woman who'd spent most of her life shut up in a dun should have had every possible trouble on the road, too. Although Lady Mallona's life had hardly been pampered and courtly, still, she'd doubtless never had to build a campfire, haggle for food, find water for her horse, or do any of those hundred other tasks that fell to travelers on the Deverry roads.

An easy task to find her, stuck somewhere with a lame horse or trying to bargain with suspicious innkeeps—except that after a full day on the south-running road, Rhodry had to admit that she seemed to have disappeared like dweomer. No farmer had remembered seeing her, no tavernman had given her shelter, no noble lord had wondered about a solitary rider traveling across his demesne.

"I'm beginning to think that she didn't go south after all," Rhodry said. "Not even to lay a false trail. May the gods blast me if I give up, though. If any woman ever deserved hanging, she does."

"I suppose." Jill thought for a while, staring moodily into the flames of their campfire. "Now, from the way she was described to us, I can't believe she'd have any luck disguising herself as a man, not during broad daylight."

"I've been wondering about that myself."

"And she's never been more than thirty miles from her home in her life. You'd think she'd get lost or suchlike."

"So you'd think."

They shared a sigh of frustration and contemplated the fire.

"I wonder if she's dead," Jill said abruptly. "Maybe she killed herself somewhere, or ran into a pack of young men who raped and murdered her."

"It would be a fitting end, so fitting that I doubt the gods would be so kind to us. Well, here, should we go all the way to Cerrmor? If she does end up there, probably she'll be arrested. Coryc made those messages pretty urgent."

"True spoken, but if we don't find her first, we don't get the bounty."

Although it was true, it was also so cold-blooded that Rhodry didn't even know what to say to it.

"Let's ride south for a bit longer," Jill went on. "There's a town not far from here, Muir it's called, and there's a temple of the Goddess there."

Rhodry swore under his breath.

"I should have thought of that," he said. "Sanctuary. Do you think she'd have the gall to seek it?"

"Why not? Gall seems to be the one thing she's never lacked."

If Mallona had indeed sought refuge with the Holy Ladies, they were going to have a fine time trying to get her out again. Gwerbret Coryc would have to confer with the gwerbret of this rhan, and if that worthy agreed, they would have to set up a judicial council that would meet outside the temple gates and present evidence to the High Priestess and the temple council. Only if the High Priestess agreed that Mallona was guilty would the Holy Ladies surrender her. Since every gwerbret in the kingdom grumbled that the priestess always sided with the woman in the case, no matter what, it was quite possible that Mallona would convince them with her lies and end up spending the rest of her life in the penitential rites of the temple. Penance was not going to be satisfying. Rhodry wanted to see her dead.

The sun was low and golden in the sky when they reached the rich farms of the temple's lands, worked by free farmers who owed fealty to the High Priestess, not a lord. The temple itself rose on a hill behind high stone walls, an enormous complex for the time, spilling half down the hillside and guarded by iron-bound gates trimmed with silver interlace and the holy symbols of the Moon. Above the walls, among the towers of the various brochs inside, Rhodry could see trees growing, the dark green bushy cedars brought all the way from Bardek and coddled to keep them alive in this colder land. Although the gates stood open, Rhodry stopped his horse and dismounted the ritual hundred feet away. Jill would have to go on alone to this place that no man could enter or approach.

Beside the road was a stand of poplars, a water trough, a rail for tying horses, and a pleasantly carved wooden bench.

"At least you'll be provided for, my love," Jill said. "It shouldn't take me long, truly, to ask a few questions of the priestesses. By law, they have to tell anyone who asks if Mallona's in there. Oh, wait! That silver chain you found? It's in my saddlebags, isn't it, not yours?"

"I saw you put it there. Why?"

"I want to show it to the Holy Ladies, of course. They'll know what it means."

Rhodry watched as Jill rode the last hundred feet and dismounted at the gates. A small flock of priestesses ran to greet her. He heard one woman shriek; then everyone began to laugh, their high pure voices drifting down the hill. They'd probably thought Jill was a lad, he figured, and he smiled at the jest himself. Surrounded

75

by the priestesses, Jill led her horse inside, and the gates closed behind her.

Rhodry watered his horse, tied it up, then sat down on the bench with a chunk of bread. It was pleasant in the warm shade, silent except for the buzz of a drowsy fly. Rhodry stretched his legs out in front of him and enjoyed the soldier's luxury of merely sitting still in a safe place.

Like most Deverry men, Rhodry knew very little about the Old Lore, that worship of an ancient goddess which had come with the people of Bel from the Homeland, where it had seemed as dark and primitive then as it did now to the modern Deverrian mind. Aranrhodda was her name, and she had a magical cauldron which was always full, which would give every man his favorite meat and drink no matter how many kinds were called out of a single batch, and which would also poison those who had displeased the Goddess or one of her worshippers.

One old story stuck in his mind. Aranrhodda had tricked the gods into giving her cauldron its dweomer in this wise: she made a magical golden piglet and tethered it in a thorny thicket. One at a time, Bel, Lug, Nudd, and Dwn tried to free the piglet and claim the prize, but every time the thorns drove them back. Only Epona and the Goddess of the Moon refused to try, because they knew their sister too well. Whenever the gods pricked themselves on the thorns and bled, Aranrhodda caught the drops in her cauldron. Finally, when they went away, cursing her soundly for the ruse, she killed the piglet and made the first stew in the cauldron using the divine blood for soup.

Just thinking about the story made Rhodry shudder. Drinking the blood of a god was one of the most impious things he could think of. Of course, the gods themselves did what they willed and lived by their own laws, ones that humanity could only shake their heads and wonder over. But it was no wonder that Aranrhodda's followers were reputed to do such grisly things: use the fetuses they'd aborted in strange spells, for one, and make up poisons to order for another, along with the usual curses and love charms. He sincerely hoped that the wretched Mallona wasn't up to her neck in this magical muck, because at heart, he was afraid to pull her out of it. Rhodry got up and began pacing beside the road.

It was sunset before Jill came back, leading her horse down the hill from the temple, all cheerful efficiency.

"Sorry I lingered so long, my love, but I heard many an interesting thing from the Holy Ladies. Mallona's not there, but the High Priestess knows about the Old Lore. What I learned might come in awfully handy. Just for starters, that chain with the feather? It's a thing you make to give to someone in your service."

"Too bad Bavydd took it off, huh? It might have brought him better luck. Here, is there a village nearby, or can we camp on the temple's roads?"

"There's a village with a tavern not far to the west. The tavernman's used to sheltering the men who escort their wives here, so we can find good lodging, or so Her Holiness told me."

"Good. I wouldn't mind sleeping on a decent mattress for a change. I don't suppose Her Holiness had any idea of where we might look for Mallona."

"West, near Lughcarn. I swear it, the priestesses hear everything worth hearing in their part of the country. This is only a hint, mind, and it might well turn out to be a false trail."

"Better than no trail at all. Well and good, then. Let's ride."

2

IN THE FINE DUSTING of soot on the windowsill, Sevinna idly printed her name, then flicked the soot away with the side of her hand. No matter how often the servants cleaned, there was always soot on everything in Lughcarn. She looked out the window to the ward of the gwerbretal dun, a small village within the city, with its barracks, stables, round huts, and even some little houses for the privileged servants, all of them topped with dirty gray thatch. The sky beyond glowed hazy and golden from the smoke of the thousands of charcoal fires burning in the iron smelters at the edge of town. Most of the iron ore that came downriver from the northern mines passed to be smelted down into ingots before being traded further, because by the king's own charter, Lughcarn held a virtual monopoly on rough smelting in the northern kingdom. The monopoly, of course, made the gwerbretrhyn rich, less so only than Cerrmor and the king's own city of Dun Deverry itself.

"Sevvi?" Babryan called out. "Is somewhat wrong?"

"Oh, naught." Sevinna turned from the window. "Just wondering if Mam and her escort were home by now."

"Probably. Are you going to miss your family?"

"Of course, but it's splendid getting to stay here, anyway."

Babryan smiled and gestured at a cushioned chair next to her own. Sevinna dutifully sat down and looked round the richly furnished room, the top floor of a half-broch entirely devoted to the

78

gwerbret's womenfolk, and the private preserve of Babryan and her sister, Wbridda, Sevinna's cousins. That unmarried lasses would have a hall of their own was a breathtaking sort of luxury to Sevinna, who had been raised in her father, Tieryn Obyn's, country dun to the north. Babryan and Wbridda had fine silk dresses, too, and lots of silver jewelry and soft wool cloaks, dyed in any color they chose. At one side of the room stood four carved chests, packed full of extra clothing. Those chests made Sevinna painfully aware of her own coarse linen dresses, all three of them, which sat neatly folded on a chair beside her bed. Her one consolation was that she was as pretty as they were, in spite of their jewelry. In fact, she looked enough like them to be another sister—blond lasses, all of them, with wide blue eyes and a heavy but sensually curving mouth that was the mark of the gwerbret's line.

"I'm truly glad you're here," Wbridda said. At thirteen, she was the youngest of the girls. "I'll wager we can find you a better husband than you'd ever find up north."

Sevinna giggled and covered her mouth with her hand.

"And what makes you think I'm looking for a husband?"

"Oh, huh! Why else are you here?" Babryan broke in. "Mam told us all about it. She doesn't want you to marry some rough northern fellow, either. Don't worry. There's lots of young men hanging around Da. I'll wager there's a truly handsome man who'll be thrilled to marry the gwerbret's niece."

"Baba, you're so cold!" Sevinna said.

"Oh, you've got to be when you pick a husband." Babryan leaned forward earnestly in her chair. "Mam was telling me. She's hoping to get me a place at court next year, you see, one of the princess's servingwomen, maybe. Oooh—who knows who I'll meet there?"

"Someone very rich," Wbridda said. "And old and ugly."

All three of them giggled, then laughed, the giggles feeding on themselves and turning into a wave of something near hysteria. I don't want to marry yet, Sevinna thought, but Da says I've got to. She laughed with the rest until at last the giggling stopped as suddenly as it had come.

"I just hope I don't fall in love with someone who doesn't favor me," Sevinna said. "But maybe I'll never fall in love at all, and that will settle that."

"Oh, listen to Sevvi." Wbridda rolled her eyes heavenward. "Baba used to talk that way, and then last year she met Lord Abryn, and all I heard was men men men. You're disgusting, Baba."

"You just wait." Babryan tossed her head. "Besides, Lord Abryn was only a passing fancy. I must have been daft. He's got hair on the backs of his hands."

"Hah!" Wbridda said. "You mean he was only a lord. Da was ever so angry, Sevvi. He practically turned Lord Abryn out of the palace, and all he did was give Baba some roses."

"Well, I should think that was quite enough," Sevinna said. "When a young man gives a lass flowers, it means something serious."

"He was a rake, too," Wbridda pronounced.

"Now here, Bry," Babryan snapped. "You're too young to even know what that means."

"I am not. I heard Mam and Da talking." She rolled her eyes significantly. " 'I'm not marrying her to a common lord, baby or not,' Da said, and then he said, 'so you'd better be cursed sure he never gives her one.' Mam was so mad! Oh, you should have heard her, Sevvi."

"You hold your tongue!" Babryan said with a blush.

"Shan't," Wbridda simpered at her. "And then Da said—"

Babryan rose from her chair and raised her hand to threaten a slap, but the door opened and Lady Caffa swept into the room. Although she was growing stout, Caffa was still a beautiful woman, with thick blond hair and eyes of the deepest violet. Her long green silk dress trailed behind her in a train and was bound in at the waist with a kirtle of her husband's green and blue plaid. At the sight of her mother, Babryan curtsied and sat down again.

"Sevinna, dearest," Caffa said, "I've summoned one of the clothsellers from the town. We must get you some decent dresses soon, and I'll need you to pick out the colors you want. Then we shall set the women sewing."

"My lady is ever so generous." Sevinna rose and curtsied to her. "I don't deserve such honor."

"Oh, hush, child." Caffa smiled vaguely in her direction. "Of course you do. You poor thing! Here you are, eighteen and not even married, and perhaps it's just as well, of course, considering what your poor dear mother has to pick from, but still! I'm so glad she finally listened to reason and sent you to me. Poor dear Maemigga."

Sevinna curtsied again, but her heart was aching. She felt like a charity project, some farmer's widow plucked from poverty and given a decent place in the kitchen. Her mother's marriage was the big scandal of the gwerbret's clan; Maemigga had loved her land-poor tieryn so much that she'd ridden off on her own one night and married him before her family could stop her. By the time the gwerbret had caught up with her, she was so obviously no longer a maiden that his grace could do nothing but formally approve the match and make sure that Obyn never forgot what he owed him, either. To the children of this love match, the gwerbret and his wife had always been kind—very, very kind—as Caffa was now, smiling as she studied Sevinna like a bit of cloth on which she planned to embroider.

"Baba," Caffa pronounced, "surely you can lend Sevvi some of your dresses until hers are ready. We have guests tonight at dinner, you see."

"Handsome guests?" Babryan said with a grin. "Of course, Sevvi. Mine are yours. We'll look through and pick one out."

"Good child. But truly, you lasses must stop thinking of little things like a man's looks. Most good-looking men are so horribly vain—well, Sevvi dear, your father's an exception, truly, but he's the only one I've ever met—and anyway, it's things like steadiness and kindness that matter in a marriage, not curly hair and blue eyes."

"Of course," the three girls chorused.

"Oh, I know!" Caffa waggled a playful finger at them. "I was your age once, wasn't I? But it's time for all of you to think of the things that matter. We shall have lots of nice chats now that Sevvi's here."

When Lady Caffa turned away, Babryan rolled her eyes heavenward, and all three girls broke out giggling.

Dinner that night was a splendid meal, as every meal seemed to be in the gwerbret's palace. The gwerbret and his family ate at a carved and polished table near a hearth inlaid with Bardek tiles. On the other side of the enormous hall, a warband of two hundred men sat listening to their own bard. Servants in spotless embroidered clothes silently and gracefully served four elaborate courses, starting with a vegetable aspic made in colorful layers as intricate as the tiles and ending with an apple cake soaked in fine mead. While Sevinna desperately tried to mimic her cousins' delicate manners, she watched this guest, who, or so Caffa had made clear, had been invited expressly to look over the gwerbret's unmarried niece. Although his title was simple, Lord Timryc was one of the king's own equerries with a large holding of land near the Holy City itself. He seemed a pleasant enough fellow, about thirty, with sandy-blond hair, a prominent chin, and undeniably kind eyes. Every now and then, he would look Sevinna's way and smile at her, a gesture that flustered her so much that she would bury her nose in her water goblet. When at the end of the meal the ladies retired to their hall, Sevinna was profoundly glad to be gone.

Caffa took the girls to her own hall, a vast round room where Bardek tapestries hung at intervals on the walls and cushioned furniture stood in profusion. The servingwomen lit candles in silver sconces, then sat down on cushions near the mistress's chair.

"Well, Sevinna dearest," Caffa said, "he seems a very nice man. Not too young, of course, but his first wife died in labor, you see. He's been consolidating his position at court, and a man like that can hold out for a good match. But anyway, I think we shall arrange a little riding party tomorrow." She glanced at Wbridda. "Now Bry, if you mind your manners and that tongue of yours, you may join us and bring your little falcon."

"My thanks, Mam," Wbridda said. "Don't worry, I won't get in the way. He looks dull to me."

"Now hush," Caffa snapped. "You may all go upstairs."

No sooner were they safely in their own hall than Babryan wrinkled her nose and stuck out her tongue.

"He's too old. You can do better than that, Sevvi."

"I hope so," Sevinna said. "I didn't like his chin, either."

"It's his beastly position that Mama's so smitten with," Wbridda put in. "But he just won't do."

"I'm glad you agree with me. Well, maybe he won't like me. My father can't give me that big of a dowry, after all."

Wbridda smiled in an oddly sly way and sat down on a chair with a flounce of her dresses.

"We can make sure he's not interested. Can't we, Baba?"

"If we have to. We've got somewhat to tell you, Sevvi. It's a secret, so you've got to promise you'll never tell anyone, especially a man."

"Of course I'll promise. What is it?"

"It's a thing we learned from Lady Davylla. She's the wife of Lord Elyc of Belgwerger."

"All the ladies are doing it," Wbridda put in. "That's why we've got to keep it a secret, you see. But anyway, Lady Davylla spends lots of time in court, and she says that even the princesses know. I don't know about the queen, though."

"Oh, she's doubtless too busy with all that court stuff she has to do. But it's ever so amusing, Sevvi, and I'll wager it works."

"What?"

"You have to swear first," Babryan said. "Just a promise won't do. Come on, Bry. Go get your little knife. We'll do it by the fire."

While Wbridda rummaged through her jewelry casket, Babryan put out all the candles so that the only light was a pool from the fire. When Sevinna and Babryan knelt down in the flickering shadows, Babryan giggled in pleasant excitement, and Sevinna caught her mood. Whatever this mysterious something was, it was much more amusing to think about than marrying a man she hardly knew. Wbridda knelt down beside them and opened her hand to show Sevinna a tiny knife with a silver handle and a blade of black obsidian.

"Lady Davylla has a Wise Woman living in her dun," Wbridda explained. "She's awfully, awfully old, she doesn't even have any teeth, but she knows everything. She makes these knives, you see. Lady Davylla gives them to her special friends, and she gave one to us."

"What are they for?"

"We'll tell you once you swear," Babryan said. "Here, we're going to have to have a bit of your hair and a drop of your blood, but it won't hurt. That knife's awfully sharp."

Wbridda cut off a tiny bit of Sevinna's hair and laid it on the hearthstone, then pricked her index finger and squeezed a drop of blood onto the hair. Sevinna sucked her fingertip.

"Now you've got to swear you'll never repeat any of this to one who doesn't know the Goddess," Babryan said.

"Which goddess?"

"We can't say yet. Just swear."

"All right. I swear I won't betray the secrets to one who doesn't know the Goddess."

"And to any man ever."

"And to any man ever."

Babryan picked up the bit of hair and threw in into the fire.

"Aranrhodda," she called out. "Aranrhodda, favor our cousin, and us, too, for bringing her to you!"

The bit of hair caught and burned with a drift of stench in the wood smoke. Sevinna went cold, wondering what she'd just done to herself, wishing she'd asked more before she'd sworn the vow, but Babryan and Wbridda were giggling. Oh, there can't be any harm in it, Sevinna thought, not if they'd do it.

"There, now you're one of us," Babryan announced. "Lady Davylla will probably ride our way soon for a visit, and you'll get to meet her. Oh, she's ever so splendid."

"But anyway," Wbridda said, "if you don't like this Timryc fellow, we'll just work a charm to turn him cold to you. You can work lots of charms when you learn how, Sevvi. There's one to turn a man cold to you, and one to make him love you, and one to make your father or brother favor the man you favor, just lots of them."

"Oh, here," Sevinna said, "I thought you didn't even care what men did."

"Well, it's all going to come in handy someday." Wbridda shrugged. "I don't want to marry some dry stick of a man just because Da says I have to. This way there's stuff you can do about it, you see. Otherwise there isn't."

Sevinna nodded. She did see, entirely too well.

On the morrow, Gwerbret Tudvulc called Sevinna into his private council chamber for a little chat. Her uncle, so tall and stout and noisy, had always intimidated Sevinna, and being dependent on his charity only frightened her the more. Tudvulc sat her down in a chair and strode back and forth by an open window while they talked. His mop of brown hair and mustaches had gone quite gray since the last time she'd seen him.

"Now here, lass. No use in mincing words, eh? I want you to take a good look at Timryc here. He's got splendid connections, a good bit of land. You'd have plenty of pretty dresses from a man like that, eh?"

Sevinna smiled out of duty alone.

"But there's no use in jumping at the first hare out of the bushes, either," Tudvulc went on. "You're my niece, got connections of your own, and you're blasted good-looking, too. A pretty face is worth half a dowry, eh? So you just wait and see what kind of game we can beat out of the forest, lass. No rush. You're always welcome at my table."

"His Grace is ever so kind." Sevinna bowed her head. "I'm willing to wait for the right match."

"Good, good. Never know about you lasses, eh? Most of you are so eager to get that crown of roses on your head you can't think straight." He gave her a twisted grin that was doubtless meant to be jolly and avuncular. "Oh, the gwerbret of Buccbrael has a young son, too. Be a cursed good alliance for both our clans, and I hear the lad's already turning the heads of the local lasses. Good-looking sort. A year or two younger than you, but young men grow faster with a wife in their bed. We'll see what we can turn up, truly."

Bowing, a page appeared in the doorway.

85

"Your Grace? There's a messenger here from the gwerbret of Caenmetyn. He says it concerns an urgent matter of justice, an escaped murderer."

"Indeed? Send him straight in. Here, lass, you run along to your aunt and have a nice little ride."

Sevinna rose, curtsied, and made a grateful escape. In the corridor, she passed the messenger, a warrior with the blazon of Caenmetyn on his road-stained shirt.

The afternoon's expedition rode slowly along the grassy banks of the Sironaver, sparkling in the sun, until they came to a spot where willow trees had been planted to give some shade for just this sort of party. The grass had been trimmed back with a scythe, too, and beds of bright flowers made pleasant curves by the riverbank. When the others dismounted, Wbridda, with her falcon on her gloved wrist and one of the pages riding behind, went off into the grasslands to hunt. As she'd been told to do, Sevinna waited a moment before dismounting. Sure enough, Lord Timryc hurried to her side to help her down from her sidesaddle. His hands were strong on her waist, his smile carefully courtly as he set her down.

"This is truly a lovely place," Timryc said. "Will my lady honor me by walking down the river to see the view?"

"My thanks, my lord. What a pretty thought."

As they walked, Sevinna found herself tongue-tied; all she could do was ask him questions about his life at court, but the questions had to be carefully phrased, as it would be most discourteous if he thought she were prying into his financial worth or standing. Fortunately, Timryc had no difficulty at all keeping a conversation going, especially when the subject was himself. Sevinna was amazed at how often he could mention the times the king had spoken to him or the queen had thanked him for some favor.

Getting back to the privacy of the women's quarters was like finding refuge from a storm. Sevinna sank gratefully into a chair and wondered if she could feign a headache to get out of sitting next to Timryc at dinner. Babryan sat down next to her and gave Wbridda a scowl.

"Go change that dress! You've got blood all over your sleeve."

"We had a good hunt," Wbridda said. "Two sparrows and a crow."

"Ugh! I don't care. Or wait! Did you get some of the crow's feathers?"

With a grin, Wbridda pulled three black tail feathers out of her kirtle and held them up.

"Those are ever so useful for charms, Sevvi," Babryan explained. "If you don't want Lord Timryc, we'll work one tonight on him."

"Oh, splendid! Because I don't."

The girls waited till late that night to make the charm. Wbridda brought one of the black feathers; Babryan, a candle end; and Sevinna, a bone stylus. They crouched down close to the hearth, and Babryan laid the candle end down a little distance from the flames.

"We'll let the wax soften."

"All right," Sevinna said. "Now here, though, this won't make his lordship sick or anything, will it?"

"Oh, of course not," Wbridda chimed in. "It's awfully hard to make someone sick or have them die or suchlike. You've got to have bits of their fingernails or hair, and you've got to have special herb oil, and you've got to work the charms nine times at midnight and all do sorts of stuff."

"All right, then. He's only an awful bore. I don't want to cause him any harm. Do you know anyone who's ever worked this charm before?"

"Oh, lots of people," Babryan said. "Lady Davylla's sisters, and then their friends. I don't know anyone who's ever worked the death curse, though. Oooh! That would be awful. You'd have to really hate someone."

"I bet Lady Davylla's Wise Woman could do it, though," Wbridda said. "Or one of her friends."

"There's some round Lughcarn, too," Babryan added. "We've got a little silver chain Lady Davylla's Wise Woman gave us, you see.

If we show it to one of the Wise Women here, they'll know that we're their friends."

"Have you talked to any of them?" Sevinna said.

"Not yet, because it's so hard to get away from Mam. Now that you're here, we'll have to think of a way to do it. We can pretend to hunt with falcons or suchlike. It'll be ever so exciting."

"Let's do it soon," Sevinna said. "Look, the wax is getting really soft."

Babryan picked up the warm candle end and kneaded it into the shape of a heart. When it was cool, Sevinna scratched Timryc's mark onto the surface, then handed it to Wbridda, who stuck the shaft of the feather into the wax. While Sevinna held the heart over the fire, the other two began to chant Aranrhodda's name. She threw the heart into the hottest part of the fire and watched as the feather singed and flared.

"Let his regard for her melt, melt, melt," Babryan chanted.

For a moment, the heart held steady, then began to twist and run. The wax flared with a plume of black smoke. Sevinna was suddenly frightened: it seemed that a face looked out of the flames, a pair of eyes, dark and grim, looking her straight in the face and marking her presence.

"Aranrhodda, Aranrhodda, Aranrhodda!" Babryan was whispering the chant over and over. "Let his heart melt, melt, melt."

The face disappeared; there was only the fire and the flaring wax along a log. Sevinna felt herself shuddering as if she knelt by a winter window instead of a roaring fire.

Black thatch covered the inn roof, the innyard stank from a dirty stable, and the innkeep kept picking at a boil on his face, but the place was the only one in Lughcarn that would take in silver daggers. All the time they were sweeping out stalls and tending their horses, Rhodry grumbled, but Jill ignored him. He grumbled about the food, too, and she had to admit that fried turnips flecked with mutton weren't her favorite dinner, but when he insisted on wiping the rim of the tankard with the hem of his shirt before he drank from it, she'd had enough.

"Oh, stop it! I suppose you think we should be sleeping in the gwerbret's broch!"

"Don't pour vinegar in my wounds. I *have* stayed in the dun, and it's the memory that aches my heart now."

"Huh. Do you think his grace would remember you?"

"Most like. Ah, by the black ass of the Lord of Hell, I hope our paths don't cross. The last thing I want is for his grace to see me now, a lousy silver dagger."

"If you've really got lice, I'd better go through your hair tonight."

"Just a way of speaking! You don't need to make light of my shame."

"Oh, now here, my love." Jill laid her hand on his arm and smiled at him. "It's just hard for me to remember how shamed you feel, because to me you're the most wonderful man in all Deverry."

Mollified, Rhodry returned the smile. Jill went back to thinking about her plans in peace. Having the local gwerbret remember Rhodry would be useful if he'd only agree to face him. On the other hand, if Lady Mallona had found a refuge somewhere near Lughcarn, it might be better if they kept as quiet and anonymous as possible. If the priestesses of the Moon were right, some very high-born women, who doubtless had connections at the gwerbretal court, were amusing themselves by pretending to follow the Old Lore. The holy ladies considered such pastimes dangerous.

"Ye gods," Rhodry groaned. "Mallona could be anywhere."

"Just that, but maybe we can find some kind of a trail. I've got an idea, you see."

Since it was market day, Jill and Rhodry walked round the town to look the place over. Lughcarn was a big city for that time, close to twelve thousand people, cobbled street after street lined with round houses, always topped with dirty-gray thatch. They passed the foundries, long half-open sheds, and fenced yards where deep pits gaped to smelt the ore, and sticks and chunks of black

charcoal lay piled in covered sheds. At the center of town, Rhodry
pointed out the gwerbret's dun. Behind the smooth stone walls rose
the tops of the broch and the half-brochs like a thick cluster of
spears. Jill counted seven towers in all, each with slate roofs. Here
and there in a favored window a piece of glass caught the light and
gleamed.

As they lingered, admiring, the iron-bound gates swung open,
and a riding party came out on matched bay palfreys, three young
lasses in linen riding dresses, draped gracefully over their sidesaddles.
Behind them came a falconer and an escort of five riders from the
gwerbret's warband. Rhodry grabbed Jill's arm and pulled her into a
deep doorway behind them.

"Those are the gwerbret's daughters. Doubtless Babryan would
remember me, and I don't want her to see me."

"Why? Did you break her heart or suchlike?"

"Naught of the sort! The last time I saw her, she was a child
with her hair back in a braid. I just don't want to have to face her."

As the lasses rode slowly by, the people on the street hurried to
get out of their way, the men bowing, the women dropping curtsies.
The lasses hardly seemed to notice; they were talking among themselves and letting their gentle horses pick their own way through the
streets.

In the middle of town, Jill and Rhodry found the market square,
cluttered with booths, built all anyhow, and farmers with produce
spread out on the ground wherever they could find a bare spot.
Through it all wandered shabby women with baskets on their arms,
elegant women with a servant trailing behind to carry their
purchases, young men hanging round and merely watching the passing show, servants hurrying on errands. Jill and Rhodry picked their
way through heaps of cabbages and baskets of eggs, walked past a
man with a stack of round yellow cheeses, and generally looked over
the various rural people come to town to sell.

Eventually, they saw an old woman kneeling on the ground
behind a blanket spread with bunches of tied kitchen herbs, basil,
chervil, and rosemary, both fresh and dried. Her gray hair was neatly

caught back with the black headscarf of a widow, and her faded brown dress was scrupulously clean. When Jill knelt down in front of her, the old woman raised a quizzical eyebrow.

"You don't look like you do much cooking, lass."

"Well, actually, I'm looking for a different kind of herb, but I was wondering if you knew a woman who deals in physic."

"Here, there's a fine apothecary in town. Duryn's his name, and he has a shop over by the west gate."

"Well, er ah, you see, I was hoping to find a woman with herb lore, not a man."

The old woman sighed in faint disgust, looked at Rhodry, who was hovering nearby, sighed again, then crossed her arms over her chest and glared at Jill.

"Now, you should have thought of such things before you ran off with a handsome silver dagger," the old woman snapped. "Oh, your poor family! Is it too late for you to ride home?"

"Far too late," Jill said, thankful that she was lying about this supposed pregnancy. "They'll never take me back now."

"Well, my heart aches for you, lass, but you waded into this mucky river, and now you'll just have to dry your own clothes. You lasses! Ye gods! Thinking you can roll around with any man who takes your fancy and not have to give the Goddess the tribute she demands. Lasses weren't like this in my day, they weren't. We knew the right side of the blanket from the wrong one. Now, it's a nasty impious thing you're thinking of, and even if I could do a thing about it, I wouldn't, and neither would any honest woman, neither. You'd best get yourself to the temple and beg the priestesses to do something about that man of yours. No doubt he'll try to run out on you, but our gwerbret will put a stop to that if the holy ladies ask him. Lasses! Ye gods, didn't you think?"

Jill hastily rose and began babbling something about having to leave. The old woman followed and caught a startled Rhodry by the arm.

"You'd best do the right thing by this lass and marry her, Silver Dagger," she announced. "Maybe she was stupid, but you lads are the scum of the earth, getting lasses with child and then riding on again. You had the fun of getting the baby, and now you'd best turn your hand to supporting it."

This tirade was attracting quite a crowd. The cheese seller strolled over, the egg woman hurried up—everywhere folk stopped and turned to listen. When a scarlet-faced Rhodry tried to stammer out some excuse, the crowd snickered and grinned. A couple of stout older men, one of them quite well-dressed in the checked brigga of a merchant, trotted over and made the old women bows.

"Now what's this, Gwedda?" the merchant said. "Has this lad dishonored this poor lass?"

"He has, and now she's with child. You men! A rotten pack, all of you."

"I'm going to marry her!" Rhodry squealed. "I swear it! Come on, Jill!"

Rhodry grabbed her arm and dragged her along as he shoved their way through the snickering crowd. Once they got clear of the market square, they ran all the way back to their inn. As soon as they got into the refuge of the dark, smoky tavern room, Rhodry grabbed her by the shoulders and shook her.

"You and your ideas! You might have warned me!"

"I figured you wouldn't have gone along with it if you'd known."

"Cursed right! All I want now is to get out of here. Everyone's going to be smirking every time we walk out on the streets."

"There's still the bounty. We can't just ride away from it."

Rhodry groaned. Jill was about to say somewhat soothing when she noticed a little boy, wearing torn brigga and the sleeveless remains of a shirt, hovering in the doorway. Thinking he was a hungry beggar child, she went over to offer him a copper. He took it tight in one grubby fist and looked her over with solemn dark eyes.

"Be you that lass who was in the market? The one they was laughing at?"

"I am. What do you think about that?"

"Naught. My Gram said that she wagers she could help you."

"Oh, does she now?" Jill knelt down to look him in the face. "And who is your Gram?"

"Just my Gram. She lives on our farm. She said I should find you, like, and tell you."

"Ah, I see. And where is your farm?"

"Not far. She's gone back with the wagon. Do you want to come back with me?"

"I do, and here, I've got a horse. You can ride it, too."

The boy grinned to reveal missing front teeth. Jill supposed that he was too young even to know what kind of errand he was running. She told him to wait and hurried back to Rhodry, who was less than pleased at the thought of her going off alone.

"I don't want to alarm old Gram," Jill said. "Besides, usually this kind of woman won't speak in front of a man. Let's not put her off. She's the only clue we've got so far."

"Oh, well and good, then. But don't drink whatever it is that she brews up for you, will you? The Lord of Hell only knows what it'll do to you."

"Oh, don't worry. I've a plan in mind."

Jill saddled up her horse, lifted the boy up to sit behind the saddle, then mounted, following his direction to go to the north gate of the city. He was so entranced with getting to ride on a real warhorse that she had to keep reminding him to tell her the right road, but they finally found the farm, about three miles to the northeast. In the middle of fields of wheat and vegetables stood a sprawling compound behind a low earthen wall, the family house, the cow barn, the well, and the pigsty all jumbled up together among the dung heaps and the haystacks. When they rode in the gate, a pair of mangy yellow hounds ran up barking to greet them. Jill dismounted and set the boy down.

"Mam and Da are still out in the fields," he said. "That's why Gram said to bring you now."

Gram herself came strolling out of the house. A stout, hard-muscled woman with gnarled hands, she was wearing a black head-scarf and a brown dress, pulled up into her dirty kirtle to leave her ankles and muddy bare feet free. She gave Jill a look of honest sympathy and turned to the boy.

"Bucket of slops and greens by the hearth," she announced. "Them chickens is hungry."

When the boy ran into the house, she gestured at Jill to follow and led her down to the gate where he couldn't overhear. Flies buzzed round them, and distant chickens cackled.

"Now what's all this, lass? Gwedda's a nasty sort with her tongue. Hah! Mincing round with her nose in the air over you, and here she's buried two husbands and so eager to get another you'd swear she was a bitch in heat, you would, and at her age!"

"She was wrong, too. I'm not with child. I was trying to tell her, but all she did was natter on and on at me, and I couldn't say much with my man right there." Jill glanced round as if expecting Rhodry to pop up and spy on her. "It's about him, you see. Here I gave up my family and everything when he asked me to go with him, and every town we ride to, he's looking over the lasses. I can't say a thing about it. What if he just left me? Oh, by the Goddess herself, it aches my heart."

"Ah. Them handsome men, all face and no heart, truly."

"So I'm finding out." Jill did her best to sound bitter. "So I thought, well, maybe Aranrhodda could help me keep him faithful. You hear about things, charms and suchlike, to keep your man in your bed and nowhere else."

"So you do. Now, how long are you going to be in Lughcarn? You can't make up a powerful spell like this one in between baking your bread and cutting your dinner meat."

"At least a few days. My man's going to go up to the gwerbret's dun and see if he can find a hire, but we've got money now, so he won't be in any hurry." She noticed the mention of money bring a smile to the old woman's face. "He spends every copper the minute he gets it, but I sneaked a bit for myself."

"Sensible lass, and if you'll listen to an old woman, you'll go on sneaking a coin here and there and laying it by, like, somewhere in your clothes where he won't find it. Now, our Lady of the Cauldron can help you keep him, sure enough, but the day's going to come when you won't want to keep him, and then what are you going to do?" She fixed Jill with a stern look. "A woman with a bit put by can find herself a husband who's got a cursed short memory for what she done before she met him. You remember that."

"I will, good dame, and my thanks, but I can't imagine ever not loving my wonderful Rhodry."

The old woman rolled her eyes heavenward at the follies of young lasses, then considered the problem, idly tracing a line in the dust with her big toe.

"I'll need a bit of his hair," she said at last. "Just a bit will do."

"I've got some. I was combing his hair last night, and I kept what was in the comb." She reached into her brigga pocket and took out the strands of Rhodry's hair, carefully wrapped in a scrap of cloth.

"Oho! You seem to know a bit about our Lady's power."

"Well, my Mam knew a Wise Woman near our house. And sometimes I heard them talking when I was just a little lass."

Smiling, the old woman tucked the bit of hair into a fold of her kirtle.

"Now, tonight, when it's good and dark, I'll take this out to yonder copse. And I'll bind it up around a charm that'll bind him tight to you. But he's a good-looking man, and we'll do a bit more. I'll make you up a pot of salve, and I'll tell you how to mark him with it when he's asleep. And then." She held one forefinger straight in the air. "If he tries to roll around with some other lass, well, then." She curled the forefinger slowly down. "He won't get much fun out of it, and neither will the little slut."

Jill gave the old woman a silver coin, then started riding back to town. She was idly hoping that the spell would do Rhodry no harm when she saw a trio of riders trotting across a cow pasture and heading for the farm. By shading her eyes with her hand, she could just make out the gwerbret's daughters. There was no sign of either falconer or escort. Now isn't this interesting? Jill thought, I wonder if old Gram's going to do another bit of business today? She thought of going back on some pretext or another, then decided that it would be too obvious.

95

At the tavern, Jill found Rhodry waiting by the fire, where he was whittling a stick into nervous shreds with his silver dagger. The innkeep watched him with a scowl as if he were thinking he was lucky it wasn't the furniture. Jill took Rhodry out to the stables on the excuse of helping with the horse.

"It all went well. I'm supposed to ride back tomorrow and pick up a love charm."

"A love charm? Better than a dose of herbs, I suppose, but what are you going to do with that?"

"Naught, of course, but I had to gain her confidence, didn't I? Here, if you start feeling sick or suchlike, tell me."

"What? What have you done? Hired some daft old woman to put a spell on me?"

"She's far from daft, but don't worry about the spell. I just told her some tale about fearing you'd stop loving me."

Rhodry shrugged the problem away. Jill decided that she'd best not tell him about the pot of salve.

On the morrow morning, Jill rode out the north gate and headed in the direction of the farm until she found a stand of trees where she could dismount and stand hidden. Sure enough, in a little while the three young ladies from the gwerbret's palace rode by, followed by their usual escort. Jill rode after, taking a roundabout way through the various dirt roads and tracks that ran from farm to farm. Finally, she caught up with them again down by the riverbank. The escort had tethered their horses in the shade of a pair of big ash trees and were hunkering down to play dice; the falconer was talking earnestly with the girls, each of whom had a little merlin on her gloved and padded wrist. Jill trotted on by to the farm.

When she arrived, circumstances favored her. Gram was busy kneading a batch of bread, a process that couldn't be stopped in the middle. Jill sat down on a battered wooden bench and wondered how long it would take the girls to get away from their escort.

"Now don't worry, lass," Gram said abruptly. "That charm's a good one, if I do say so myself. Just as I was finishing it up, the moon, she rises, and the moonlight comes through the trees and falls right on it."

"That's wonderful. I just worry so much."

"Course you do. Now, I'll just make this into loaves, and we'll let it rise while we talk things over."

Once the loaves of bread were formed and draped with a damp cloth on a wooden board, the old woman went into another chamber. Jill could hear her rustling about; then she came back with a small clay pot stoppered with a bit of old rag and a small object wrapped in black cloth. She handed Jill the wrapped object, then sat down next to her.

"Now, don't you ever unwrap that cloth. It'll spoil the dweomer if you do. You carry that with you, and we'll see if your pretty silver dagger has eyes for another lass again." She set the pot on the table. "I'll wager he's a hard-drinking man, so you wait until he's sound asleep and snoring from his ale, and then you put this on his back. I'll show you the pattern to draw."

With the pattern came a silent prayer: Aranrhodda, Aranrhodda, Aranrhodda, rica rica soro, alam bacyn alam, Aranrhodda rica. Since the old woman could tell her nothing about what this chant meant, Jill had trouble memorizing it. By the time she did, the morning was well on its way to noon, and the old woman hospitably offered her a bit of ale and cheese.

"If that man of yours isn't going to wonder where you are, that is. Don't want to make him turn nasty and beat you."

"Oh, he'll be looking for a hire all day. That's why I knew I could get away."

They settled down companionably to their lunch. It was easy to ask innocent questions and get the old woman to reminiscing about various times she'd used the lore.

"Now, here," Jill said at last, "suppose I run into trouble somewhere else along the road. Do you think I'll be able to find another Wise Woman?"

"Depends where you ride. But usually you can find one of us if you look hard enough."

"Of course, you'd hardly know. It's not like you could travel and meet places or suchlike."

"True enough, but every now and then, you hear a bit of news."

Jill was wondering how deeply she dared pry when they heard horses riding into the farmyard. The hounds leapt up and barked their way out the front door with Gram right behind them. When Jill hurried after, she saw the three lasses from the gwerbret's dun dismounting while Gram kicked the dogs away.

"We got one for you," the youngest-looking announced. "Here, Gram."

The lass handed over something wrapped in a bit of cloth, oozing a few drops of blood.

"Now that's kind of you. He looks like a good big raven."

"He is. And I got my falcon back before he spoiled too many feathers, too."

The oldest of the lasses suddenly yelped and pointed to Jill, standing in the doorway.

"Nothing to worry about," Gram said. "Just a lass, for all she's got that dagger and them men's clothes."

"I'd best get back to my man," Jill said. "My thanks, Gram, for all your help."

"You're welcome, Jill. And don't you let that man of yours know where you've been. I don't want him beating you for it."

When Jill mounted her horse, she was aware of the three noble ladies watching her wide-eyed in curiosity. Jill bowed to them from the saddle, then rode out, turning into the road and trotting fast for the river road. On the way back to town, she pitched the pot of salve into the river, but she kept the charm to show Rhodry and put his fears to rest.

When she got back to the tavern, they went straight up to their dusty wedge-shaped chamber and closed the shutters over the window. They sat down on the floor, away from the bedbugs in the straw mattress.

"Here." Jill handed him the charm. "She says that if you unwrap it, you'll spoil the dweomer, so you'd best do just that."

Handling it as gingerly as a horse turd, Rhodry pulled the bit of cloth away to reveal a tiny stick, whittled into an unmistakable phallic shape and bound round with the strands of his hair.

"Oh, by the hells," Rhodry snapped. "And what was this sup-posed to do to me?"

"Can't you guess from the shape? You can just toss it into the fire downstairs."

"I'll do naught of the sort! It might have some strange effect on me."

"Rhodry! I swear you believe it's real."

"Well, how do I know it isn't real enough in its way?"

They compromised on burying the charm out behind the sta-bles, where it was unlikely that anyone would ever dig it up again. Although Jill teased Rhodry for his concern, she wondered why she was so sure that the charm was useless—her usual instinct, she sup-posed. All her life, she'd been able to tell what dweomer was and what dweomer was not, just as she had always been able to see the Wildfolk. Rhodry tamped the earth over the charm with the heel of his riding boot and stamped on it hard for good measure.

"Now, kindly don't go buying any more of these from her, will you? Did you learn anything worth knowing while you were there?"

"Nothing directly about Mallona. But the gwerbret's daughters came riding up while I was there, and they seem to be up to their pretty elbows in this muck."

"What? Now, this could be dangerous. Someone should tell his grace."

"Not just yet, not until I've had a chance to worm what they know out of them. So remember, do hold your tongue about old Gram when you're talking to the gwerbret."

"Talking to the—here, I can't face Tudvulc again! I'm not go-ing up to the palace, and that's that."

Jill laid her hand on his arm and gave him the sweetest smile she could muster.

"Please, Rhodry? It's so awfully important."

"Oh, he's so handsome!" Babryan said breathlessly. "I'd forgotten about Eldidd men! Those dark blue eyes!"

99

"He's a rotten silver dagger, Baba," Wbridda snapped. "You shouldn't even talk that way about him."

"I don't care. He's noble-born, after all, and I'll bet his brother banished him for some silly reason. Don't you think Rhodry's handsome, Sevvi?"

"Well, sort of, but he frightens me. He's so strange, somehow. And I wager he's a harsh man in battle. I'll wager he can be truly cruel."

"Men are supposed to be that way," Babryan said. "Don't be silly."

The girls were sitting at the fireside in their hall, where they'd fled as soon as they could make a decent exit from the dinner table and Lord Timryc. Sevinna had suspected the worst during the meal, when she'd seen Babryan staring at this exile of a silver dagger whom the gwerbret had pitied enough to seat at his table. Now the worst was being confirmed: Babryan threw her arms round her knees and stared moodily into the fire.

"I wish he didn't already have a woman."

"Well, he does," Sevinna said. "And a woman that looks like she could beat you to a pulp if she wanted to, too."

"How nasty!" Babryan stuck her tongue out at Sevinna, then returned to the moody stare. "Besides, I'd never want to break her heart or suchlike. She must have defied her father and ridden off with her Rhodry. Just like your Mam did, Sevvi."

"Not at all! My father wasn't any dishonored silver dagger."

"My apologies, truly, I didn't mean that. You're so growly tonight, Sevvi. I'll just wager you think he's handsome, too."

Sevinna crossed her arms over her chest and did her best to look dignified, but Babryan laughed at her.

"Oh, don't be such cats!" Wbridda broke in. "Neither of you can have him, anyway. He might have been a gwerbret's son once, but he isn't anymore."

This was true enough to make Babryan lay aside her mood and sit up, but she chewed on her lower lip as if she were thinking something over.

"Now, we saw Jill there at Gram's, getting a charm. I'll wager he's unfaithful to her all the time."

"Baba!" Sevinna said. "I'm not being catty, truly, I'm not, just worried. What are you thinking about?"

"Naught." It was Babryan's turn for the dignified hauteur. "What did you think I was thinking about?"

"Oh, *you* know!"

They were well into a fit of giggles when the door opened and Lady Caffa came in with Jill right behind her. Babryan blushed scarlet, then rose with the other girls and curtsied to her mother. Sevinna surreptitiously studied Jill. She seemed some years older than herself, and her obvious physical strength placed her as a dweller in some utterly different world.

"Now, darlings," Caffa said, "your father's offered poor Rhodry his shelter for a while, so Jill is going to be spending lots of time with us. I shall want you to be hospitable to our guest, and I'm sure we'll have lots of lovely chats. You must have seen so many interesting things on the road, Jill."

"I have, my lady. Riding with my Rhodry has been awfully exciting."

"What a brave way to put it. I know it must have been terribly hard on you."

Jill gave her a meek smile, as if agreeing, but Sevinna found the smile suspicious, as if she were a wolf pretending to be a lap-dog.

Yet on the morrow, Jill settled so easily into the life of the woman's hall that Sevinna wondered if she'd been wrong. Although the gwerbret gave these odd guests a chamber of their own, Jill turned up in a borrowed dress in the women's quarters after breakfast, when Caffa held a kind of court. Her daughters, guests, and servingwomen sat round on cushions as she went over the accounts with the chamberlain, discussed menus with the head cook, and generally kept her fingers on the pulse of the life of the dun. During the session, Jill sat next to Sevinna and watched the proceedings narrow-eyed, as if she were memorizing everything she heard. In whispers, Sevinna pointed out this person or that to her and explained why they were there.

"This is awfully exciting," Jill said at one point. "Your aunt seems to know everything worth knowing about the whole town."

"She does. Whenever my uncle's away somewhere, she rules pretty much as his regent."

Later that afternoon, when her cousins were busy with their mother, Sevinna, as a substitute hostess, took Jill out to show her the garden—a rare thing in those days, even though it was just a square of lawn with floral borders and a stone sundial in the middle. Since Jill had never seen a sundial before, Sevinna explained how it worked and read off the legend engraved around the edge: time flies fast, so catch it while you can.

"Sevvi, you know how to read!"

"I do. I wheedled my father's scribe into teaching me the letters and suchlike when I was little. I was so afraid of what my father would do when he found out, but he just laughed and said I could waste my time if I wanted to."

"He sounds like a kind man, truly."

"He is, and I honor him, but of course, we're not rich or suchlike."

"Your uncle certainly is. I've never been inside a dun like this one before."

"Indeed? Does your clan live in one of the northern provinces?"

"Well, my father lives in Eldidd, but I'm not noble-born or suchlike. He was the captain of Rhodry's warband before Rhodry got exiled. I went with him when he rode away."

Jill's tale led to Sevinna telling about her mother, and from there to the life of her whole clan, and the noble clans in the neighborhood, and the local gossip. Sevinna found herself rattling on and on while Jill listened with a flattering attention, speaking only to ask questions.

"Now, I'm just dying of curiosity," Jill said finally. "I'll tell you why I was at Gram's house if you'll tell me why you were there."

"Fair enough. We wondered if you were buying a love charm or suchlike. Rhodry's awfully good-looking."

"He is. It seems that every lass in the kingdom thinks so, too. He's all I have in the world, after all, and I'd just die if he left me someday. After all, a woman's got to fight with what poor weapons she can, doesn't she?"

"We do. You see, I'm here because my uncle's going to make my marriage for me. I don't want to have to marry some man I don't like just because he's got the right kin. So I'm learning how to make charms and suchlike."

"Oooh!" Jill's eyes grew wide. "You actually know how?"

"Just a little bit right now. We all—oh, here, I can't tell you more than that unless you've sworn the oath to Aranrhodda."

"Of course I have. Why do you think Gram was helping me?"

"Oh, splendid! Well, look, tonight you'll have to come up to Baba and Bry's hall. We can talk about it then, because Lady Caffa doesn't know, you see. Baba's sure that her mother would be furious."

"I'll hold my tongue, I swear it. Oh, this is going to be splendid fun."

"Ye gods," Jill said. "These noble ladies are always eating! It seems like they just finish one plate of sweetmeats when a servant brings another. It would be awfully easy to poison someone if you wanted to."

"And why are you thinking of poisons?" Rhodry said.

"Because of Mallona. Why else?"

They were sitting in their chamber in Tudvulc's broch, a little room and poorly furnished. Tudvulc's chamberlain was terrified of offending Rhodry's powerful brother by being too hospitable to a man he'd exiled, and Rhodry saw no reason to argue about it. Besides, the room was tucked into an obscure segment of one of the half-brochs, where they weren't likely to be overheard, compensation enough for the lack of embroidered coverlets.

"The gwerbret tells me that the ladies are going a-visiting soon," Rhodry said. "Have you heard that?"

"I have. They're going to show Sevinna off to possible suitors in another demesne. Lady Caffa takes her responsibility to her niece very seriously. They'll be staying with someone called Lady Davylla. As far as I can tell, she's the one who taught Babryan and Wbridda about all these love charms and things. Ych! It's all such silly stuff!"

"How do you know?"

"I'm not sure." Jill shrugged uneasily. "But I do know it, just somehow. There's no dweomer in it at all. But that doesn't matter. What does matter is I overheard Caffa talking to Babryan about some other guest Davylla had."

"A guest? So? Women of their rank visit back and forth all the time."

"This guest seems to have just been put aside by her husband, and she's supposed to be ill, but no one's ever heard of her before. The wife of some very obscure lord, Caffa said. And a very obscure cousin of Davylla's, someone Caffa's never met. But Caffa knows just everything about everybody."

"Oh. Ye gods! Do you think it could be?"

"Do we have any other trail to follow?"

"None, truly. It's off to Lady Davylla's town we go."

"I do think we'd best get there ahead of them, too, just to look round, like. Can't you tell Tudvulc that you feel unworthy of the honor he's paying you, and that we'd best ride on, undeserving wretches that we are?"

"Naught easier, since that's the way I feel."

On the morrow, Rhodry sought the gwerbret out and found him in a private council chamber, where he was talking over a matter of bridge taxes with the head of the merchant guild. Rhodry knelt at the gwerbret's side and waited until the merchant took his leave, all bows and smiles.

"Your Grace," Rhodry said, "I've come to beg your permission to leave your broch. You've already done far too much for a dishonored man like me."

"Horseshit! 'Twas naught, naught. Get up lad, and take a proper chair. You're welcome here as long as you want to stay."

"My humble thanks." Rhodry got up and sat. "But truly, it's time I did take leave of your grace."

"Somewhat to do with this murderess you're tracking down?"

104

"Just that, but I'll beg His Grace to keep the matter to himself. We've found a hint that the lady might be to the west of here. May I consult with His Grace on a point of the laws?"

"Of course."

"What if our murderess has taken shelter with a high-ranking lady who's determined to protect her at any cost? This lady might persuade her husband to refuse to surrender his guest. After all, his honor would be at stake."

Tudvulc stroked his grizzled mustache while he thought.

"A cursed wasp's nest," he spat out at last. "If she's out of Coryc of Caenmetyn's boundary of jurisdiction, he'd have to persuade the local gwerbret that taking the lady was worth a war with one of his vassals. That would be a very difficult thing to persuade any man to do."

"So I thought. And Coryc would never be allowed to ride down with his own men and wage the war."

"Would he even want to? This woman sounds like a hell-fiend, truly, and an impious little bitch, but is punishing her worth an outright war, especially with another gwerbret, say, if that gwerbret took up his vassal's cause? He might send to the king's justice, of course, but that'll take years to sort out in the court."

"Just so. I'd hate to see her get out of this without so much as an angry word. Well, we'll have to persuade this lord that the lady isn't worth his and his wife's protection."

"If she's a witch, that might be hard to do," Tudvulc said, grinning. "She might ensorcel him, eh? Hah! The nonsense these women believe. I'm cursed glad there's none of that going on in my dun."

It took all of Rhodry's will to stay silent.

"Well, good luck, lad," Tudvulc went on. "You're going to need it, eh? Now listen, Rhodry, don't be such a stiff-necked bastard from now on. I'm willing to shelter you, and you know cursed well Blaen of Cwm Pecl would take you in. No need to wander the roads like a wretched beggar. Come to me or Blaen, get yourself a position with one of us. I can always call you my equerry or suchlike. Always need another good man around, eh?"

"His Grace is most generous. But I've poured myself this cup of shame, and I'll drink it down."

"Don't be a dolt, man! Doesn't matter to me if your brother takes umbrage at me sheltering you. I don't have any alliances with Rhys, won't need one, either. Eldidd's a blasted long way away. You think it over once you've caught this foaming bitch."

"My thanks, Your Grace, for your generosity to a shamed man. I'll think about your offer."

Rhodry rose and bowed, then fled to the ward. He was tempted, seriously tempted, by Tudvulc's generosity, but he knew that taking it would cause political problems touching the High King himself. Rhodry's brother Rhys, Gwerbret Aberwyn, hated him so bitterly that no doubt he'd find a way to challenge any lord, no matter how powerful, who took his younger brother in. The challenge would be the king's affair to settle, at great cost to His Highness. Exile or not, silver dagger or not, Rhodry considered himself the king's vassal still, and one who had sworn a sacred oath to put his liege's needs above his own. With a toss of his head, he shrugged the temptation off and strode back to their chamber, where he found Jill waiting.

"That's that, my love. We'll be on the road on the morrow. No doubt you'll be glad of it, too. This must have been tedious for you, sitting about with the womenfolk."

"It wasn't. I like them all, truly, and you can't blame them for worrying about the right match. I tell you, Rhoddo, I'm more deter- mined to hunt Mallona out than ever. I still pity her, but she's like a fox among chickens. What if one of these ladies stood in her way?"

"Well, it wouldn't be pretty, would it? We'll do our best to make sure the lovely Lady Mallona gets a long neck from the gwer- bret. Here, did you arrange to get in touch with the lasses once they reach Belgwerger?"

"I did, and they assure me they'll find some way for me to meet Davylla at least, if not her guest. It should work out well."

Although Belgwerger was a decent size, with close to eight thousand people, its lord's dun looked definitely shabby compared to the iron-supported splendor of Lughcarn, and the town itself had none of the feel of a place where money flows like a river. Rhodry and Jill found a quite decent tavern where the innkeep wasn't too proud to take a silver dagger's coin. There they spent an edgy pair of days, trying to keep out of sight while watching what might be happening in the town. Several times they saw Lord Elyc riding out of the dun with his warband, but never did they see any of his womenfolk.

Finally, as they were lounging near the east gate of the city on a late afternoon, the traveling party from Lughcarn rode in: the three lasses on their palfreys, a servingwoman for a chaperon, a couple of pages, a small cart of clothes and traveling gear, a pair of servants, and fifteen men of the warband, all looking profoundly bored with their duty as they brought up the rear.

"No wonder it took them so blasted long to get here," Rhodry muttered. "Traveling with a wretched cart!"

"Just so," Jill said. "Here, I'm going to make sure they see me."

On the streets, the crowd was hurrying out of the way, stepping into doorways and alleys as the procession made its slow way along. Jill worked through the crowd until she was at the edge of the street, then bowed as the lasses passed her. All three of them giggled and waved, and the servingwoman allowed herself a small smile in her direction. Once they were past, Jill came back and caught Rhodry's arm.

"Well and good, my love. If I don't hear from them soon, I'll go up to the palace and bribe a servant to take them a message."

Sevinna was surprised to find Lady Davylla young, with a pretty round face and a thick head of chestnut hair. At the dinner to celebrate their arrival, her ladyship kept the talk light, amusing her guests with talk of various weddings and other social events in her husband's demesne, as well as chatter about her young daughter. Only once did the talk turn to her mysterious new dependent.

"I take it Lady Taurra must still feel ill," Babryan said, "since she's not dining with us."

107

Davylla shot a small smile in Elyc's direction and changed the subject.

After the meal, they retired to Davylla's hall, a pleasant round room, though sparsely furnished compared to the women's quarters in Lughcarn. The servingwomen lit candles in the wall sconces, then retired when Davylla gave them leave to go. The girls sat down on cushions round the lady's chair.

"Now, you've got to promise not to breathe a word of this to anyone," Davylla said, "but Lady Taurra's not truly ill. The poor woman, how she's suffered! Her husband suspected her of having a lover, you see, so he turned her out of his house and sent her back to her kin. All they did was mock her for her shame, and she simply couldn't bear it, so I offered to give her refuge."

"How simply appalling for her," Babryan said. "She didn't really have the lover, did she?"

"She didn't. Poor Taurra thinks that he was simply tired of her and took a chance to put her aside."

The girls all shuddered.

"Taurra must have had an awful time on the roads," Wbridda said. "Or did her brother give her an escort?"

"He didn't, the beast!" Davylla said. "He was trying to force her into a Moon Temple, but she's got a different goddess to serve, so she just rode out on her own. It took her days to get here, the poor dear, and oh, it was so dangerous for her to be doing that."

"Oh, now here, Davylla dearest, I survived," said a soft voice.

Sevinna twisted round and saw a tall, graceful woman just coming in the door. Since she was a cast-off woman, she had her hair down and caught back in a simple clasp like a lass, even though she looked old enough to be the mother of a grown child. The hair was raven-dark, touched with gray at the temples, and her eyes were a deep cornflower blue, the mark of Eldidd blood somewhere in her clan. She made Davylla a curtsy, then sat down on a cushion by Sevinna.

"Well, doubtless our goddess was looking out for you," Davylla said. "But still, who knows what could have happened to you, wandering around like a common peddler?"

Taurra smiled, and there was something odd about that smile, as if she knew some private joke that would be unpleasant to hear. As she looked the girls over, Sevinna's unease deepened at the hard assessment in those dark blue eyes. Oh, here now! she told herself, doubtless she's just bitter about what happened to her.

"I trust you lasses honor our Lady Davylla highly," Taurra said. "She's the most wonderful woman alive to take in a wretch like me."

"Not a wretch at all," Davylla snapped. "I shan't listen to that, Taurra. It's your beastly husband who's the wretch, and that's that."

"Lord Gwell is no longer my husband, and I suppose I should count myself fortunate."

Taurra began to ask the three girls polite questions about themselves, as if she were turning the conversation away from her painful past. Sevinna supposed that such was the reason, anyway, because she seemed not in the least interested in their answers. As the evening wore on, Sevinna wondered if she really liked this woman. She was annoyed with herself for not liking her; after all, she'd suffered terribly and deserved pity, but there was something about the stiff way that Taurra held her head, something about the slow way she answered questions, something about the way her eyes would narrow as she looked at someone else, that made Sevinna feel like a cat faced with a dog.

"Baba?" Sevinna said. "You should tell Lady Davylla about our friend Jill."

"So I should," Babryan said. "My lady, the oddest thing happened just last week. A silver dagger came to our dun, and here it turned out to be Rhodry Maelwaedd, Lovyan's son."

"By the Goddess herself!" Davylla gasped. "Now, fancy that!"

"And he had a lass with him. She ran away from her family and everything to ride with Rhodry."

"Indeed?" Davylla allowed herself a grin. "I see that Rhodry hasn't changed much. I met him several times at court, you know. Oh, honestly, the way he had of looking a lass over!"

In a flood of giggles and interruptions, Babryan told how they'd made a friend of Jill and how she, too, wanted to learn Aranrhodda's lore. Sevinna noticed Taurra listening with a small fixed smile, her delicate mouth pressed thin as if she were in pain.

"They're in Belgwerger now," Babryan finished up. "So we wondered if you'd like to meet her."

"That might be most amusing, even if she is common-born," Davylla pronounced. "Perhaps we can send a page to find out where she and Rhodry are staying."

"Or would that distress Lady Taurra?" Sevinna put in.

"Why would it?" Taurra turned dark eyes her way. "Frankly, I should like very much to see this lass. Probably she needs the Old Lore to handle a man such as this Rhodry seems to be. Perhaps I can offer her some advice."

On the morrow, Lady Taurra kept to her private chamber all morning, and Sevinna was frankly glad of it. While Lady Davylla was busy with her servants, Babryan and Wbridda took Sevinna to visit Clamodda, the Wise Woman who lived in a hut inside the ward of the palace. Since Clamodda had spent most of her life on a farm, she would have been uncomfortable living inside the palace itself, preferring a tiny wooden hut among the other servants, or so she told the girls. A tiny, wrinkled woman with wispy white hair, she'd lost all of her teeth years ago and was now losing her sight.

"The eyes aren't so keen anymore, my ladies. But thanks be to our Lady Davylla, I won't starve before the gods see fit to take me to the Otherlands." Clamodda peered into Sevinna's face. "Now, here lass, you seem to be as pretty as your cousins here."

"I'll hope so," Sevinna said. "My thanks."

"I do hope you're courteous to our Lady Davylla. Best woman in the world she is, and the kindest. I'll be doing my best for her, I will. It's a son she needs now, not another daughter, you see. Oh, you should have heard her husband, carrying on and berating her when the little lass was born. Well, we'll just see about that, we will. We'll just see if the next one isn't a son, as nice and fat as you could want, too. I'm a-working on the charms right now, I am."

"We'll pray so, too," Babryan said. "And we'll leave you to your work."

110

Arm in arm, the girls wandered out into the ward, where they found a page searching for them.

"There's a silver dagger at the gate, asking for Lady Sevinna. Should I have the captain chase him away?"

"It's a her, silly!" Sevinna said. "I'll bet it's Jill, anyway."

The girls followed the page down to the gates, where, indeed, Jill was lounging against the wall in her dirty men's clothes. Sevinna ran to her and caught her arm.

"Jill dearest," Sevinna said, "it truly gladdens my heart to see you."

"My thanks, but what's wrong? You look so worried."

Only then did Sevinna realize that indeed, she did feel that something was wrong, and maybe badly so. Before she could say so, Babryan and Wbridda ran up, calling out greetings, to sweep Jill along with them up to the broch. They took Jill up to their chamber above the women's hall, then sent a maidservant with a message to Lady Davylla. Jill started to ask after their mother, but Babryan was too excited to have time for pleasantries.

"Oh, Jill, we've met Lady Taurra, and she's not ill at all. The poor woman! What a tale it is."

"Indeed?" Jill said, all wide eyes. "Tell me."

As Babryan rattled off the story, Jill listened, feigning a little squeal of amazement every now and then. Sevinna was sure the squeals were feigned, anyway. She wondered how she ever could have thought that Jill was just an ordinary lass like they were. She realized that meeting Lady Taurra had put her on her guard, like a doe who hears one hound barking and begins testing the wind to smell out the pack.

"Do you know this Lord Gwell?" Jill said.

"We don't," Babryan said. "But there's lots and lots of lords in the kingdom, aren't there? Why?"

"Just an idle wondering." Jill gave them all an impartial bright smile. "But does she truly know the Old Lore?"

They were happily discussing love charms when Lady Davylla came to their chambers and brought Lady Taurra with her. After

Babryan introduced Jill, Davylla took them all down to the woman's hall where they'd be more comfortable and sent a servant for a plate of dried fruit dipped in crystalized honey. They all sat down on cushions by the open windows, where the sun came in pleasantly with a bit of cool breeze.

"Now, Jill dearest," Davylla said, "I've actually met your Rhodry down at court. I wonder if he'd remember me?"

"Oh, he does, my lady. When I told him where I was going, he said to give you his regards, if you'd take them from a shamed man and a silver dagger."

"Well, I will, but it's rather naughty of me." Davylla flashed a grin. "Rhodry was always so charming."

For a while, they chatted about Rhodry and his mother, the Lady Lovyan, who was trying to get the king to intervene and recall her son from exile. Sevinna noticed Taurra watching Jill with a pleasant enough smile, but she would glance Jill's way and then somewhere else, as if she didn't want anyone to catch her doing it. The maidservant came in and began to hand the dried fruit round, offering the plate to Lady Davylla first, then the lasses, and finally Taurra and Jill.

"Just put that down on the table," Davylla said. "And you may leave us."

The servant put the fruit on a low table near at hand, then curtsied, and left. Sevinna nibbled on a dried apricot and listened to the others talk; she was too uncomfortable to say much herself. Lady Taurra seemed to have little to say, either, although once or twice she made some comment to Davylla. Sevinna supposed that she would have little in common with the young lasses. She supposed. Babryan got up once and passed the plate of honeyed fruit round again. Gradually, the talk drifted from Rhodry and court gossip to the real interest of this little group: the Old Lore.

"Baba and Bry showed me the little knife your Wise Woman made them," Jill said. "I hope that wasn't naughty of them, but I was awfully interested."

"Not naughty at all. Poor Clamodda can't do that fine work anymore, you know, with her eyes. Fortunately, she trained a lass out in the countryside to do it. It's just amazing what some of these simple farm folk know!"

With a small smile, Taurra got up and fetched the dried fruit, offering it around the circle. By the time it came to Jill, there was only one piece left.

"Odd," Davylla said vaguely. "I thought there was lots more. Eat that up, Jill darling, and I'll send someone for more."

"My thanks." Jill took the dried slice of apple. "Here, I'll take the plate and fetch the servant, my lady."

"She should be just out in the corridor."

Sevinna surreptitiously glanced at Taurra. She could swear that there was a bulge in her kirtle, as if something were hidden in it. Jill came back and resumed her place.

"You've got a bit of honey on your kirtle, Lady Taurra," Jill said.

"Oh, so I do, how messy of me!" Taurra idly dabbed at it with her forefinger. "Do you have a handkerchief, Davylla dearest? I've quite forgotten mine."

Her eyes met Jill's in a flash of dueler's hatred.

While Taurra was busy dabbing at the spot, Jill slipped the apple slice into her brigga pocket. No one seemed to notice but Sevinna. What is going on? she thought to herself. Things seem to have turned so peculiar! Although everyone pressed her to stay, Jill insisted on leaving soon after, saying that Rhodry had told her expressly to come back early, not late. Pleading courtesy, Sevinna walked with her down to the ward. They lingered in the open door of the central broch for a moment.

"Jill," Sevinna said, "you've got some game afoot, don't you?"

"Whatever makes you think that? Tell me, Sevvi, do you like Lady Taurra?"

"I don't. I don't know why, but I don't."

"Good. You've got more sense than your cousins and the Lady Davylla put together. Now listen, Sevvi. Be very careful while you're here, will you? Don't ask me why. Just keep your eyes open and watch what you say to Lady Taurra."

"She's not the sort of woman I'd care to cross."

"Good. Don't. Now, I shan't be able to see you again for a

while, because Rhodry and I are riding out this afternoon. We're going to Hendyr. Do tell Lady Taurra that, will you, if she asks? Rhodry can usually pick up hires guarding merchant caravans out of Hendyr."

Although Sevinna of course agreed, she wondered why she was so sure that Jill was lying to her. When she went back into the great hall, she met Lady Taurra on the staircase. With a smile, Taurra came to greet her.

"And did you say farewell to your friend?"

"I did, indeed. She and Rhodry are riding down to Hendyr, so the gods only know when I'll see her again."

Taurra nodded with the first sincere smile Sevinna had seen out of her all day.

"I don't think it's poisoned at all," Jill said. *"I think she was just playing* with me, daring me to say one word there in front of the others. Or it may not have been Mallona at all. Maybe she just took a dislike to me. I mean, I'm this common-born dirty lass, sitting among the fine ladies. Maybe I was imagining the whole bit about poisoned fruit."

"Maybe, but I doubt it. She certainly matches the description of Mallona we've got."

They were up in the chamber of their inn, kneeling on the floor and examining the slice, which lay in a patch of sunlight.

"But even if it's not her," Jill went on, "she's a strange woman, anyway. Rhoddo, I know you hate it when I talk about dweomer and stuff, but I could feel danger in that room. It came pouring off her like a stink."

Rhodry looked up, angry, but he said nothing.

"What it is, is she's desperate," Jill went on. "You know, when I was little, Da and I were staying in a dun where he had a hire, and one of the lord's dogs got stepped on by a horse. It crushed his paw, and when the kennelman went to help the poor creature, the dog bit him, ever so badly, too. It went all septic, and the kennelman lost his hand over it. I've never forgotten that, it was so awful."

"And Mallona reminds you of the dog?"

"She does. Oh, I know what you're going to say—she's not a poor helpless animal but a murderess. You're right, and that makes her even more dangerous."

"I'm glad to see you realize it."

"But we've got to be sure it's her. What we need is a witness. How far are we from Dwaen?"

"Three days' ride. Why?"

"I want you to go fetch him. He's a justice-minded man, and I'll wager he'll come back with you. Look, we've got to have a noble-born witness. Davylla won't have to believe a silver dagger or a servant or rider or suchlike, but she'll have to believe a tieryn. He'll be riding on the matter of Coryc of Caenmetyn's justice, and so her husband will have to take him in."

"That makes sense, truly. You know, our innkeep has an extra horse here in the stables. I could use some of that coin Dwaen gave us and buy him for an extra mount. Although, wait! What if the lady slips away while we're gone?"

"Where would she go? She'll never find a hole this comfortable again. Besides, that's why I'll be staying here."

"What? Are you daft? I don't want to bring Dwaen to Belgwerger to find you dead."

"I'm going to be careful, don't trouble your heart about that. But she's right there with Davylla and the gwerbret's daughters. For all I know, she might poison one of them for the fun of it."

"Ah, horseshit, she wouldn't dare! You're not staying alone. I won't even hear of it."

"Rhodry, my beloved." Jill smiled and caught his hand between both of hers. "You know I won't if you really say so, but be sensible."

While Rhodry haggled with the innkeep for the extra horse, Jill took the apple slice and went down to the stable, where she found the innkeep's son, a skinny lad, all Adam's apple and big nose.

"Tell me somewhat." Jill held up a couple of coppers. "How do you trap rats in your stable? Do you use those little wicker cage things?"

"We do, and then I drown them when I've got them. Why?

115

There's not a rat in your chamber, is there? I'll get a trap up right away if there is."

"That's not it. Here, can you keep a secret? I've got a rival for my man, you see, and she gave me a present of some honeyed fruit, but I don't feel like eating it without having someone else taste it first. Can I bait one of your traps with the slice?"

"Why not? If it's poisoned, then that's one less rat I have to drown."

Jill handed him the coppers, then followed him into the stable. Near bags of oats were the traps, disguised under wisps of hay and baited with cheese rind. Jill substituted the apple for the cheese and marked the trap by tying a wisp of hay around one of the withes.

When Rhodry left, he took his extra mount, so that he could make better speed by changing his weight from horse to horse. Even so, it would take him a long hard ride to reach Dwaen, and the return journey would be even longer with the tieryn and his men along. Jill walked down to the gates and waved him off, then returned to the inn with the cold chill of a dweomer warning down her back.

Despite the warning, the night passed with no trouble. At dawn, the lad brought Jill the rattrap. Inside, there was a big gray rat, squirming and biting at the withes, baring its long front teeth and scowling with little red eyes at its captors.

"He ate the whole bit, but he's alive and nasty."

"So he is. Here's another copper, and my thanks."

The lad hurried off to drown his prey in a water bucket. So, Jill thought, either the bitch was toying with me, or I'm dead wrong and it's not Mallona. Yet despite her lack of evidence, she'd never been so sure of anything in her life, that a poisoner and murderess was living on Lady Davylla's charity. In the rising light, the pale towers of the dun gleamed over the roofs of the town, impregnable and strong—except to a traitor within.

3

EVERY NIGHT, THE GIRLS and Lady Davylla gathered in the women's hall, where Lady Taurra taught them strange lore—the virtues of different plants, the chants for different spells, the correct colors and metals to choose for talismans. Although Sevinna enjoyed learning about the various love charms and potions, at times they touched on things she found—not frightening, exactly—but unsavory. To curse a rival for your man's affections, for instance, you were to catch a rat, keep it in a cage for three days while calling it by the rival's name, then bury it alive while chanting the proper spells, and all at midnight in a lonely place. Sevinna had no love for stable rats, but still, it seemed a cruel thing to do to a beast. Much to her surprise, Wbridda and Babryan shared none of her scruples.

"Oh, honestly, Sevvi," Babryan said. "I'd never really do such a thing, and I'll wager Lady Taurra wouldn't, either."

"It's just fun to hear about it," Wbridda put in. "Well, not fun, exactly, but you know. Like ghosts. When the bard sings about someone walking through the great hall with his head in his hand, it's splendid, but if you truly saw it? Oooh, how nasty!"

Almost as if she had picked up Sevinna's doubts, Lady Taurra went out of her way to be friendly to her. Often she would insist Sevinna walk with her in the garden or come to her chamber alone to see some special thing. Taurra had a way of catching one's gaze with hers and holding it while she smiled. Her eyes seemed to hint

117

at secrets and of power, as if she had looked upon strange things and might someday share them. After a few of these looks, Sevinna came to wonder if she were misjudging the lady. After all, she had every right to be bitter and hard after the way her husband had treated her.

No matter how thrilling all this talk of lore might be, Lady Davylla never forgot that the real purpose of this visit lay in showing Sevinna off to possible husbands. Davylla had a young cousin, Comyn, who held an honorary rank of tieryn because of his position in the royal court. She was planning on putting him forward as a candidate.

"It's not that he's so handsome, dearest, rather a man's man type, you know, but he's in a very good situation with the king's guard and can keep a wife well."

"What does my uncle think of him?"

"Now, I don't believe they've met. I shall have to remedy that."

"You know, Davylla dearest," Taurra broke in, "there's a little ritual we could do to help Sevinna choose. Sometimes a lass can even see her future husband's face in a mirror if the Goddess is gracious enough to show her. It's just the full moon now, so we could do it."

"Oh, how very exciting! Let's!"

"There's one obstacle, though," Taurra went on. "We really should leave the dun and go to some wild place, and at night."

"Oh, well, don't forget. My husband's off with one of his allies on that matter of justice. We'll be able to slip out easily enough."

All that afternoon, while the others prepared the necessary implements for the rite, Sevinna was wondering if she could possibly get out of it, perhaps by feigning a headache. Her reluctance must have shown, because Taurra took her aside at one point to reassure her.

"Now, really. Don't tell me you're afraid of our Lady of the Cauldron."

"Not afraid." Sevinna lied blandly. "But one must be properly respectful, mustn't one? I don't want to take the Goddess's favors too lightly."

"Nicely spoken. You know, Sevinna dearest, I think you might have true calling for the Old Lore. Your cousins are such lovely lasses, and so earnest, but it takes someone very special indeed to serve the Goddess properly. Don't tell them I said this, mind, but someday you could have ever so much more power than they ever will."

It was very flattering, especially when Lady Taurra was smiling so gently and her eyes were so intense, as if she were looking deep into Sevinna's soul.

"My lady is very kind," Sevinna said.

Taurra gave her a little pat on the arm and went on staring into her eyes. Suddenly, Sevinna found it hard to look away.

"We're going to be such friends." Taurra's voice turned as soft and as penetrating as oil. "I simply know it, such friends. Aren't we, dear? Tell me you'll be my friend."

"Of course I'll be your friend."

Taurra gave her one last pat on the arm, then left the chamber. Sevinna sat down on her bed and felt her head throb in earnest. When she tried to remember what Taurra had said, she found it gone from her mind.

That night, even though the chamberlain moaned and fussed, and the equerry blustered and wagged his finger, the women insisted on riding out without an escort, and since neither servitor could directly order Davylla to stay, ride out alone they did, just an hour after the moon rose. They left the city and followed the river road through the silvery night until they came to a tangled spinney of hazels growing close to the water's edge. There they tied up the horses and walked farther on.

"This looks like a good spot," Taurra announced. "Now, here, Sevinna dearest. You come stand where you can see the moonlight on the river."

When Sevinna took her place, the other women stood back, but Taurra took a stone-bladed knife out of her sack and knelt. Chanting as she worked, she cut a circle in the turf round Sevinna's feet. She took a bronze mirror out of the sack, laid that down nearby, fussing over it until it caught the moonlight, then cut a second circle round the mirror. She got up and joined the others, handing them each a bundle of herbs tied with strips of black cloth.

"Now, watch the mirror, Sevinna," Taurra said, "while we chant."

The women formed a ring around Sevinna and began to circle, their voices soft and light, their steps solemn as they danced gravely widdershins. Aranrhodda! Aranrhodda! The chant was like a drug, muddling Sevinna's mind. She looked at the moonstruck mirror and tried to see something in the curved and distorted surface as the chanting went on and on.

"Kneel down," Taurra called out. "Kneel down and look."

Feeling as if she were drunk, Sevinna did as she was bid. The moonlight caught the mirror and turned it silver, a misty color on the pitted surface. The women chanted and sang as they moved in their round dance. Suddenly, Sevinna wanted this thing over with.

"I see something!" she squealed.

Taurra stepped up the chant and led the women faster. In the distorted surface, Sevinna could see a pattern of shadow much like a face. She realized that if she'd been in love with someone, it would have been easy to convince herself she saw him there. With one last wail of Aranrhodda's name, the chant stopped, and Babryan rushed over.

"Who did you see? Was he handsome?"

"He looked nice, but not handsome. With dark hair, and big dark eyes, and he seemed youngish and awfully kind. He was smiling at me, but he seemed to have a very lordly air about him."

Babryan squealed and caught her hand. The others clustered round, Wbridda and Davylla talking, Taurra standing a bit to one side and smiling in a distant sort of way.

"Oh, this was so wonderful!" Sevinna said. "My thanks, Lady Taurra. We must do this for Baba and Bry, too."

When Davylla slipped her arm through Taurra's, they began talking about the herbs that they'd used for the rite. Feeling a bit sick, Sevinna walked a few steps away and glanced at their horses, who suddenly stamped and tossed their heads. Something, someone, was moving in the copse. Sevinna stood frozen and wished they'd brought guards as she watched a figure slipping out of the trees and running to the riverbank. Yellow hair, bright in the moonlight, and a flash of silver at the belt—Jill!

"Sevvi, dearest!" Davylla called out. "Come along. We must get back before the chamberlain worries himself into a snit."

"Of course, my lady. I was just watching the moonlight on the water. So lovely."

On the ride back, Sevinna decided that she wouldn't tell anyone about having seen Jill. All of a sudden, she remembered Jill's warnings about Taurra—so suddenly that she wondered how she could have forgotten them. She would have had little chance to discuss it, anyway, because all the way home Babryan chattered about the rite and begged Taurra to do the same for her.

"Of course, Baba, sweet, but we'll have to wait till the moon's perfectly full again. In the meantime, we'll have some nice chats and teach you what you need to know."

Babryan smiled, as bright as the Moon herself.

A wedding meant feasts for the noble-born guests and largesse for the poor of the demesne. While Slaecca and Ylaena planned details, Dwaen leaned back in his chair and nursed a tankard of the dun's darkest ale. Every now and then, when his mother asked his opinion about cost, he would shrug and tell her to spend whatever they had. At length, when the women rose to leave the great hall, Slaecca lingered by his chair.

"Ah, Dwaen, my only hope is that I'll have the joy of seeing you married, too, before I die, and that might not be long now, at my age."

"Mam, hold your tongue. Ruses don't suit you."

Slaecca snorted and crossed her arms over her chest, but the gods spared Dwaen a tedium. The page burst into the hall and raced over.

"Your Grace!" Laryn was too excited to kneel. "Rhodry the silver dagger is here, and he knows where Lady Mallona is."

"Ye gods!" Dwaen rose, slamming the tankard down in a spray of ale. "Just Rhodry? Where's his lass?"

"I don't know."

Dwaen raced outside to find Rhodry sitting on the cobbles in the ward. The silver dagger's hair was plastered slick with road dirt, and his shirt stuck to him with sweat, old and new. Behind him stood his own bay gelding, head down and weary, and a near-foundered roan. When Rhodry tried to get up, he stumbled into a splayed kneel. Dwaen knelt and steadied him by the shoulders.

"What have you done? Ridden all night?"

"Longer than that. Your Grace, we think Mallona's in Belgwerger, and we're going to have a cursed rotten time prying her out, too. I've come to beg your aid."

"Granted, of course. Get up. Let's go inside and get you some food. And then you'd best sleep."

"Can't. No time, Your Grace. Jill's there alone, keeping watch on her."

Dwaen slipped his arm round Rhodry's shoulders and helped him stand, then led him inside, yelling at a servant to fetch the silver dagger meat and ale. While he ate, Rhodry told the story of their hunt.

"It truly might be her, mightn't it?" Dwaen said. "Huh. It looks like great Bel will bring her to justice, after all, and I'll do everything in my power to help him. Rhodry, I don't care what you say. You've got to get some sleep. I've got to send messengers to Coryc and ready my men. We can't leave immediately, anyway."

Dwaen sent Laryn upstairs with Rhodry to find him a bed, then called Lallyc over for a conference. He had to send messengers off to Coryc first, then get the men and extra horses ready to travel—and fast. It didn't take dweomer to know that they had no time to waste upon the roads.

Ever since the moonlight ritual, Sevinna had been aware of Taurra turning her attention to Babryan and flattering her in the same way that she'd formerly flattered Sevinna. With Baba, the treatment seemed more effective. Sevinna could see the younger girl becoming withdrawn and silent, turned in to herself on some private line of thought. She spent more and more time with Taurra, less and less with the other girls.

The third afternoon, Babryan returned to their chamber after one of these private sessions with her face dead pale. She flopped into a chair by the window, where the sun streamed in, and reached up to rub her cheeks with both hands.

"I feel so cold," she announced. "Do you feel cold, Sevvi?"

"Not at all. Do you want a cloak round you?"

"Oh, maybe not." Babryan yawned hugely. "I need a nap. Ye gods, I hope I'm not getting some fever."

"Come lie down, then, and get under a coverlet."

Sevinna got her settled, hovered round for a moment, then realized that Babryan had fallen straight asleep. Since in those days any illness might be a dangerous thing, she was frightened, wondering if there were fever in the dun, but she remembered her own peculiar experience with Lady Taurra, and the headache she'd got on the day of the mirror rite. She hurried down to the ward and sought out one of the kitchen maids.

"Gwarra, I have a favor to ask of you, and I'll give you a copper, too."

"Well, gladly, my lady."

"There's a silver dagger down in town, and I badly want to send her a message. If I gave you a note, do you think you could take it to her? It's got to be kept awfully secret."

Gwarra smiled at the sight of coin.

"That blond lass, is it? Of course, my lady. I swear I won't say a word to anyone."

But as Sevinna was walking back to the great hall, she looked up at the broch to see Lady Taurra standing in the window of the woman's hall and looking down. Oh, Goddess preserve! Sevinna thought. She saw me! And the Goddess to whom Sevinna was praying was no longer our Lady of the Cauldron, but the Holy Moon Herself.

· · ·

There were times when Jill regretted not knowing how to read. She stared
at Sevinna's note, turned it this way and that, and wished that
Rhodry was there to interpret these strange marks on the bit of
parchment. She looked over the crowded tavern room and wondered if any of the merchants and craftsmen there could read, and
even more, if she dared trust any of them. Perhaps she could go to a
priest, but a priest would ask awkward questions about her connections with the gwerbret's womenfolk. Yet, as she thought about it,
she could puzzle out one meaning of the note: Sevinna had to be
troubled if she'd risk sending it. Tucking it into her pocket, she
hurried out of the tavern room and walked up to the dun.

At the gate, though, she received a rude welcome. The two
guards looked her over, then moved, the one stepping round behind
her, the other grabbing her arm.

"This must be her. Are you Jill?"

"I am. What's it to you?"

"You're coming with us. The gwerbret's equerry wants a word
with you."

They marched her along to a small chamber on the bottom
floor of one of the half-brochs. By a long wooden table stood a tall
blond man whom she recognized as Lord Elyc's equerry—Sevinna
had pointed him out during her last visit to the broch.

"Very well," Cenwyc snapped. "Her Grace the Lady Davylla
informs me that her guest, Lady Taurra, has lost a jeweled brooch.
The last time she saw it was when you were in the dun last."

"Well, I'll swear to you that I never took it, and you can search
all my gear, too."

"No doubt it's long been sold. Listen lass, I know our noble
ladies like to amuse themselves at times with the common-born.
Doubtless they found you interesting, just like you'd hoped. I've seen
clever thieves like you before, getting into some lady's confidence
and then stealing her blind."

"I'm naught of the sort. If I were the kind of woman you think I
am, I'd have fled town long before this."

124

Cenwyc set his hands on his hips and looked her over with cold blue eyes.

"Ask the Lady Sevinna if you don't believe me," Jill said. "She'll speak for me."

"She already has. But it's easy to fool a young lass, and I'm not listening to her, no matter how much she carries on. My lord's not in the dun. When he returns, you can tell your fine tale to him."

With a snap of his fingers, Cenwyc summoned the guards, who marched Jill out of the broch and across the ward. By the wall was a stone structure much like the one at Coryc's dun: a small prison for town beggars and any riffraff awaiting the gwerbret's judgment. They shoved her into a cell and barred and bolted the door behind them.

Restlessly, Jill paced round the space, about eight feet by five, the floor covered with reeking straw, the odor as thick as the flies come to sample it. From the one barred window, she could see the rise of the stone wall and nothing more. *You underestimated our dear Mallona, didn't you?* Jill thought, *and now you're going to pay for it.* She sat down on the cleanest part of the straw and hoped that Rhodry and Dwaen rode in before Mallona was able to poison her.

"Now, Sevvi dear, I'm as disappointed as you are," Davylla said. *"But it was foolish of us to trust someone like that, and here we are."*

"My lady, please! I know it couldn't be Jill who took that jewelry, I just know it."

"So sweet of you to be loyal. But so misplaced. Oh, how awful! Here it's spoiled your lovely visit. Let's not talk about it anymore."

Since she was a guest, Sevinna allowed the subject to be changed, but guest or not, she was a tieryn's daughter and used to having her own way in women's matters. As soon as she could, she slipped away from the other women and went down to the ward, where she bribed a page to show her the prison house. At the door, a beefy guard made her a bow. Sevinna set her hands on her hips and glared at him.

"I want to speak with Jill, the woman you stupidly think is a thief."

"Now here, my lady, you don't truly want to do that."

"If I didn't want to do it, I wouldn't be standing here telling you I did. Now listen, my man, I don't care to be kept waiting."

The guard chewed on the edge of his mustache and looked this way and that.

"If you're rude to me much longer," Sevinna snarled, "I shall go straight to Lord Cenwyc."

"Not to be rude, my lady, honestlike, but you don't want to go in there. It stinks, it does."

"Then is there a window in the miserable cell where you've put her? Take me round so I can speak through that."

This compromise won the day. With a melancholy sigh, the guard walked Sevinna round the prison house and pointed to a small window. By standing on tiptoe, Sevinna could just see in.

"Jill!" Sevinna said. "Oh, by the gods, this is awful."

Jill jumped up and ran to the window.

"I didn't steal anything."

"Of course you didn't. That's why I came to see you. What are we going to do? Where's Rhodry?"

"Off on an errand, and I blasted well hope he gets here soon. He'll be bringing a friend of ours with him, but I don't dare tell you more about that. Here, where's Lady Taurra? Does she know you're doing this?"

"She doesn't. Why does she want you arrested? I just know she's behind this. She never mentioned losing the beastly brooch before today."

Jill considered, rubbing the side of her face with the back of her hand.

"I don't truly know why. Oh, Sevinna, this is so horrible! The only food they gave me was a bit of stale bread with green places on it. I just couldn't eat it."

"Don't worry, I'll smuggle you somewhat better myself."

"Oh, would you?" Jill seemed on the edge of tears. "I'll be ever so grateful. But please, be careful. I don't want you to get into any trouble over me."

"Not a soul will know, I swear it. It's easy for us to get food any time we want, after all."

"So it is." Jill turned suddenly grim. "Which reminds me. Are you all well?"

"All of us but Baba. She's gone all mopeylike. I don't understand it."

"Mopey?"

"Tired all the time, but she's not ill. She's been spending lots of time with Taurra, though."

Jill clutched the bars tight with both hands.

"Listen carefully. If Baba starts getting ill in any way, for the love of the gods tell me. It's truly important. And please, the moment you see Rhodry, tell him where I am."

"I will, I promise. And I'll do my best to get you out of this, too. I don't know what I can do. We're going to be going home in two days, so maybe I can speak to my uncle."

"Two days? Well, maybe Rhodry will get here before then. And I can go hungry for a couple of days if I have to."

Sevinna was honestly surprised that food would mean so much to her that she'd starve rather than eat prison food, but she'd always heard it was terrible stuff. She left the prison and hurried across the ward to the kitchens, but before she could reach them, she met Babryan and Wbridda, out for a stroll to see the gwerbret's falcons. In the sunlight, Babryan's face was still decidedly pale.

"I thought Baba needed some air," Wbridda announced.

"So she does. I'll join you in a bit."

"Why not now?" Babryan said. "Sevvi, what are you doing out here? You haven't been to see that awful Jill, have you?"

"Of course not! It aches my heart to think she deceived us all."

Sevinna saw no way out of walking with them, but in the end, she was glad of it. As they came to the gates, they saw one of the guards coming in, leading Jill's distinctive golden horse, laden with a pair of saddlebags and a bedroll.

"Those are Jill's things, aren't they?" Wbridda said. "I hope none of the men steal them or suchlike."

"Oh, hold your tongue," Babryan snapped. "She's awful, and she deserves whatever she gets."

"Baba, I don't see why you're being so nasty. For all we know, there's some mistake. After all, why would a noble-born man like Rhodry fall in love with a thief?"

"He's done awful things, too. Da should never have let him stay at our dun, never!"

Wbridda started to reply, then merely shrugged. Sevinna marched over to the guard.

"What are you doing with those? Where did you get them?"

"Fetched them from the inn at Lord Cenwyc's orders, my lady. As to what, his lordship hasn't told me yet."

"Then let's go find out, shall we?"

The man turned the horse over to a waiting page, but took down the gear. Sevinna followed him inside to Cenwyc's usual reception chamber. The lord rose and bowed to her, but she could see how irritated he was with the sight of her. The guard dumped Jill's gear onto the table and made a hasty retreat.

"Cenwyc," Sevinna snapped, "I want to watch while you search for the brooch."

"Oh, those clever thieves sell things as soon as they get their hands on them, my lady. No use in looking."

"And where would she sell it in town without you knowing?"

Cenwyc started to answer, then hesitated, looking oddly troubled. All at once, Sevinna recognized his expression, so much like Babryan's after one of her special lessons.

"Think, my lord!" Sevinna crossed her arms over her chest and glared. "Who told you that? About thieves selling things, I mean."

"Told me? What do you mean, told me? Don't be silly!" But he hesitated and thought. "Well, that's odd, now that you mention it. Must have been Lady Taurra, when she was telling me about the brooch in the first place. I do remember, now that I come to think of it."

"Indeed?" Sevinna summoned up all her courage. "Well, I think we should have a look into this, my man. I can't believe his lordship would be so slipshod about an important matter."

128

Nowhere in the saddlebags or bedroll did they find any piece of jewelry, not so much as a copper pin.

"Huh," said Cenwyc. "Well, I'll send men to ask round town and see if she sold it anywhere. I've been told she never left when that man of hers did, so if she sold it, it would have to be here. Odd, very odd. Well, you've made your point, lass. If it does turn out that she was never seen selling anything, or if they don't find it buried round that inn where she was staying, then I'll have a word with my Lord Elyc when he comes home. Lady Taurra might have mislaid the thing."

"Perhaps so. How silly of her!" Sevinna arranged a bright and winsome smile. "Oh, I do thank you so, my lord, for letting me watch you. I'd best go join my cousins."

Cenwyc bowed rather absentmindedly, then picked up the gear and slung it into the curve of the chamber wall, where it could lie out of the way.

Sevinna found her cousins down by the falcon house, and they resumed their walk. It was some time later when they passed by the broch again to find Lady Taurra coming out of it.

"There you all are," the lady announced. "I was just looking for you. Shall we all go to the garden for a nice talk?"

Although the other girls went with her, Sevinna begged a headache, hurrying inside before she could be stopped. She was planning nothing more than going back to the women's hall, but as she passed Cenwyc's reception chamber, she noticed the door open and his lordship gone. On sheer impulse, she stepped inside, glanced round, and noticed that someone seemed to have moved Jill's gear along the floor.

"How very odd."

She knelt down and opened the saddlebags only to make sure that none of the servants had stolen anything out of them. Tucked to one side gleamed Taurra's jeweled brooch.

"Fancy that!"

Sevinna got up fast, looking round to make sure that no one had noticed, then stuffed the brooch into her kirtle and hurried out. As far as she could see, only one person in the dun could have or would have put the jewelry there. No doubt Taurra would have later made some new remark to Cenwyc that would have him searching the bags after all, and there the brooch would have been, clear evidence that would have got one of Jill's hands chopped off in the public square.

For some time that day, Sevinna brooded clever ways to ensure the brooch was "found," then decided that simplicity was always safest. Up in the women's hall, Babryan and Taurra had left a sack of herbs and feather charms lying on the floor; Sevinna slipped the brooch between it and the wall. Sure enough, right before the girls went down to dinner, Babryan picked up the sack, then squealed aloud.

"Oh, look at this! It's Taurra's brooch!"

Feigning surprise, Sevinna rushed over with Wbridda right behind.

"It is, indeed," Sevinna said. "By the Moon herself!"

"Huh, Baba," Wbridda sneered. "So. It wasn't Jill at all, was it now?"

"It wasn't." Babryan blushed scarlet. "I'm sorry, Bry. You were right, and I was wrong. Here, we'd best take this down with us straightaway."

They found Lady Davylla sitting at the head of the honor table in her husband's absence, with Taurra to her left and Lord Cenwyc to her right. When Babryan laid the brooch onto the table, Davylla leaned forward with a little squeal.

"Taurra, dearest! Here it is."

"Why, so it is." Taurra picked up the brooch and smiled, but never had Sevinna seen such a forced smile in her life. "Where did you find it?"

"Up in the women's hall, my lady. Near that bag of our— things."

"How stupid of me!" Taurra squeaked. "Oh, dear, I've done Jill such an injustice! I feel so absolutely doltish. How could I not have seen it there?"

She looked up, glancing at each girl in turn. When she fastened upon Sevinna, her eyes burned with such rage that Sevinna stepped sharply back in an unthinking admission of guilt. With a little smile, hastily stifled, Taurra looked away.

"I'm so terribly, terribly sorry." Taurra spoke in a small and broken voice. "Oh, Davva, how can you ever forgive me? I've caused you all such trouble! I'll never be able to look poor Jill in the face again, truly."

"We must get her out of that awful prison." Davylla turned to Cenwyc. "My lord?"

"As my lady wishes." Cenwyc rose, then bowed. "I'll turn her back out on the road where she belongs."

"What? Naught of the sort!" Davylla rose to face him. "You'll bring her directly to me, where I can apologize to her."

"My lady is being most unwise. Truly, the wench seems innocent of this theft, my lady, but her kind's not to be trusted."

The stalemate held: Davylla was far superior in rank, but Cenwyc was, after all, a man. Sevinna hesitated, then decided that since she'd already shot the bow, she might as well swing the sword, too.

"My lady? Perhaps Jill won't want to face you. May I go along with the equerry and give her your apology, rather like your envoy, shall we say?"

"Sevvi, dearest, I should be ever so grateful." Davylla sighed. "I truly don't know what to do. Do you think it would insult her if we offered her money?"

"No doubt. I'll just have a word with her."

Taurra put delicate fingers over her mouth, as if in shame, but when their eyes met, Sevinna felt her stomach clench cold.

With a sullen sort of courtesy, Lord Cenwyc escorted Sevinna out to the prison house and ordered the guard to bring Jill out while a page saddled her horse and fetched her gear. In a few minutes, Jill appeared, striding briskly out, her head held high, her eyes so haughty when she looked Cenwyc's way that one would have thought her noble-born.

"Very well, lass. There's been a mistake. The missing brooch has been found, and you're free to go."

"My most humble thanks, my lord," Jill snapped. "I trust his lordship will think twice in the future before he commits injustice in the gwerbret's name."

Cenwyc merely scowled at her. Sevinna hurried forward and caught her arm.

"Let me walk with you to the stables. I'll tell you how the brooch was found, if Lord Cenwyc will be so kind as to let us have a word alone."

"As my lady wishes, of course." Cenwyc bowed. "I'll return to her ladyship."

The two girls began walking toward the stable, but slowly, whispering as quietly as they could.

"I saw Taurra put the brooch in your saddlebags," Sevinna said. "Or well, I didn't truly see her, but we'd looked through your gear, and the brooch wasn't there. Then I saw her near the room where your things were lying. When I looked in the bags, there it was. So I put it where Baba could find it."

"I see. Taurra doesn't suspect you, does she?"

"I have the most awful feeling she knows I did it. She's awfully clever, Jill, and I'm not much good at hiding things."

"Oh, by the gods! I'll be forever grateful to you for this, but you've just made yourself an awfully dangerous enemy. I hope Cenwyc isn't going to run me out of town."

"That's what he wants to do. I don't know if Davylla will let him or not."

"If I go, you've got to be careful—truly, truly careful."

"Well, what can she even do to me, here in the dun?"

"Poison you, that's what. Please, believe me! Taurra isn't what she's calling herself. She's dangerous, and she's already poisoned one person that I know of—her lover, it was."

Sevinna caught her breath with a gasp and felt cold panic round her heart.

"I'd denounce her, but no one's going to believe me," Jill went on. "That's where Rhodry went, to get noble-born witnesses. Is there any way you can all go home? I don't want to leave you lasses here."

"Well, there isn't. I mean, I'd have to tell Davylla what you said, and you're right. She's never going to believe it."

At the stables, they found Sunrise saddled and ready, with Jill's bedroll tied on behind. The page handed over the reins, then trotted off to the great hall and his dinner. By then, twilight hung cold over the dun. Flickering light began to spill out the windows of the great hall as inside, torches were lit.

"Did you want to go inside?" Sevvi said. "Davva's waiting for you, you see. She really does want to apologize."

"I don't think I want Taurra to get a look at me." Jill was staring over Sevinna's shoulder to the main gates of the broch. "How much do you weigh?"

"What? Not much over a hundred weight. Why?"

"I've got an idea. Come on, walk with me into the town, will you?"

"Oooh, do you think I dare?"

"I don't think you dare not to. Please? I've got an idea. Look, the guards have gone off somewhere. It's now or never."

Sevinna hesitated, but she was remembering the hatred in Taurra's eyes. Even more she remembered her herbs—lots of herbs—and the mastered lore to go with them.

"There's no time," Jill said. "Someone's bound to come out here as soon as soon. Will you come with me or not?"

One last hesitation, and the memory of Taurra's small smile of triumph.

"I will. Let's hurry."

They rushed out the gates with Sunrise clopping after them into nearly empty streets. Most of the townfolk had shut themselves up in the safety of their homes for the night. Jill jogged along fast, making Sevinna pant to keep up, until they were out of sight of the dun gates.

"They'll be shutting up the town soon," Jill said. "Quick! Get up behind my saddle. I'll help you. We're light enough so the horse can carry us both."

Sevinna didn't even stop to consider where they might be going. With Jill's help, she scrambled up behind the saddle, sitting astride with her dresses awkwardly bunched round her hips. Jill swung herself up in front and urged the horse to a smart trot. They wound their way dangerously fast through the streets until they saw the town gates, open but guarded, ahead of them.

"Put your arms around my waist," Jill said. "And hang on."

Sevinna clasped her tight just as Jill kicked the horse hard. Yelling, the guards leapt back as Sunrise hurtled through the narrow gateway. They were out, galloping full tilt down the dangerously rutted road. Sevinna heard the guards screaming at them to halt, but she was too frightened to look back.

"Hang on!" Jill yelled.

She turned Sunrise off the road into a stubbled field. Sevinna clung to her as the horse leapt some low obstacle, stumbled, then gained his balance and raced forward. When Sevinna risked a glance round, she saw that they were turning to the east, where the moon was just rising. When they reached the scanty forest cover, Jill let the sweating horse slow to a walk and pick his way down a dark trail.

"I never would have tried this with an ordinary horse," Jill said. "But he's truly amazing, his stamina, I mean. Well, now we've got a bit of a lead. It'll take Cenwyc a while to get the riders together to come after us, too."

"Well, I hope so." Sevinna heard her voice shaking. "I suppose this is awfully exciting."

Jill laughed.

"Trust me, Sevvi. I swear it, you'll be better off sleeping in a ditch tonight than eating at the same table with Lady Mallona."

"With who?"

"That's Taurra's real name. She's a murderess from up in Gwaentaer, and Rhodry and I have been hunting her down for the bounty on her head. Lord Cenwyc was right enough about one thing. I'm not truly fit company for the likes of you."

It was impossible, and Rhodry knew it, for the tieryn and his warband to ride as fast as a speeded courier for the entire journey. Every sensible rest and delay stabbed him like a javelin point. Every day's traveling stretched to a seeming month, though in fact, only four nights passed before they came to the road that would lead them straight to

Belgwerger, some twelve miles on. Near the crossroads stood the dun of a lord that Dwaen knew well.

"We should stop here for the night," the tieryn said to Rhodry. "It's late afternoon, and the horses are tired."

"True enough, Your Grace. As Your Grace wishes."

"Even though you're thinking of strangling me as I ride?" Dwaen turned in the saddle to grin at him. "I never thought I'd see a cold-blooded man like you so troubled."

Rhodry could only shrug for an answer.

They rode on. On its low hill across a meadow, the lord's dun loomed closer and closer. At the lane leading to its gates, Dwaen paused his line of march and turned in the saddle to call back to the men following him.

"We're going to stop for a rest and a meal in a few miles, lads. Then we're riding straight through to Belgwerger. If I pound on the gates in the king's name, the night watch might let us in. If not, we'll be there when they open in the morning."

Rhodry laughed in a long peal. If they hadn't been on horseback, he would have thrown his arms around Dwaen and hugged him.

Eventually, they found fresh water, a stream running through a fallow meadow beside the road. After they unsaddled the horses and let them roll, they watered them and set them at nose bags of oats. The men had to make do with whatever stale leftovers from the noon meal that they had left in their saddlebags. Rhodry and Dwaen ate standing up, strolling a little ways away from the others.

"Now, truly, it might be a good thing to sneak into town at night, anyway," Dwaen said. "I don't want Mallona getting word of our coming and running out the postern gate."

"This time we'll hunt her down if she tries, Your Grace. But she doubtless knows that she's safest under Davylla's wing."

"Well, I'm going to have plenty to say to Lady Davylla."

"True enough. If she'll listen."

Dwaen started to reply, then broke off at the sound of hooves coming. When Rhodry looked down the road, he saw to the west dust first pluming, then resolving itself into a horse that carried two riders. Jill's horse! Rhodry recognized Sunrise's color before he could actually see Jill. With a shout, he raced to meet her as she turned her mount into the meadow. Behind her sat a dirty and bedraggled Lady Sevinna.

"Saved!" Jill crowed out. "Here, Sevvi! The gods are on our side."

Rhodry reached up and helped Sevinna down. She staggered, so sore from the unaccustomed posture of riding astride that she could barely stand. Jill swung herself down and laughed, dancing a few steps.

"It gladdens my heart to see you, Tieryn Dwaen," Jill said. "May the lady and I throw ourselves on your protection?"

"My dear Jill, I haven't ridden all this way just to spurn you. From what do you need protecting?"

"Lady Mallona, mostly, but I'll wager Lord Elyc's men are close behind us. They think I kidnapped Sevvi, you see. Your Grace, allow me to present Lady Sevinna, niece to Gwerbret Tudvulc of Lughcarn. Mallona was going to poison her."

Sevinna caught her filthy skirts and made the tieryn a curtsy, which he returned with a bow.

"You'll forgive my appearance, my lord. We slept in the woods last night."

"A lady like you would be beautiful in rags," Dwaen said. "Which indeed, that dress most resembles."

Rhodry handed Jill the piece of cheese he'd been eating, while Dwaen offered his flatbread to the Lady Sevinna.

"This is the best we have to offer you at the moment, my lady. But we'll be going to the shelter of that dun there." Dwaen jerked his thumb back in the direction in which they'd come. "There's not much use in pushing on to Belgwerger now."

The dun turned out to belong to a certain Lord Rhannyr, a childhood friend of Dwaen's—they had served as pages in the same dun, a situation that made either bitter enemies or lifelong friends of men. Surrounded by thick stone walls, it held only a squat broch and a few outbuildings, but it was shelter nonetheless. Rhannyr himself, sandy-haired and freckled, ran out into the ward to greet them.

"By the gods, Dwaen, it's been years! To what do I owe this most welcome honor?"

"Trouble," Dwaen said with a melancholy sigh. "May I bother you to close your gates? We're being chased, you see."

Rhannyr took one look at the Lady Sevinna, riding next to the tieryn on one of the extra horses, grinned as if drawing conclusions, and began yelling at his men to bar the gates and set a guard on the walls.

Rhannyr's great hall occupied only half of the ground floor of the broch. Smoke-stained wickerwork partitions set it off from the kitchen, and through them they could hear the servants talking and swearing at their work. Rhannyr took Dwaen and his immediate party over to the table of honor at the hearth, told his captain to feed the men in the warband, then stuck his head in the kitchen door and yelled to the cook that they had hungry guests.

"Mead and meat soon," Rhannyr announced, sitting himself down next to Dwaen. "You'll forgive my lady for not joining us. She's due to have another baby in a week or two."

"Another one?" Dwaen said. "Ye gods! That makes four, doesn't it?"

Rhannyr allowed himself a smug smile, then turned to Lady Sevinna.

"It troubles my heart to see a lady in distress. How may I be of service to you and your tieryn?"

"Well, he's not my tieryn, my lord," Sevinna said. "But I happen to be fleeing from a murderess."

Over the meal, Dwaen and Rhodry took turns telling their fascinated host the story, or as much of it as they knew. Rhodry would rather have heard what Jill had to say, but just as she was about to tell her part of the tale, they heard the shouts of the watchmen at the gates.

"There they are," Jill said. "It took them a beastly long time, I must say! Elyc's men can't track as well as a blind peasant."

Wiping his hands on his brigga, Rhannyr got up just as a young rider ran, yelling, into the hall.

"My lord? There's fifteen men at the gates, and Elyc's captain's with them, and by the demons in the Hells, they're furious."

When Rhannyr went out, Rhodry and Dwaen followed him up to the catwalk on the wall directly above the gates. Down below, sullen on tired horses, the men in question bunched in ragtag formation. Rhannyr leaned over the rampart and yelled.

"Good eve, Ocsyn. What brings you to me?"

"A matter of kidnapping, my lord," Ocsyn yelled back. "One of my lord's guests, a young woman, was stolen away from the dun by a silver dagger. We tracked her to a place down the road where it looks like she met up with another party, and their tracks lead here."

"So they do, because she's inside, but she hasn't been kidnapped. She fled of her own free will." Rhannyr laid a hand on Dwaen's shoulder. "This is Tieryn Dwaen of Dun Ebonlyn, and the lady is under his protection."

"Oh, by the black ass of the Lord of Hell! Well, begging your pardon, my lord, but we've been chasing her all over the cursed countryside, and now you tell me the lady's eloped!"

"Naught of the sort," Dwaen yelped.

Rhannyr laughed and slapped him on the back. Down below, Ocsyn scratched his head while he thought things through. From the back of the warband, someone yelled at him to tell his grace about the messengers.

"Right enough," Ocsyn said. "Here, my lords, the equerry sent messengers off to fetch Lord Elyc home, and then he sent another pair to Lughcarn to fetch Gwerbret Tudvulc, too, because this lady is Tudvulc's niece. I'll warn you, Tudvulc's a bad man to face when he's angry."

Dwaen groaned, rather loudly.

"You always were the very spirit of gallantry, Dwaen," Rhannyr said, grinning. He leaned back over the rampart. "Ocsyn, are you and the lads hungry? I'll send food out to you, but I'd best not offer you the shelter of my dun tonight. Things are complicated enough already."

"Just so, but we'll take the food gladly, my lord."

When Rhodry climbed down, he found Jill waiting.

"There's naught like a good thick wall to make men polite," she remarked. "If they'd caught us on the road, we'd have been in for it good and proper."

"Just so. I'm glad Tudvulc's on his way. He knows me, and he knows we've been tracking poisoners, and so he'll believe us easier than Elyc will."

"Let us hope." Dwaen joined them. "Because if he doesn't, this is going to leave a stain on Lady Sevinna's honor."

"Well, true," Jill sighed. "But I thought it would be better than having her killed."

"A thousand times better," Dwaen said. "Oh well, if worse comes to worst, it's time I married, anyway."

When both Jill and Rhodry stared at him, he smiled in a vague sort of way and strolled back to the great hall.

After a good wash, a night in a decent bed, and some real meals, Sevinna felt recovered enough to walk with Jill out in the ward, such as it was. A few cobbled paths led through mud and horse leavings. Servants strolled back and forth with buckets of slops or an armload of firewood; a page trotted past, scratching himself as he attended to some errand or other. Jill and Sevinna found themselves dodging chickens and trying to stay upwind of the pigsty.

"I know it's sensible to stay here and let Elyc and my uncle come to us," Sevinna said. "But ych!"

"It's not Lughcarn, is it?"

"It's not indeed! On the other hand, I'm not in much of a hurry to have my uncle get here. I do hope he doesn't beat me."

"Well, he won't as long as Rhodry can talk to him first and explain things. Tell me, Sevvi, what do you think of the tieryn?"

"Dwaen? I've heard of him, of course, just from cousins and suchlike. They all said he was daft, talking about the gods all the time."

"I suppose they did, but what do *you* think of him?"

"I rather like him. He seems a decent sort, and he's not bad looking."

"Good. Because if your uncle is unreasonable, you're going to have to marry him."

"Oh, by the Goddess!" Sevinna felt suddenly short of breath. "You're right, aren't you?"

"I'll wager the scandal's spreading already. My apologies. I never thought of what it might mean to your honor when I came up with this idea."

"Better dishonored than dead. Don't trouble your heart about it for a moment."

And yet, of course, it did trouble her own heart, that after the love charms and Old Lore, after the assessing of suitors and the scheming of female relatives, her marriage might well come down to a stranger chance met on the road, and all because of scandal and Lord Rhannyr's sense of humor. To her surprise, she found that Dwaen had been thinking along the same lines. After the noon meal, when she sat alone by a little window in the great hall, he sought her out, fetching a stool so that he could sit beside her chair like a page.

"Er, well," he said, "I thought I'd best tell you about my dun and lands."

"Why? I mean, I'm always glad of his lordship's conversation, but uh, well, I—"

"Please, my lady. There's no need for us to cross swords and spar. We both know that the gods have placed you in an awkward situation. Well, they've placed me in one, too. Here I am, tieryn in my own right, with no wife and no heirs, because the lass that I always thought I'd marry, from the time we were children, truly, well, she died of a winter fever."

"Oh! My heart aches for your grief."

Dwaen shrugged and looked away, brushing his dark hair back from his forehead with a broad hand.

"It was over two years ago now. You wouldn't be living with another woman's ghost or suchlike. I'll never mention her again, I promise you, but I thought you should know."

Sevinna suddenly wondered if there were another lord in the kingdom who would be so scrupulous about his lady's feelings. Dwaen looked back at her and smiled.

"I've got rather a lot of land, actually. You could live well in my dun."

"But my lord, this is so sudden—"

Their eyes met, and they burst out laughing.

"Sudden, indeed," said Dwaen. "But here we blasted well are. The thing is, I know somewhat of your uncle and your father, and I doubt me that I bring the kind of alliances they need."

"Oh." Sevinna considered, chewing on her lower lip. "Well, it's kind of a nasty problem, then. But if the scandal spreads, then no one will marry me."

"Exactly. I suppose we could always pretend that we really did elope."

"I suppose. We'd probably best wait and see what my uncle thinks about it all."

Nothing very good, as it turned out. They all spent an uncomfortable day and night waiting at Rhannyr's willing, if overextended, hospitality before Gwerbret Tudvulc and half his warband charged in. Sevinna was up in her guest chamber, talking with Jill, when they heard the clattering and cursing out in the ward.

"Oh, Goddess defend me!" Sevinna said, looking heavenward. "That must be my uncle."

They rushed downstairs and outside to find the ward mobbed with men and horses. Not only was Tudvulc there, but Lord Elyc as well, met on the road home, apparently, and swept along by the gwerbret. Just outside the door to the great hall stood Rhannyr and Dwaen, with Rhodry behind them. Sevinna would have run out, but Jill caught her arm.

"Let's stay in the doorway," she whispered. "They'll see us soon enough."

Red-faced and growling, Tudvulc dismounted and strode over to Dwaen and Rhannyr, both of whom bowed as deeply as they could bend. A last few chickens fled squawking at his approach.

"You I know." Tudvulc waved a hand at Rhannyr, then turned on Dwaen. "You! What are you doing with my niece?"

"Protecting her from harm and naught more, Your Grace."

"Hah! What do you think I am, a halfwit?"

"Never, Your Grace. If you feel her honor's been in the least degree besmirched, then I'll marry her gladly."

"Cursed right you will!" Tudvulc looked round, saw Sevinna, and growled again. "Ye gods! As bad as your blasted mother!"

And that was Sevinna's betrothal ceremony. When she caught Dwaen's eye, he shrugged and grinned. In spite of everything, she found herself smiling in return.

"Now then," Tudvulc bellowed. "Elyc, where are you? We've got to ride straight to Belgwerger."

On the edge of the crowd, Elyc turned his mount in the gwerbret's direction.

"What about the horses? They're tired, and Rhannyr can't remount us all."

"Too cursed bad! Your wife and my daughters are in that dun with a poisoner."

Since Rhannyr's vastly pregnant wife had no need of them, Sevinna rode back on that lady's palfrey and in her proper sidesaddle. Tudvulc and Elyc headed the march, with Sevinna and Dwaen riding side by side just behind them, leaving the silver daggers and the warbands to sort themselves out however they wanted. Chivvying and growling, Tudvulc kept them moving at a good pace, too, marching his improvised army up to the city gates well before sunset. As they hurried through the town, the citizens fled out of the way like Rhannyr's chickens.

They trotted into the dun, where pages and servants rushed to greet them and sort out this plethora of unexpected guests. When she looked up at the broch tower, Sevinna saw figures in the window of the women's quarters. One of them had to be Taurra, she assumed, watching and wondering at the uproar below. Once they were close to the broch and out of the worst confusion, Dwaen swung down and helped her dismount.

"My thanks, my lord."

"Most welcome, my lady."

When they exchanged a smile, the events of the past few days suddenly became real to her. Oh, by the Goddess! she thought. This man is my husband, and I barely know him. She turned away with a scatter of tears.

When she'd got herself under control, Dwaen slipped his arm through hers and escorted her into the great hall, where frantic servants were dragging extra benches up to tables. Yelling for ale, Elyc grabbed a page and sent him upstairs to fetch Lady Davylla and her womenfolk down to the hall. Sevinna allowed Dwaen to seat her at the table of honor, then looked round for Jill, who was standing with Rhodry beside Tudvulc and talking intently to the gwerbret. Every now and then, Tudvulc grunted in agreement. At the far side of the hall, the weary riders were sorting out who would sit where as quietly as they could. Elyc sat himself down at the head of the table of honor with a long yawn.

"We're going to clear this wretched mess up right away. While we were riding to Rhannyr's dun, Tudvulc was telling me about this poisoner. If this Taurra's her, then she's no guest of mine."

By the time that the ladies came down, the men were all seated, drinking ale in grim silence. In a rustle of silks and a flash of jewels, the women hurried into the hall, Lady Davylla and Wbridda in the lead, Babryan and Taurra just behind. Taurra had put on a plain dress, dark-colored, shabby from mending, and swept her dark hair back in a simple copper clasp, the very picture of a humble bewildered penitent, but she walked in proudly, head held high, her eyes calm, as if she were sure of her innocence before the gods. Sevinna felt a ripple of fear mixed with awe, as if she were going to see a wild boar brought to bay.

Taurra glanced round and saw Dwaen. She stiffened, her eyes flashing rage, her hands clasping as if she would claw him. Dwaen rose and made her a bow.

"Well met, Lady Mallona. I doubt me if you truly want news of your husband, Lord Beryn, but I'll offer it to you."

"What?" A bewildered Davylla turned this way and that between them. "Who is this man? Elyc—"

143

"Sit down and be quiet!" Elyc snapped. "This woman's lied to you and deceived us all, and I'm putting a stop to it right now."

"I take it then that my lord has already judged and condemned me," Mallona said in her quiet strong voice. "And all on the word of a man he doesn't know."

"I have a good bit more evidence than Tieryn Dwaen's word. You may sit, too, while we discuss this."

"I prefer to stand. Like the accused I am."

Servants stepped forward with a chair for Davylla, who sank into it, gathering Babryan and Wbridda round her to huddle on the floor by her feet. The girls were staring at Mallona, and Babryan's mouth worked as if she would cry. Mallona smiled at them and stood her ground in front of Elyc, her hands clasped calmly in front of her.

"Since my lord has so generously fed and sheltered me," Mallona said: "Let me beg only for his justice."

"That you shall have, I swear it. The charges against you are grave: murdering your lover, the merchant Bavydd, up in Gwaentaer, after your plot to murder the tieryn here came to naught."

Mallona tossed up her head like a startled horse and turned slightly to look down the table, her eyes pausing long on Dwaen, on Jill, and then reaching Sevinna with such a surge of hatred that Sevinna had to summon all her will to speak.

"My Lord Elyc? She also made false claims against Jill, this silver dagger, that caused her to be arrested and mistreated by your own equerry, Lord Cenwyc."

Elyc glanced around the hall, saw Cenwyc standing ready by the hearth, and beckoned him over. Cenwyc knelt at his lord's side.

"The Lady Sevinna speaks the truth, my lord. A small charge, compared to these others, but it speaks of a woman trying to elude justice."

"I see."

Cenwyc rose, bowed, and stepped back out of the way. In her chair, Lady Davylla went pale, her hands tightening on the folds of her dress. The girls huddled closer to her.

"Very well," Mallona said. "I see that I have no choice but the truth. I am Lady Mallona, wife to Lord Beryn, and truly, I did murder the man who seduced me and forced me to plot against my own lawful husband. Ah, ye gods and goddesses, I call you witness on my side! How could I say Bavydd nay, when he was threatening to tell my husband of my infidelity and have me cast onto the roads if I didn't plot with him?" Her voice cracked, a little tremor of tears. "I grew to hate him, grew to bitterly regret the day I ever succumbed to his lying flatteries and kisses." Suddenly she flung herself down by Elyc and clasped his knees. "I know His Grace can never forgive, but perhaps he can understand how lonely a woman grows, shut up with a coarse man who cares only for his hunting and his feuds. Bavydd was like a snake. He wormed his way into my life by bringing me news of my poor outcast brother, and what woman doesn't want to have news of her own true kin?" Tears welled. "Bavydd was so kind at first, but then, when I found out what sort of man he was, it was too late."

It was so beautifully done that at first Sevinna was inclined to believe her. Elyc's expression softened, then turned puzzled as Mallona stared straight into his eyes.

"Then I found out that Bavydd was making trouble between my lord and his liege, Coryc. I felt like a fish in a net, Your Grace, flopping and flopping. And my son." Her voice broke again. "My only son had just died, and I was distraught. All I could think of was ridding myself of the man who'd come upon me like a curse. And so I killed him. And then there was nothing left to me but flight." She paused to let tears roll down her cheeks. "Ah, by the gods, my lord! I know I must pay for this murder, but I beg you, don't let me hang. Let me go to a Moon Temple, where I can spend the rest of a miserable life tending the Goddess's garden and praying to her for forgiveness. That's all I ever ask of you."

Elyc bent down and reached for her hands. Before he could touch them, Rhodry swung clear of the bench and strode to his side.

"My Lord Elyc! This sad story seems to ache your heart, but there are a few small things the lady has omitted. She would have killed Tieryn Dwaen if she could have. And to escape your justice, she would have let my Jill's hands be cut off in the public market-place, leaving her maimed for life."

With a shriek of rage, Mallona bounded to her feet and swung at Rhodry, a hard claw with her nails. He dodged, grabbed her wrist, and swung her round, twisting her arm behind her back until she went limp. Lady Davylla began to cry, a soft whimper under her breath. Babryan leaned back against the lady's knee, so pale that it seemed she would faint.

"Your Grace?" Rhodry said. "This lady's lapdog has the teeth and claws of a wolf, and about as much heart as one, too."

"Cursed right, Silver Dagger!" Tudvulc could hold his peace no longer. "Elyc, may the gods blast me if I flaunt my rank in your hall, but think, man!"

"Just so." Elyc rose to face the lady. "Well and good, then, woman. You will be turned over to Gwerbret Coryc of Caenmetyn to pay the full penalty for these heinous crimes. Tieryn Dwaen has come here with armed men to escort you back to his liege lord for that purpose. In the morning, I'll give you over to his charge and offer him whatever aid he needs to return you to your lawful punish-ment."

Mallona burst out weeping, throwing her head from side to side, writhing and sobbing as she desperately tried to look at Davylla. With tears running down her face, Davylla rose and ap-proached her husband, kneeling at his feet and clasping his knees.

"My lord? Only one thing I would beg you. Don't throw her into that prison house. Let her have a chamber for the night."

"For your sake, my lady, I'll do that, and besides, no matter what she's done, she's noble-born."

The chamberlain stepped forward and bowed.

"My lord? I know a little room that can be barred from the outside, and I'll have the shutters over the window barred, too." He glanced at Dwaen. "Does that suit His Grace?"

"It does, my lord, and my thanks."

Elyc himself went with the servants, and Rhodry followed, to make sure that Mallona's temporary prison was a secure one. When

Sevinna rose, Dwaen joined her, smiling as he laid his hand on her arm.

"Well, my lady, I'm afraid it won't be much of a wedding procession, but will you come home with me when I ride?"

Sevinna glanced round and found her uncle glaring at her.

"Perhaps I'd best go to my father's home first, my lord, and you can fetch me there."

"Very nicely put, lass." Tudvulc turned the glare on Dwaen. "Still hasn't been a word said about the blasted dowry or your marriage gifts, eh?"

Gathering her skirts around her, Sevinna swept off to join the other women, who were waiting for her near the staircase. For a long moment they stared at her, pale faces, reproachful eyes, soft trembling mouths.

"My lady?" Sevinna said to Davylla. "Think of me what you will, but Mallona was a spider in your glove, not a friend. I only spoke against her for your sake."

"So it seems. Why did you ride off like that?"

"To keep her from poisoning me. I'm the one who exposed her ruse to trap Jill."

"She never would have!" Babryan broke in. "I don't believe it. She'd never have hurt you, and she didn't poison that lover, either!"

"Baba, don't be a dolt," Wbridda snapped. "Or do you think she confessed like that because it was good sport?"

Babryan began to cry, then turned and ran for the stairs.

"I never liked her, anyway," Wbridda hurled after.

With a sob, Babryan raced upstairs, turning round the spiral and disappearing. More slowly, the others followed. When they reached the guest chamber, they found the door barred. From inside they could hear weeping.

"Baba, darling," Davylla called out. "Now be sensible and open that door. Sevvi and Bry have to sleep, too, you know."

The weeping stopped, but there was no answer. Davylla knocked and ordered and begged as well, but the only reply was a furious "Go away! I hate you!"

"Ah, well," Davylla said at last. "There are plenty of beds in other chambers. Here, perhaps it would be best, anyway, if you two shared a chamber nearer my own. I have plenty of nightdresses, too."

"She'll be better in the morning," Wbridda agreed. "We can talk to her then."

Although Sevinna hated to leave Babryan alone with her wounds, there was no getting her cousin to open the door, and she allowed herself to be swept off by Lady Davylla. As soon as she was lying in a comfortable bed, she fell asleep without any worries for either present or future, but all that night she dreamt about Dwaen.

Since Jill and Rhodry had been given a chamber of their own, Jill was planning on sleeping as late as courtesy would allow, but the gray of first dawn still filled the room when she woke to hear someone pounding on the door. Grumbling and swearing, Rhodry sat up just as Dwaen burst in.

"Rhodry! Lady Mallona's escaped."

"What, Your Grace?" Rhodry sat bolt upright. "How could she?"

"Someone unlocked the door from the outside. On your feet, man—there's not a minute to lose."

"If His Grace would be so kind as to turn his back so my lady can dress, we'll be as quick as ever we can."

The tieryn strode over to the window and stared out. While Jill and Rhodry dressed, he told them how a page had wakened him only a few minutes ago, saying that the servant who went up to feed the lady had found the door unbolted and the prisoner fled.

"Elyc and Tudvulc are going to question the womenfolk," Dwaen finished up. "It must be one of them, and I'll put my wager on that little Babryan."

"So would I," Jill said. "But how did Mallona get out of the dun?"

"A stolen horse and men's clothing again, probably. There hasn't been time to question the gatekeeper yet."

148

They were all hurrying down the staircase to the great hall when they met a page hurrying up.

"Your Grace, the Lady Babryan's gone, too."

Jill felt as sick as if she'd bitten into tainted meat.

"The faithful little dolt! You're right, Your Grace—there's not a minute to lose."

The table of honor framed a tableau of hysteria. Lady Davylla and Wbridda wept and clung together; Elyc and Tudvulc paced back and forth and shouted at each other. In the background hovered Cenwyc and a crowd of frightened servitors, while across the hall the men ate standing up and straining to hear every word. Sevinna ran over and caught Jill's arm.

"I've been searching the chambers. All of Lady Mallona's herbs and stuff are gone, and so are Baba's traveling cloak and riding boots. They took the blankets off Mallona's bed, too."

"Do you know if Mallona had a weapon?" Jill said.

"A dagger. It was a long one with a metal handle, because she used it for the rites. That's gone, too."

"I'm less worried about steel than I am about herbs," Rhodry broke in. "Oh, ye gods, where do they think they're going? How do they think they're going to get away with this?"

"I doubt me if either of them's thinking at all," Dwaen said. "Especially the Lady Babryan."

"Just so." Sevinna turned to him, her voice quivering in rage. "Mallona's been working on her. She's got ways of doing that. She tried them on me, but it didn't avail her much. I beg you, my lord, don't think unkindly of my cousin for this. I swear she's been ensorcelled."

"Never did I think anything else," Dwaen said. "And for your sake, I'll bring her back safely or die in the attempt."

Sevinna dropped him a curtsy, then hurried back to her aunt. With an impatient bellow, Tudvulc waved them over.

"The grooms are getting the horses ready. You'd better eat fast, lads." He grabbed a couple of chunks of bread from a bowl on the table and threw them, one at a time, to Jill, Rhodry, and Dwaen.

"When I catch this fiend who's got my daughter, I'm going to skin her alive!"

"I trust His Grace is merely overcome by his feelings," Dwaen said. "The penalty that great Bel decreed is hanging."

Tudvulc snarled wordlessly.

"Well, Your Grace, the laws say—"

A yell from the door stopped Dwaen's disquisition.

"My lords! He's dead! Gello—he's been stabbed."

"The gatekeeper," Rhodry muttered. "Poor bastard."

Old Gello, as frail as a stick, lay broken on the floor of his little hut beside the gates. He'd been stabbed once from behind and thrown face down, so that a pool of blood stained his shirt.

"It's still wet." Dwaen knelt down and laid a hand on his face. "And he's barely cold."

"What?" Elyc sputtered. "How could—"

"My lord?" Rhodry broke in. "It means they waited till he opened the gates. Just at dawn, not all that long ago at all."

"We've just missed the bitch," Elyc snapped. "Ye gods, her gall!"

Tudvulc chained a string of foul oaths worthy of a bard. Elyc turned and yelled to his men, clustering out in the ward.

"Get every man in the dun into the town! You, you, and you—run like the hells were opening under you! I want the town gates closed!"

Jill glanced at the sky, where the true dawn was just beginning to brighten. With luck, some, at least, of the town gates might never have been opened.

In a tumult of shouted orders, Elyc and Tudvulc began organizing the search. Dwaen grabbed Jill's arm, and with Rhodry trailing after, led her round the curve of the broch where they could hear each other speak.

"I don't like this!" he snapped. "How could she have killed the man and then just walked out the gates? There's too many folk about, even at first light. She must have known they'd never make it to the road unseen."

"Just so," Jill said. "Unless she had a friend in town, somewhere she knew she could hide."

"She's been here weeks, and she must have left the dun now and again," Rhodry put in. "To go to market for those herbs if naught else."

"They must have dashed like foxes for an earth," Jill said. "Well, if—oh, ye gods! An earth, indeed. What if they've never left the dun?"

"Ye gods!" Dwaen whispered. "As bold as all that, to wait till we've all charged out, and then stroll out after us?"

Rhodry tossed back his head and howled his long mad laugh. Yelling at the top of his lungs, Dwaen ran to fetch his warband and start them searching. As Jill jogged after him, she heard Tudvulc start to bellow, then break off. She and Rhodry reached the lords in time to hear them start yelling at their men to search the dun.

They found them in the boldest place of all, the chamber where Mallona had been imprisoned the night before, up high in one of the half-brochs. The men had charged like whirlwinds through every other building by the time that Jill found a kitchen maid, all wide eyes with excitement, who admitted seeing a lady in a cloak going in the door to that tower.

"Was it Lady Taurra?"

"I only saw her back, like. I thought maybe it was our Lady Davylla, come to bid the murderess farewell."

"Not too likely, lass." Jill turned away and yelled back to the others. "My lords! Rhodry! Come on!"

Shoving the lass out of the way, Jill charged inside and clattered up the spiral staircase. She could hear the sound of the men, swearing and shoving as they followed. At the landing, she hesitated, but just one door stood closed. She flung it open only to stop short at the threshold. Mallona was standing in a shaft of sunlight in the center of the room. In front of her, Babryan slumped in a chair like a heap of discarded dresses. At first Jill thought her dead, but the lass breathed, her mouth half-open. Her fevered eyes turned Jill's way in an agony of pleading. At her throat, Mallona held the long-bladed ritual dagger.

"One more step, you little meddler, and she'll die." Mallona's voice was as strong and quiet as ever.

From the oaths and boots trampling behind her, Jill knew that the men were mobbing the landing. When Tudvulc shoved his way through to stand in the doorway, Mallona turned calm eyes his way.

"Your daughter's been poisoned, and only I know the antidote. Let me go, and I'll give it to you. Here's my bargain. Fetch me a horse, and that smelly silver dagger will ride with me outside the town. There I'll give her the vial, and she'll take it back to you. Don't worry, there's plenty of time, at least till noon, before Baba dies."

"You whore to pigs and dogs," Tudvulc whispered. "You impious bitch!"

"And if you and your men follow me and Jill," Mallona went on. "You'll never get the vial, because I'll break it. Swear on your sacred honor that I go free, and Babryan lives. How would bards sing of your name if you let a child of yours die?"

Tudvulc was shaking, his face scarlet, the veins on his forehead bulging and pulsing. Elyc laid a heavy hand on his shoulder and dragged him back a step.

"If you kill me now, you'll never know which vial is the right one," Mallona remarked with a small smile. "I have many different herbs."

Jill stepped back to let Elyc have her place. She bumped into Dwaen, looked round but saw no sign of Rhodry. She could only assume that he'd got stuck on the staircase in the crush of warbands.

"It gripes my very soul to say it, Your Grace," Elyc said, "but I see naught to do but take her terms."

Tudvulc tried to speak, then merely nodded his consent.

"Swear it then." Laughing, Mallona held the dagger close to Babryan's throat. "Swear on your honor, oh, your ever-so-sacred men's honor! Swear on your swords, swear on your very clans that neither you nor your men nor your servants will do one single thing to impede my escape."

"So I swear," Elyc said.

"And I," Tudvulc growled out. "Someday the gods will take my vengeance for me."

"Oh, I'm prepared to deal with the gods when my time comes. It's your oaths I want now. Jill, swear the same, or I'll kill your pretty little Baba."

"I swear on my silver dagger that I'll do exactly what you've described."

"Done, then! Shut that door while I make my preparations."

Elyc reached in with one fist and slammed the door shut. Tudvulc went on shaking; Elyc looked as if he would weep; Dwaen crossed his arms over his chest and prayed softly to his god for vengeance, his eyes shut, his face raised toward Bel's heaven. All at once, Jill heard a shriek, then a crash and thump from the chamber. Thinking that Mallona had stabbed Babryan after all, she sprang forward and flung the door open. Babryan moaned, unharmed, but Mallona lay on the floor with a vial clutched in her hand and a silver dagger in her back. Laughing like a fiend, Rhodry climbed in the window and knelt down beside her.

"You never asked me to take a vow. I'm not sworn man nor servant, am I? Only a silver dagger. And you should have held your ugly tongue while you were fetching that vial."

Rhodry grabbed her wrist and pulled the vial free. Mallona raised her head, struggled to turn over, but when she gasped, blood broke on her lips in bubbles.

"You'll have one wish," Jill said, striding in. "You won't hang."

Gasping, choking, Mallona pushed herself up, her hands paddling in her own blood, and raised her head to stare at Rhodry.

"Aranrhodda," she whispered. "Aranrhodda rica rica, crissi bregan crissi . . ."

She coughed and writhed, her bowels emptying in a reflexive gush, so that like Bavydd of Cerrmor, she fell to lie dead in her own excrement. Jill shoved her fist in her mouth just in time to stifle a scream, because she saw, as clearly as a winter's mist though no more, a dark woman's form, with long hair that streamed out all round her face, come to tower over her worshipper's corpse. Mallona's soul, a naked woman made of pale blue light, rose from her dead body like smoke rising from a fire. Jill saw it throw itself into Aranrhodda's arms, which folded round it like wings. The vision lasted but a few beats of a heart, but Jill could have sworn that the Goddess's eyes turned Rhodry's way and marked him.

"Well, here, Your Grace," Rhodry said. *"It wasn't truly that much of a* thing, and I feel dishonorable for stabbing a woman in the back. All I did was go into the next chamber, then climb out the window and go along the wall. The stones were so rough, they were as good as a ledge to stand on. I could hear her taunting poor little Baba, too, and I saw her holding up the right vial and telling the lass to pray that she lived to drink it. So I braced myself in the window and threw the dagger, and you know the rest."

"So I do," Tudvulc said. "And I hold you honorable, because that was no woman, but a fiend from Hell. I'm going to see that you're well rewarded for this bit of work."

"My thanks. Because the coin means more than the honor to a silver dagger."

"Ye gods, man! Will you stop berating yourself for your brother's stubbornness? Here, what about that post in my court? I can't let the man who saved my blood kin's life just ride away. Even Rhys should be able to see that."

Rhodry merely shook his head in a no. He refused to weaken, no matter how tempted he might be.

"Well, you know your own mind, I suppose," Tudvulc said with a sigh. "One thing, though. Will you ride our way for the wedding?"

"We might at that, Your Grace. Jill would like to, I know."

"Huh." Tudvulc suddenly smiled. "By the by, meant to tell you. I do understand—now—that Sevvi wasn't running off with that Dwaen fellow. Told her so, told her we'd find another man if she wanted and blast the scandal! But she says she likes her tieryn perfectly well, and so there we are. The Goddess must have brought us together, says she. Hah! Probably going to be a good match, eh?

They can sit around and talk about the gods together. Daft, both of them."

When Tudvulc laughed, Rhodry joined him, but mostly for the courtesy of it. As soon as he could, he made a polite escape from the gwerbret and went to find Jill.

She was sitting in the window of their chamber up in Elyc's broch, turned sideways to look down on the ward. The sight of her there, up so high with naught between her and a fall, made him uncomfortable, even though her position seemed perfectly secure. When he shut the door, she turned her head his way.

"You look so pale," he said. "What's so wrong, my love?"

"I don't know. I was just thinking about Mallona's death."

"Oh, here, you've seen far worse deaths than that!"

"I know. You're going to think me daft, but I still feel sorry for her."

"What? You are daft, then! She would have had you maimed without thinking twice and then killed Babryan, too."

"Would she? Well, one thing's sure, if her clumsy charge of thievery had held up, I would have lost a hand." Jill shuddered, rubbing one wrist with the other palm. "But she wasn't making that charge in cold blood. I doubt me if she was thinking at all, by then. She was so panicked, seeing her last safety gone. And as for Baba, well, we'll never know the truth of that."

"And what about the gatekeeper?"

"You have me there. The poor old fellow!"

"She's an evil woman, Mallona. Don't you believe that?"

"Probably so. I can't really defend her, because, well—" She hesitated for a moment. "When she died, I thought—I saw the oddest sort of vision, as she lay there. The goddess came to claim her, Aranrhodda, I mean."

"Well, splendid! They can sit round in the Otherlands together and gossip over their pot of herb brew."

"Don't! Oh, Rhoddo, hold your tongue! Never mock like that, oh please! It's so dangerous."

"Dangerous?" He tossed his head, tried to grin, would rather have spat on the floor. "Oh, come now, what is this? More of your blasted dweomer?"

Jill started to speak, then began to cry in a shudder of tears. Rhodry ran to her, pulled her up, and pulled her into his arms.

"Oh, here, here, I'm sorry, my sweet, please forgive me, I'm sorry. I didn't mean to mock you."

"It's not me that matters," she sniveled out. "When it comes to mocking, I mean."

"Well, then, I don't mean to mock the Goddess either. My apologies to her as well. It's just all this talk of all this wretched dweomer! It gets on a man's nerves, it does."

"Don't you think it gets on mine?" She looked up, sniffing back more tears. "Oh, Rhodry, I love you so much. All I ever want is you. Truly."

He kissed her, savoring her words as much as the feel of her mouth on his.

Yet later, of course, the memory of those words would return, a bitter haunting, when her dweomer finally tore them apart, as indeed the entire memory rose, all those many years later, when he looked into the golden eyes of a shape-changer, and knew against all reason, all possibility, against everything his intellect knew of life and death, that his old enemy Mallona lived again, and that she remembered him as clearly as ever he did her.

That evening, while the dragon slept after feeding upon a doe she'd hunted down, Rhodry sat awake without a fire and stared into the dark, all glowy with moonlight and as bright as a summer twilight to his half-elven sight. Round him on the high plain, the land stretched silent toward the white peaks, glimmering under the stars. He was remembering all the cryptic hints that Jill had, much later in their lives, given him about such matters. She'd suggested more than once that each man or woman lives far more lives than one, that the gate to the Otherlands swings both ways, no matter what the priests may have taught to the faithful.

"No!" And oddly enough, he found himself speaking Elvish rather than the language of men. "No, no, no! It can't be true!"

He refused to believe such a preposterous thing, absolutely refused. The wind picked up, stroking his hair as if to reassure him that the world was still solid and real despite whatever fancies he might be having. Yet deep in his heart, a feeling—or perhaps it was an insight—nagged and gnawed, that perhaps, just maybe, perhaps all the death-dealing that he'd done in his long warrior's life was the most ridiculous thing in the world, because nothing had ever been or ever would be settled or finished, once and for all, by blood and the sword.

"No! It can't be true."

And if it were true? All his life one thing had defined Rhodry—death and his ability to deal it. He saw it very clearly, that night, how his honor, his rank, his very manhood had always rested on his talent for war. Yet if death meant nothing, if war settled nothing, if old hatreds lived and old feuds haunted like ghosts no matter how much blood was poured out to propitiate them—well, then! what was he, who was he?

He leapt to his feet and walked, pacing round and round, staring at the stars that glittered high above him, cold and utterly indifferent to the fate of men and elves alike. He would talk about it with Jill, he decided, once the siege of Cengarn was lifted, and he could reach her. He would ask her outright this time; he would take up her wretched hints and her challenge. He'd never been a coward before. Cursed if he'd be a coward about this!

Once he made the decision, he could put his mind at rest, could kneel down and spread out his bedroll as if this were a night like any other. He put all his trust in Jill and what she would tell him, just as a sick child puts all his trust in his mother to heal him; and trusting in her, he could sleep.

It was just at dawn, and a long way west from Cengarn and south as well, so far away, in fact, that it would have taken men and horses half a year to march there, that Evandar materialized on the shore of the Southern Sea, at a cove where a river ran down from the north to form the harbor of Rinbaladelan, City of the Moon. Most of the river still flowed in the stone conduits that the elven folk had built to contain it, but here and there Time had broken the levees and allowed the water to spread. On top of the stone banks, shrubs grew in windblown soil; flowering vines draped old stairways and ramps; here and there, trees put down roots that would in time crack apart the masonry. Soon, Evandar supposed, the original swamp would reclaim the estuary and spoil the perfect crescent of the harbor.

He walked along the white sand at the tide line until he reached a mound of sand-covered stone, some twenty feet high, where once a lighthouse had stood. A slippery climb up broken stairs brought him to the top and a good view of the ruined city. Behind him the blue sea broke over water-worn stone, the drowned bones of jetties and seawalls; ahead, forest in green waves lay over mounds and gullies that had once been buildings and streets. On the highest hill, like a fist, the ruins of the observatory poked through the trees, still dominating the city in death as it had done so in life. From where he stood, Evandar could just pick out a few stone structures, each well over a hundred feet tall—a crumbling stairway clasped by underbrush; a peculiar curving track, like an upside-down arch, that had once guided light from important stars to the eyes of learned men; slender pillars that still marked the rising and setting of equinoctial suns—though their positions were a bit off after this lapse of time. Each pillar stood crowned, these days, by the untidy nests of herons and storks, while lesser birds dwelt in the star tracks.

It was from the observatory hill that the founders of Rinbaladelan had first laid out the city plan, an elaborate scheme of circles and ellipses, drawn from the movements of the so-called "wandering stars." Since the city had fallen some eleven centuries earlier, tree roots and winter storms had effaced the pattern, just as the sleeve of a careless scribe wipes out half of what he's written. Evandar was the only being left who knew where a map lay. Fetching it, at the appropriate time, would constitute a crucial turn in the maze of schemes he'd set himself to walk. The conquering Horsekin had called the observatory a palace of magic, if Evandar remembered rightly, and believed that the elves used it to summon demons.

They were all dead now, the Horsekin conquerors, wiped out by their very victory. After the city had fallen, and its few surviving defenders been tortured to death, the Kin had thrown the corpses of friend and foe alike into the harbor to rot. They settled down in Rinbaladelan to live in a city for the first time in their lives, crowded into the ruins of their conquest with broken sewers and not the faintest idea of the need for same. They'd never seen a ship before, either, and harbors were a mystery to them—except for fishing in. The sea had given them a fine crop that next year, with the suppurating dead to feed it.

It had been an interesting little plague, all in all. Evandar smiled as he remembered the dying of the Hordes, the Meradan, as the elves had termed their enemies. The women and children died first, crawling on hands and knees while their swollen bellies poisoned them. Later, Evandar walked among the dying warriors and taunted them as they lay puking and sweating in their stolen jewels. The survivors of the first plague fled north to infect the Horsekin living in the ruins of Bravelmelim, who had died in turn, and its survivors fled again until a chain of death wound round the brief Horsekin empire and strangled it.

By then, Rinbaladelan, the first thing on earth that Evandar had ever loved, lay long past help or repair—or so he'd always thought, until some seven hundred years later, when he met Dallandra, the second earthly thing he'd come to love. She'd spoken of the crafting of fine things that lasted beyond the moment of their imagining; she'd turned his eyes to the lands of men and dwarves, where master craftsmen still understood the smelting of metals and the quarrying of stone. Dallandra had given him ideas, grand ideas full of vast imaginings, and he'd begun to scheme out ways to realize these ideas, not in his own shifting empire of images, but upon the solid earth and in the world of Time. After all, if souls could die and be reborn, why shouldn't a city do the same?

Evandar needed more than craftsmen, of course, to make his city live—he needed citizens to settle Rinbaladelan and do the work of the rebuilding. Most of the descendants of the elven people now lived out on the high plains of the Westlands as nomadic horse-herders, remembering their former splendor but sharing none of it. A dying race, worn out with loss and danger, soon they would be gone, a memory blown on the winds of Time, unless somehow and against all odds he could revitalize their race and bring them souls willing to be born among them. For three hundred years now, he'd been braiding a complex net of schemes to do just that.

"And then the bitch nearly goes and spoils everything," he said aloud to the ruins. "That charming harridan, that hag of great strength, she who was once my wife, Alshandra."

At her name he spat onto the sand. The siege of Cengarn was only the beginning of her troublemaking. She'd promised her followers new conquests as their reward and turned their greedy eyes to Deverry and the rich lands of men. Where was he going to get the artisans and settlers he needed, if the stupid shrew plunged the whole country into war? And what would happen to that third thing he'd come to love, Rhodry Maelwaedd?

Evandar disliked acting directly upon the earth. He preferred to give a charmed gift here, utter an oracle there, pretend to be a god to the Gel da'Thae, a Guardian to the elves, a mysterious dweomermaster to men and dwarves so that he could say cryptic things and set obscure riddles—in short, to play only the most subtle melodies upon the harp of Wyrd. Yet, if he refused to act, if Cengarn fell, what then would happen to all his plans? He would have to decide soon whether to act or no. Decisions and haste were two things he particularly hated.

Muttering to himself about the injustice of it all, Evandar walked down to the tide line, picked his way through the driftwood and strings of dead kelp to the water, but instead of walking into the quiet waves, he stepped up above them and strode along the dapple of sunlight upon sea until, in but a few moments, he disappeared.

The wind rose. Up on the hill, the trees nodded over the ruined observatory, as if reminding it of Evandar's promise, that someday the city would be reborn.

PRESENT, RISING
The Northlands, 1116

FORTUNA MINOR

*In all lands of our map this figure does
bring aid to those in distress and a turning
for the better in many things, yet always at
a price, which, depending upon those figures nearby, may be far higher than the
querent wishes to pay. In the land of
Quicksilver it also denotes a going out into
strange ways.*

—The Omenbook of Gwarn,
Loremaster

"Where are we going, master?" Arzosah said.

"What do you mean, where? To the dwarvehold, of course. Lin Serr, just like Evandar said."

"You'd follow his orders?" She slapped her tail against the ground with a boom and a roil of dust.

"Why not? He knows things I can't see. Now hold still. I've got one last knot to tie."

With a whine, she settled down and let Rhodry finish arranging the ropes for the riding harness. He tied on his gear, then considered. Although out of habit he was wearing his sword, he decided that they'd flown close enough to the war, now, for him to consider combat. The sword, securely lashed, went into his bedroll. He slung a quiver of arrows at his hip and a curved elven hunting bow over his back.

"You'd best tie yourself on if you're going to be using that thing," Arzosah said. "They take both hands, don't they?"

"They do, and you're right. Here, I should think you'd be glad if I fell to my death."

"Of course I'd be glad. I'd be free, then. But you ordered me to do all in my power to keep you safe, and giving you good advice is within my power. Alas."

"Ah. I see. Well, my thanks."

On impulse, Rhodry reached up and first patted, then scratched her scaly brow, which curved round her eye sockets, in the same way as you'd scratch a dog on the head. She rumbled and leaned into his touch.

"You like that, eh?"

"I can't reach to scratch there myself. Oooh, do the other side, please?"

He walked round her head and obliged, while she let her eyelids droop and kept rumbling till he was done.

"Now, if you're good," Rhodry said, "I'll do that again tonight."

"Done, then—a bargain, Dragonmaster. So we fly south today?"

"We do. And keep a good watch for Horsekin."

Ever since they'd left the place that had once been Haen Marn, they'd been following the track left by an army. Once they were flying again, Rhodry could see it clearly. Across the scrubby downs, it ran like a road, a muddy wound bitten into the grass by the hooves of hundreds of horses and the wheels of many wagons. Just ahead, though, lay forest, as the hills dropped lower and lower toward the plateau when Lin Serr stood. The track led straight into it and disappeared. Rhodry could assume that the raiding party had found the trees rough going; they would have had to chop a road for their wagons and scrounge fresh fodder for their stock.

"Drop down! Let's take a look at the forest."

Arzosah allowed herself to glide until she flew only a few yards above the trees. Sure enough, Rhodry could see clearings and two wagons, as well, left shattered in the improvised road. Farther on, he could just make out another wagon and a scatter of objects.

"Big clearing over there!" Arzosah bellowed. "Shall I land? I don't smell any Horsekin near here."

"Then let's go down and see what they left behind."

As Arzosah settled, a cloud of terrified ravens flew up squawking, but these were ordinary birds, come for the dead horse he could see near the shattered wagon, which lay half in a stream. As soon as Rhodry slid down from her back and looked round, he recognized the little valley. Only two months earlier, he'd hiked through it. During that last visit, he'd found a road marker, a slab of black basalt, polished glassy and graved with dwarven pictographs that announced it stood on the road for Haen Marn. Rhodry glanced round and at last saw it, half-hidden by underbrush at the valley's edge.

"Rhodry?" Arzosah said. "I don't suppose you'd mind if I finished up that horse."

"Ych! It's all gassy and overripe!"

"I rather enjoy meat that way. It's a savory, like."

"Well, it's no good to anyone else, sure enough. You'll be able to fly, though, if you eat it?"

"After a bit of a rest, not much more than one of your hand's breadths of the sun moving in the sky."

He'd ridden to war too often to risk starving his mount when combat lay ahead.

"Eat away. Just watch out for maggots."

"Why? I like maggots."

"Whatever pleases you, then."

Even though the dragon was a tidy feeder, slicing her meat with a delicate fang, then chewing quietly, Rhodry preferred to get away from the smell of rotted horse while she ate. He wandered over to the marker stone and swore aloud. Moss and the pitting of weather had mottled its once-slick face with white and green; rain had worn the slab itself away, shrunk it down and dug out its shoulders. He had to run his fingertips over the pictographs to find them and trace them out. It seemed that a thousand years had passed over this stone while he'd spent but the turning of two moons away from it. If Evandar hadn't told him of the siege of Cengarn, he would have panicked, wondering if he'd been cast into a magical sleep like the heroes of old tales. As it was, he supposed that everything linked to Haen Marn had suffered at its leaving.

"No hope for it now," he said aloud. "Angmar, my love, I only pray you're well, wherever you may be."

Tears burned in his throat, but he choked them back. With a toss of his head, he strode back to the broken wagon to see if he could learn anything about the enemies he was facing.

Quite a lot, as it turned out. Behind the heap of slats and

shattered wheels lay smashed wooden boxes and a long narrow bundle, covered with a cow's hide that had been painted with strange runes. Rhodry flipped the hide away, then staggered back. Underneath a dead man, and a human being at that, lay on his back, but he was no victim of the wagon accident. As battle-hardened as Rhodry was, the sight nearly made him retch. The fellow had been stripped naked, then staked out, hands and feet pierced through with iron-tipped spikes. From breech to breastbone he'd been slit, then opened like a book, a few inches at a time, it seemed, and his internal organs pulled free to lie in tidy rows to either side—guts by his hips, liver and stomach to either side his waist, lungs split and laid beside his chest. His heart, however, was missing. Judging by the agony still graved into his face—his tongue and lips were so caked with black blood that he must have bitten them repeatedly—he had lasted a good long time. Ants swarmed over everything.

Rhodry shuddered like a wet dog and moved away. He swore a couple of times, spat on the ground for good measure, then looked up to find Arzosah considering him with one coppery eye.

"That's how they send messages to their gods," she said. "After they stake him, they chant the message over and over, then send him off to the Deathworld to deliver it."

"If I were him, I'd lie, just for revenge. What do they do with the heart?"

"I have no idea. Eat it, maybe, or work magic with it? I watched them do the message rite once—up in the mountains, that was—but then they put the heart in a box and took it away."

"I see. Here, can you fly a little ways? I don't want to stay here with this thing."

"I can manage a few flaps, but then I'll have to rest."

"Fine. Let me just wash my hands in the stream."

"Why? You didn't touch that thing, did you?"

"Of course not. I just feel like I need a bit of a wash."

Worse lay in store for them later that afternoon. After Arzosah's rest, they headed south again, flapping and gliding at a pace slow enough for her to keep testing the wind. The Horsekin, she assured him, had a distinctive scent, traceable from a long way off. The land here dropped steadily down in a long roll of foothills to a wide plateau, where dwarven men worked communal farms to feed their underground city of Lin Serr. Some days past, Rhodry had seen from far off a pall of smoke hanging over this rich farmland. Now he found his fears justified. From his high perch on dragonback, he could see, among the green fields and pastures, the irregular swathes of black cinders that meant pillaged farms. Nowhere did he see a single cow or sheep. Nothing moved but the wind, rising as the sun sank toward the west.

"Land!" he called out to Arzosah. "At that first burnt farm there. Maybe someone's left alive."

No one was, and in the event, he was glad of it. When they landed in another huge scatter of ravens, he found the ruins of house and barns cold, with only wisps of gray ash, not smoke, blowing in the evening wind. Over everything hung the sickly sweet reek of burning, tinged with dead flesh. He walked back and forth, his silver dagger in his hand just for the comfort of it, saw here and there a dead man, lying hacked or broken, killed, all of them, from cuts of some bladed weapon wielded from above—he could postulate a horseback charge with long swords. Some of the corpses still clutched flails or wood-cutting axes, the only poor weapons they could grab. Some the flames had reached, but whether they were mercifully dead or only wounded when they'd caught fire, he couldn't tell.

Beyond the largest heap of timbers and crashed walls he could see what seemed to be poles of some sort, standing stuck in the ground, and he could make out shapes attached to them. His stomach clenched, anticipating.

"It's not pretty," Arzosah said. "What they do to prisoners they take alive, I mean. I found some once, flying over Horsekin country."

With the dragon padding after, Rhodry forced himself to walk round and see for himself. He'd been expecting severed heads; what he found was much worse, a thicket of death, twelve poles and corpses in all, each pole stained black with old blood. Each prisoner had been stripped and then impaled, while still alive judging from

166

the agony in their twisted faces, on long spears that had been thrust into each man's anus and straight on through, so that the iron tip now stuck out between their shoulder blades just at the neck. Each corpse hung half-eaten by ravens, the remaining skin a mottled gray, and the flesh the maroon of cut meat.

"They stand them up and let them die," Arzosah said. "Do you think it takes a long time?"

"Anything more than a bare moment would be too long." Rhodry was surprised that he could speak at all. "Why? Ye gods, why?"

Arzosah lifted her wings in the long rustle that did her for a shrug. Rhodry found himself staring at each man in turn; he'd shared a meal with them, when he was on his way to Haen Marn. Here hung the young lad who'd served cheese from a basket lined with herbs; there, the old man who'd joked with him about his elven blood. All at once, Rhodry realized that he was dreading a specific thing. He strode forward, weaving his way through the spears from corpse to corpse.

"What are you doing?" Arzosah called out.

"Looking for friends. But thanks be to every god in the sky and under it, they're not here."

"We saw other burnt places."

"So we did, but we don't dare take the time to look for them there."

"Who?"

"These two friends of mine. Otho and young Mic. They had an errand to run, taking payment for a debt to Haen Marn, you see, after I left it to look for you. Then they had to get home again."

"Well, let's hope the Horsekin didn't catch them on the road."

"Just so. Let's get out of here. I'm too sick even to swear, and for a silver dagger, that's a bad omen."

By then, the summer light lay golden over the ruins and the dead, and bright on the grass, green beyond the burning. When Rhodry looked up, he saw the sun picking out drifts of cloud in the western sky. He clambered up onto the dragon's back and slipped his lower legs under a pair of ropes, tied another round his waist, and braced himself as she took to the air. Once she found her gliding rhythm, he could think.

He was remembering his doubts of the night before, when the thought that life and death might be two sides of a door seemed to mock his warrior's craft. Now those doubts were gone. He had seen what his enemy did to their own slaves, seen how they treated prisoners. These were the same beings who held the siege of Cengarn. If the city fell to them? He refused to let himself imagine it possible. This was what his long life of war had led him to, as straight as the flight of an arrow, that he and other men like him should stand between the city and this army. As they flew, following the long track across the plateau, he watched the sun sink in a sea of blood.

That night, he made a fire for their camp, just for the light against the dark. When he searched through his gear, he found one last scrap of flatbread, barely two mouthfuls, but he'd ridden hungry before. He knelt close to the fire and fed it twigs, a few at a time, till he could lay in the dead branches he'd found.

"I can fly at night," Arzosah said, "if you want to push on for this Lin Serr place."

"They shut it up at sunset, and besides, for all we know, it's besieged."

"Or fallen."

"Nah, nah, nah, not Lin Serr. They could hold off a siege for a hundred years if they had to. You'll see what I mean when we reach it. Huh, though, a thought just dawned on me. Should I be having this fire? It's like a beacon, truly, if there are some roaming squads around."

"I would have smelled them. Rhodry, an odd thing! I begin to think that they're all gone. The Horsekin, I mean. We haven't seen a thing move, and I've smelled naught."

"Well, they arrived up here by dweomer, didn't they? Mayhap they've left the same cursed way."

Since the fire had taken, he moved back and sat cross-legged in the dirt to watch it burn. Arzosah sighed and rested her head on her paws.

"I'm hungry," she announced. "We've flown a long way since I ate that horse."

"I'm hungry, too, but we can ignore it."

"You are *so* mean, Dragonmaster!"

"What I've seen today would make any man mean. Ye gods, I keep remembering other wars I've fought. Petty things, all of them, or so they seem now, compared to this."

She raised a doubting eye-ridge.

"Well, they were," he went on. "Some arrogant lord's feud, mostly, men wrangling over who'd get the taxes from a bridge, or who'd be elevated in rank, or swearing vengeance for some slight or another. Stupid things, stupid, stupid things, though, you know, I never would have called them that before."

"Were lots of men killed in them?"

"They were. Too many."

"Well, you don't need to look so sad. The blame of it isn't yours."

"Of course not. And I never felt this way back then, when I was riding the wars, I mean." He shook his head, baffled. His life had never allowed him much time for thinking, after all, especially of this abstract sort. "It was seeing those farmers, somehow, that made me realize. Now *this* is a war worth riding."

"Vengeance, you mean."

"That, too. But I meant, to keep it from happening to anyone else. Ye gods, vengeance won't be bringing them back to life, will it?"

Arzosah laughed in a long thunder.

"I never thought I'd hear an elven man say such a thing," she said. "Amazing."

"Don't be snide! You're after a vengeance of your own."

"Of course, but I know I'm doing it for me, not for my poor dearest mate. You people always seem to think the dead will be pleased because you're avenging them. They won't, you know. They can't be. They're dead."

Rhodry started to snap at her, realized that he had nothing to say, and contented himself with putting another branch on the fire. Although the dragon fell asleep soon after, he stayed staring at the flames until he ran out of wood, and his mind was leaping this way and that just like the fire, with strange thoughts forming and rising, only to fall again. When at last he slept, he dreamt of Jill, who spoke to him at length, but in some language he couldn't understand.

In the morning, Rhodry's guess about dweomer proved right. As soon as the sun rose, they followed the army's tracks as it curved steadily south and east, heading away from Lin Serr, until all at once, out in the middle of a meadow, the trail ended as abruptly as if the army had been snatched away by birds and carried off. Perhaps, for all Rhodry knew, they had. Straight as a carpenter's rule the muddy track ran, straight as a carpenter's rule lay the end of it, with naught but grass beyond.

"This is exactly the way their trail started," Arzosah remarked. "Back by Haen Marn."

"Just so. Ye gods, it makes my blood run cold, thinking how much dweomer they must have! Though it's Alshandra that's doing this, if you ask me."

"Who?"

"Evandar's wife. She's gone mad, and the Horsekin think her a goddess."

"Living with Evandar would drive any female daft."

Rhodry knelt down at the end of the trail and studied the grass. On one side, there was naught but trampled mud and horse droppings; on the other, tall grass, green and healthy, nodding in the noontime heat. In between, though, lay a thin stripe of grass turned brown—but not by hooves. It looked as if it had been touched by the first freeze of autumn, left all brown and parched, but still living. Baffled again, he shook his head and rose, wiping his hands reflexively on his brigga as if he'd touched something foul.

"Well, we can't follow them, can we? Let's head back to Lin Serr."

·   ·   ·

170

"It's a matter of obligations, and that's that," Envoy Garin said. "We signed a treaty with Cadmar of Cengarn for mutual aid in times of war. A time of war is what this is, and we owe him five hundred axmen and another hundred and fifty pikemen, all of them with supplies for forty days, and conveyance for the lot."

"I'd never deny it," Brel Avro said. "But what are we supposed to do? March our men into certain death? The city's besieged good and proper, or so the scouts tell us. How are we supposed to reach Cadmar, eh? Just answer me that."

In the shadow of an overhang of raw rock, the two dwarves were standing on the wide terrace outside the doors of the dwarvehold they both served, Lin Serr. Behind and around them on three sides, a huge horseshoe of gray stone rose, embracing a flat basin a good mile across. In front of them, on the other side of a broad terrace of pale stone, zigzag stairs led down the cliff face some hundred feet to this park land of grass and trees, crossed by a river. Hundreds of years past, dwarven workmen had dug the basin out of living rock and released the river from its underground caverns. The city itself, however, lay hidden in the cliffs and the heart of the mountains behind.

"You have a point," Garin said at last, and reluctantly. "But Cadmar has human allies. He's a well-liked man, and I'll wager they're mustering an army right now. Joining up with them's the least we can do."

Brel ran slow fingers through his beard, streaked here and there with a gray to match the stone.

"I don't trust these men, Envoy. Never have, never will."

"You don't have to trust them. Our contingent can keep to itself, and I'll be there to do any negotiating at councils of war and so on."

"Hum. Well, maybe so. I—ye gods! What's that?"

Garin looked up and gaped. A dragon was flying over the hills. With a peculiar motion—a beat of black wings, a leap, a glide—it flew high and steadily, closer and closer, until the dwarves could hear the thwack! of naked wings on still air like the beat of a slack drum. Just behind its neck, wedged among scales, perched a human rider.

"It's Rori!" Garin whispered. "By the beard of the Thunderer himself, I never thought he'd do it, but it's Rori."

With the warleader right behind, Garin took off trotting down the stairs, zigzagging back and forth as the dragon circled, then landed out in the park land on a graceful glide. The two dwarves reached the ground just as Rhodry, his bow slung over his back, slid down from the enormous beast's neck. Although Garin started over to greet him, the dragon swung its head round and stared right at him. Garin stopped so fast that Brel ran into him.

"It's so huge," Garin said. "Ye gods, it's as big as a Deverrian house."

"They're not known for their daintiness, dragons," Brel snapped. "Now get a move on, man!"

With the warleader laughing at him, Garin drew himself up and strode forward, quite boldly once the dragon waddled over to the river and turned its back to drink. He reached out to shake Rhodry's hand, but the moment he got a look at his friend's face, his celebratory mood vanished.

"What's so wrong?" Garin spoke in Deverrian.

"Don't you know?" Rhodry answered in the same. "Your farmlands! They've been pillaged, and your people are all dead. It was Horsekin."

Garin's breath deserted him in a cold stab. Brel swore with three foul words.

"And you want me to take men away?" Brel hissed in Dwarvish. "For some worm-riddled human lord?"

With a long sigh Garin recovered himself.

"A treaty's a treaty, and you know it as well as I do. As for the other, well, Lin Serr can muster more men than five hundred. *And* we've got a few treaties of our own to call in." He turned to Rhodry and spoke again in the language of men. "I'd hoped to see you again in better times than this, Silver Dagger, but I thank you for the report. Here, I forget myself. This is Brel, our *avro,* or warleader. It's an office rather like your cadvridoc."

When Rhodry bowed to him, the startled avro bowed back.

"But as for the farms," Garin went on. "No one's come in for some days now, you see, but that's normal enough."

"But I sent out messengers," Brel snapped. "Three days back. They haven't come home, either. I'd best sound a general alarum and straightaway."

"Rori, where are the Horsekin now?"

"Gone." Rhodry turned his hands palm upward. "I've got a tale to tell you, envoy, that's blasted hard listening. Here, tell me somewhat first. Did Mic and Otho get back here safely?"

Again the cold stab, a kind of ice-fire, running up his spine—all Garin could do was shake his head in a no. Rhodry stared at him for a moment, then dropped his face to his hands and wept, while the dragon came padding back to his side, as if in concern.

Up in Evandar's country, which lay beyond the physical world in the reaches of the etheric plane, a silver river flowed through a meadow, dotted with daisies and buttercups. Near the riverbank stood a pavilion of cloth-of-gold, glittering under a summer sun. To be more precise, images of these things existed, though they were far more substantial than simple pictures or thoughts. Evandar had built these forms with energy drawn straight from the currents of the upper astral, which shapes the etheric the way that the etheric shapes the physical. Over the thousands of years of his existence, he'd continually channeled energy into them until they had an existence of their own—not as solid and as stable as matter, certainly, but a presence and a duration, there in their proper plane.

The bodies his people wore were woven of the same thread. Unthinkably long ago, in the morning light of the universe when Evandar and his people were struck, sparks from immortal fire as all souls are, they'd been meant to take up the burden of incarnation, to ride with all other souls the turning wheels of Life and Death, but somehow, in some way that not even they could remember, they had, as they put it, "stayed behind" and never been born into physical bodies. Evandar had instead built them this place, the Lands, as they called them, and fashioned them bodies of a sort, modeling everything after the elven race and the elven culture he loved so much. They were a beautiful people, with hair pale as moonlight or bright as the sun to set off their eyes, violet, gray, or gold, and the long delicate curled ears of that earthly race. For the most part, their skin was as pale as milk, just touched with roses in the cheek, but some had seen the human beings of the far southern isles, and those wore a rich, dark skin like fresh-plowed earth under a rain.

It was hard to say how many of them there were. They lived lives at times separate, at others merging into one another, rising into brief individuality only to fall back to a shared mind. Only a few had achieved, as he had, a true consciousness. One of those was a blue-eyed fellow, more human in shape than elven. Although he looked like a full-grown man, and a warrior at that, tall and built broad, he was in a sense newly born. Only a little while before had he achieved enough of an identity to take a name, and now he stood beside Evandar and announced it.

"I would be known as Menw, because in the other world where we do walk at times, there was a great warrior of that name who befriended me."

"Done, then," Evandar said. "Menw you shall be. In honor of the setting of your name, you shall ride beside me as we seek out the howling harridan, that scraggly shrew who nags two worlds, my wife, Alshandra."

All round him his men leapt up, laughing and jeering. Suddenly a host sprang into existence, called by that laughter, of swordsmen and archers, dressed in silver mail and carrying weapons, or the images of weapons, made of silver as well. When Evandar raised his hand, a silver horn appeared, dangling from his fingers by a leather strap. He raised it and blew, summoning horses.

"The hunt is up!" he called out. "Havoc! I cry havoc!"

The cheer roared in answer like the beating of a winter sea. The Bright Host mounted and rode out in the musical chime of silver armor, silver gear, bridles ringing, and swords flashing in a light turned suddenly pale, a greenish light that thickened to mist at the far edge of the view. At a fast trot, they plunged into a forest.

Even though the ancient trees stood gnarled and grasping, and the bracken grew thick among thorn and vine, the horses never stumbled nor slowed, and not a single twig tangled itself in horse gear or the riders' clothes. On and on they rode in the eerie corrupted light, past huge stones set among the trees, and ruins that hinted of dead fortresses and dead kings.

As they traveled, other warriors joined them, slipping out of hollows and thickets or riding up boldly on hidden roads. These wore black armor, but of some enameled stuff, never iron. A mix of beast and man they were, some furred and snouted like Westlands bears, others sporting glittery little eyes and warty flesh like a Bardek crocodile. Some seemed almost human until they raised a paw, not a hand, in salute; others were like great wolves, running along the ground behind the horses. A fair number seemed stitched together from three or four creatures—the head of a boar with human hands and a dog's tail, perhaps, or dwarven torsos on animal legs, human heads, cat heads, dog faces, braided manes like the Horsekin, dwarven hands, elven hands, ears like mules, hair striped like a tiger, but whatever their appearance, all were armed and ready for war.

At the last, carrying a herald's staff wound round with ribands, rode an old man, a hunchback, his face all swollen and pouched, his skin hanging in great folds of warty flesh round his neck. He urged his palfrey up to keep pace with Evandar's golden stallion.

"My lord!" His voice rasped like sand under a boot. "The men of the Dark Host have remembered their vow. We come to serve you."

"Well and good," Evandar answered. "And I shall make you a promise. In return and once the war is over, you shall have new bodies to wear, all harmonious and of a piece."

They cheered him in a screech of voices and cries.

"My lord?" the herald continued. "Your brother will meet you at the beacon that marks what used to be the boundary between your lands and his."

"Used to be?"

"Well, my lord, now they all belong to you."

Evandar smiled, pleased that they remembered this as well.

The beacon stood in a clearing, a tall and ancient tree half of which grew like spring in green leaf, while half burned, clothed in fire along every branch and twig—yet never was it consumed. Underneath the green boughs sat a warrior on a black horse. Though he was wearing black enameled armor, his helm hung from a strap at his saddle-peak, and his gauntlets lay in his lap, so you could see that he was more than a little vulpine, with pointed ears tufted with red fur and a roach of red hair running from his forehead over his skull and down to the back of his neck, while his beady black eyes glittered above a long, sharp nose. His hands, too, were furred on their backs and tipped with black nails. When Evandar blew his horn for the halt, the vast army milled round, then came to rest. Oddly enough, there was room for all of them in the clearing.

"Shaetano!" Evandar called out. "My own dear blood kin! Well met, well met!"

With a growl, the fox warrior rode over and paused his horse beside Evandar's.

"Any news of Alshandra and her bronze pack of rebels?" Evandar went on. "Here in the Lands, I mean. I've plenty of news of her doings down in the world of men."

"I've seen her, sure enough, riding along at the head of her piss-poor excuse for an army." Shaetano paused, glancing round at the men who used to ride in his. "You've mustered the lot of us, I see."

"Every one I could rouse. This is war, brother, and that should gladden your heart."

"So it does." Shaetano pulled black lips back from pointed teeth in a grin. "And so what shall we do? Ride to the battle plain?"

"Do you truly think they'll be drawn up ever so nicely to wait for us? Tonight, we ride the border."

Under the light of a sudden moon, hanging pink and swollen near the horizon, the army cheered, waving swords and clubs alike. The wolf runners bared fangs and howled.

"Very well," Shaetano said. "And where shall I ride in the army?"

"Here, next to me. You shall ride at my left hand, as Menw rides at my right, and at the feasting we shall sit together, too."

"What? Am I to be honored, brother dear?"

"Not in the least. I merely don't trust you at my back."

On the morrow, just as the sun was rising over Lin Serr, a hundred dwarven warriors, led by Brel Avro himself, marched out to bury the dead up at the pillaged farms. Although Rhodry offered to go with them, he could do nothing, truly, but intrude upon private grief. In the end, he decided to stay at the dwarvehold. By this time, Arzosah was famished, and he sent her out to hunt, with a strict command to bring her kill back to Lin Serr's park land to eat it there. She flew off with a roar, leaving him to a private talk with Garin.

"I've tried to get the Council to allow you into the high city," Garin said, sighing. "No such luck, I'm afraid. All they'll give you is the run of the public hall here and the envoy's quarters you had before."

"I'll go on sleeping outside. Allow me to spare your people my tainted elven blood."

Garin winced and considered. They were standing just inside the huge double doors, carved with the history of Lin Serr, that led to the entrance hall, a cavern carved from living rock and lit by a bluish-silver glow. In the spill of sunlight through the doorway, Rhodry could just see, inlaid into the cavern floor, a circular maze that was big enough for a man to walk.

"I'd sleep better knowing you had a roof over your head," the envoy said at length. "You're too vulnerable out there. You've got enemies, you know."

"Ah, Alshandra's far away. Besides, I've got the talisman."

"That'll only protect you from scrying, not from someone using their own two eyes, like. What if this raven creature pops out of nowhere, takes a good look at you, and pops back to fetch Alshandra to do you harm? Come now. You told me how the raven met you on the road here. Well, what if she followed you down?"

Rhodry started to answer, then paused, caught by the truth of it.

"There's the old watchtower," Garin went on. "Our wyrm

177

could nest on top of that, and you could camp in the old gatehouse, surrounded by heaps of iron."

They both turned and looked out at the entrance to Lin Serr. The cliffs rose round in a horseshoe whose ends didn't quite meet; at the gap to the south, a gentle slope of land rose from the park land and out to what was normal ground level, that is, level with the tops of the cliffs forming the artificial basin. Just inside, before this tongue of land began its rise, stood a stone tower, seemingly a natural spire, freestanding with one end of the horseshoe to one side and the gap between the ends to the other. It was in fact worked stone, carved like a statue from one living rock. When Lin Serr was a-building, the tower had overshadowed a gateway, but over centuries of peace, the dwarves had widened the entranceway, leaving the tower standing alone.

Still attached to the cliff at the end of the horseshoe stood the gatehouse in question. This second tower sported two smaller round structures, in shape much like brochs, down at its base—the old guard rooms, crammed with stored weapons, single-bitted axes, spearheads on old and splitting wooden shafts, knives of various shapes, all too old to use but too good to throw away. If Rhodry took up residence in the empty chamber above so much iron, Alshandra would never be able to reach him.

"You get a good look round from up there," Rhodry said. "I wouldn't mind moving in."

"Good. Still, I feel we owe you somewhat, for the bringing of the news, if naught else."

"I'd never demand a price."

"I know it, you know it, but does the Council need to know it?"

They shared a grin.

"Well, then," Rhodry said, "could you get me a proper harness for my new mount? She keeps complaining about the ropes I've rigged up. They're not fine enough for a lady like her."

They both laughed.

"No doubt we could," Garin said. "Our craftsmen have never made a dragon harness before, but I suspect they could rig one up. Can't be much different than for horses, not in principle, anyway.

You go down to the grass and wait for our demanding wyrm, and I'll just go see what the guildsmen have to say about this."

Arzosah returned with two dead deer, not her usual one, and by the time she'd finished gorging herself on raw venison, she was so drowsy that she made no objection to being fitted. The master armorer, the master tanner, and their two apprentices clambered round with ropes, making knots at crucial points to mark her measure and talking all the while in Dwarvish. Occasionally, Garin would translate a question—did Arzosah want brown leather or black? would she like bronze buckles or steel?

"I must say," the dragon remarked at last, "that this pleases me mightily. If I must wear a harness like some smelly mule, at least I'll have a decent one."

"I only wish I were a rich lord, to give my lady jewels and gold," Rhodry said, grinning. "But I doubt if you'll ever find better workmanship than we'll get here at Lin Serr, even if the harness is a plain one."

"You know, Rori," Garin put in, "I think we could muster a decoration or two, at that. Before he left for Haen Marn, Otho made his will, and as I remember, he left some gems to you."

"What? I thought he hated me."

"I asked him about that. He did, he said, but on the other hand, he'd hated you for so long it was like you were blood kin." Garin's voice wavered. "Just like the old man, eh?"

Rhodry was caught twixt tears and laughter for a moment; then any urge toward mirth vanished.

"I just had an evil thought. What of Otho's mother?"

"Ah. She died a few days after you left here for Haen Marn. She'll never have to know how her son met his death."

"Good."

For a little while, they stood looking out over the grassy park land and the river, bright in the sun. Rhodry sighed and waved a hand at the bustling craftsmen.

"How long do you think making the thing will take?"

"A couple of days, they say."

"Huh. Well, if Arzosah will condescend to wear the ropes one more time, tomorrow we might fly down and take a look at this siege. I wonder if Cadmar's allies are assembling somewhere near the city?"

"It'd be a good thing to know, sure enough, but I wouldn't go down there alone."

"Why not? If we fly high above the encampment, they won't be able to touch us."

"Truly?" Garin raised a bushy eyebrow. "Now, if this was some ordinary fight, like, I'd agree. But there's dweomer involved, shape-changers, and that Alshandra creature. I've seen what she can do. How do we know they can't work some magic to bring our wyrm here down? And then there you'd both be, flopping along on the ground with not a friend who could reach you."

Rhodry was about to argue, but Arzosah got in first.

"He's right, Dragonmaster. Oh, please, I know I have to obey you, but please, don't make us go alone. Look at how those wretched Horsekin killed my mate. They're not to be trifled with, dweomer or no."

"Well, that's true spoken."

"We'll be marching soon enough," Garin went on. "Cengarn's walls will hold for a while longer, lad."

Rhodry hesitated, wondering if he wanted to explain. As long as he had some task on hand, whether traveling or fighting, he could forget about Angmar and Haen Marn, the woman he'd come to love, the place whose magic was bound up with that love.

"What's so wrong?" Garin said. "You look heartsick."

"Ah, well, it just gripes my soul, sitting up here in the mountains, not even knowing if Cengarn stands or how it fares."

"It still stands. I can tell you that. Some of our women have a little dweomer of their own, you know."

"I do know." Reflexively, Rhodry laid his hand over the talisman he wore under his shirt. "Didn't Otho's mother give me this stone?"

"Well, there you are then."

"But here, Cadmar's allies? His main alliance is with Gwerbret Drwmyc of Dun Trebyc, and I've never met a more justice-minded man. He'll do everything he can to fulfill their treaties. Some lords might weasel, but not Drwmyc."

"That gladdens my heart." Garin paused for a grin. "Now, five hundred dwarven axmen are worth a thousand human beings, but from what I gather, there's a cursed lot of these flea-bitten Horsekin round the town."

Rhodry laughed at the jest, but he was thinking hard, trying to estimate just how many men Drwmyc might be able to scrape up, down in the rough borderlands of the kingdom. Not enough—that was the one thing he could be sure of.

That very night, Garin's prudence proved its worth. Rhodry's chamber in the old gatehouse was small, round, and dusty-bare except for his own gear, but it had a grand view out across Lin Serr's park land. He was sitting on one of the enormously thick window ledges, watching the moon rising over the distant cliffs, when he saw movement out in the grass. Although an ordinary man would have seen nothing, Rhodry had inherited his vision from his father's people. When he looked carefully, he could make out a pack of strange creatures trotting across the grass and heading straight for the gatehouse. Bronze gleamed in moonlight. Smiling a little, he drew his sword and waited.

Down at the base of the tower they assembled, a shuffling pack of misshapen warriors dressed in bronze armor and waving bronze knives. In the moonlight, he couldn't see them clearly, but he knew from previous experience that they were a jumble of human and animal bodies. They looked up, pointing with hand or paw. At the sight of Rhodry in the window, they began to curse and shout in a babble of languages, swirling round in an eddy of malice.

"Come up, then," he called out. "Come up if you're so brave."

They screamed and gnashed, howled and cursed, while they danced back and forth before the door. Suddenly, with a roar, Arzosah dropped from the high tower and flew. With one last shriek, the pack disappeared back into whatever world it was that they came from. The dragon swooped out into the park land, then turned and flapped back, settling up on the high tower's roof again. Rhodry leaned out his window and yelled.

"My thanks!"

"Most welcome, but I wasn't worried about you." Her vast rumble drifted down to him. "They were keeping me awake."

Rhodry had been right to worry about the situation in Cengarn. The next morning, at about the time that he was telling Garin how Alshandra's creatures had threatened him in the night, Jill was sitting in the window of her chamber, high up in one of Dun Cengarn's towers. Except for a small shelf housing some twenty books, a fabulous number in those days, it was an ordinary sort of chamber, a half-round of a room with stone walls on the curved side and woven wicker on the straight, and furnished with a narrow bed, a chest, a charcoal brazier, a table, and one chair—perfectly ordinary, except of course it was filled with Wildfolk. Sprites and sylphs flickered through the air, some visible, others a bare crystalline glimmer; gnomes curled up in the patch of sun from the open window like cats or sat on Jill's bed, amusing themselves by picking at the frayed edges of the blankets.

A couple of gray gnomes sat in the lap of the guest occupying the chair, and she was far from ordinary as well. Not only was Dallandra a member of the race that men call Westfolk, or elves, but she was the only dweomermaster in Deverry whose power matched Jill's. With her ash-blond hair and steel gray eyes, she was a beautiful woman, too, if one could overlook her eyes, slit vertically with dark irises like a cat's, and her ears, long and furled. For the sake of privacy, they spoke in Elvish, which no one else in the dun could understand.

"What are we going to do about Meer?" Dallandra was saying. "I cannot convince him that I'm not a goddess. He keeps throwing himself onto the ground every time I come near him, and one of these days he's going to hurt himself. I mean, he *is* blind."

"Tell him that he's so favored by the gods he need only kneel in your presence."

"Jill, this is no time for jests!"

"I'm not jesting. I truly don't think you have any chance of convincing him that you're mortal. You might as well put your divine status to good use."

Dallandra scowled, then laughed. "Perhaps so. Besides, I know what convinced him, and I have to admit, it was fairly spectacular. It was when Rhodry first captured our bard, and he and young Jahdo were penned up in that awful dungeon here. I felt so bad for them, and Evandar wouldn't do a thing for them, of course. So I appeared in their cell and told them that things would be better soon."

It was Jill's turn for the laugh. "Just like a goddess in an old hymn, comforting prisoners. Dalla, you've brought it on yourself."

"Maybe so. But I've managed to change Jahdo's mind, you know. Once he got a chance to talk with me, he could tell that I'm not some divinity."

"Jahdo's got a lot of common sense for a child, but our Meer sees gods everywhere. His people do, after all. That's what Alshandra took advantage of."

"And so did Evandar. He deliberately set himself up as a god, too, you know. He's the one who manifested back in Meer's home city and sent the bard on his quest in the first place."

"Here!" Jill snapped. "I never knew that."

"He told me about it at the time, but I had no idea what he was up to. He loves to speak in riddles. But I've pieced the meaning out now. Evandar appeared right in a temple, as bold as brass, and told the priestess to send Meer off on some errand. He's the one who guided Meer and Jahdo into Deverry and had them take the route that would lead them to Rhodry and his men. Evandar's up to something, Jill. I don't know what it is, but he's got some sort of horribly elaborate strategy in mind to reach some mysterious goal. And he doesn't care what he does to whom, just so long as he gets what he wants."

"And you love this man?"

Dallandra rose, pacing back and forth in the wedge-chamber. The displaced gnomes sat down on the floor and pouted.

"I do," she said at last. "I know it's daft, but I do. At heart he's good and warm, but he has no idea of consequences. How could he, Jill? He's never lived incarnate. He knows nothing of suffering, or frustration, or illness—none of those things have a feather's weight of meaning for him."

"Any more than they do for Alshandra."

"Exactly."

Jill shuddered and turned on the narrow ledge to better catch the afternoon sun. From her perch, she could see out over the dun to the distant east wall of the city. Beyond that she could just catch a glimpse of white tents and red banners on a little rise, a group that seemed to be the encampment of the Horsekin leaders. She idly wondered if they worshipped their false goddess somewhere among them, or if Alshandra could approach so much iron.

"Dalla, a question for you! How can Evandar come and go so easily? He just walks right into cities, and Rhodry says that Evandar's ridden next to him when he—Rhodry, I mean—he's been fully armed. But Alshandra can't abide the touch of iron, and none of her folk can, either."

"No more can Evandar's men. They all have silver weapons and suchlike. I haven't the slightest idea, Jill, not the slightest. He keeps his secrets, even from me, until he feels like telling them."

At a knock on the door, Jill swung her feet back to the solid floor of the chamber.

"Who's there?" she called out in Deverrian.

"Yraen, my lady," a dark voice answered. "The gwerbret's wife sent me to see if you could come attend upon the princess."

Jill muttered something foul under her breath, then raised her voice again.

"Come in, will you?"

With a deferential nod of his blond head, Yraen stepped in, shutting the door behind him. Well over six feet tall, and in a warrior's prime of life, Yraen was, in his way, a good-looking man, though the way was cold and grim enough to scare off most women. His ice-blue eyes glittered with some suppressed rage, and thick blond mustaches hid most of his full mouth. At his belt, the hilt of a silver dagger glittered as coldly as his eyes.

"What's all this?" Jill said.

"Carra's worrying about the prince her husband again, my lady. We were all down in the great hall when she started weeping over him. So the gwerbret's wife took her back to the women's hall and sent me to fetch you. We were wondering if you had, uh well er you know, news."

Scrying, of course, was what he meant but refused to name.

"I haven't had a chance to glean any news today," Jill said, "about much of anything. Ye gods! Weeping right out in the great hall? She's got to learn to control herself better than this. We've got the men's morale to think of."

"Jill, please!" Dallandra spoke in Elvish. "You're as cold as Evandar at times, really you are." She switched to Deverrian. "Yraen, Jill's tired. She has more important things on her mind than young Carra's temperaments, too. I'll go the women's hall and deal with it."

"My thanks, my lady." He made her a bow.

When Dallandra left, Yraen lingered in Jill's chamber. Although he was the Princess Carramaena's personal bodyguard, he— or any other man, for that matter—was forbidden to follow her into the women's hall unless the princess's husband was in attendance there. Unfortunately, the prince, and his warband with him, had been cut off outside the dun when the siege began, leaving them no choice but to return to the Westlands and their people, where they could gather warriors for the relieving army. Jill had scried them last a few days ago, making an unthreatened way south.

"I don't mean to offend you, my lady," Yraen said, "but I don't suppose you've any news of Rhodry, either."

"None. No more have I seen any of Cadmar's allies riding to relieve us. Ye gods, man! I'll tell you as soon as I do."

"I know. I'm sorry. It's just the cursed siege. You're right enough about morale. The waiting's a hard thing for us to bear, us fighting men, I mean."

"I know." Jill softened her voice. "I'm not what you'd call fond of it, either. But we can't sally, not with the numbers against us, and so here we all blasted well are."

"True, true."

185

He nodded, glancing vaguely about him, seemed to be about to speak, choked it back, looked round again.

"Yraen, what's so wrong?"

"Naught, naught." He forced out a smile. "Beyond our situation, anyway."

"You look like you want to ask me somewhat."

"My apologies, and here the other sorcerer did say you were tired. My apologies."

Bowing all the way, he backed out of the room, then shut the door so hard the wickerwork trembled. The gnomes began to mock him, lining up, bowing backward, until one bumped another, and a small brawl of pinching and squealing began.

"Stop it!" Jill banished the lot with a wave of her hand. "Ye gods, now what in all the hells could be wrong with Yraen?"

Jill found her answer later in the day, when she went down to the great hall to fetch herself a scant ration of bread. Dun Cengarn's great hall occupied the entire ground floor of the main broch of the complex. On one side, by a back door, stood enough tables for a warband of well over a hundred men; at the hearth, near the table of honor itself, were five more for guests and servitors. The walls and the enormous hearths were made of a pale tan stone, streaked and stained with smoke from torch and fires. All round the windows hung panels of interlacement; between them, roundels of spirals and fantastic animals. The honor hearth was the greatest marvel, though, embraced by an entire stone dragon, its head resting on its paws, planted on the floor, its winged back forming the mantel, and its long tail curling down the other side.

At the moment, the honor side of the hall stood empty, except for a serving lass wiping down the tables with a rag, but over at the other, riders clustered round the open barrels of ale while the chamberlain's men rationed out scant servings. Jill could wrap her aura about herself like a cloak, and by moving quietly and sticking to the shadowy half of the room, she passed through, virtually invisible. Yraen certainly never noticed her; he was standing near the back door and keeping a watch on the spiral staircase that led to the upper floors of the main broch.

As Jill was fetching her loaf back again, she saw Yraen suddenly smile and take a few automatic steps toward the stairs. The Princess Carramaena was coming down, wearing a dark blue dress kirtled with a simple sash of cloth of gold, since the Westfolk never marked their clans with plaids as Deverry men did. She wore the kirtle high, too, to allow for her swelling pregnancy. She was a lovely lass, Carra, not quite seventeen that summer, all blond hair and rosy cheeks, with big blue eyes and a ready smile that even Jill could admit to be charming. She looked round, smiling impartially at the great hall below, and waited for her dog, a big wolflike gray creature, to catch up with her. Unseen by the door, Yraen watched her every gesture, his lips half-parted in something close to grief.

Oh, horseshit and a pile of it! Jill thought. The little bastard's in love with her.

Bread in hand, Jill left by another door and hurried across the ward to the stairs that led up to her tower room. Although she considered asking the gwerbret to find Carra a new bodyguard, she couldn't do so without telling him the reason, and she refused to shame Yraen. Besides, there was no doubting the cold truth that a bodyguard who loved his charge so hopelessly would throw his own life away to save hers, if things ever came to such an evil pass.

Still, the situation was bound to turn dangerous, with the two of them shut up in the dun and Carra's husband far away. Even supposing that the siege was lifted, and supposing again that both men lived through that battle, Yraen would be face to face with his beloved's husband. Prince Daralanteriel was no man to trifle with. No doubt he would see nothing wrong with protecting his wife's honor by murdering the mercenary soldier who'd dared to love her. There was nothing Jill could do with him. Yraen listened to advice about naught, generally, and now he was bound to be doubly stubborn, not so much for what he was now but for what he'd been, back in another life—Carra's husband. It had been hundreds of years ago, but seeing her again had brought all the buried memories alive in his soul at least.

What Carra thought of him, Jill didn't know, though she reminded herself that she'd best find out. She, at least, was malleable.

Yraen brought her naught but grief then, she thought, and if things go on this way, he'll bring her naught but grief now. Carra loved her husband with all her heart, but at the moment, who knew if she would ever see her elven prince again?

Carra had barely seated herself at the table set aside for the dun's womenfolk when Yraen appeared to take up his usual place on the floor, slightly behind and to the right of her. Lightning wagged his tail with a thump on the braided rushes, as if greeting a peer.

"Yraen, I do wish you'd take a chair," Carra said. "It aches my heart to see you sitting on the floor."

"This is fine for the likes of me." He twitched his lips in the expression that did him for a smile. "Besides, anyone trying to reach you would have to trip over me."

"Oh, nonsense! Nobody's going to attack me right here."

"We've already ferreted out one traitor in the dun, haven't we? Who's to say there aren't any more?"

"Well, truly, I suppose you're right."

In a few moments, the gwerbret's wife, Lady Labanna, a stout woman, her gray hair neatly pulled back into an embroidered kerchief, hurried over with her servingwomen trailing after.

"Carra, dear, I do wish you'd waited for the rest of us. It's not seemly for you to come down to the great hall alone."

"But I wasn't truly alone, my lady. I have Lightning, and Yraen's always here."

Labanna favored dog and silver dagger alike with a sour smile, then sat down in her place at the head of the table. At her signal, a serving lass brought bread and watered wine.

Slowly, the hall filled up for the evening meal, riders and servants at their hearth, gwerbret and his noble-born servitors at his. Cadmar himself came in late, stopping by his wife's table for a word before moving on to head up his own. Even though he limped on a twisted right leg, the gwerbret was an imposing man, standing well over six feet tall, broad in the shoulders, broad in the hands. That evening he repeatedly ran one hand through his slate-gray hair as he whispered to his lady. Carra could hear bits of their conversation over the general noise and clatter—a predictable worrying about when the relieving army might ride their way. Even when it did arrive, there was no guarantee, of course, that the battle would go their way.

"Just have to wait and see," Cadmar finished, turning away. "Naught else we can do."

Labanna watched him go with haunted eyes.

"I'm so sorry," Carra burst out. "I'm not worth all this trouble."

Yraen rose to a kneel and growled.

"Hush, child!" Labanna snapped. "No one blames you."

"I blame myself. If it weren't for me, you wouldn't be besieged."

"Hush, hush, that's not true." Labanna leaned forward with a wry smile and caught her hand to squeeze it. "If it weren't for the treaties between my lord and your husband, we wouldn't be besieged. That's a very different thing."

"I suppose. I just—"

"It's honorable of you, child, to worry for our sakes. But you must remember that these days, it's your position that counts, not you. You're not that obscure lass with no dowry anymore. I realize it's difficult for you to get used to."

"It is, truly." Carra felt her mouth trembling and forced it to stop. "If it weren't for the baby, I think I'd just turn myself over to them, and you'd all be safe."

"Hush!" Labanna laid a warning hand on her arm. "You must never allow yourself to think such things." She glanced at Yraen. "Make sure you keep a close watch upon your lady from now on."

"I will, Your Grace. You need have no fear of that."

Satisfied, Labanna sat back in her chair and turned the talk to other things while the meal was served. Although normally Cengarn's dun set a generous table, with the siege, the chamberlain measured out each scrap of food. When the thin slices of meat arrived, they were spiced so heavily with pepper and Bardek cinnamon to cover the scent of spoilage that Carra couldn't eat hers. Without thinking, she tossed it to Lightning, then realized that Yraen, silver dagger as he was, had been given none. What should she do, apologize and call attention to her selfishness, or let it pass and let him think she hadn't even noticed? She could not make up her mind, felt tears of sheer frustration gathering. I *cannot* be a princess, she thought, I just don't know how. All at once, she realized that the other women were looking at her in concern. She nearly wept.

"I feel unwell." Carra rose, gesturing to Lightning. "I simply have to get out of all this noise."

Yraen leapt up and caught her elbow just as the room spun round her in a blaze of candlelight. Although she did faint into his arms, she woke again almost immediately to find the room still spinning. She could hear the yelping of concerned voices round her, but at first the words roared without meaning. Yraen hoisted her up like a sack of meal and settled her head against his shoulder. The luxury of his strength, his concern, his simple human touch went to her head like another faint. She clasped her arms round his neck to steady herself.

"Take her up to her chamber, Yraen." Labanna's voice seemed to be coming from a long way away. "I'll follow you up. Page! Where's a wretched page? We need to fetch Jill."

With Lightning bounding ahead of them, Yraen carried her upstairs, first past the landing of the women's hall and then up another spiral to the chamber she once had shared with her husband. Fortunately, she'd left the door unbarred, so he could kick it open and maneuver her inside. He laid her down on the bed, then went to the window to fling open the shutters for some air and light. A little breeze was blowing, blessedly cool. Carra struggled with her kirtle, which was pinned with a small brooch. When she tried to unclasp it, she stuck her finger.

"Here, here," Yraen sat down next to her. "Let me."

His broad fingers, all calloused and battle-hardened, were clumsier than her own, but at last he got the brooch free and the kirtle untied. Carra sucked the bleeding tip of her finger and watched him try to fold the cloth.

"Just throw it onto that chair," she said at last. "It doesn't matter."

"Very well."

For a moment, he sat beside her, the cloth of gold in his hands, and looked out the window at the sky. Through the open door, she could hear voices, panting up the stairs. She wanted to apologize to Yraen, but if she did, their talk would inevitably dredge up the painful truth that he loved her. The moment ended; he rose and strode across the room just as Jill appeared in the door with Labanna right behind her. The dweomermaster carried a cloth sack that smelled of herbs.

"I'm sorry," Carra burst out. "I know I've been weak again."

"Do hush," Labanna said. "It's all right."

Jill said nothing, merely laid her hand on Carra's forehead.

"Well, you're clammy and cold, sure enough. Labanna says the meat set you off."

"It was all the pepper. I'm sorry."

"Stop apologizing." Jill considered for a moment. "But you're fairly well along now. These queasy spells should be passing off."

"It was the noise, too, and everything so crowded. Really, I'll be fine in a bit." Carra bit back another apology just in time. "I just felt so odd."

"Odd?" Jill went stock-still. "How? Queasy, you mean?"

"That, too, but just odd. I couldn't think right."

"Carra, this might be very important. Try to remember. You say you couldn't think right. Do you remember why?"

"Well." All her shame at having put her dog before a man who loved her flooded back. "Sort of. I was trying to decide a thing, you see, and I couldn't, and I just felt so worthless, all of a sudden, like I couldn't do anything right."

"Did you ever feel that—well, this will sound very peculiar, I know—but did you feel that someone was interfering with your mind?"

"What? I didn't, truly." All at once, she realized what Jill must mean. "You mean, someone like another sorcerer?"

"Just that."

"I didn't, but, ye gods! Do you think it might happen?"

"It's not very likely. I was just making sure." Jill walked over to the window and looked out as if she were studying the view. "You'd best rest, Carra. Yraen, you guard the door. I'll have someone bring you food."

"Jill?" Labanna said. "Wouldn't she be better off in the women's hall?"

"Once you're all in it, she will be. But for now, I want her in a room that Yraen can enter if he has to." Jill stopped, thinking something through. "My lady, and you, too, Silver Dagger, if you could leave us for a moment? Just shut the door, too, would you?"

Once they'd all left, and the room was quiet again, Carra felt well enough to sit up, pulling the pillows behind her to rest against. Jill sat down on the chair.

"Carra, what do you think of Yraen?"

Carra bit her lip and turned her head away.

"You're not in love with the man, are you?"

"What? Of course not. Oh! You know how he feels."

"I do, and it worries me. I'll warn you somewhat—your husband is a proud man and a jealous one."

"I do know that." Carra forced herself to look at Jill again. "And truly, you don't need to worry. I don't love Yraen. Truly."

Jill raised a questioning eyebrow.

"Well, besides," Carra went on, "I feel so rotten all the time with the baby and suchlike. And here we are, right in the middle of everyone all day, and I sleep in the women's hall at night. I mean, even if I did love him, and even if I was the sort of woman who'd betray her husband, where would we go?"

Jill laughed.

"You have a very fine core of common sense," the dweomer-master said. "I need to remember that, and so do you. Now, you rest here till the other women come back upstairs, then go to the women's hall. In the meantime, I'll have Yraen come in. If he says he feels danger in the air or suchlike, listen to him. The reason that I want him to be your guard is that he's had some experience with the peculiar kinds of magicks we're facing here."

"I will."

"Good. But somewhat's still wrong. I can tell by the look on your face. Out with it."

"I just feel so cruel, knowing Yraen loves me. He knows I'll never love him. And he has to sit on the floor when we eat, and walk behind me everywhere, and sleep on the floor, too, in front of the door to the women's hall. It's dreadful."

"Cruel? Well, you know, I hadn't thought of that, but I suppose it is painful for him. Huh. Very well. I'll think about this."

When Jill left Carra, she gave her sack of supplies to a page to return to her chamber, then went up to the roof. Although she'd just renewed the dweomer seals that noon, she wanted to check them on the off chance that they'd been breached to allow an enemy to attack Carra's mind. She stood in the middle of the roof, faced east, and raised her inner sight to etheric level.

Over and around her, the golden dome shimmered unbroken with all its seals of the Elemental Kings still safely in place. Jill turned in a slow circle, studying each seal and segment, but she found not the slightest sign of tampering. Yet danger pricked at her like a touch of ice, a deep stab of dweomer-warning. She sat down cross-legged, because she would have to be in a stable position if she should need to go into a trance, then considered the sky beyond the dome. To her etheric sight, it hung silvery and alive, swirling with energy and the darting forms of innumerable Wildfolk. The long beams of light from the setting sun shot through, seemingly as solid as silver rods.

In the midst of all this confusion, it was hard to see, yet Jill felt the warning intensify when she peered out to the east. She waited, on guard, until all at once, she saw a white mist forming high in the sky. She dropped her sight down, found no trace of the mist on the physical, and brought it back up to the etheric in time to see the opalescent mass billowing outward from some other plane, as if an invisible blacksmith were using a bellows to blow smoke through a crack in the wall of sky. Jill went tense and rose to a kneel. Light-shot and pearly, it sank toward the golden dome in a single cloud.

All at once, the cloud cracked open like a tapped egg in a cook's strong fingers. Out stepped the figure of an enormous woman as calmly as if she were stepping onto solid ground instead of midair. She was dressed like an elven huntress, in tight doeskin trousers and a belted tunic, with a quiver of arrows slung at her hip and a bow held loosely in her hands. Her honey-blond hair hung to her waist in swept-back Horsekin fashion, laced with little charms and thongs, but it had to be Alshandra. Like Evandar and indeed most of their race, she preferred to appear in elven form, mostly because those incorporeal beings had no true form of their own. Here on the etheric, she shimmered in an aureole of silver light.

Jill forced herself to breathe calmly, slowly, to gather power from the Light and to focus her mind as Alshandra drifted over the apex of the dome and looked down at the seal set there. Jill was expecting this powerful being to banish the thing with ease, and she knew she'd have but a bare moment to set it back before an attack, but Alshandra moved on with a toss of her honey-blond mane. She drifted round the dome widdershins, moving slowly and deliberately, pausing every now and again to study one of the lesser sigils or the seal of a quadrant.

Moving slowly herself, Jill got up and turned to follow her as the Guardian—or so the elves called Alshandra's and Evandar's race —made her survey of Cengarn's magical defenses. She was unsure if Alshandra even saw her until the Guardian stared in her direction and sneered with a curl of her lip before turning away and resuming her slow drift round.

Well and good, then, Jill thought. This gives me a moment to arm myself.

Slowly, casually, glancing round as if she were interested in naught more than the weather, Jill walked over to one of the bundles of arrows, all tipped with good steel points, and slowly crouched down to pick one up. The thong round the oiled hides had soaked up oil. Swearing under her breath, Jill drew her silver dagger and slashed the thong, but the flash of magical metal caught Alshandra's attention. With a howl of rage, the Guardian swung round and rushed over the top of the dome, sliding down to stand facing Jill

194

and just a bit above her. Jill thrust the bundle of arrows up, holding it like a two-handed torch, right through the dome—which, of course, remained unharmed.

With another shriek, this one of pain, Alshandra flung herself backward, but she stopped her inelegant tumble to hover some twenty feet away. The touch of iron, and its magnetism, only worked against her kind at close quarters. For a long moment, they faced off, Jill on her side of the dome, Alshandra on hers. Alshandra sneered, tossing her head again, then turned and drifted off through the sky. The mist began to form round her, a few wisps at first, then a streak here, a puff there, until the egg-shaped cloud hung huge in the sky. For a few beats of a heart, it drifted, then began to sink earthward and eastward, heading for the red-bannered tents upon the ridge. As it moved, it changed, growing solid and steady, gleaming with the silver touch of real water drops as it swelled and billowed into fog.

Jill dropped her sight to the physical plane. Sure enough, the mist now hung visible, and every man on town walls and out among the Horsekin camp to the east had seen it, too. In Cengarn, the alarum went up—men yelled, temple bells clanged, silver horns blared. Armed men poured out of the dun below Jill's perch and rushed for the walls. The Horsekin began to cheer, or at least, to make a sound that seemed to be their version of cheering. Halfway between a wail and bark, the sound could perhaps be best written as "Hai! Hai!" over and over. More and more took up the cry; some drew daggers and raised them in salute. Down in the besieging army, a vast swell of movement began, as the Kin began turning and surging toward the mist in a roar of their barking cheer.

Out of the mist and some forty feet above the ground, Alshandra appeared, hovering in the air, her arms flung high in benediction. The Kin within sight of her began to scream and stamp their feet; the Kin round the other side of the town began to moan, as if they knew what vision was being denied them, but their discipline held, and they kept to their posts. Alshandra called out three words in their language, then disappeared as suddenly as she'd come. The Kin began to moan and sway, holding their hands up high in imitation of her gesture.

Yet, nearly forgotten, the mist continued to billow and swell up on the east ridge. It drifted this way and that, touching the tents, then pulling back, until at last it came to rest on a long and level spit of land. Jill could only swear helplessly as out of that mist poured warriors, men of the Horsekin all, rank after rank of them upon their enormous horses, the riders glittering with mail and waving their long swords aloft as their allies below began to cheer again, surging back from the ridge to make room for the muster. All over Cengarn, silence fell. No horns, no yells of defiance rang out; only silence as deep as if the very walls held their breath.

On and on the line marched, five abreast, the horses setting down their tufted feet with fine precision as they negotiated the slope and strode down the side of the ridge. Jill lost count quick enough—some hundreds of riders, maybe even a thousand in all, riding into camp, while the sun sank a fair degree lower in the sky, and Cengarn neither spoke nor cursed. At last, the final rank reached the flat, but something that was perhaps worse came after— wagons rumbling through, laden with supplies, to pull up behind the tents on the ridge, and scrawny packhorses after that, bringing bundles of provisions down to the waiting warriors. At the very end came lowing, bleating herds of frightened animals—cows, sheep, a few goats—chased along by human-looking herdsmen. So. This detachment had been plundering farms. Jill felt sick, wondering where the steadings lay. She could guess that the farm folk were long past her help.

Twilight began to turn the east gray while the sun sank to touch the western horizon. At last, at long last, the final cow and herder came through. The mist blew away, breaking into long tendrils, touched pink by the dying light, and disappeared. From the remnants flew one last figure—an enormous raven, circling round the tents once with a flap of its wings, then settling to disappear among them.

"Jill?"

Jill yelped and spun round to find Dallandra standing some feet behind her.

"My apologies!" Dalla said. "I didn't mean to startle you."

"It's all right. Have you been here long?"

"I have. Too long. I saw the whole thing. Jill, answer me honestly, will you? What kind of omens have you received? Are we all doomed?"

"No omens at all. Things still must hang in some balance."

Dallandra walked to the edge of the roof and stood looking down. Far below, the town was beginning to come out of its enchantment. A vast susurrus of talk and cursing and tears rose round the hill, as a few at a time, the men began returning to the dun. Most walked head down and silent.

"If Alshandra can bring her men through on the mothers of all roads," Jill said at last, "can't Evandar help us the same way?"

"I'm sure he could, if he would. To tell you the truth, I've been trying to contact him, but I can't seem to reach his mind." Dallandra's voice shook badly. "I hope she hasn't—well, got the better of him."

"Could she? I thought he was much the stronger of the pair."

"Of the pair, truly. But she has allies."

"I see. But can't you open roads?"

"Of course, but not on that scale. I can open a gate, like, for a few brief moments, long enough for a few people to slip through. I could never bring in an army or lead the town folk out. And I don't dare leave you alone for long, anyway. It'll take more than one dweomermaster to defend Cengarn against—" Dallandra waved her hand in the direction of the tents—"that."

In the growing darkness, they picked their way downstairs, shutting the trap after them. Jill sent Dallandra off to the great hall to talk with the gwerbret and, with luck, reassure him and his men both. She herself went to consult with Meer, the Gel da'Thae bard, who knew lore as valuable as another warband. Although the Gel da'Thae came from the same racial stock as the Horsekin tribes, they were a civilized people, living in the towns they'd made for themselves near the ruins of the elven cities in the Westlands.

Jill had just come out on the landing near his chamber when she met Jahdo, the bard's servant and guide. He was a skinny little lad who couldn't have been more than ten summers old, and messy at that, with his torn and dirty clothes and shaggy dark hair.

"Oh, my lady!" Jahdo blurted. "You must have seen. The dweomer cloud! All those men and horses!"

"I certainly did. I'm coming to talk with your master about it."

"That gladdens my heart. He's truly troubled, and I'm dreadful a-scared."

Apparently, the boy had lit the candles in the wall sconces before leaving the chamber, because the wedge-shaped room danced with pale light. Meer was sitting on a carved chest near the window. When Meer was standing, he towered at seven feet tall, but now he sat slumped, his long arms lying heavy across his lap. His skin was as pale as milk in contrast to his black hair, as coarse and bristling-straight as a boar's. At the bridge of his enormous nose his eyebrows grew together in a sharp V and merged into his hairline. His hair itself plumed up, then swept back and down over his long skull to cascade to his waist. Here and there in this mane hung tiny braids, tied off with thongs and little charms and amulets. The backs of his enormous hands were furred with stubby black hair, too, and wisps showed at the neck of his loose Deverry shirt. His face, however, was hairless, merely tattooed all over in a complex blue and purple pattern of lines and circles. When the door slipped out of Jahdo's grasp and slammed, the bard didn't even bother to turn his head toward the sound.

"Meer?" Jahdo said. "It be Jill."

At that he did move, growling a little as she walked over and raising his head. His eye sockets were empty pools of shadow in the uncertain light.

"I take it," Jill said, "that Jahdo described the nasty little show we had earlier."

"He did," Meer rumbled. "I don't mind telling you, good sorcerer, that my heart lies heavy and cold within me. Ah, ye gods, how could ye have deserted us, how could ye have handed us over to these impious hordes! Why, oh why, won't you strike this false goddess dead, as justice and reason both demand?"

It was a good question. Jill only wished she had an answer.

"Well," she said aloud, "the gods have minds that none of us can fathom, mortals that we are."

"True, true. Mayhap they test us, to find the strength of our devotion." Meer shook his head with a jingle of charms and beads. "Alas for these wicked times, that a demoness should flaunt herself in the light of the holy sun!"

"Er, well, true spoken. I've come to ask you about somewhat, good bard. There were a good two thousand men holding the siege before today, and Alshandra's just added hundreds more to her army. How many more warriors can the Horsekin muster? Cadmar has allies, true, but we're up here on the edge of the kingdom, and human settlements are sparse."

"Ill news, sorcerer, ill news indeed! What about this High King of yours?"

"We sent messengers before the siege began, but who knows if they reached safety before Alshandra noticed them? If they've been captured, it's up to Cadmar's allies now, to send more, I mean. And the heart of the kingdom lies a long, long way away. The High King will come if need be, and he'll bring plenty of men with him, but it could take months."

Jahdo whimpered, then stuffed the back of one hand in his mouth to keep himself silent.

"I see." Meer considered for a long time. "Well, the Horsekin are spread all over the northern plains. They can muster a horde of warriors, truly, ten, twenty times the number sieging us now."

Jill felt so faint that she had to sit down. She perched on the edge of the bed and clasped her hands between her knees. Meer smiled as if, blind or not, he knew perfectly well the effect he was making. He raised one hand in the air.

"But fear not! The warriors can muster all they wish, but only a bare portion of them will ever attack us." He paused, then dropped his oracular tone. "It's the horses, Jill, not the men. No Horsekin warrior fights on foot unless he's desperate and dying. You've seen our horses. Bred for war they are, and bred that way for hundreds, nay, for an aeon of years! Can a horse such as that eat grass alone and still carry his armored master into battle?"

Jill laughed, just softly under her breath.

"Up on the high plains?" she said. "Is grain easy to grow?"

"Hah! Only on the southern borders. Besides, no Horsekin, nor Gel da'Thae either, would ever farm. Farming is for slaves. And slaves are what the Horsekin keep to raise what little grain they have. Another thousand horses, I'd say, and no more can these savages muster."

"Savages? That reminds me of somewhat I wanted to ask you. You keep calling them that, but they know siegecraft, they carry good weapons, and as far as I can tell, they've got the best organized army I've ever seen."

"What does that have to do with anything? Savages they are, who will not worship the true gods and who follow the false."

"Well, you see, among my people, the word savage means a poor sort of person, a brute, truly, someone who lives wild and roughly."

"Ah. I knew it not. Well, brutes they can be, cruel and loathsome, and given to whoring after strange gods, but poor they are not, exacting tribute everywhere they can, stealing from some, trading with others."

"And what about their armies?"

"They live for war and study war and have given their hearts to war. Every man watches his nephews from birth to see which are fit for war and which will be gelded for other crafts."

"Gelded?" Jahdo burst out. "You mean like horses and steers?"

"I do, lad, I mean just that. Savages I called them, and with some reason. And their women share out the best men, that their daughters may be fit to lead by the council fire and their sons to fight on the battlefield." Meer tossed back his head and keened, a wail that rattled the bronze sconces. "Alas, that the gods have handed over our lives to such as this, to spill them or to enslave them as they will!"

"The war's not over yet, good bard. So far, we've still got our lives, and we'll win yet."

"Ah, hold your tongue, mazrak! I know you lie only to spare my grief, but lie you do."

"About what?"

"I know not our sins, for lo! what man can ever know the telling of his people's sins, but the gods have deserted us, sure enough."

"As you wish, then." Jill got up. "I'd best get down to the great hall and tell the gwerbret about the horses."

Before she went to bed that night, Jill went up on the roof and renewed the seals again, just as the astral tides were changing from those of Elemental Water to those of Elemental Earth. When she was done, she lingered for a few moments, staring out at the Horsekin camp, dark and silent under the stars. They would have set guards round, of course, but she couldn't pick out a trace of movement from her distance until she looked east.

At the end of the ridge, a long ways away from the pale shapes of the white tents, she saw a tiny point of light moving, back and forth, forth and back, as if it were a lantern held in someone's hand as that hypothetical someone paced out of sheer nerves. Jill walked to the edge of the roof and watched the light while she sent her mind out, almost randomly, to see what traces of feeling she might pick up from the lantern-bearer. For a long time, nothing, and then it seemed she felt the touch of another mind on hers, nothing as strong as a greeting or a thought, just an awareness of a human being —and male, at that—as if she were in a room and had sensed someone enter from a door behind her.

The man remained unaware of her. At moments, she lost the feel of his presence; at others it returned with a waft of emotion. He was troubled, disgusted even, by something—what it might be this primitive scrying could never tell her. The disgust, however, mingled itself with regret, a thoroughly human wishing that things were otherwise. Occasionally, the point of light would stop its restless traveling, and at those moments she would clearly perceive that he was looking up at the dun and longing to be inside it. Could he perhaps be a slave? It was unlikely that any slave would be wandering round by himself at night.

Eventually, with one last sending of regret, the man walked away, the lantern swinging beside him. Briefly, a tent glowed as he carried his lantern inside; then he must have blown it out, because there was only darkness. Jill sighed, wondering if she'd ever know who he was. She doubted it.

On a huge heap of cushions, made of purple-dyed leather and strapped together with golden, tasseled cords, Rakzan Hir-li was lounging, his enormous body dressed only in a long tunic of rough brown cloth. Over a small pillow, his bleached mane of hair spread out, all braided and greased and studded throughout with beads and charms. His heavy blue eyes drooped under their furred brows, and now and then he yawned, exposing his long teeth, filed to points, but Lord Tren of Dun Mawrvelin knew better than to think him sincerely drowsy. While they finished the rations of bread that did them for a breakfast, the lord sat on a leather stool in front of the Horsekin warleader's couch, while behind it stood two human slave-soldiers, each armed with a long spear. The long, narrow tent itself was draped with purple and gold hangings, once splendid war booty, now smoke-stained and as greasy as their owner. Morning light came through between them in dim slits.

"The muster is now finished," Hir-li pronounced, "and I can't keep putting my captains off. They come to me and ask, is not the purpose of war to attack?" He paused for a sly smile. "What do you suggest that I tell them?"

"That the purpose of a siege, my lord, is to wait and force terms."

Hir-li scowled, making the purple and blue tattoos covering his face ripple and swell.

"So I see, so you see, but they do not see. I think me that we must have a little blood to satisfy them."

"As my lord wishes, of course, but Cengarn is a rock. If a man keeps kicking a rock, which breaks first? The rock or his foot?"

Hir-li laughed, nodding agreement, sitting upright in a motion strikingly supple for one so large.

"It's a good saying, Lord Tren, a good saying. Among your own people, are you considered an eloquent man?"

"Among my own people, my lord, I am considered exactly nothing."

The rakzan raised a furry eyebrow, then smiled.

"And so you've joined with us."

"It's one reason. My brother's death weighs upon me, for another. He was killed in Cengarn by a stinking mercenary. I don't care if they called it fair combat or not."

"Ah, of course. Rhodry. The famous silver dagger."

"I don't care if he's famous, either. I want him dead."

"The high priestess told me of this." Hir-li considered, his scarred and patterned face unreadable. "I will warn you. There's another thing my captains say, that you don't worship her with all your soul."

Tren started to speak, but Hir-li held up a hand for silence.

"I am not asking you for any answer or protest. I merely repeat what they say."

"For that, my lord, you have my sincere thanks. And has the high priestess said the same thing?"

Hir-li never answered, merely got up and turned toward the back of the tent, where a human eunuch crouched beside a battered wooden chest. The rakzan spoke in his own language; the slave scurried forward with a long sleeveless surcoat, crusted equally with gold thread and sweat, and helped his master into it. Over the coat Hir-li strapped a heavy leather belt with a bejeweled lunette at the front and his gold-hilted saber at his side. He sat again to allow the servant to pull on his high leather boots while Tren waited, saying nothing. At last, the rakzan spoke in Deverrian.

"One of your men tried to desert last night."

Tren rose without thinking.

"He will have to be turned over to the Keepers of Discipline. It would be best if you didn't argue."

"I understand. Did my lord think I would argue?"

Hir-li considered, sucking a long fang.

"I don't know what to think of you, Tren, except for two things. One, you're valuable. Two, most men grovel around me. You look me in the eye and try to keep to your old ways."

"And is that a good thing or a bad?"

The rakzan smiled, briefly.

"Most men would never dare ask that, either. Come along."

They stepped out into the bright sunlight glaring off the welter of white tents and threaded their way through the captains' camp, as the grouping on the ridge was called. Here and there they met a slave, carrying water or some such thing, who hurriedly dodged out of the warleader's path before he could swing a massive paw their way. Although at well over six feet tall Tren towered among his own people, his head came only to Hir-li's shoulder. Tren was a lean man, too, a dagger to the rakzan's sword, with the long muscles of a swordsman, and a narrow face, narrow gray eyes, oddly slender ears, and short-cropped hair so pale it was close to white. Although no one had bothered to tell him why, the Horsekin considered his coloring a good omen.

"One more thing," the rakzan said abruptly. "Last night I looked out of my tent and saw you walking back and forth at the end of the ridge, carrying a lantern."

"So I was."

"Why?"

"I couldn't sleep, and the camp's too crowded to walk in the dark."

Hir-li said nothing, leaving Tren to wonder if he believed what was, after all, the simple truth. Sleep, and particularly the act of falling asleep, had become a nightly torture, when he would lie alone in the dark of his tent with only his remorse for a companion. How had he been such a fool, to follow his brother Matyc into treachery? If only he had known just whom he was allying himself with, if only he'd seen more of the Horsekin than those few prophets, religious men all, talking of wise things, telling wonderful tales of a goddess who deigned to come into the world to meet her worshippers face to face. If only, if only—the words ate into his honor like burrowing worms.

Slaves had smoothed a rough road and cut a few dirt stairs down the side of the ridge to give the captains an easy walk down into the main camp. At the foot of the ridge, on the east side of

Cengarn in the level plain, lay a parade ground. In this vast circle of open land, the subordinate officers of the Horsekin's minutely organized army came each morning to receive orders and to make their reports to the rakzanir or captains. As Tren and Hir-li made their way downhill, Tren could see those officers, the Keepers of Discipline, standing waiting, while all round the edge of the circle a crowd was gathering. In the long boredom of a siege, any show came welcome.

Stripped naked and tied hand and foot like an animal ready for slaughter, there lay at the officers' feet a human being, a blond fellow, young—Tren's stomach wrenched when they came close enough for him to recognize Cadry, a man who'd ridden in his warband from the time he was little more than a lad. He was aware of Hir-li, watching him slantwise in appraisal.

"That's the man?" A life filled with secret hatreds and resentments kept Tren's voice rock steady.

"So I've been told. We'll see what the Keepers say."

They stopped on the other side of the bound man from the Keepers, each of whom wore a long red surcoat over his tunic and boots. One of their number, with a purple feather pinned to one shoulder, stepped forward and began delivering his report to the rakzan. Even after weeks in the Horsekin's company, Tren could only decipher the odd word or two of their speech. Finally, Hir-li cut the man short with a wave of one massive hand.

"He says that just before dawn, they found this fellow trying to creep out of the encampment, over on the north side where the terrain's rough enough to give a man a chance to hide," Hir-li said. "They have witnesses."

"Indeed?" Tren looked at Cadry. "Do you deny this?"

Cadry wrenched himself round like a caught fish and managed to get his elbows under his back. He propped himself up enough to tilt his head back and look Tren full in the face.

"I do not, my lord. If you had any honor left you'd do it yourself. Ah, by the *true* gods! If you had any honor, you'd lead us all out, away from these stinking creatures and back to our own kind."

Tren's life and the life of every man in his warband depended

205

on his reaction. He kicked Cadry in the mouth so hard that he heard tooth and bone crunch under the blow.

"Hold your tongue, you blaspheming dog! Have you forgotten about *her?*"

His eyes filled with tears, Cadry flopped back on the ground and bled. Tren set his hands on his hips and merely looked at him, saying nothing, showing nothing. Hir-li said a few sentences to the Keepers, but Tren, of course, had no way of knowing what. For all he knew, Hir-li was inventing rather than translating his words. The leader of the Keepers replied briefly.

"They ask if you have objections to his death."

"Tell them I demand his death."

Hir-li repeated—something. The Keepers nodded, grunting in what seemed to be satisfaction. On the ground, Cadry sobbed once, then lay still, his eyes fixed upon the sky, so pure and far above them all. Hir-li glanced at the officers and barked an order that seemed to displease them, from the way they glowered.

"I told them to kill him fast," Hir-li said to Tren. "To get it over with, as your people would say."

"Indeed? Why?"

Hir-li grinned hugely.

"No wonder you speak to me of rocks, Lord Tren. Your heart is made of one."

He turned and spoke to the Keepers, who went on looking sour. All round, the Horsekin in the crowd groaned and muttered, as if in disappointment. Hir-li considered them, then suddenly laughed and shouted, bellowing a message as loud as he could. The Keepers cheered, the waiting warriors cheered, laughing, drawing swords in a sudden rattle and holding them high, cheered again, "Hai, hai, hai," until the sound and the news spread through the entire camp.

Up on the rooftop of Cadmar's dun, Jill heard the shouting, but only as a distant sound, a sigh on the wind and little more. She was distracted enough to ignore it, because by daylight, she could see that the Horsekin had placed their reinforcements into the northern camp, formerly their weakest point. Cengarn was ringed good and proper, now. As she so often did in difficult times, she found herself thinking of Nevyn, her teacher in the dweomer and indeed, one of the greatest dweomermasters that the world had even known. Thanks to powerful magicks, he had lived over four hundred years, and during that unnaturally long life, he'd gathered together a vast amount of lore which his own researches and experiences had enriched. What would he have done, here in this siege?

Jill thought for a long time, pacing back and forth on the rooftop. Would he have used his alliances with the High Kings and Lords of the Elements to bring rain and plague, or perhaps fire and havoc, to the besiegers? She doubted it, since the enemy army included innocent slaves and servants—since, indeed, the army itself was deluded by Alshandra's madness rather than being evil. Would he have risked facing the enemy sorcerer in astral combat? Not if a loss would have meant depriving the city of his protection. What about challenging Alshandra herself? Nevyn might indeed have won such a battle. She could not. She was forced to realize that he would have done exactly what she was doing—wait—wait and watch for that one moment when all the hints and omens would come together in her mind and show her the one true thing that must be done.

Shaking her head, she left the roof and went downstairs. She was just leaving the main broch when she met Jahdo, who'd apparently been looking for her, judging from the way he brightened at her approach.

"There you be, my lady," Jahdo said. "I did come to ask you a question for my master's sake."

"Ask away, then, if it's somewhat that needn't be kept secret."

Jahdo glanced round at the busy ward, considered, then shrugged.

"I do see no reason for it to be, my lady. Meer did wonder if you could give me a written thing, a note, he called it, to introduce us to the dwarven gentlemen what be staying down in town. They do have a way of casting omens, or so he heard, that he would like to know of."

"That's more like our Meer, truly. It gladdens my heart to hear he's got his appetite for lore back. Let's go up to my chamber, and I'll write it out."

"My thanks, my lady. It do be a marvel, that you can read and write. Now, that be somewhat that I'd like to learn, someday, but no one's going to be teaching the ratter's lad letters."

"Indeed? Well, if I had time, I'd teach you. I didn't learn how to read until I was way older than you are now, you see. I was a grown woman, and it was a bit hard at first."

"I'll wager, I'll wager. I do know how precious every scrap of your time do be, my lady. But oh, it would be splendid, if someday you could teach me."

"Well, I'll tell you what. When this war's over, you remind me of my promise, and I will."

The boy grinned as bright as a rising moon, but Jill felt a coldness wrap round her heart, as she wondered if either of them would live long enough to sit down to that tutoring.

The note turned out to be a pair of wooden tablets, smeared with wax. Jill wrote her message with a stylus, put the tablets wax side together, and tied them up with a thong.

"A dwarven invention, this," she remarked. "You can use them over and over, you see. Here you go, lad. Ask for Jorn."

With the tablets safely in hand, Jahdo hurried out of the dun gates into the town. At the best of times, Cengarn was a confusing place, with streets that curved round the hills and dipped randomly into the valleys between them. Round houses, sheds, shops, most roofed with thatch, stood where people chose to build them, some set off with woven withey fences, others right on the streets. Here and there stretched bits of grass, and trees grew here and there, as well, nodding over chicken coops and public wells. Now, of course, with the siege, farmers, cows, chickens, children, sheep, wagons, improvised tents, dogs, lines of washing hung to dry, extra horses, cooking fires, stacks of hay filled every spot and nook and spilled half out in the street, while loose creatures and children ran round between other people's houses.

It took Jahdo a long time to find his way, asking directions every time he saw someone who looked like an actual townsman, to the dwarven inn. Round back of the hill topped by the public market—a campground now—he found a rise so steep it came close to being a cliff. Set right into it, between two stunted little pines, stood a wooden door with big iron hinges and a big iron ring. Jahdo grabbed the ring and used it to pound on the door. After a few minutes, a dwarf with an enormously long black beard opened up and fixed him with a suspicious eye.

"I do have a note from the dweomermaster up in the dun," Jahdo stammered. "For the man known as Jorn."

"Ah." The dwarf stepped back. "Well, come in, then."

Jahdo followed him into a stone hallway, lit with the eerie blue glow of phosphorescent fungi gathered into baskets and hung along the walls. Much to the boy's surprise, the air inside smelled fresh and sweet. At length, they reached a round chamber, some fifty feet across, scattered with low tables and tiny benches round a central open hearth, where a low fire burned and a huge kettle hung from a pair of andirons and a crossbar. The smoke from the fire rose straight up to vent holes in the stone ceiling. At one of the tables lounged a dwarf who was on the lean and lanky side, with a brown and curly beard.

"Message for you, Jorn." The innkeep jerked his thumb at Jahdo. "From the dun."

Jorn read Jill's message, then smiled.

"Well, now," he said. "If your master would like to learn geomancy, I do know a bit about it. Get him started, like. But the man who really knows how it works isn't here, alas. He went off with Rhodry to look for that dragon months ago, before the siege came, like. Otho's his name, and—"

The floor shook. Jorn swore in Dwarvish and swung himself clear of the bench to stand just as the shaking came again. It felt as if a giant hand had slammed into the side of the hill from outside. The innkeep turned dead white.

"An earthquake?" Jahdo said. "We do get them in my home city, but I didn't know they happened here."

209

"They don't," Jorn said. "Worse'n that, lad, much worse. The Horsekin are up to somewhat, I'd say. They're ramming the walls, most like."

Jahdo felt as if all the blood had drained from his body. It was an attack, then. As they all stood straining to hear, a sound at last filtered through the thick walls and under the hill, a faint susurrus like an unnatural wind.

"Fair lot of shouting outside," the innkeep muttered.

Suddenly, Jahdo remembered that he had duties.

"My master! It be needful for me to get back to the dun."

"Then you'd best hurry," Jorn said. "I'll just be arming myself and heading for the ramparts. If we turn the bastards back, then tell your master I'll be glad to teach him what I know. If we don't, well, it won't matter, will it? Now run!"

Jahdo did, racing down the long hall, letting himself out the heavy door. As soon as he opened it, the noise broke over him. Shouting, screaming, cows lowing, dogs howling, weeping, war cries —all of it punctuated by the boom, boom, boom of something huge hitting from the east. Jahdo ran and dodged and twisted his way through the streets. The refugees milled round; soldiers poured from dun or militia hall and rushed for the walls. Silver horns blared; men yelled and shrieked and yelled some more. The streets swarmed as those civilians caught down by the walls began to stream uphill and toward the center of the town, while the militia and men from the dun struggled downhill toward their posts. Jahdo ducked between two houses, crawled under a wagon, shoved his way past a group of weeping farmwives, jumped up onto a barrel, and waited while a squad of warriors raced past, wearing mail but settling their pot helms as they ran. He glanced round and realized that his barrel stood at the overhang of a rough slate roof.

A jump and some concentrated scrabbling got him onto the roof, where he could inch himself up to the peak and finally see. The house he clung to stood halfway up a slope facing east, and it was at the east gate of the city that the attack seemed concentrated. Cengarn men lined the ramparts and shouted war cries and insults as they hurled stones down at the attackers or leaned over to stab and shove at enemies that Jahdo couldn't see. Behind them, other men handed stones up ladders or milled round, waiting a turn up. Every now and then a Cengarn man screamed and fell; his fellows on the wall would shove him down and help a replacement up.

The noise spread; from the north as well as the east, came the thwack, thwack of battering rams pounding on gates, the screaming and yelling of the soldiers, the wordless chanting of the Horsekin outside. Below Jahdo's perch, the town folk and the refugees huddled together. The center of town fell silent as the people grew terrified, barely speaking, barely moving, though here and there a woman wept, and somewhere a baby was sobbing, over and over. Suddenly, from the east, almost directly over the east gate, in fact, flew a shower of fire—whether flaming arrows or balls of pitch, Jahdo couldn't tell from his distance. He wanted to scream as the fire fell among thatched roofs—and went out. He could only stare in utter amazement as every scrap of burning turned cold and died the moment it fell. Down below, the town folk who'd seen began to cheer and howl, laughing like demons.

"Dweomer," Jahdo whispered to himself. "Our sorcerers be working it, I do believe."

Another sound went up, this one distant from beyond the walls, another kind of howling—rage and frustration. Silver horns blared in Cengarn; the defenders began to shout and cheer only to cut the cheering short as another charge came. Remembering Meer, Jahdo clambered down from the roof, managed to get his feet on the barrel again, then fell when it tipped. Cursing under his breath, he picked his aching self up from the cobbles. The palms of his hands were scraped and bleeding. He could remember falling this way back home, but at a time when nothing terrible was happening, and his father had picked him up to comfort him. Jahdo turned and wept, leaning on folded arms onto the wall. It seemed that if he only wished hard enough, only wept hard enough, he would suddenly find himself home, but the screams and the war cries pounded on and on, like waves on some distant beach. When he opened his eyes, he was still in Cengarn. He choked back one last sob.

"I've got to get to Meer."

His eyes refused to dry as he headed uphill, rubbing his face on his shirtsleeve. He passed clots of refugees, huddled in doorways, huddled in alleys, weeping and trembling, their children and their animals huddled round them. No one so much as asked him for news, and still the distant screaming went on and on. When he reached the dun, he glanced up to see a few men standing guard on the walls. The gates stood closed, but when he banged and howled, the gatekeeper pulled one just wide enough to let him slip in.

"Where have you been, lad?" the old man snapped. "Your master's been calling for you."

Jahdo ran across the ward and rushed into the great hall. The dun's womenfolk stood or sat near the dragon hearth, huddled together just like the farmwives, noble lady and serving lasses alike. Her face as pale as death, Princess Carra sat slumped in a chair with her dog leaning against her knees, but there was no sign of Yraen. Meer stood right behind her, clutching his staff in both hands, as if he'd taken over the silver dagger's guard duty.

"Meer, Meer, it's Jahdo!" Jahdo ran to them, remembered to make a bob of a bow to the princess. "Your Highness."

Carra raised one hand but said nothing, merely went on staring out at empty air. Lady Labanna seemed to be about to speak, then stayed silent. When Meer reached out a hairy hand, Jahdo caught it and guided it to his shoulder, then leaned against the bard. Here in the dun, the battle noise drifted up from the town muted like an evil wind, howling and whistling round the towers. The sound of the rams seemed only distant drums, beating to some alien song, keeping time with Jahdo's heart. He could feel himself shaking under Meer's strong grip, but the bard himself stood perfectly still. Every now and then, Lightning growled; no one spoke.

All at once, the distant howling changed, grew lighter, more human somehow, and silver horns called. The drumbeat stopped. Labanna ran like a lass to the door of the hall.

"Guards, guards!" she called out. "What news?"

Although no one inside could hear the answer, she relayed what scraps of action that the men could see from their high perch. The Horsekin seemed to be—no, they were falling back to their camps. Some of their siege towers were burning. There were a lot of dead Horsekin on the ground, or maybe they were but wounded. Either way, their fellows were leaving them there and pulling clear of the walls.

All at once, Carra got up. She tossed her head, and her hands were clenched hard into fists.

"I hate them," she hissed. "I hate them all! I wish I could swing a sword, I wish I could stand on the walls and kill one myself. I'd like that, stabbing one and seeing blood!"

"Your Highness!" Ocradda grabbed her by the shoulders. "You're distressing yourself."

The other women flocked round her, and suddenly the silence broke. In a flood of chatter and nervous laughter, washing over Carra's outburst like a bucket of water thrown onto a floor to carry some filth away, the servingwomen swept Carra up and hurried her upstairs. Labanna, however, returned to the hearth.

"I cannot say I blame her highness," she remarked to no one in particular. "Ah, well, the gods will bring what they bring."

"Just so, my lady." Meer swung his head round in her direction. "And well said."

"No doubt the men will stay on the walls for some while, but I think we may count ourselves safe for the time being."

"So it would seem, and the princess's brave words have given my heart strength. When the next attack comes, my lady, my place will be on the walls."

"My good bard! I don't mean to be insulting, mind, but I doubt if you could fight—"

"Of course not! But I can invoke the curse of a sworn bard, one acknowledged by gods and men alike, upon the impiety being committed here by these foul swine, these ravening beasts of the northlands, these demon-ridden scum. If a flicker of life remains in their ugly souls, perhaps my words will reach and move them to think better of their deeds."

"Perhaps so. I thank you."

As the sound of cheering grew louder, they fell silent, listening to the victory coming toward them from the walls.

• • •

"Well, they all know we've got dweomer on our side now," Dallandra remarked. "May the knowledge spoil their night's sleep!"

"It would have been splendid to see their faces, sure enough," Jill said, grinning, "when those sparks went out. From now on, one or the other of us has to answer every alarum."

"True spoken. How long before the next attack? Do you have any idea?"

"Well, if this were an ordinary Deverry war, not for a very long time indeed. But who knows what the Horsekin think? They don't have cities of their own, Meer tells me, so for all I know, they've never even run a siege before."

Dallandra nodded, considering. They were sitting in Jill's chamber with frightened Wildfolk clustered round them in gathering dusk. Outside, the last of the sunlight was gilding the western towers and sending long shadows over the ward, where a few servants hurried back and forth without the usual laughter and chat.

"I was expecting our raven to show herself," Jill said. "I'm surprised she didn't give you a fight of it over putting out those fires."

"So am I. You didn't see her, then? You were the one up on the roofs."

"Not a feather's worth of her. I wonder just what sort of dweomer she knows, I truly do. She can shape-change, she knows the dweomer of roads, but what of all the other lore? Is she a woman of the Horsekin? If so, their magicks are crude, or so Meer tells me."

"Why are you so sure that it's another woman we're facing?"

"I met her once when I was flying in my hawk's form and she was the raven. The falcon could somehow tell that this other bird was female." Jill smiled briefly. "It's odd how we mazrakir become the animal we're mimicking—odd, and a dangerous thing."

"That's never happened to me."

"This sort of dweomer suits your people better than mine. It can be dangerous for a human being to fly too often. You know, that gives me an idea. The raven I saw acted very much like a real bird.

Do you think that might mean she's human, the shape-changer, I mean?"

"It could. We really know next to nothing, don't we?"

"Just so. If she was there at the battle, why didn't she start those fires again, the ones you put out? Doesn't she know how? Was she gone rounding up more warriors? Was she just holding her hand to make us wonder? We have no way of knowing."

They exchanged a troubled glance.

"There were over eighty Cengarn men wounded and thirty killed outright," Dallandra said at last. "The chirurgeon tells me that twenty of the wounded are sure to die. It seemed to me that a lot more Horsekin than that were killed. One of the guardsmen counted up a hundred, just on the east side."

"No doubt. Our men have the position. It's hard to fight climbing up a ladder. Interesting, isn't it, that they chose the east gate for their attack?"

Dallandra looked puzzled.

"That used to be the weakest point in the defenses," Jill said, "until Jorn and his men sealed it up with some sort of dweomer stone they know how to make. They did it after the traitor in the dun had been exposed and killed, you see."

"Ah. So the Horsekin wouldn't have known. I do see. Is there anything more we can do, or do we just have to wait for the next time?"

"Just wait, I'm afraid." Jill tried to smile. "But I think we can sleep well enough after today. The walls are going to hold. That's one thing we do know."

"Unless Alshandra finds a way to bring her men over the walls from above."

"If she does, we'll be there to greet her."

Dallandra nodded, thinking something through. Yet again Jill found herself wishing that Nevyn were there. Even if he'd only counseled them to wait, his very presence would have been a comfort—the one person in her own long life that she'd ever been able to trust completely, the one person who had always put her welfare above his own while at the same time demanding that she continually live up to everything she was capable of being. As she thought it over, she supposed that he'd been the one person that, in return, she'd ever truly loved. She felt her eyes fill with tears and wiped them away fast on the back of her hand.

"What's wrong?" Dallandra said.

"Naught. I'm just weary, as well we all might be."

"Well, that's true enough."

"Tell me somewhat. I've been trying to find out the nature of the Guardian, what they're made of, I mean." Jill nodded toward the table, where several of her books lay. "You've told me that Alshandra has a soul of sorts. That means her various forms must be like our bodies, right?"

"Housing the soul? Just that, or so I've always assumed. They can feel etheric pain, for instance."

"Indeed? Huh, I wonder then. Suppose we could destroy Alshandra's astral form. Would it set her soul free to be reborn then? Reborn and gone, I mean, on to some new life, good and far away from us?"

"It should, certainly. But destroying her form's not such an easy thing." Dallandra tried for a wry smile and failed. "She's not as vulnerable as one of us, out on the etheric. Break up our body of light, snap the silver cord—and there we are, dead as a stone in the road. But she doesn't have a physical body, so she'd have to be absolutely torn to pieces for the same thing to happen."

"I doubt if either of us have the strength to do such a thing. I doubt if we'd have enough strength together."

"I doubt it, too—very, very much indeed. Not even Nevyn could have defeated her."

"You think so?"

"I do. You know how much I respected your master, Jill, but she's from some different order of being than we are—elves or men, it doesn't matter. She's stronger than us all."

The Wildfolk eddied round them like white water round a rock, then disappeared. The two dweomermasters sat without speaking until night filled the room with darkness.

In the deep mid of the night, after she'd finished renewing the astral seals over dun and town, Jill scried for Prince Daralanteriel. She expected to see him and his men sleeping, but though she found him easily enough, he was wide awake, sitting by a fire in an elven camp with men and women both clustered round him. So! he'd caught up with one alar or another. The prince was talking, waving his hands, tossing his raven-dark hair, and his excitement was like a fire playing over his strikingly handsome face. The people round him nodded in agreement or turned to whisper to one another as his mood spread. As Jill watched, a tall man carrying a staff pushed his way through to the fireside—pale hair, violet eyes— Calonderiel! Jill felt herself grinning with relief. So, Dar had found the one man of all the Westfolk who had the power to call for all-out war. From the twist to Calonderiel's mouth, from the way his hands clasped the staff as he listened to the young prince, Jill knew that the warleader would summon his people to ride to Cengarn's aid.

But how soon? When she widened the scope of the vision, she could see only empty grasslands under a dull moon. They could be hundreds of miles away, and besides, it would take Calonderiel time to muster his bands of archers, who lived scattered all over the grasslands. Jill swore aloud, scattering a gaggle of Wildfolk. By the time the elven force arrived, the battle for Cengarn might well be over.

In *Evandar's country, a bare hour seemed to have passed since the army* left the beacon tree behind. On this side of the border tree, the forest stretched dead—the trees, black hulks; the shrubs and bracken, spongy peat; the ivy bronzed, clinging to brittle branches. Even the Dark Host rode silent in this wood and kept a watch on every tangled thicket and shadowed dell. Menw kept glancing up at the sky, dark with tattered clouds.

"My lord!" he suddenly cried. "Look! At the edge of the forest!"

Evandar rose in his stirrups and followed the point of his lieutenant's sword. Through the misshapen trees, he could just make out the form of an enormous hawk, its gray-dappled belly flashing as it swooped off. With a whoop, he urged his army forward, but by the time they burst out of the woods, the bird had disappeared. Not so much as a speck dwindling in the copper-colored sky marked her going.

"So," Evandar said. "Alshandra's spying on us in her bird form. I wonder where she may be?"

"No doubt back in the world of men," Shaetano sneered. "Or off somewhere we don't even know about. Do you truly think we can catch her? She learned the dweomer of the roads from you, brother dear, and now she's got many a world she can travel through."

"So she does, but Elessario only lives in one of them. We have a lure for our hawk, to keep her close."

Evandar raised one arm and yelled for a halt. Off to their left, the river had sunk and dwindled to a white-water stream, cutting a canyon some twenty feet below the road. Off to their right, the sun hung swollen, as if it swam through the smoke of some enormous fire. Ahead lay plains, as flat and seeming-infinite as those in the Westlands, stretching on and on to a horizon where more clouds—or was it smoke?—billowed like a frozen wave, all copper-red from the bloated sun.

"Ah, the battle plain," Evandar remarked. "Where once we met, you and I, to discuss this thing or that."

Shaetano drew back his lips in what might have been a grin.

"I don't see Alshandra's rebels anywhere about," Evandar went on. "If it weren't for the iron, I'd wonder if she took them down to join the Horsekin army. That *would* be a pretty sight at Cengarn's walls, her pack of monsters all mingling with the ugliest flesh and blood I've ever seen."

"My lord?" Menw said. "If it was the nighthawk who came to spy, couldn't they all be hiding in the clouds?"

"Counsel like that earned you your name, sure enough." Evandar raised his silver horn. "Let us go see."

When he blew five notes, the army charged forward onto the battle plain, but as their horses galloped, they climbed, racing higher and higher into the sky, not flying, exactly, rather blown by some huge wind like a river of dead leaves whirled into the air ahead of an autumn storm, or perhaps the army had become the crack of a huge and glittering whip, snaking through the air. Up and up they rode, swirling round on a huge spiral through the coppery smoke until all at once they burst into clear air and silver light.

When Evandar called the halt, it seemed their horses stood on a solid surface, but round their feet and legs billowed mist. Ahead of and all round the army towered huge pillars of cloud, as if they stood in a forest of white brochs. Here and there among them, sunlight fell in golden shafts, while above shone broken tiles of blue sky. The pillars and brochs were drifting, though, some moving one way, some another, merging only to break apart again as they sailed through the air. Shaetano turned in his saddle and stared.

"They could be anywhere," he whispered. "We could hunt here forever."

"Indeed, brother? Then we'd best get on our way."

Lord Tren's warband had been assigned a campground on the flat not far from the east ridge—a place of honor, or so Tren had been told, but he suspected it of being merely a place where they could be watched. During the abortive assault on the city, Rakzan Hir-li had kept the Deverry men back, too, out of the fighting, as if perhaps he wondered if they'd try to desert right over the town walls. The day after the attack, Tren, along with the other captains, met to discuss the day's fighting. Although everyone treated him cordially, so few of the Horsekin spoke his language that he had no true idea of what they might be thinking of him. When the council ended, just as night was falling, he fled their company to join his warband in its camp.

Some of these men had ridden for him and been housed in his small dun, but the majority had once been his brother's men, come over to him after Matyc's death. They sat huddled round their cooking fires, saying nothing to one another, though a few men sat by themselves, staring out at nothing. His captain, Ddary, a stolid man with close-cropped brown hair, joined him as he walked through the tents. Although Tren tried to speak with the men, most merely listened, mouths set and tight, staring at the ground as if they were waiting for him to be finished and gone.

"You can't blame them, my lord," Ddary whispered. "We all saw what happened to Cadry, tied up like that and stabbed. They let him bleed to death like a beast."

His voice ached with reproach. Tren glanced round, wondering how many of his men had been subverted for spies. The Horsekin made it a policy to sponsor friendly ears in every squad.

"He spoke against her holy war," Tren snapped. "Do you deny that he got what he deserved? Would you say such a thing aloud?"

Ddary might have been slow, but he wasn't stupid.

"Never, my lord. The Keepers did what they had to do, sure enough. Blessed be she, who watches over us all."

When Tren glanced his way, their eyes met in something much like agony. Tren looked up at the sky, darkening to a velvet gray. Off to the east, a few stars were coming out.

"I'd best get back to the other captains. They're waiting for the high priestess to return."

Ddary's hands twitched, as if he were forcibly keeping himself from making the warding signs against witchcraft.

"I see, my lord. Where is she, if I may be so bold as to ask?"

"I've no idea. She keeps her own counsel."

But there's not a man of us who wouldn't like to know where she's got to, Tren thought. We could have used the bitch's help this afternoon. Sorcery! It makes a man's blood run cold. He spat on the ground, whether the Goddess was watching or not.

Up at Lin Serr, Rhodry was coming to much the same conclusion. That night, he stood at the window of his tower room and watched the stars while he thought of Angmar, remembering the brief months they'd shared, praying to every god that she was well, wherever the island's mysterious dweomer had taken her. He wondered about Enj, too, keeping his watch up in the mountains. At that moment, with his hiraedd lying upon him, he doubted if either of them would ever

see Haen Marn again. At length he lay down and slept, but he
dreamt of Angmar, and the view from their bedroom window of the
lake, so vividly that when he woke, he nearly wept to find himself
not there.

That morning, since he was shut out of the main city and thus
any councils of war that might have been taking place, there was
nothing for him to do but fume, pacing back and forth in his quarters up in the gatehouse or wandering through the old watchtower.
He found himself wishing that Alshandra's peculiar creatures would
come back and give him a fight, but apparently their experience
with the iron-filled gatehouse had scared them off. Finally, he went
down to the riverbank and the dragon's company. In the hot morning sun, Arzosah stretched out and lazed, turning from one side to
the other as if she were meat on a spit, browning by a fire. To give
himself something to do, Rhodry groomed her as he would have
done a horse. With handfuls of oiled rags from the gatehouse store-
room, he rubbed her down till every scale gleamed, while she
stretched and rumbled in the sun.

"Revenge will come when it comes," she remarked. "A dragon
lives many a long year, while the Horsekin live but few."

"My heart longs to make them live even fewer," Rhodry
snapped. "I'm sick as I can be of all this delay."

Later that afternoon, he did receive some news, when Garin
came down from the city. Rhodry looked up to see him hurrying
down the long stairs and strolled across the grass to meet him by the
river.

"One of the women passed along a message this morning,"
Garin said. "Seems like someone did a little scrying. There's been an
attack on Cengarn, but it was beaten back easy enough."

Rhodry stopped walking and swung round to face him.

"When was this?"

"Two days past, round noon or so. They couldn't tell me much
about it, of course."

"Of course."

"All this wretched dweomer! Well, it comes in handy, every
now and then. Too bad our enemies have it as well."

For a long moment they stood looking up, but nothing moved in the cloudless sky, not natural bird or shape-changer.

Rhodry saw no sign of the raven woman all day, but that night she invaded his dreams. Once before a woman—or to be precise, a female spirit in that case—had taken over his dreams. Although it was years past, he remembered it well enough to recognize the sensation when it happened again. He was having an ordinary dream, where he walked along the shore of Haen Marn's lake with Angmar, neither of them speaking, merely delighting in each other's company like the dragon in her sun. At one point, he bent down to pick up a stone from the shore, and when he straightened up, she was gone. He ran this way and that, hunting all over the island, which suddenly turned into Dun Aberwyn, as places will do in dreams. He ended up in the garden behind the main broch, where stood the fountain with the marble dragon.

Sitting on a bench, framed by roses, the raven woman was waiting for him. She reminded him of Mallona, though younger and somehow coarser, with raven-dark hair and lovely eyes, but her mouth was too full, her neck too thick, and her smile too sly. She had blunt heavy fingers, too, peasant's hands, he found himself thinking, folded over some shiny object hidden in her lap.

"Well met, Rhodry Maelwaedd," she said. "Is it that you know who I be?"

"I don't know your name, if that's what you mean, but I think me we've met before."

"We have at that. It does surprise me that you remember."

"I'm more surprised you do, frankly."

"My Goddess, she does show me many a hidden thing. There be power upon her beyond your imagining."

He merely shrugged, glancing round. The walls of the brochs seemed to have closed in round the garden, penning them in with no gate or door. A low ceiling blocked out the sky as the garden turned into a chamber with a single chair and a woman's riding gear scattered on the straw-strewn floor. She rose, laughing, her hands still clutched tight over her mysterious holding.

"Never will you escape from here," she snapped. "You did trap me once, and now I've trapped you."

"Indeed? I'm bound to wake up sooner or later."

She tossed her head up, her eyes narrowing in rage. Rhodry laughed, making her a mocking sort of bow.

"What did you think? That I wouldn't know I was dreaming? That I'd believe in you and your wretched little spells?"

She cursed in cold fury, then began to chant in some language that he'd never heard. With her right hand, she began to sketch a strange pattern in the air, while in her left she held out a little glass vial, gleaming with silver light. Out of sheer reflex, Rhodry slapped at her arm with a wide sweep of motion. His hand seemed to pass right through her flesh, but the vial fell spinning to the ground and shattered.

He was wide awake, sitting up in his blankets in the gatehouse and sopping with cold sweat. He got up, swearing with every foul oath he could muster, ran both hands through his damp hair, and staggered over to a window. Out to the east, the sky was just beginning to lighten. He leaned onto the sill until the sun rose to banish the dark. With one last shudder, he turned back, picked up his brigga from the floor, and pulled them on, then reached for his shirt and saw something gleaming on the stone, a curved fragment of silvery glass.

"Oh, horseshit and a pile of it!" Rhodry whispered.

He hunkered down and inspected the floor, but he found only that one piece. Even in the brightening sun, it seemed to glow with its own private light. And what would she have done with that vial, he wondered, trapped his soul the way witches were said to do in the old tales? Or was it merely poisoned? He found his sword belt, started to draw his silver dagger, then reconsidered. He had another knife as well, a crude bronze blade bound to a wooden handle, which Dallandra had given him a long while ago. He drew that from its crumbling sheath and slid the point under the fragment to pick it up for a closer look, but the moment the bronze touched the silver glass, the fragment puffed up, hissed, began to steam, and with an evil smell boiled away like a drop of water on a hot griddle stone.

223

Rhodry was too stunned to cry out or swear. He sat back on his heels and stared at the knife point. When he risked touching it, the metal felt cool and hard, just as it always did. Jill had told him once that this particular knife had great dweomer upon it; she'd said something about it existing in several worlds at once, but since he hadn't understood what she'd told him, he'd forgotten exactly how it might do so. From now on, he decided, he'd sleep with that knife in his hand.

After he finished dressing, he went outside to the park land and called Arzosah down from her high perch. She flopped ungracefully into the dew-damp grass next to him and yawned, shaking her wings.

"I don't suppose you saw or heard any ravens flying over last night," Rhodry said.

"What? Of course not. Ravens don't fly at night." She yawned again, then caught herself. "Oh. You mean *that* raven. I did not, and truly, I would have, because it was chilly and damp up there, Dragonmaster, and I did not sleep well at all."

"If you didn't sleep all day, you'd sleep better at night."

She flounced her wings and curled her upper lip to expose one long fang. Rhodry held the ring up with a gleam of sunlight.

"We're going to go flying," he said. "I want a look round. If she was working dweomer last night, she has to be round here somewhere."

"What? She did what?"

While he tied on her rope harness, Rhodry told the dragon about his "dream." She immediately agreed with his interpretation.

"No ordinary dream at all! She drew your soul out of your body, all right, and I'll just wager she was trying to trap it, there in that world where sorcerers work their magic. I've never seen anything like that peculiar stuff the vial was made of, but I'm sure it was dweomer. Ych! This is awful! If she manages to trap you, then she'll get the ring, and serving her would be loathsome. I'd hate it." She stamped her front feet. "Hate it, hate it, hate it!"

"Then you'd best help me track her down, hadn't you?"

They flew for a long time that morning, until the sun was

halfway twixt horizon and zenith. They swooped up high over Lin Serr's plateau and saw tiny figures below them, the dwarven burial party working at one of the burnt farms, then circled back, drifting on the air currents over the hills and currents to the south and east of the dwarvehold. They never saw the raven, though it was possible that in her woman's form she lay hidden in the cover of the deep forest. Finally, when the sun was sending long shadows from the west, Rhodry gave it up as a bad job and went back to Lin Serr. They landed by the river, where he untied her harness.

"What are you going to do?" she said. "You've got to sleep some time."

"True spoken. I don't know, actually. I might go find Garin and ask him to see what dwarvehold's womenfolk have to say about this."

"Good idea. May I go hunt, Master? I spied some nice fat deer down in the hills."

"Very well. Just come straight back here to eat them."

"And if I find the raven, I'll eat her. I think she knows it, too."

After she flew off, Rhodry coiled the harness and carried it back to the gatehouse. He'd grown so used to thinking of iron as a protection that he was paying little attention to much of anything as he climbed the stairs, but of course, it was only Alshandra's and Evandar's people who couldn't abide the presence of that metal. When he walked into his chamber, the raven woman was waiting for him. Stark naked, her long black hair draped over one shoulder, she was standing in the curve of the wall twixt two windows. From the disarray of his blankets and gear, he could guess that she'd been rummaging through everything he owned.

"You're bold as brass, aren't you?" he snapped.

She laughed, then looked full into his face, caught his gaze with hers, and held it with dweomer. Her stare seemed to pierce his eyes and impale his very soul, so that for a moment he couldn't frame a single thought. He felt the slap of her mind as a physical blow, making him stagger. With a wrench of will, he looked away and tossed the bundle of ropes he carried straight at her. Although they fell short, she yelped and jumped back—all the time he needed. He drew the bronze knife in a smooth motion and charged. Shrieking, she dodged to one side. He barely missed, would have stabbed her with his next lunge, but his own ruse tripped him. He caught a foot in the ropes and stumbled just enough to let her duck past.

"You bastard of a silver dagger!" She leapt up to the window ledge. "You've not seen the end of this."

She flung herself out the window. Spitting every foul oath he knew, Rhodry shook the rope from his foot and rushed to the ledge. When he looked down, he expected to see a corpse spattered on the grass below, but instead the raven flew, swooping up past the window with a harsh cry. For a long time, he leaned onto the sill and watched as she flapped off, flying hard and steadily back south toward Cengarn.

It was about an hour after dawn of the next day that Lord Tren, walking at the edge of the captain's camp, saw the raven flying home on slow wings. He stopped and watched her circle once over the army, which greeted her with cheers and upraised arms. She never flew directly over the city itself, he noticed; he supposed that she feared a lucky arrow shot from the defenders. Flapping once, then settling into a long glide, she came to earth not far from him at the open door of her tent, so like a real bird, hopping a little, shaking her wings, but so huge, that he shuddered. When servants rushed out to chase him away from the high priestess's presence, he was glad to go.

Yet that night, after she'd granted Hir-li an audience, Raena, the name by which the men knew the high priestess, had Tren summoned. He followed a perfumed maidservant's lantern through the dark camp to the high priestess's tent, a particularly large one and set well apart from the others. In the night, it glowed softly from light within. At the tent flap stood two human eunuchs with long spears. The servant held the lantern high with one hand and pulled back the flap with the other.

"If the captain would enter?"

Tren ducked his head and stepped in, straightening up in a pale

226

silver glow that seemed to come from everywhere and nowhere, as if light clung to the very walls and tent poles. Not far from the entrance, in the midst of this moon gleam, Raena sat on a chair made of curved wood and linen slings. Behind her he could see chests, a bed, various weapons and clothes, lying scattered on a carpet of red and gold. At her feet sat a thick leather cushion. She snapped her fingers and pointed.

"You may sit."

"Her Holiness is very kind."

Tren sat. She was wearing a long tunic, all embroidered with Horsekin-style designs in red and gold, and her long dark hair plumed back from her brow in Horsekin fashion, too, braided with charms and trinkets. Her short, almost stubby hands lay in her lap, unmoving as she considered him.

"Hir-li did tell me this noon that one of your men committed blasphemy."

"He did, Your Holiness. He was put to death for it."

Raena nodded once, as if considering what he'd said, then nodded again, and again, and again, her head bobbing back and forth, her body swaying with the motion, forward, back, forward, back, while Tren stared gape-mouthed. With one last plunge, she bent double, her head face-down in her lap. He half-rose, wondering if he should call for the servants. All at once she sat up, but with a strange sinuous motion, as if a rope were attached between her shoulder blades to pull her torso up. At the last moment, her head snapped up as well. She sat back in her chair, but another soul looked out from her eyes, and an alien smile curved her mouth. When she spoke, her voice rang hollow and booming.

"Lord Tren! I speak to you through the mouth of my priestess."

Abruptly cold, Tren slid off the cushions and knelt to lift trembling hands to his Goddess, truly made flesh for this little while. She laughed in a long cackling peal and raised her hands to return his salute.

"Do you wish the death of your brother's killer?" The voice pealed like bronze. "Do you crave his blood?"

"I do, O Beloved One, with all my soul."

227

"The priestess will give you what you need to bring him down as he flies. She, too, wishes this man's death, as do I."

Tren was stunned—as he *flew?* Did she mean to say that this Rhodry, this misbegotten silver dagger, was another shape-changer?

"But if you receive this gift, you will have bound yourself to serve me and to slay my enemies, no matter who they may be, no matter how it might ache your heart. You must kill in my name. Do you hear me? Kill. I want blood. You must kill."

He started to speak, but Raena's head flopped first back, then forward. She gurgled, drooling, spitting, her body wrenching in the chair, then twisting back. Tren leapt to his feet and grabbed the writhing woman just as the chair threatened to tip and dump her upon the ground. When her head flopped onto his shoulder, he felt warm drool seeping through his shirt. Was she choking to death? He had never felt more helpless.

He scooped her up and carried her to the bed, then laid her down face forward, grabbing blankets and wadding them up to stuff under her neck and chest. She lay so still that he risked putting his hand along the side of her face. Although she felt chilly, she was warm enough for life.

"Raena?" Tren whispered. "Your Holiness?"

He would have bellowed for servants, but he feared that she'd be mortified to be seen this way. He certainly would have been. All at once, she raised her head and stared at him.

"Water?" Her voice cracked, but it was her own voice.

Tren got up, glanced round, and found a clay pitcher and a wooden cup. He had to support her while she drank, both hands wrapped round the cup like a little child.

"The Goddess demands a great deal from her priestess, I see."

She nodded and held out the cup for more water. He poured, then slipped his arm under her shoulders again to hold her up.

"My thanks." Her voice rasped. "Be you mindful of the great honor she did pay you?"

"Very much so, Your Holiness. Shall I call your maidservants in?"

She shook her head no, handed him the empty cup, and sat up, sighing, pushing her mane of hair back from her face with both hands.

"See you there that long chest at the back of the tent?" she said. "Open it. The gift she did promise you be wrapped in red cloth."

Tren did as he was told and found, wrapped in reddish-brown linen, an elven longbow and a quiver of arrows. He stood, measuring the long yew staff—just a few inches shorter than he was and with a good strong pull. Tucked in the quiver's mouth were a pair of bow strings. Raena swung her legs over the side of the bed and sat looking at him.

"Do you ken the using of such a thing?"

"I do, Your Holiness. There's more than a little blood of the Westfolk in my clan's veins."

"Oh, I'm well aware of that." She smiled briefly. "But do you remember what she said? If you do take that bow, it will be needful for you to kill at my order."

"Of course. Why wouldn't I?"

"I know not." She tilted her head a little to one side. "Yet an omen did come to me, saying that you might stay your hand from the task I would put you."

"Your Holiness, I assure you. I'm the Goddess's man, heart and soul."

She started to speak, shrugging, yawning, then flopping back onto the bed, stretching her arms out over her head with a long sigh.

"Er, Your Holiness seems tired. I should leave her."

"Not just yet." She smiled at him. "When the Goddess takes me over, she leaves me hungry. Come lie down."

Her tunic, hiked up round her thighs, stuck to her fleshy body with sweat. He stood for a moment considering her and wishing she looked less like a farmwife, lying in the haystack after a hard day tending pigs. Yet it had been a long time since he'd had a woman, and besides, scorning this one could prove dangerous. He sat down beside her and kissed her on the mouth. She laughed and threw one leg round his waist. The sex had something of the farm about it, too, at least to Tren's way of thinking, short, rough, and noisy. When they were done, she rolled away from him and yawned.

"You may go now. Take the gift of the Goddess, and call my servants."

By the time that Tren had finished lacing his brigga, she'd fallen asleep, slack-mouthed and snoring. Although he tried to convince himself that he still found the Goddess awe-inspiring, he kept remembering Raena, drooling onto his shoulder.

"Rori! Rori, where are you?"

Garin's voice drifted up faintly to the tower room. Rhodry went to the window and knelt on the ledge to lean out and see the envoy standing in the bright morning sun at the tower's base. With him were the master tanner and the master armorer and their apprentices, carrying some large burden.

"The harness!" Garin bellowed. "Come down!"

"I will, then."

With a yell to Arzosah to fly and meet him on the grass, Rhodry hurried down the long staircase. He'd had a dreamless sleep the past few nights, when he could sleep at all. It seemed that every few minutes he'd wake, thinking he heard the raven shrieking over Lin Serr. In the sunlight, though, with the tanner and armorer bustling about, showing off their shiny handiwork, perilous dreams and shape-changers seemed very far away.

"Let's try it on, shall we?" Rhodry said to the dragon. "Will you let them work the buckles and suchlike? I've no idea how this thing goes together."

"Very well. But they'd best be careful of my beautiful scales."

Once it was fitted, Arzosah pronounced herself satisfied with the new harness, an elegant thing of black leather set off with polished bronze buckles and the little gold dragons, inlaid round the martingale, that Otho's bequest had bought her. Rhodry found it much easier to ride in a proper saddle, though this arrangement of pads and leather loops rode and felt far different than any horse saddle he'd ever used. He still knelt more than sat, but securely so now. As they soared and dipped over Lin Serr, he realized that, at long last, he'd grown used to dragonback.

Now that he wasn't worrying about falling hundreds of feet to his death, he could try out his various plans for fighting during the battles ahead, but there he was in for a series of grim discoveries. First, he tried using his hunting bow. When he shot in the direction they were traveling, the wind that Arzosah's forward motion created blew the arrows right back at him, though all lopsided and harmless. When he tried twisting in the saddle to shoot behind, he nearly impaled her wing. Arzosah shrieked like the clash of a hundred swords on shields.

"Oh, do be careful," she whined. "You almost hurt me, Dragonmaster! Those things are little, but I'll wager they sting."

"I'll wager so, too. Very well. We'll try fighting with a long spear."

But unless she flew so low that she was in danger of being stabbed from below, and on her vulnerable belly at that, his spear thrusts would never reach an enemy. Next he tried carrying aloft a pouch of big stones to throw, but again, the wind stirred up by her enormous wings made it just as likely that he'd hit a friend as a foe. Swearing with every silver dagger's oath he knew, he let her land in the park land for a rest, only to discover they'd gathered an audience of five dwarves, Garin among them. When Rhodry dismounted, sliding down from the dragon's neck, he told her to go drink at the river, then walked over to join them.

"Things look bad," Garin pronounced.

"They do, at that. Ye gods, you hear all those bard songs about the glorious heroes of old, fighting from dragonback, but the blasted bards never say exactly how they did it!"

"I don't think there is any how." Garin waved a vague hand at the other four dwarves. "I don't think you've met these gentlemen, but they're weaponmasters, *the* weaponmasters, if you take my meaning."

Since Rhodry did, he bowed, a gesture they acknowledged with grave nods. The eldest of the four, all bushy white eyebrows and white beard, stepped forward and spoke to Garin, who translated.

231

"He says to tend your mount, then come meet with him in the armory. Rori, if he invites you in, the Council can't say one rotten word against it. This is Varn Avro Krez, the greatest warleader Lin Serr's ever had."

As if he knew he was being flattered, the old man snorted in disgust, then turned and stomped off, his confederates trailing after.

"He's turned command over to Brel," Garin went on. "But he served as avro for some hundreds of years. They say that once someone shot an arrow at him, but he flicked his great-ax up and knocked it from the air."

"I believe it. You can see his mastery, somehow, in his eyes."

After he'd removed the harness and stowed it to the armorer's satisfaction, Rhodry rubbed Arzosah down. He knew that a true weaponmaster would expect to wait while he cared for his mount properly. Once she was resting in her beloved sun, he and Garin hurried across the lawns and zigzagged up the stairs to the main entrance of the city. At the double doors, the guards acknowledged them both, nodding pleasantly at Rhodry as they strode through. They crossed the main hall, avoiding the maze, then hesitated at the alcove containing the main staircase down. The guard stepped forward and made some remark to Garin, who grinned.

"He says that old Varn's already put the fear of the gods into him, and so you can pass by."

The massive stone stairs led down straight and steep to a narrow landing below. To either side of the marble floor, tunnels branched off, while ahead, another flight of stairs plummeted down like a waterfall of white stone into a river of gloom.

"We turn to the right," Garin said. "To tell you the truth, it gladdens my heart that we're not going all the way down to the deep city this time. The climbing back up again gets to a man's knees."

"So it does."

They walked briskly down the wide tunnel, lit by baskets of silver-glowing fungi in carved niches. Rhodry would have preferred to linger. Although the walls themselves were plain, made of highly polished white marble, each alcove sported carvings, and each differ-·

ent. One piece of stonework would seem to be woven of salamanders, all writhing round, biting each other's tails, carved from green and black marble so that you would have sworn they were alive; the next might be roses, so delicately carved of pink that you might have smelled their perfume. Each door that they passed was inlaid in different colors of polished stone to produce pictures so cunningly drawn that it seemed you could reach right into them, as through a window. Once they passed a young dwarf pushing a wooden handcart filled with fresh fungi mounded up so that it seemed he carried the moon. In that brighter light, Rhodry got a good look at one door and saw a garden, blooming with as many different flowers as the colors of stone would allow.

The door to the armory was, predictably enough, inlaid with a battle scene. Dwarves were storming the ramparts of a mountain town while strange warty creatures strove to push them and their ladders down.

"Trolls," Garin said, pointing. "Well, or so the old saga calls them, not that I've the slightest idea what they mean by it. But see that fellow there with the gold great-ax? That's one of the gods, though I can't tell his name to a stranger."

The god in question was just gaining the top of the wall and splitting a particularly ugly troll in half while he was about it. Rhodry decided that the dwarven gods were a bit more to his taste than Alshandra and her lot. When Garin pushed the door open and ushered him inside, Rhodry found the armory itself disappointing. Except for the polished stone walls, it looked much like any other armory he'd ever seen, a long narrow room filled with wooden rack after rack of weapons, all oiled and ready, while shields lay neatly stacked in the corners. At the far end a small door stood half-open.

"Ah," Garin said. "He must be in there."

As they walked down between the long rows of axes and swords, Garin snagged one of the glowing baskets and carried it like a lantern. They stepped through the door and found themselves in a small square room, where broken shafts and blades lay piled on what seemed to be a workbench. Rhodry could make out another door on the far side.

"Odd," Garin said. "I know he said he'd meet us in the armory."

"Well, maybe he's gone on a little further."

That door proved to open onto a landing, from which a narrow flight of stairs plunged down into darkness.

"Surely not!" Garin whispered. "He wouldn't have gone—well, I don't know where else he'd be. Rori, he must have somewhat truly important to tell you, that's all I can say. I'd best go first, since I'm carrying the light and all."

A voice floated up from below. Garin called back, the voice answered, the envoy turned incredulous. For a moment he argued; then he shrugged, turning to Rhodry and speaking in Deverrian.

"Varn's down there, all right. He says that if you dare, you should pick up the mock sword he left for you on the worktable and go down after him. He wants to see the stuff you're made of. I'll follow in a bit."

Rhodry laughed in a long chime of berserker mirth, echoing down the stairs. He found the sword, a proper hilt fitted with a wooden blade, lying in the clutter on the bench, and hefted it, a good length for his own height and reach. When Garin offered him the basket of light, he waved it away, then sat down and pulled off his boots.

"If I carry the light, he'll see me coming, while I'll be blind."

Garin swore with such passion that Rhodry was just as glad he didn't understand.

"You'll be killed if you fall," Garin said at last.

"Well, you know, I've got some of the elven feel for dweomer in my veins, and somehow or other I know that if I fail this test, there's not much use in my being alive."

Each step was narrow, and the risers seemed of different heights, too, so that Rhodry had to feel his way with a bare foot, one step at a time. As he moved past the pool of glow from the top of the stairs, his eyes began to adjust and find a different kind of light, oozing up from below, this more blue than silver. He felt as if he were easing into water, and about halfway down he heard water, too, the roar and thunder of a river, plunging over some precipice lost in

234

the dark. He felt himself grinning; he'd never be able to hear Varn over that noise, but then, the weaponmaster wouldn't be able to hear him, either. He paused and peered down. From this height, he could just distinguish a cavern floor, broken by mounds of rock and stalagmites, silhouetted in the eerie blue. Nothing moved among them.

In a few more steps, the stairs turned damp underfoot. His riding boots would have meant his death, had he been wearing them. Down ten steps more, another five, and the stairway suddenly disappeared from dead ahead of him. Moving fast would have meant his death as well. The stairway spiraled in a half-turn for some ten steps more and brought him to a new view. Through towering pillars of rock, he could place the source of light. The entire underground river churned with phosphorescence, a seethe of silver and blue that streaked across the darkness of the enormous cavern through which it flowed. Down another five steps, two more—he gained the rough floor of the cavern to find it scattered with stones.

Some of them bit into his bare feet, too, but not enough to draw blood. If he stepped just wrong, they would roll and rattle to give Varn the alarm. And where would the old man be hiding? The entire cavern was a maze of broken pillars and natural stalagmites, any one of which could hide a dwarf. Suddenly, Rhodry grinned and spun round, his sword up and ready for a parry, to find Varn waiting, right there at the end of the stairs. Rhodry might have searched for hours out in the cavern while the old man watched, enjoying his jest.

Varn nodded, then grunted out a single word. He carried a wooden great-ax, balanced with his left hand at the end of the shaft for a fulcrum and his right, partway down for the guide, because he was holding it with the blade well down, almost to the floor. As the dwarf stood and waited, his ax seemingly at rest, Rhodry found himself remembering Cullyn of Cerrmor, who stood the same way at the beginning of a duel or mock combat, the point of his broadsword trailing on the ground, so that no matter what attack his opponent might make, he'd come from below their stroke to flick it aside.

When Rhodry lowered his blade to the same position, Varn

laughed, grinning approval in the pale light. From behind them, Rhodry heard muttering and grumbles as Garin made his slow way down the stairs, yet he never looked away from Varn, who merely smiled and never looked away from him.

"Hola!" Garin called out. "There you are. Eh, what's this? I gather naught's happened."

"That's not for me to say," Rhodry said.

The puzzled envoy repeated his question in Dwarvish. Varn laughed and relaxed his stance, speaking a few quick words.

"He says that everything's happened," Garin translated. "You'll have to explain this to me later, Rori."

"And so I will, but please, tell him that I've never received higher praise, not once in my life."

When Garin translated this last, Varn nodded, well-pleased. As usual, when they spoke, Garin translated back and forth between them.

"You've proved somewhat to me here," Varn began. "I think you might be warrior enough to understand what I have to say. We, too, have tales of heroes fighting from dragonback, but I see now that they're naught but a tale-singer's fine words, all empty air. Perhaps with enough time we could find weapons to match your mount, but there is no time, Rori Dragonmaster. You had best consider yourself a scout for this battle and naught more."

"Never! How could I ever hold my head up again if I rode to war only to hang back? It's the honor of the thing! Here, I can just ride the dragon to battle, then take a horse and fight like other men."

"You disappoint me after all."

Rhodry felt it like the slice of a knife. He took a few steps away, the wooden sword dangling from one hand. Through the maze of stone, he could see the cold burn and seethe of the silver river. When Varn spoke, the authority in his voice called him back even before Garin translated.

"What did you just show me, here at the bottom of the stairs?" Varn said. "I thought you understood the thing you need to understand, if we're to win this war."

Rhodry considered, then forced himself to voice the bitter truth.

"There are times when doing naught is all a man can do."

"Just so! Very good, lad. There's hope for you after all, eh? When you and the dragon first came here, Garin told me about this strange creature Evandar and his meddling. If he can truly read the future, and everyone seems to think he can, then he must have some use for this wyrm."

"Not that he ever told me or any dweomermaster, either. He saw an omen, he said. He didn't know himself what it meant."

"Even so, an omen is a powerful thing. If you leave her behind in order to satisfy your vanity, you might well be leaving the victory stabled with her."

"Vanity?" For a moment Rhodry was too enraged to speak.

Varn snapped a few sentences out. Garin winced and gave what Rhodry could guess was an edited translation.

"He says to tell you that you blasted well know exactly what he means."

"So I do, and truly, he's right. But you can't know how deep this cuts. I want blood and vengeance. I'm no dweomerworker, to sit about idly wondering how to fulfill some wretched omen or other! It gripes my soul."

Garin translated again.

"No doubt," Varn answered. "If it hadn't griped your soul, I would have been disappointed in you. But do it anyway."

The old man turned and walked off, disappearing among the towering stones into shadow. Rhodry didn't need Garin to tell him that the audience was over.

"Well, might as well start the climb back up," Garin said.

"Just so. Huh. Last time I came to Lin Serr, I was taken blind down to the women's quarters, and this time I get to find my own way here in the dark. If I come back again, will you have any other secrets to show me?"

"Oh, not truly. The Halls of the Dead, maybe."

Rhodry felt a touch of ice run down his spine, just from the way Garin's words seem to hang in the damp air.

"Will you do me a favor?" Rhodry said at last. "If I should die near here someday, and if it's at all possible, will you see that I'm buried in Lin Serr?"

"Providing I'm still alive myself, like. I'll promise you that if you'll do the same for me."

"Done, then."

They shook hands on it with the silver river for a witness.

On the morrow, late in the afternoon, Brel Avro and the burial party finally returned. One look at their hard-set and grim faces told Rhodry all he needed to know. They'd seen what he'd seen, up at the farms, and like him, they were ready for war.

Through the silver world of Elemental Air, Evandar's army rode in utter silence. Their horses' hooves made no sound; the men were too frightened to speak. All round, cumulus clouds drifted by, towering over them, casting vast shadows. Every now and then, two clouds would part to reveal a sudden long view of a white sea—a fog below, spreading out to the horizon, gleaming under a sun that had never shone in an earthly sky. During the ride, Evandar noticed his brother growing more and more restless, turning in the saddle, look-ing round him with wild eyes, tossing up his head, laying his free hand on the hilt of his sword. At last, Shaetano could stand the silence no longer.

"This is useless! We could be lost here forever. Even if they are here, we'll never find them."

"Indeed?" Evandar said. "Look there."

Out across the sea of fog, an island lay in view, rising dark gray and craggy. Round it thunderheads piled and darkened, while light-ning flashed like scythe blades. Evandar raised his horn and blew, collecting his drifting army.

"To the isle! To the isle!"

With a whoop, he kicked his horse to a gallop and plunged off the road into the sea—or upon it, because the horses traveled on its surface like a road. Clattering and shouting, the army swept across the gray—then suddenly slowed to a walk that grew slower yet, as their horses suddenly staggered. Under them, the cloud-road billowed and swelled as if it were a linen sheet, shaken out by a servant over a bed. For a moment they hung suspended in midair, trapped by the moving ground.

Evandar raised one hand and sang an incantation in the name of the Lords of Air. All at once, a marble bridge appeared under the horses' hooves. With a clatter more deafening than thunder, the army galloped again, charging toward the isle.

"They're here, sure enough!" Evandar yelled over the din.

Shaetano bit his lip as if to suppress a curse. Menw grinned and drew his sword with a flourish. At the signal, the rest of the army did the same with a flash like lightning as their horses clattered off the bridge and onto the dark gray sand of the island's beach. When Evandar glanced up, he saw, drifting far overhead, the tiny shape of a bird.

"Look there, brother," Evandar said. "Think that's Alshandra?"

"What? I don't see anything."

"You don't, eh? No matter."

Ahead, a silver billow of hill rose, its flanks streaming pale mist. Perched at the summit a castle loomed, not the conjoined brochs of Deverry, round and towering inside a proper dun, but a strange edifice, built square, with sharp corners to its walls, and the only towers were peculiar skinny ones, perched on top of the big square palace inside or clinging to the edges of its pointed roofs.

"Pitiful," Evandar sighed. "Absolutely pitiful."

He waved his hand once in the air and summoned a gale. Slamming into the walls, pounding at the towers, it blew the castle into shreds and whirled the chunks away. Shrieking and screaming, tumbling out of the broken walls like dice shaken from a bag, Alshandra's rebels plunged in an untidy mob. Thunder boomed and echoed as they rolled down the hill and plunged off the island, screaming as they fell into and through the foggy sea, down and down.

"After them!"

The falling rebels swirled down with the horsemen riding hard after, just as the wind will drop its tower of leaves in a long spiral

239

onto the ground. Out on the battle plain, the rebels fell to earth, scrambling up and shrieking in a plume of copper dust. Their bronze armor and bronze swords glittered under the reddish light as they gathered into a milling mob, each fighting to squeeze into the center and safety.

"Surrender!" Evandar called out.

For an answer, they gabbled and swore. The horsemen charged. Here and there, some braver creature with an ax or sword made a stand; most fled, shamelessly throwing their weapons away as they scattered. Shields and breastplates, knives and helms, all littered the battle plain and gleamed, the pale gold of dead leaves.

Although Evandar screamed orders to let them go and reform, there was no holding back the men of the Host. Bright or Dark, elven image or beast, they raced off after the rebels—except for the few who dismounted and ran to gather bronze trinkets. Only Menw and Shaetano answered his call. The three of them paused their snorting, blowing horses on the edge of the battle plain and watched the rout.

"She escaped," Menw said.

"She was never there," Shaetano growled. "Or the castle would have repelled my brother's attack."

"Both wrong. I saw her flying round overhead, but there was no catching her. She deserted her pack. She has no more use for them, truly, with Elessario safe in Carra's womb and about to be born."

The two of them goggled at him. Evandar grinned.

"I didn't want this wretched ragtag excuse for a rebel army prowling round my borders, working malice while my back was turned. One thing at a time. I learned that from Dallandra, truly: one thing at a time."

A few at a time, the men of the conjoined Host rode back, walking tired horses across the plain, where the dust swirled thick over the last of the rebel weapons and buried them. Far fewer warriors returned than had joined the chase; some had wandered away, others had fallen back into a shared existence, as flames will spring out of a fire when a wind rouses it, only to merge again into the general burning.

"Now what?" Shaetano said.

Evandar glanced at Menw.

"We've chased her from the air and trounced her pack here in the land of fire," the lieutenant said. "In the land of earth, your pavilion stands, and our women wait for us. She'll not stay there long. I say we look for her in the sea."

"And I agree." Evandar raised his horn. "Back through the forest, then. We'll follow the silver river down to the shore."

"I do not understand this delay." Cadmar spoke quietly, but the tendons in his jaw bulged from the effort to keep his voice down. "Jill, I'd expected a relieving army before this. I truly did think Drwmyc would have ridden to our aid straightaway. I've never stinted him when he's called upon me, and if Cengarn falls, the whole north country's in danger."

"We did see those two messengers approach, and your men told me they seemed to be wearing the gwerbret's colors."

"True spoken, and we thought they'd got away safely, too. What if we were wrong? What if they ran into a Horsekin patrol?"

"The enemy might have caught them on the road, sure enough."

"And if they did, my allies don't even know our enemy's strength, do they? Ah, ye gods! If only we could send them messages, but well, that's the worst of being sieged, isn't it?" The gwerbret managed a rueful sort of smile. "Ah, by all the ice in all the hells!"

"Your Grace, I'll think on it, but truly, I'm not sure what can be done."

Jill took her leave of the gwerbret and started back to her chamber. She was planning on scrying, though not for the gwerbret of Dun Trebyc and his men—since she'd never seen them in the flesh, she couldn't scry them out. As she was stepping out of the great hall, she nearly ran into Yraen, lounging against the wall in the sun. He straightened up and made her a bow.

"Is your lady about?" Jill said.

241

"She's in the women's hall with Lady Labanna and the others, so she gave me leave to go."

"Well, truly, there's no need for you to sit in front of the door like a dog or suchlike."

"So she said. Uh, well, just now?" Yraen glanced about, almost furtively. "Well, I was just coming into the great hall, you see, and so I overheard your talk with the gwerbret, about his allies and the delay and suchlike. And well, I've a thought or two about that."

"Then spit them out, if you please."

"It's going to sound daft."

"I'm the best judge of that. Come along, tell me."

"Well, the first hire that Rhodry and I ever rode together, it was about three years ago, now, but it was a feud, and we rode for a certain Lord Erddyr. He's one of Gwerbret Drwmyc's vassals, you see."

"Hold a moment. Is this the hire where Rhodry had that wretched enchanted whistle?"

Yraen gaped.

"Enchanted?" he said at last.

"Well, what else could it be? Certainly plenty of strange beings thought the thing worth fighting over. You see, Rhodry told me some of this before he left."

"Did he tell you what happened during the gwerbret's adjudication? About the badger-headed creature, I mean, who tried to murder him, right in front of Drwmyc?"

It was Jill's turn for the gape.

"He did not," she said, and grimly. "Our Rhoddo has a rather poor way with a tale at times. He mentioned that a badger-headed thing was hunting the whistle, but he said naught about the gwerbret being right there."

"Not just the gwerbret. Every lord in that part of Pyrdon, because this feud had drawn a lot of lords in, and it'd killed a fair lot of them, too. They were all there in the pavilion, and the creature appeared practically at Drwmyc's feet, you see, and tried to kill Rhodry. And Rhodry killed it instead with this bronze knife Dalla had given him. The creature had murdered this other rider, you see

242

—I nearly forgot that bit—and stolen his clothes. That's how it got into the pavilion and so close to the gwerbret. We found the rider's body, and ye gods! Was there a panic!"

"I see." Jill felt profoundly weary. "And now the gwerbret's faced with Cadmar's tale of dweomer warriors and dweomer danger, and he's got to convince his vassals to ride north with him when he doesn't have much stomach for it himself."

"I'd wager a good bit of coin that's the case. And ye gods, they still must be short of men, too, the lords who rode that feud, I mean. It was a cursed bloody affair, because it all got out of hand, some-how, well beyond what the honor of the thing demanded."

"Feuds always do get out of hand—somehow. Here, Yraen, you have my profound thanks. If you remember anything more like this, do tell me straightaway? It's not daft at all."

"I will, then. It just sounds so strange, when you tell it in cold blood, like."

Later that afternoon, with Yraen's remembrance still very much on her mind, Jill received a visitor. She was working up in her tower room when Jahdo opened her door.

"My lady?" the lad said. "There's a dwarven gentleman down in the great hall. He says it's needful that he see you. What shall I tell him?"

"What's his name?" Jill said.

"It's Jorn, my lady, the one you did send me to, about the omens and suchlike."

"Then bring him up straightaway."

In some minutes, Jorn came hurrying in, leaving Jahdo puffing on the stairs behind him. The dwarf bowed to her, then shut the door.

"I've come to see if there's more that me and the lads can do to help out," Jorn said. "There's six of us caught here in town, you see, not counting our innkeep."

"Here, sit down. You've helped a fair bit already, what with the dweomer stone you laid in behind the east gate."

"Wasn't dweomer." Jorn snorted profoundly. "A secret, it is, but dweomer it is not."

He sat down in the chair and leaned back, cocking one ankle over the opposite knee, while Jill took her usual perch in the window.

"We've been thinking," Jorn said, "and we've come up with two ideas, like. You know the stream that flows through town?"

"Of course. I worry about the wretched thing every day. Or about the place where it goes out through the walls, I mean. A portcullis is all very well, but—"

"It might not be much protection when our ugly friends out there start ramming the walls? Just so, just so. Well, we've been thinking about turning that weak point into a weapon. We could do a little digging and building to make a basin and a dam. I won't bore you with the details, but when it looks like the big attack's on its way, we could back the stream up for a bit, half a day, say, then let the water flood out all at once."

"Aha! That would give the attackers somewhat to think about, eh?"

"Especially if they were standing right round that little arch in the wall." Jorn smiled briefly. "The ground on the other side of the wall would stay muddy, too. It would make for some bad footing."

"So it would. I'll take you to the equerry. He can detail some men to help with the actual digging."

"Good, good. Now, here's the second idea. Cengarn's built on hard stone, a proper foundation, like, but there's one spot to the north where our lads have been thumping on the dirt and heard what sounds like an old fissure. It's likely that we might have easier digging there."

"Aha! A sally port?"

"Not too likely. I doubt if we can make it wide enough to get more than one man out a time, you see. But we might be able to dig you a back door for sneaking out a messenger. We're all wondering what's happened to Cadmar's allies."

"You're not alone in that."

"No doubt." Jorn allowed himself a thin smile. "If a messenger's going to get out of here, it's got to be soon. They're doing a right good job on those ditches round their camp. Once that ring closes, no one's going to get out without them knowing."

"True spoken. Unless maybe to the north. They're never going to be able to enclose those hills."

"Which is why we were poking round the north wall."

"Of course. This is a splendid offer, Jorn, but it strikes me as dangerous. Cave-ins and suchlike happen."

"Well, they do, they do, but it'll be dangerous for the messenger most of all, if we can get one out." He paused for a wry smile. "But another danger's to the north wall. You never know what weakness you'll find, when you start poking round like this. We don't want to sap our own walls."

"Ye gods! If it came down—even if it caused the barest breach—"

"Disaster, truly. That's why I came to you first. I wanted to ask your opinion, like, before we go talking to the gwerbret."

"Well, let me think about it. But you do have my thanks for the offer."

Better yet, he'd given her an idea that might well prove more valuable than a risky mine. There was more than one kind of tunnel in the world. Jill escorted the dwarf downstairs, found the equerry, and left them happily discussing plans for the stream, then went to find Dallandra, who was, it turned out, sitting on the roof of one of the secondary brochs. Jill closed the trapdoor in the middle of the roof behind her, then joined Dalla near the edge among the heaps of stones.

"Was that one of the dwarves I saw come in?" Dallandra said.

"It was, and he started me thinking. Could you open a road through Evandar's country and get a messenger out to Cadmar's allies?"

"Easily, but what if Alshandra were waiting for us?"

"Imph, now I hadn't thought of that. But if I renewed our seals right before you began, it's not likely that Alshandra and her tame shape-changer would even know."

"Not likely, but possible."

245

"And the messenger and his horse both will have bits of iron all over them."

"Now that *is* true."

"We'd need a man who's seen dweomer of this sort before."

They looked at each other for a moment.

"Yraen," Dallandra said at last.

"Just so. Ye gods, I hate this! For all we know, we're sending him to his death!"

"Death's waiting for all of us right here, isn't it? If we don't get this siege lifted soon. What were you telling me about the second planting?"

"That's true. If the farmers don't get that crop in the ground soon, this entire city's going to starve, sieged or no."

They left the roof, and on their way down, Jill found a page and sent him hunting for Yraen. In some minutes, the silver dagger joined them in Jill's chamber. He stood uneasily in the center of the room and looked back and forth between the two dweomermasters.

"Yraen, I've somewhat to ask you," Jill said. "If you don't want to do this, by every god in the sky, tell me so, and I'll find another man. There won't be the slightest bit of shame on your head for turning a task like this down."

He merely smiled.

"We're going to try to get a messenger out of the dun with dweomer." Jill saw no reason to mince her words. "The kind Evandar uses when he opens roads through another world."

"I've ridden one of those before."

"So Rhodry said. It occurs to me that you know the land and the lords round Dun Trebyc, too. Do you think Erddyr will remember you?"

"He should. I saved his life in that wretched feud."

"Did you now? That's a handy thing. Are you sure you want to do this, though? You could be riding right to your death."

"There's worse things than that, for a man like me."

"Like the duty you have now?"

He shrugged and looked away. It was as much of an admission

as he could ever make, Jill supposed, and more of one than she'd ever expected.

"Done, then," she said. "I'll need to get sealed letters from the gwerbret and suchlike for you to carry. Dalla, when's the best time for this little ride?"

"Broad daylight," Dalla said in Deverrian, then switched to Elvish. "Before sunset, on the full astral tide of Fire."

"Then we'd best hurry. I've got to find Carra another guard, too, though this time, I think I'll rotate the duty among a whole squad." Jill returned to Deverrian and Yraen. "Get your gear together and a horse. You'd best wear your mail and a helm, too. Meet us—" She glanced at Dalla. "Where?"

"Now that's a good question. Are there ten feet together in this wretched dun or town where we won't be seen leaving?" Dallandra frowned for a long moment, then grinned. "Well, why even leave the stables? There's a long aisle twixt wall and stalls, isn't there?"

"So there is," Yraen said. "And no doubt the grooms will run like mice when they see a sorcerer coming."

Yraen would have preferred to have left the dun without saying farewell to Carra, or failing that, to have had a private word with her, but as it was, they said the worst of all possible good-byes. With the women-folk round her, she came down into the great hall and stood some ten feet away, watched without saying a word as Gwerbret Cadmar handed over the silver message tubes, and personally thanked Yraen for attempting this risky delivery. When Yraen rose from his kneel, he allowed himself a glance at Carra and found her on the edge of tears. With Jill muttering at him to hurry, he bowed in the princess's direction, then started to follow the dweomermaster out of the great hall.

"Yraen!" Carra came running after him. "Yraen! Wait!"

He hesitated, glancing at Jill, who pointedly looked away. He stopped, turning just as the princess caught up to them, her golden hair wisping round her face.

"Be careful." She laid her hand on his arm. "Do be careful, Yraen."

It was a fatuous thing, but what else could she say? Already the other women were bustling up, Labanna glowering at her royal charge's improprieties, that Carra would speak to, much less touch, a silver dagger in the middle of the great hall.

"I'll do my best," he said. "And you do the same."

"I will."

A squad of old women, as determined as warriors, surrounded her and marched her away. Yraen turned on his heel and strode out of the great hall.

Dallandra was waiting for him in the stables, where he'd left his saddled horse, and sure enough, there wasn't a servant to be seen. Yraen settled the messages inside his shirt and against his belt, then led the snorting gray out.

"You'll be glad of a bit of a run, won't you, old lad?" He patted the horse's neck. "So will I."

Jill and Dallandra were speaking together in some language that he didn't know. He waited, wondering if he'd ever see Carra again. He wasn't sure if he wanted to or not. At last, the two dweomermasters stopped talking. While Jill went to the doorway and took up guard, the elven woman took the horse's bridle.

"Mount up, Yraen, but let me lead you along. We're going to be walking into a mist of sorts—do you remember that?"

"I doubt if I'll ever forget it, my lady."

"Good. At some point, I'm going to let the bridle go and yell at you to ride. When you hear that, gallop like all the hells were opening under you, because you know, they just might be." She smiled briefly. "When you find yourself in country you recognize, you should be safe enough—unless you see Horsekin, of course."

"Of course." Yraen turned and waved at Jill. "Farewell."

"And may you fare well, Yraen, for all our sakes."

Dallandra clucked to his horse and began leading it forward in the narrow dark curve along the line of stalls. They had about thirty feet to walk before the wall, but they'd gone only a few strides when the mist formed, an opalescent billow, all silvery white shot with lavender and the palest blues. The horse tossed his head and snorted, but Dallandra soothed him with a few meaningless sounds. Another stride, another, and the mist lay all about them, thick and cool on his face, beading in little drops on the horse's silvery mane. Another few steps, and more—they should have ridden straight into the stable wall, but the horse's hooves no longer clopped on boards, rather thudded on dirt. Ahead, sunlight gleamed, thinning the mist. Dallandra walked with them a few steps farther. Through the mist, Yraen could see a pair of trees, nodding in a rising wind. Dallandra laughed and let the bridle go.

"Ride!"

Yraen kicked the horse hard, and the gray leapt forward, dashing free of the mist and pounding down a proper packed-dirt road. When Yraen glanced back, he saw a wisp of the pearly mist hanging over a meadow, where white cows with rusty-red ears grazed in bovine indifference. The mist blew away. He slowed his stable-bound horse to a walk before it foundered itself in the sheer joy of being free, then rose in the stirrups for a good look round. He recognized the road immediately as a place he'd seen before, but he couldn't put a name to his location. For all Dallandra's talk of the hells opening, no one shared the road with him, and no more did he see enemies in the surrounding meadows.

But Jill had warned him that there might be enemies invisible to his human sight. He sat back into the saddle, then transferred both reins to his left hand and drew his sword with his right. There was never any harm in riding ready for trouble during a time of war. Automatically, he swung the sword in a wide arc to loosen his arm. Though he saw not a thing, he felt the steel blade catch and drag for the barest of moments on—something. Something which shrieked, a thin sound like a mewling seabird. The hair stood up on the back of his neck.

"Be gone!"

Like a madman in the seeming-empty road, Yraen swung his sword round and about, sweeping it through the air to this side and that, twisting in the saddle to swing it behind him, while his battle-trained gelding walked steadily on, no matter who or what shrieked and howled and whimpered. All at once they were gone, whatever they'd been. The sword swung through nothing; the cries stopped. Panting and sweating, Yraen paused his horse in the middle of the road and realized that a child was watching him. Dressed in a dirty brown smock, the boy carried a wooden crook—the cowherd, no doubt. He stood as if ensorcelled himself, his mouth slack, his eyes wide, in utter stupefaction at what he'd just seen.

"Here!" Yraen called out. "Where does this road lead?"

The boy considered, unblinking. "Which way?" he said at last. "Both ways."

"Ah." Another long pause, then a point. "Dun Trebyc, that way." Another point. "The hills, that way."

"Then my thanks to you."

Yraen turned his horse in the direction of Dun Trebyc. As he jogged off, he was hoping that the child was telling the truth, wondering, in fact, if the child were a real child or just some dweomer illusion, invented by an invisible enemy. Yet now that he had a name for the road, he could remember it better. He and Rhodry had actually ridden this way with Lord Erddyr, when they'd been traveling to Gwerbret Drwmyc's adjudication, only a few years past.

What Yraen couldn't know was that he'd fought only a skirmish, that the real danger lay behind him in the mist. Dallandra had just released his horse and sent it forward when she heard the howl, shrieking out of the mists around her. She spun round and saw an enormous wolf, all red eyes and white teeth, charging straight for her. Dallandra leapt into the air and changed as she leapt into the image of the linnet, calling out as she swooped upward on gray wings. In an instant, Alshandra became the nighthawk, screaming again as she rose, wings beating, to gain height in the misty sky. Dallandra dropped, hit cool grass, and changed back into her woman's form.

Ahead, a dark spot in the swirling mist, stood her gate. She ran for it, heard the whir of wings as the nighthawk stooped, ran and ran, felt her heart pounding and her lungs aching like fire as the huge bird, its talons flashing like knives, swept down upon her. Dallandra leapt and threw herself through the gate just ahead of the slashing beak.

She felt herself falling, tumbling, heard herself scream, too, in honest fear, then landed hard in straw and horse sweepings at Jill's feet in the dim stables. She could only lie there, gasping for breath, feeling her ribs burn, while Jill flung up her hands and called out a strange invocation. The mists swirled, then vanished, choking off the cry of a hawk.

"She was waiting, then?" Jill said.

Nodding, Dallandra sat up, bracing herself with both hands.

"Did Yraen get through though?"

Dallandra nodded again, then got to her knees with a last gulp for breath. Jill caught her hand and hauled her to her feet.

"How long?" Dallandra gasped.

"Some while, actually. I've terrified the grooms." Jill paused for a grin. "Telling them that they'd be blasted with magic fire if they so much as set one foot into the stables. They believed me, poor souls."

Dallandra ran both hands down her sides.

"Naught's broken," she said at last. "But ych, do I smell of horses! I think me I'd best go look at my bruises in a bath."

At about the time that Jill and Dallandra were leaving the stables, Yraen was reaching Dun Trebyc. He rode to the crest of a hill and saw below, all misty in the lowering sun, a walled city spreading on either side of a river that wound like a riband through a patchwork of farms. From his height, Yraen could pick out the cluster of gray stone buildings that had to be the gwerbret's dun, four conjoined brochs standing in the middle of a walled ward, just outside the town proper on his side of the river. He sat for a moment to savor what was likely to be the last moment of peace left to him, then chirruped to his horse and rode downhill. As he trotted up to the dun, he pulled the silver message tubes out of his shirt and held them ready. At the gates, a pair of guards stood lounging against the nearby wall, yawning.

"I'm from Cengarn!" Yraen called to them. "For the love of every god, take me to Gwerbret Drwmyc!"

The two leapt to their feet as if they'd been poked with hot irons.

"Ride in, ride in," one of them yelled. "I'm running right behind you."

In a cobbled ward, half-full of tethered horses, Yraen dismounted just as the guard caught up with him, bellowing for pages. One lad took his horse, another ushered him through the huge oak doors of a broch tower. Inside, he found a great hall far larger than Cengarn's and packed with men, some sitting on the floor for want of room at the tables.

"Messages, Your Grace!" the page called out. "Messages from Cengarn!"

Every man in the hall stood and cheered as Yraen strode over to the table of honor. He handed the messages over as he knelt at Drwmyc's side.

"Is the siege lifted then, Silver Dagger?" the gwerbret said.

"I only wish, Your Grace. I managed to get through the enemy lines on a ruse and naught more."

Drwmyc swore, then called for his scribe. The page gave Yraen a tankard of ale and a chunk of bread. Yraen drank half of the one right off, then sat back on his heels and more courteously began nibbling on the other. While the scribe read the letters out, the great hall fell into a desperate sort of silence with every person in it straining to hear. Yraen glanced round, idly counting up the fighting men, picking out those guests who seemed to be noble-born. The lords were scattered over the hall with their men, at this early hour, rather than assembled at the table of honor for the meal. All at once, he realized that one person seated at the table of honor was staring not at the scribe, but at him. His heart sank as he recognized her, Lady Graeca of Trev Hael, seated among four noble ladies down at the table's end. Once, when he'd been but sixteen and she not much older, they'd been betrothed, but in the end her father had found her a better match than him among the lords of the northern border.

What was she doing in Pyrdon? Visiting some noble friend, he supposed, and caught there by the risk of war. She was still very beautiful, with her lustrous dark hair and green eyes, her full lips a little parted in astonishment at seeing him again. All at once, she seemed to realize her indecorum and looked sharply away. Yraen finished his bread and hoped that she would hold her tongue about his identity, but a small hope it was. Graeca had never been much for tact.

The scribe finished the last letter, and the hall boiled over, men shouting and swearing, women weeping and babbling. Drwmyc rose and pounded on the table of honor. Silence fell.

"Very well," the gwerbret called out. "Soon, men, soon we'll ride north!"

Riders and lords alike cheered him. He held up both hands for quiet.

"We've moldered here long enough. The muster's as complete as it'll ever be, my lords, and we'll deal with the slackers when we ride home."

More cheers rang out. So that's the delay, Yraen thought. Some of his vassals have been shirking! He rose to his knees and looked round the hall, found near one side Lord Erddyr, as stout and gray as ever, standing at the head of a table, and next to him the one-armed Tieryn Comerr. All at once, Erddyr laughed, nudged Comerr, and pointed at Yraen. Comerr smiled, more than a little grimly, and nodded. The gwerbret sat back down, picked up his own tankard, and leaned over to speak.

"What's your name, Silver Dagger?"

"Yraen, my lord." He shot a glance at Graeca, who was leaning forward to listen. "And truly, that's all the name I have anymore."

"Well, iron you are, in your soul, eh? You've done a grand thing, getting these messages through. I—hold! I know you. You used to ride with—oh, ye gods, what's his name, that berserker, the other silver dagger."

"Rhodry of Aberwyn, Your Grace, and he killed Lord Adry in that feud, some years past."

"The very one. Has his Wyrd taken him, then?"

"Not that I know of, Your Grace. He was—" Yraen hesitated briefly "—riding another message for Gwerbret Cadmar before the siege began, so I truly don't know what did happen to him."

"I see. Well, that's the fortunes of war, eh?" Drwmyc seemed more than a little relieved that Rhodry was far away. "Here, page! Take Yraen over to the men and see that he's fed. What have you done with his horse?"

"One of the grooms took him, Your Grace," the boy said, bowing.

"Good, good. Well, find our silver dagger somewhere to sleep, too, when he's done."

Glad to escape from Graeca's stare, Yraen followed the page across the great hall. With so many men there for the muster, Yraen supposed that the gwerbretal barracks would be full to overflowing, and indeed, the page told him outright that he doubted if he could find him a bed.

"I can sleep out in the ward, lad. It's not going to rain tonight."

"Well and good, then. There's a thousand men here, you see. Well, they're not all in the dun, I mean. You must have seen the camp when you rode through the town."

"I didn't, truly. I came in the south gate."

"Oh, I see. The camp's on the north side of the river."

"But a thousand men at the muster? That's all?"

"Maybe a hundred or so over a thousand. That's what the marshal said, anyway."

Yraen felt sick and suddenly weary. There were at least twice that number of Horsekin camped round Cadmar's walls—at least. When he glanced back at the table of honor, he saw that the ladies were retiring, and the noble lords rushing to cluster round the gwerbret. Despite the cheers earlier, none of them were smiling now. No doubt they could all add Cadmar's news to the size of their own army and count out doom.

"Is there any chance of raising more men?" Yraen said.

"Well, his grace called in his big alliance with the gwerbret in Dun Drw, and a messenger rode in some days ago and said they were on their way."

"Splendid! How many men will that bring?"

"Oh, lots and lots. Another five hundred."

The weariness claimed him again. He'd forgotten how sparse things were here on the western border, forgotten how few lords, how few men lived spread over such a vast expanse of forest and farm.

"Yraen, you bastard!" A familiar voice called out, laughing. "Come over here and have some dinner."

It was Renydd, Erddyr's captain, waving at him from a seat at one of the tables. Yraen shook hands, then joined him, sitting himself down on the bench opposite.

"You turn up like a witch's curse, huh, the moment there's talk of dweomer," Renydd said. "Where's Rhodry? Still in the land of the living, I hope."

"As far as I know, he is. He was gone from the dun when the siege began." Yraen hesitated, then decided that the last thing he wanted to do was talk of dragons. "I'm assuming he's part of some ally's army by now."

"Most likely. Here, have some of this pork. Once we're on the march, who knows what we'll be eating."

As the evening wore on, Yraen was profoundly grateful that no one asked him much about his supposed escape through enemy lines. Whenever the question started to rise, he'd turn it aside with a few mutters about having had a silver dagger's luck or maybe the favor of the gods. He did invent a merchant who'd supposedly given him a horse. The men round him were far more interested, anyway, in what he knew about the enemy. While the lords clustered round the gwerbret at his table, the various captains of the warbands stood round Yraen, and the mood of the hall grew grimmer and grimmer as the evening wore on. Most had never heard of Horsekin before, but none saw any reason to disbelieve him.

"Ah, well," Renydd said at last, "I swore I'd die in my lord's service, and that's that. No one lives forever, eh, lads?"

The men round nodded, saying little, and drank hard.

Pleading weariness, Yraen left the great hall early. He picked up a candle lantern by the door, then found his bedroll out in the stables. With his gear slung over one shoulder, he was looking round the ward for a softer place to sleep than the cobbles when a young page, carrying a lantern of his own, hurried up to him. In the dancing light, he could see that the boy was smirking from ear to ear.

"I've got a message for you, and the lady gave me a whole silver piece to keep it secret."

"The Lady Graeca?"

"It is. She wants you to follow me."

Yraen debated, but curiosity won. The page led him through the mobbed maze of outbuildings and sleeping men, towers and tethered horses, carts and pigsties, to the main complex itself, then round the back of that into a narrow space between two of the half-brochs. As they walked, Yraen kept looking round, expecting to find her waiting in some secluded spot outside, but the page led him right into one of the towers and up the stairs. At a polished wood door the boy pointed, then winked and took his leave.

Before Yraen could knock, the door opened to reveal a small reception chamber, lit by candles in sconces. Giggling like a lass, Graeca hurried him inside and barred the door fast.

"I've sent my maid away, you see. Maryn, what are you doing here? Where have you been? Why are you carrying that beastly silver dagger?"

Yraen sighed and flopped the bedroll onto the floor. It had been so long since he'd heard his actual name that it no longer seemed to belong to him, as if perhaps the heroic king of the old chronicles, for whom he'd been named, had come back from the dead and asserted his right to bear it alone. Yraen set the candle lantern down in the hearth, empty on this warm summer's night, then glanced round. On the far side of the chamber, a half-open door led to some other room.

"What are you doing here yourself?" he said instead of answering. "Visiting Drwmyc's lady?"

"Of course. She happens to be my sister, you know. Or well, I don't suppose you'd remember that."

There were a pair of chairs standing on a Bardek carpet in the curve of the wall. Yawning, he flopped into one and stretched his legs out in front of him. For a moment she stood, studying him. Her unbound hair fell over slender shoulders.

"I must be filthy from the road," he remarked. "My apologies."

"Oh, please, I'm quite used to that by now, married off to a lord up here." Her voice iced. "Things are very different than at court."

"Your husband's a fair bit richer than ever I would have been."

"Do you think that mattered to me? I wept when they broke our betrothal, you know. Father already had an alliance with your clan, and he wanted one up here in the north, and that's all that mattered." She shrugged, perching on the edge of the other chair. "But you never answered me."

"If you brought me here to badger me, I'm leaving right now."

"Is it badgering to ask a man I haven't seen in four years where he's been?"

Yraen allowed himself a brief smile. She waited, saying nothing, her head cocked a little to one side.

"Marro, please?" she said at last.

"There's not much to tell. I rode away from Dun Deverry because I was sick in my gut of court life. I became a silver dagger because a man's got to eat along the road, and what else did I know but sword craft?"

"But a prince turning into a silver dagger?"

"A very minor prince, my lady. Let's not forget that. The younger son of a younger son, and I could have died of boredom, waiting round for my turn to carry the king's falcon on my wrist and little duties such as that."

Utterly bewildered, she stared.

"No one ever did understand you, Maryn," she said at last. "You were always such a strange lad."

"Stop calling me that! The only name I have is Yraen."

She sighed, running both hands through her hair to push it back from her face.

"I'm glad I've seen you again," she said. "I'm glad to know you're alive and well." She looked up, her eyes glinting tears. "For now, anyway. This war—"

"I won't lie to you, my lady. Things bode ill. Very ill. When were you planning on returning to your husband's dun?"

"In a few days. Why?"

"Don't. Stay here. If we fail, if we can't turn this besieging army back, they'll be riding south, and Trev Hael's in their path."

She lay back in the chair and laid a trembling hand at her throat.

"I'm sorry, but you deserve to know the truth."

"I've got children there, Mar—, well, Yraen. Three of them."

"Send for them."

"I will, on the morrow." She rose, tossing her head in the familiar gesture of women of her rank, who reminded themselves many times over a lifetime that they were a warrior's daughter and a warrior's wife. "That reminds me. Drwmyc sent messengers to the king about this siege, well over an eightnight ago."

"Did he? Good. Grandfather needs to know. How is he, by the by?"

"Doing splendidly for a man his age. Your mother's well. I don't suppose you care about your father."

Yraen smiled, a bare twitch of his mouth, then rose.

"I won't take up my lady's time any longer. I need to find a place to sleep."

She laughed, then covered her mouth with one hand.

"Oh, ye gods, don't be daft!" Yraen snapped. "If someone finds out—"

"I've sent my maid away, and bribed the page, and besides, if things are as grim as you say, then who's to care where either of us sleep tonight?" She ran her hand along his arm. "I'm in no mood to be alone."

"Well, truly, I'm not either."

Yraen caught her by the shoulders and kissed her, her mouth still familiar, despite the years between them, and as greedy as he remembered it as well.

· · ·

258

The Horsekin camp lay bound in apathy and hot sun, while it tended those things that even the most glorious army must deal with here on earth. Every tenth man had been detailed to go fill in the old privy ditches near the edge of the camp and dig new ones. Others led horses round to the river that ran west of their camp and watered them. Out in the parade ground, where the food wagons were drawn up in a long line, Ddary was distributing rations to the warband, handing each man wrapped packets of flatbread and cheese, each stamped with the army seal, then slicing up the haunch of cooked beef they'd been allotted as evenly as he could. Tren himself handed out salt twisted in bits of cloth. When they were finished, and the men on their way back to their camp, Tren gave the rations officer a special wooden stick, which the Horsekin solemnly notched and returned. Tren bowed; the rations officer bowed. Tren moved aside to let the next captain take his place.

"Ye gods," Ddary muttered. "They do like their little ways, don't they?"

Lord and captain walked back to the camp together, but slowly, finding more privacy there in the mob that spoke not a word of Deverrian than they would have among their own men. A gaggle of Horsekin in gold-threaded surcoats came stomping by, knocking anyone in their path out of it.

"Ah, my fellow officers," Tren said. "Ye gods! We have the Overseers and the Keepers of Discipline and the rakzanir—officers everywhere you look. A wretched lot of extra mouths to feed!"

"Well, the Overseers do fight, my lord. Just to be fair."

"True. They're not all useless."

Some yards away across the parade ground, a fight broke out, a quick swirl of brawl like a dust devil. Yelling at the tops of their lungs, a handful of Horsekin swung and slugged one another. Tren saw a knife flash; the shouting changed to urgency. Red surcoats flapping, the Keepers shoved their way through the crowds and grabbed the brawlers, pulling them apart.

"Not precisely useless, my lord," Ddary said, sighing. "I wish the Goddess would show herself again. It's the only thing that keeps them happy, like."

"Well, that and an attack. Expect one soon, captain. And this time we're going to be in the thick of it. The high priestess herself has requested it."

Ddary swore, looking round him with bleak eyes.

"We'd best comport ourselves well, too." Tren dropped his voice. "There's more than one way for a man to die in battle."

"I take your meaning, my lord. I'll pass the word on to the lads, well, the ones I can be sure of, anyway."

"Let the ones you're not sure of lead our part of the charge."

They exchanged a fast smile. Tren would have said more, but by then they were walking too close to human slaves, some of whom spoke a dialect of Deverrian, to risk more honesty.

Every morning, like a warrior laying out his armor, Meer prepared himself for the next attack on Cengarn. On the carved chest in the chamber that he and Jahdo shared, he would lay out his small goatskin drum and its padded stick and his buckskin tunic with the charms and talismans studded all over it. Jahdo would fill a leather water bottle with fresh water, too, and put it next to the drum. When the alarum finally sounded, then, early on a sunny morning, they were ready. Meer had just told Jahdo to take the remains of breakfast away when they heard silver horns blow and a great shout go up from the dun walls.

"To arms! To arms!"

The sound of distant screaming from the town drifted in through the sunny window. Jahdo leapt to his feet, his heart pounding in time to the calling horns. More slowly, Meer rose, lifting his arms high.

"May the gods be with us, lad. It is time for me to join the fight as a bard's calling demands."

With Jahdo's help, Meer stripped off his cloth shirt and put on the ceremonial tunic that marked his rank as bard and loremaster. He picked up the drum, gave it an experimental thwack, and pronounced it sound. Jahdo led him down the staircase and into the great hall, where a last few warriors were settling pot helms over their padded caps and grabbing swords.

"What's this?" young Draudd called out. "Is the bard going to come sing to us while we fight?"

"Hold your tongue, you arrogant young colt," Meer snarled. "I am a true bard marked out by the gods, and my words carry some force with the savages at our gates."

In the company of Draudd's squad, they hurried down through the swirling panic of the town. Since word reached them, passed along from militiaman to townsman, that the fighting was once again heaviest at the east gate, Draudd ran his men there with Meer and Jahdo scrambling to keep up. The captain of the town guard, Mallo, was standing at the foot of the ladders up to the catwalk, yelling orders.

"Ye gods!" he snarled at Meer. "I've no time to waste worrying about you, good sir, nor your lad neither."

Meer drew himself up to his full height and boomed.

"The gods themselves have sent me here to curse those who would profane these walls. Will you stand in my way and theirs?"

Mallo growled under his breath, but he gave way. Getting Meer up the ladder wasn't easy. He had to feel his way up each rung, and at the top, two warriors had to haul him onto the catwalk. With the drum strap slung round his neck, Jahdo scurried up after. Mallo found them a place a good ways away from the heavy fighting round the gate itself, where Meer could stand on a wide stretch of catwalk and Jahdo could crouch down behind the wall and watch in relative safety.

In a swirl of men and horses, the attack was coming in two prongs, one toward the east gate, one toward the south. Down below Jahdo's position, the Horsekin cavalry were driving their infantry toward the walls like cattle. As he peered out between the merlons, Jahdo could see sabers flash among the leather cuirasses of the foot soldiers. Here and there an infantryman screamed; once a man fell, blood streaming from a head wound. At a shouted order, the foot soldiers swung their ladders up and lifted them over their heads, then broke into a trot. A rain of stones and flaming pitch greeted them.

Meer stepped forward. The wind caught his huge mane of hair and swelled it out behind him; his multitude of charms and talismans glittered like stars. He held his drum high over his head and began to strike, and with every stroke he boomed out a word, a sharp bark in the Horsekin tongue. Jahdo was sure that over the shouting and hoofbeats, the pounding of the rams and the cursing of the defenders, no one would hear him, but it seemed that out among the cavalry someone saw him. A new kind of cry went up from the attacking regiment, a shriek of alarum and—though perhaps Jahdo just imagined it—shame.

Meer was breathing in time to the drumbeats. Each huge breath he drew seemed to be pulled down from the sky to heave and swell his chest. Each time he breathed out, he sent a curse over the attackers. Jahdo had never dreamt that anyone could call out so loudly, so piercingly, could send a voice so far on such an enormous wave of sound. The defenders round the east gate began to fall silent; the attacking regiment held their place, moving neither forward nor back for a few moments of relative quiet.

In those, the curses began to be heard. Jahdo could see a horseman here or there suddenly toss up his head and start backing his mount or trying to turn out of line. The foot soldiers began to mill around and lose their forward thrust. One unit, off to the north edge, dropped its ladder and shamelessly ran. Meer chanted on and on, as if his voice were a stormy sea, pounding on a beach to tear the sand away and break down some puny seawall. The front of the Horsekin line began to eddy and swirl, moving sideways, not forward. The men in the other prong of the attack off to the south started to turn, to peer at what might be happening and to listen. On and on, Meer cursed and howled, calling down the wrath of every god in the sky or under the earth.

Out among the cavalry Jahdo saw a shove of movement—a single man riding fast, forcing his gray horse through the paralyzed line. Round him they rallied and began to move, yelling at each other, yelling at the infantry, pushing a squad forward with this new rider in their midst. The defenders on the walls began to shout in answer. Meer's voice was lost as the fighting picked up to the south, but at the east gate the infantry still milled aimlessly. Jahdo kept watching the attack and this new commander, or so he thought him then, on his easily visible gray horse, pushing a slow way forward, surrounded by a box, as it were, of four horsemen to clear his path and protect him.

Somewhere between fifty and a hundred yards away—Jahdo could guess it well out of sling-stone range—the riders in the box formation drew their horses to a halt. As the leader dismounted in the safety of his men's array, Jahdo thought he might be a human being just from the supple way he moved and the proportion of his legs to his upper body. The fellow began fiddling with some long thing tied beside his saddle—Jahdo couldn't see what, because the dust plumed as the cavalry pressed forward, parting round the four riders and the dismounted man like water round a rock. Meer paused for breath, lowering the drum to rest his arms.

"Meer, I do see some odd thing out there. There's a tall man at the back of the cavalry, like, and he's got some kind of long pole or suchlike in his hands."

"As long as he be not another bard to challenge my cry to the gods, I care not. Hand me that water bottle, lad."

Jahdo unstoppered it and put it into Meer's hands, then retrieved it when the bard was finished. Meer wiped his mouth on the back of his hand, then picked up his drum and raised it high again. Down below the walls, the infantry saw him and raised a cry, more despair than battle lust. Meer took one of those amazing breaths, pounded the drum, and began to chant. Jahdo scrunched down behind a merlon and looked out. It took him a moment to find the strange man and his gray horse. The battle line had moved up past him; except for one other fellow, mounted and holding the gray's reins, he now stood alone.

And he had strung the bow.

"Meer!" Jahdo shrieked. "Not a pole. It be a longbow! Meer! Get down!"

In his trance of chant, the bard never heard him. Jahdo sprang up and grabbed his arm—too late. An arrow fell, silent in the shouting, and struck Meer full in the chest. The bard cried out a death shriek, delivered with all the force of his chant-trance, to ring out over the battlefield. Another arrow sped to its target and knocked Meer back. The bard twisted, shoving Jahdo behind the safety of the merlons with his last bit of life, then fell, his back arching, his arms flung out, his drum falling before him into the city as he seemed to sail down and hit the cobbles, a broken twisted thing.

Down on the battlefield, the Horsekin screamed in raw terror. The line broke, infantry churning and pulling back, horsemen turning to gallop away from the impious sight of the murder of a bard. Jahdo never knew what happened to the archer, any more than he could ever remember climbing down the ladder to the ground. Suddenly, he was running to Meer's body, falling to his knees into a pool of blood to stare into the bard's dead face.

"Meer!" He heard his voice wail like a stranger's. "Meer, Meer, Meer!"

Men came running. Mallo grabbed Jahdo's arm and hauled him up.

"Lad, lad, there's naught you can do for him. Help me pull him away from the walls. You'll both be trampled, staying here."

Choking and gagging on his own tears, Jahdo followed orders. Once Meer's body lay under the relative safety of a wagon, he fell across it and keened, sobbing out a long wordless litany of grief. Draudd and the squad from the dun ran to join him. The young warrior was sick-pale and shaking as he knelt by Meer's corpse.

"Forgive me my jest," he stammered. "Never did I think you'd come to harm, good bard, or I never would have mocked. Forgive me in the Otherlands tonight, when you reach them."

As soon as he saw Meer fall, Tren slung the bow over his back and mounted, yelling at Ddary to do the same. They turned their horses and fled the field just ahead of the general rout from the east gate. Tren let his horse run where it would, following Ddary; he was weeping too hard to see or care where their retreat would take them. He had slain a bard. That the bard was a foreigner made the crime no more tolerable. He had murdered a sacrosanct man—at his Goddess's bidding, truly, but still he had committed the worst crime in Deverry, worse even than murdering your blood kin.

"They gave me no choice." He was howling out the words, not that anyone could hear him. *"She* gave me no choice."

But his honor screamed back that he'd had a choice, that he'd taken the cursed bow and promised its price, and all for his own revenge.

When the eastern attack crumbled, the men in the southern drive found their flank unprotected and were forced to retreat as well. Cengarn's defenders yelled and jeered as the Horsekin pulled back, screaming curses at walls and warriors alike. From her place on the catwalk near the southern gate, Jill studied the retreat. This Horsekin army was of a kind new to her. Although she'd seen organized legions down in Bardek, those were all infantry, and citizen volunteers at that. An army with two kinds of slaves in its rank, some willing recruits rather than mere servants, lay beyond her experience.

"Your Grace?" she said. "The men with those long red coats? I'd say they're the truly important leaders. They carry whips, and I notice that the men listen to them, no matter what the captains in gold may be doing."

"Good point," Cadmar said. "I'll see that our men know who to pick for targets. We don't have a wretched lot of arrows and javelins in the dun. We have to get a high price for each one we loose."

"Truly. Well, you didn't need my dweomer for the fight today. I wonder what made them break so soon?"

They learned, of course, as soon as they returned to the dun. Since Cadmar stayed at the walls until the field was deserted—in case the Horsekin retreat was a trick—it was several hours before Jill rode back in his company. As she was dismounting in the ward, Dallandra came hurrying out.

"Jill, horrible news! Meer is dead."

Jill tried to speak and failed. She tossed her reins to a waiting page and rushed inside.

By then, the women in the dun had washed the bard's body and laid him out on an improvised bier in the great hall, where he would lie overnight before they buried him on the temple hill in town. A few at a time, the men came to pay their respects, then all stood round, drinking and shaking their heads, that they were facing an enemy heinous enough to murder a bard. Carra was sobbing over Meer's body, and the sight of her made Jill come close to weeping herself, for the first time in a great many years. Since she refused to indulge herself, she listened instead, finally piecing out the story from Draudd and the men in his squad.

"An elven longbow?" Jill said at last. "Here? You're sure?"

"I am, my lady. I'll swear it on any god you like."

"That bodes ill."

"Doesn't it?" Draudd rolled his eyes heavenward. "Ye gods, my lady, the size of these creatures! Can you imagine just how heavy a bow one of them could pull?"

Jill could, and she winced. Out of the corner of her eye, she saw some sort of scuffling on the stairway and turned, irritably wondering who was profaning the wake. Two servants came clattering down, their arms full of Meer's possessions, with the aged chamberlain, Lord Gavry, proceeding more slowly after. Jahdo came with him, arguing and sobbing all at the same time. Jill started over in time to hear what the trouble was: some of those goods were the boy's, but Gavry had no time or patience to care.

"Listen, you little snot-faced cub!" the old man snapped. "You're naught but a servant, and your master's dead. You don't have a place here anymore. I'm minded to speak to my lord, and he'll turn you out on the streets to starve."

"Let him! You do steal from me."

Gavry swung, slapping the boy across the face, and marched on. Jahdo burst out weeping and raced out the back door of the hall. Gavry started to hurl some oath after him, then caught Jill's expression and shriveled.

"Er, ah, well, my good sorcerer, the gall of the little snot, arguing with his betters, and all about some goods he claims are his. How would I know the truth of that? Servants and people of that sort always lie."

Since Jill had been born one of "that sort," her mood darkened further. Gavry stepped back fast.

"I doubt very much if he does lie, my lord." Jill forced her voice level. "The bard's drum and suchlike will have to be buried with him, but don't you dispose of any of that other gear till you've spoken with me. Not one piece of it."

Leaving a stammering Gavry behind her, Jill stalked out of the hall and began looking for Jahdo. After a long search, she found the boy out behind some storage sheds by the dun wall. He was huddled into a corner, his arms wrapped round his knees, staring out at nothing. When she walked up, he turned his head away. Jill sat down on the ground next to him and merely waited until, at length, he looked at her.

"I mourn him, too, Jahdo. He was a great man, and a good friend, and I'll miss him."

Jahdo nodded, blinking back tears.

"It's a hard thing to lose a friend," Jill went on.

"It is that, especially here in this rotten place."

"What?"

"In Deverry. Truly, my lady, I do hope I give no offense, but were I home, this thing would be a rotten sight easier to bear."

"Well, no doubt. If you had your family—"

"That be not what I mean." Jahdo paused, choosing words. "Ever since we came to Deverry, Meer and me, I've been thinking. First we were prisoners, and we were naught until you did speak up for us. You and Rhodry, too, though he were but a silver dagger himself. And then we had a place, a good place, because Meer were a bard and I did tend a bard. But now he's dead."

"Ah. And now you have no place again?"

"Just that. I do understand somewhat now, a thing my Da always told me. We are but ratters, he would say, the lowest of the low, but no matter. We have our place. We are citizens, citizens of Cerr Cawnen, and every bit as good as the grand folk who do live on

Citadel. No one can turn us from our place, he would say. Well, there be no citizens, here in Deverry. There be only lords, and truly, in them I do see the Slavers that always I heard about, no matter how kind a single lord like Cadmar might be. And all the rest of us, we are naught unless the lords, they do give us some place."

Jill was too staggered to answer for some moments. She'd always known that the lad had wits far beyond the ordinary, but this outburst showed her the great man he'd someday become—if, of course, he lived to grow up. Jahdo glared, defiant.

"You're right as rain, lad," Jill said at last. "Right as rain. And when you get home to Cerr Cawnen, I hope you tell everybody what you've seen and learned here, so they value what they have there."

It was his turn for the surprise, his defiance sagging to a gawk.

"But I wouldn't go talking about it now, not in the dun," Jill went on. "It'll get you into trouble, sure enough, if the lords hear you."

"Well, truly, I do know that."

"Good. Tell you what. For now, till the war's over, you can come be my servant, and then you'll have a place again. How's that?"

"Oh, splendid! I do thank you, my lady, from the bottom of my heart. Never have I begrudged working for my food, because my Da, he did teach me so."

"Done, then. Now let's get your things moved into my chamber, before the chamberlain grabs them again."

That evening, clouds blew up from the south, a promise of rain, scudding before the wind in the last of the sun and sending long shadows racing across the besiegers. As Tren trudged up the ridge to the captain's camp, he felt as insubstantial as one of those shadows. No one came near him; no one spoke to him; no one looked him in the eye. Any man he met by chance ducked away from him fast. Bad geis—he could almost hear them thinking it.

In Hir-li's tent, the other captains were already assembled, kneeling on the ground while the warleader paced back and forth, haranguing them. When Tren came in, Hir-li stopped, watching as the human lord took a place near the door and the two Horsekin closest him moved away. Off to one side of the rakzan, the high priestess sat in her wooden chair. Tren wondered if the Goddess would take over her priestess's body and address her officers again— he rather hoped not. Behind her stood a squad of Keepers, hands on the hilts of their sabers.

Hir-li spoke to a young human slave, a blond lad with a narrow face, and sent him down the long line of captains. Although Tren went tense, wondering if he were to be assassinated right there, the lad turned out to be a translator. He crouched directly behind Tren and whispered the gist of what was being said in what intervals he could find.

"The priestess has already explained that she ordered you to kill the bard," he murmured.

"Good. Will you convey my apologies to Hir-li for being late?"

The boy stood and did so, then knelt again. Hir-li looked Tren's way and raised one hand in greeting, then returned to his harangue.

"The master's angry about the way the First Regiment acted when you killed the bard," the lad whispered. "He's about to call out the officers who were in charge."

Hir-li barked an order. Two Horsekin in gold surcoats rose and stepped forward, their faces betraying no feeling at all.

"He's telling them that keeping the men brave was their charge." The boy paused, listening. "And they failed." Another pause. "The Keepers will open their bodies up and take their hearts and send their souls to the Goddess for judging."

Tren winced. No one else, not even the doomed Horsekin, made the slightest sound or gesture. At Hir-li's wave, the squad of Keepers grabbed the two officers, pulling off their surcoats, then binding their hands behind them. The assembled captains allowed themselves a slight sigh as the pair were marched off.

"What will happen to the regiment?" Tren whispered.

"Every eighth man will be raised on the long spears. That's what always happens. It's all luck who. They line them up and then start the counting out wherever the Keepers decide. No one can move once they start counting."

"Ah. I see."

Hir-li spoke again, more calmly this time, pausing often to bow to the high priestess.

"They need leaders to volunteer for a dangerous mission up in the hills," the boy told Tren. "The men from the First who live through the counting out will go fight, to redeem themselves, like. But they need new captains."

Two Horsekin officers stood and bowed to the warleader. To judge from the scant amount of gold thread woven into their surcoats, they were of some low rank and eager for a chance to better their position. Hir-li nodded his approval of the volunteers, then bent down to listen as the priestess murmured a few words.

"Lord Tren?" Hir-li called out. "Her Holiness wishes you to accompany her on this raid. She says that you'll have a chance to kill the man who killed your brother."

Tren rose, smiling.

"The Goddess's will is my will, Rakzan Hir-li."

And in this case, he was speaking the truth.

The silver river that flowed past Evandar's pavilion broadened as it approached the sea. The army saw no tributaries feed into it; the river merely grew deeper and wider, though the water flowed slower and slower, until at the estuary it oozed like quicksilver through green rushes till it merged with a peacock-blue ocean, lying under lavender light. At the shore, slow waves crept up, foamed silver, and placed themselves, seemingly a drop at a time, upon pale sand.

"Downward!" Evandar cried.

At his signal, the men walked their horses into the lacy surf. The horses snorted, tossing their heads, then suddenly calmed when their hooves found sure footing. A long turquoise road led down an easy slope, down and down into the water, under the water, through the water, so that the army seemed to ride in a world turned to green glass. The sunlight dimmed as the road sank, till at the bottom among the waving fronds and tendrils there shone an emerald twilight. In the gloom, figures darted by, but whether they were fish or dolphin or humanlike was impossible to tell. Ahead, the road stretched level toward a mound of dark at the end of their vision.

"And I'd wager that she hides inside," Evandar remarked. "Menw, you and the men stay here. My brother and I will go see what we can see."

Shaetano tossed up his head and looked this way and that, but he said not a word against the plan—he didn't dare, Evandar assumed. They dismounted, turned their horses over to Menw for safe-keeping, and walked together toward the undersea hill. They'd gone not a few yards when Shaetano's foot kicked something lying on the road. When it drifted up with a flash of light, he stooped and caught a little bell, worked of gold with a handle of amethyst.

"And who would have dropped a trinket like that?" Evandar held out his hand. "Give it over, brother."

With a snarl, Shaetano did so. Evandar slipped it inside his shirt as they walked on. To either side of the road, the drifting shapes swam closer, hovering above the water weeds and waving kelp. In the murk, they could make out the flash of a golden eye here, the glitter of a silver fin there, but no one called out or said a word to them. They'd gone a fair ways farther when Shaetano's foot slipped. He dropped to one knee, then rose, laughing at his clumsiness.

"And what did you pick up, brother?" Evandar held out his hand. "It looks like a silver horn to me. How careless these people are, to scatter their roads with treasures."

Shaetano drew his lips back from his fangs, but he handed over the horn.

They could see now that the hill stood all crusted with red coral. Purple and yellow anemones bloomed among the branches; tiny fish darted back and forth in front of a silver door, set into the side of the mound, and not more than three feet tall.

"We'll never get through that," Shaetano snarled. "While we're wasting our time down here, Alshandra could be working harm to your precious Elessario, you know. I say we'd best go look for her somewhere near the child."

"Do you, brother?"

Evandar stooped down to peer at the door, engraved with strange symbols and letters. On it hung a silver ring. He was just reaching for it when he heard a deep-pitched musical note throb through the water. He straightened up and spun round to find Shaetano tossing away a curled conch, striped purple and blue—or rather, he was attempting to throw it. In the water, it drifted down slowly, accusing him.

"My apologies," Shaetano stammered. "It was just a shell. I didn't think it would make a noise."

"Indeed, brother?"

When Evandar turned back to the door, he found it gone. Coral and kelp crusted the flank of the hill as if naught else had ever been.

"Well, brother," Evandar said, "you're right enough. We'll never get in there now. Let's go back and fetch our horses."

A subdued army rode up the turquoise road. All round them, the sea turned silver as they burst through the surf and urged their horses out onto the sand. Overhead, a gull wheeled, crying out in mourning before she flew away, heading inland only to disappear in a glint of sun.

"Hah!" Shaetano barked. "She fooled you again, brother of mine."

"Not her, but you," Evandar said. "When you blew upon the conch."

With a snarl, Shaetano wrenched his horse's head round and jogged off toward hard ground. Among dunes where sea grass grew coarse and olive green, Evandar gathered what remained of the conjoint host. Just like an arch of foam will spring out from the breaking waves only to merge back when the water hits the lands, so had more of their collective lives joined together. When he glanced round, he could count some two hundred left all in all, men both of the Dark Host and the Bright. Evandar rose in the stirrups and called out.

"Very well. Soon you'll be free to return to the pavilion for feasting and song. But come ride with me a little while more, and I'll show you a marvel."

At a slow walk they set off, straggling in an untidy line across the dunes. Ahead hung a veil of opalescent mist, swirling round but strangely confined, as if caught twixt two invisible pillars. As they rode through, the air turned cool and rich, smelling of dirt and wet grass. They came clear of the mist into the rolling meadows of western Eldidd, just at a bright cool dawn, and paused their horses.

In the misty sunrise, the flower-dappled grass stretched out to a semicircle of trees round a little pond, where a few water birds glided, calling to one another. Beyond rose the emerald hills, brindled with the darker green of trees in their folds and coombs. Peace lay palpably over the scene, the sort of peace made more poignant by being so brief, a moment of music in the endless clash of life with life. Even Shaetano fell silent as if to listen.

"It's very beautiful, isn't it?" Evandar said. "And it's your birthright. Did I not promise you new bodies, all harmonious and of a piece? You shall have them here, in this green country."

For a moment, the silence hung like the mist among the distant trees. All at once a man cheered, then another, voices ringing out through the dawn. With a laugh, Evandar flung up a hand to quiet them down again.

"When the time comes, we will ride here together. For now, home!"

In a wave of shouts and cheers, they turned their horses and galloped back through the misty veil. They emerged onto the bank of the silver river and could see, far ahead, the gold pavilion waiting and the ladies of the two Hosts, dancing in a rising sun.

"Menw, lead the men home, and take our horses," Evandar said. "I must have a word with my dear brother."

Shaetano winced and swore, but he dismounted upon an order and tossed his reins up to the lieutenant. Evandar did the same.

Once the Host had trotted off, they walked over to the river and stood looking down at the water, slow among the rushes.

"I'll be hunting Alshandra on my own," Evandar said. "While I'm gone, I don't want you working malice behind me."

"Shall I come with you then, brother dear? Or will you kill me here?"

"Neither." Evandar smiled gently. "I shall leave you to flourish."

A puzzled Shaetano seemed on the edge of speaking, but Evandar threw both hands into the air and clutched the astral light —or so it seemed to him, this working, that he could gather handfuls of light from the sky and pull them down. With a yelp, Shaetano tried to jump away, only to find himself rooted, shivering and screaming at the sight of his brother's hands gushing silver. Evandar tossed this captured light over his brother's vulpine form, and as it fell, it seemed to thin out to a fabric, a shroud, wrapping Shaetano so quickly that he was trapped. Bark wound him round and stilled his shivering. Leaves sprouted from the branches of his upraised arms, roots burrowed into the earth from his booted feet. With an anguished howl, he peered out of the cleft of the trunk for one brief moment; then bark and sprouting twigs covered his face.

"You'll be perfectly safe, you know," Evandar said to the oak. "You shall flourish beside the river till I lift the enchantment. Though you'd best hope, brother of mine, that I win this little battle with Alshandra. Otherwise, you'll stay a tree forever. So wish me the best of luck when you happen to think of me."

The branches shook and rustled in rage, then stilled as the soul within took on the nature of the tree without and abandoned rage and motion both. Evandar laughed and danced, so well-pleased with his jest that he never noticed the raven, flying by high above him as she passed through his country on an errand of her own.

PRESENT, FALLING
Cengarn, 1116

TRISTITIA

*An evil omen, some say the most evil of all
those that can possibly fall into any of the
lands of our map. And yet, such is the nature of Nature, that no thing be unmitigat-
edly evil nor immaculately good, if certain
peculiar configurations of omens do occur,
then this figure does bode well for two most
disparate matters, fortifications and de-
bauchery.*

—The Omenbook of Gwarn,
Loremaster

IN THE PARK LAND below the gates of Lin Serr, a muster was proceeding. Three abreast, dwarven warriors lined up behind the red and gold standards of their companies, while at the rear, two-wheeled carts, each pulled by a pair of dwarves, formed into a marching order—seven hundred fifty fighting men instead of the five hundred promised. The news of the slaughter at the farms had produced too many insistent volunteers to deny them all. Although the men wore leather caps and carried their axes, their armor rode on the carts. With the dragon gliding overhead to scout, they didn't need to worry about being taken by surprise. What counted now was speed.

Up at the head of the line, Garin stood talking with Rhodry, while Arzosah lounged nearby, yawning hugely in the brightening dawn.

"We can march faster without mules," Garin said. "And with the farms gone anyway—"

"Just so," Rhodry said. "When we get near Cengarn, I'll fly on ahead and see if I can find the relieving army. It's got to be assembling by now. Cadmar's allies are honorable men, and they won't be leaving him to rot."

"I hope so. Well, there's Brel, getting ready to give the signal. I'd best go take my place in line."

As Garin joined the axmen, he glanced up and saw birds wheeling, black specks against the high sky. He couldn't help wondering if one of them was the raven sorceress, come to spy.

South from Lin Serr ran a proper road, made of paving stones set into thin concrete—the dwarven invention that Deverry men called "dweomer stone." On this surface, the carters and the axmen alike fell into a fast trot that would have winded a human being after a few miles. Fortunately, on this trip, Garin no longer had to worry about Rhodry keeping up with the march. Far overhead, the silver dagger and his mount circled and swooped, flying some miles off to the east, circling back, flying off to the west again, to keep watch for the shape-changer.

The watch paid off on the morrow morning. After they broke their night's camp, the contingent had made only a couple of miles when the dragon came flying back. She landed full across the road, forcing a halt. Rhodry slid down and came running to Brel and Garin.

"Ambuscade!" he called out, and he was grinning like a child. "They've drawn up next to that narrow bit of road about ten miles from here, the place with all the trees and underbrush."

"Oh, have they now?" Brel said. "Well, we'll just see who surprises whom."

"Now wait," Garin said. "How can mounted men fight in trees? How did they hope to hide their wretched horses, for that matter? What did they—"

"Here!" Rhodry held up a hand for silence. "Let me finish. They're not mounted, except for a couple of captains. It's infantry with long spears, disposed on the flat side of the road. It looks to me like they were hoping to pin you against the cliffs on the other side."

"Infantry?" Garin snapped. "How did they get up here so fast, then? Oh. Ye gods. More of that god-cursed dweomer."

"I'd wager a fair sum on it." Rhodry was grinning. "I saw a raven flying some distance off, but it never flew close enough for me to tell whether it was bird or shape-changer."

"Huh," Brel said. "Doesn't much matter. Pin us against the cliffs, eh? Well, I say we pin them between a pair of jaws."

The three of them hunkered down in the road to draw plans in the dirt with a stick. Brel would lead some three hundred axmen straight down the road as if they suspected nothing, while Garin would take the rest of the men to fall upon the waiting ambush from behind.

"Shouldn't you lead the rear attack?" Garin said to the warleader. "I'm afraid I'll botch it. A general I am not."

"True." Brel nodded. "But I don't want you killed right off, Envoy. It's going to be dangerous, marching right into the trap. That's my job."

Garin shuddered, cold in the bright sun.

"Your job," Brel went on, "is staying alive to handle all the talking and courtesies once we join up with the allies. I don't like shoveling manure, and I'm no good at it, either. You get our men in position behind the ambuscade, and then you get to the rear. Do you hear me? That's an order."

Garin considered arguing. Brel was glaring at him.

"Well, I'm not much of an axman, anyway," Garin said. "Done, then."

"Good," Brel said. "Now, what are we going to do about this blasted sorcerer? I don't want her giving our game away." He glanced at Rhodry. "Can you and the wyrm keep her occupied?"

"We can try."

"Now wait," Garin broke in. "What if she lures you off into some magical country and traps you there?"

Rhodry started to answer, then merely considered. The dragon swung her head round to join the conversation.

"She's terrified of me," Arzosah said, and rather smugly. "I don't think she'll want to get close enough to work dweomer. Besides, if she does, I'll smell it."

"Umph," Garin muttered. "Well, I don't know—"

"Garro," Rhodry broke in, "there's no such thing as a war without risk. Doesn't much matter if it comes from magic or a blade, does it?"

"It matters to me," Garin snapped. "I don't know why, but it does. But I'm not the dragonmaster here, and besides, I honestly don't know any other way to keep the witch from spying."

All morning, the First Regiment, or rather, the five hundred men, human beings all, who were left after the Keepers had imposed the discipline of counting out and the long spear, crouched in their ambuscade. The land sloped up from the road some few feet into heavy underbrush and trees, a perfect position for a trap, or it would have been for men who weren't so demoralized that they stank of fear. Since the high priestess in her form of the sacred raven would warn them when the enemy was actually approaching, Tren was free to walk among the men and try to do something to lift their spirits. Arms crossed over their chests, the newly appointed Horsekin officers merely watched, glowering.

The human soldiers spoke a form of Deverrian, oddly archaic, oddly pronounced, a survival among the slave community of the days before the Horsekin had taken their ancestors prisoner, but they could understand Tren, especially since he was talking in platitudes. I have faith in you, men, we'll redeem your regiment's honor, we'll show them how we men can fight—that sort of thing, and some at least responded, smiling a little, risking a few words back to this human lord whom Rakzan Hir-li favored so highly. Most merely stared numbly and answered not at all. Just the day past, they'd been forced to watch friends of a lifetime die slowly, screaming.

"My lord?" a squad leader said at last. "The raven priestess, she be due back, bain't?"

"So she is." Startled, Tren glanced up slantwise at the sun, which hung directly overhead. "She should have been back before this."

Tren turned to consider the Horsekin officers, who had sat down, by then, in the shade of the pines. In the heat, the forest stood quiet, except for the buzz of flies, too quiet. He glanced up again—not a bird in the sky, whether common or magical.

"Somewhat's wrong," Tren said abruptly. "Get the men on guard. All of you—squads on alert!"

In a clatter of breastplates and shields, the spearmen got to their feet, reaching for weapons. The Horsekin officers yelled taunts Tren's way, then slowly got up, so slowly that they were the first to die when the dwarves burst out of their cover and charged down the slope. In a silence more grim than any war cries, the axmen at the point swung and chopped them down like trees, legs first, then quick blows to the head. A couple of squads raced past, trying to plant and brace their spears against the swing of axes, against the rush of a downhill charge of dwarven warriors bent on vengeance for slaughtered kin. Useless sword in hand, Tren ran this way and that, trying to get his men arrayed.

No chance, no chance at all—a spearman's battle line has to be properly formed, with each man's shield overlapping the man on his left to make a tight wall; it must be organized and set before it can hold. The men of the First were milling and yelling, stabbing futilely as they tried to form a line, dropping their shields to grab their spears two-handed as the great-axes swung low, slashing men to the ground, shattering the wooden hafts. Tren began yelling for a retreat into the road and flat ground before the battle had barely begun, but suddenly screaming broke out behind him. He swirled round and saw another pack of dwarves racing into the roadway, then turning to charge up the slope.

Only the forest cover saved any of the men. On the broken ground, among the trees, the dwarven axmen were prevented from forming a tight line in their turn, which would have mowed the mob down like a scythe. As it was, the entire battle broke into a disorganized brawl—and a lethal one—as here and there a few spearmen managed to set their backs together and make a fight of it. More tried to flee, and side by side stabbed and thrust a way clear for themselves through the enemy line. Others ran for the trees and got free before the dwarves could stop them. Tren tried to make a stand, yelling at the top of his lungs, then tried to organize a proper retreat, then simply tried to find a horse—but the few they'd brought with them on the dweomer road had all fled or been downed by the relentless slash and swing of the great-axes.

"My lord, my lord! Run!"

One of the men he'd befriended was screaming at him over the general melee. Tren had just time to glance round. When he saw that the dwarven pincer movement had closed and bitten off a victory, he ran as shamelessly as any of them, stumbling uphill and toward the south, screaming surrender and hoping against hope that their enemy would understand the word. He dodged among trees, heard the enemy howling and jeering behind him, stumbled over dropped spears and thrown shields, kept running and dodging until he gained, at last, the top of the rise. When he looked back, no one was pursuing; they'd made their point and taken their road back, and that, apparently, was all they wanted.

Gasping for breath, Tren kept jogging south, yelling at the men he passed, rounding up a few here, a few there, until in a grassy valley, a couple of miles from the broken ambuscade, he managed to pull together about a hundred men of the First. They milled round him, formed up in a ragged square, spears at the ready and outward, when he ordered them. From some distance away, they could hear battle sounds, faint and dying away as they listened.

"They won't be following," Tren called out, "but stay on guard anyway."

Because they knew nothing else to do, they obeyed. Still panting for breath, Tren walked round the formation and considered their condition. Half were unarmed, many were wounded, no one had a scrap of food or a blanket with him, but they were alive. Alive and free. Free. For one brief moment, Tren could feel freedom like a taste in his mouth, as sweet as mead and as heady. He could take this troop and march north, leave the Horsekin behind and fortify his brother's dun—his dun, now—with this new warband, where they'd never dig him out again. He felt himself grinning, then remembered Ddary and his oath-sworn riders. The grin faded of its own will just as the raven called from overhead.

When the priestess in her sacred raven form swooped down, cawing and circling, the men cheered her. She'd appeared like an omen, just as he thought to break free, and in that precise appearance Tren saw his Wyrd, trapping him. He saw no reason to fight or argue.

"Well and good, men," he called out. "The priestess will lead us home again. Follow me."

With a wave of his sword, he led them across the valley, where a misty curtain hung over the magical road that would take them back to their masters. As they walked it, Tren was thinking up a good lie to save the men behind him from the fate the Horsekin dealt out to failures. They say that elven blood makes a man eloquent; be that as it may, his talk of powerful dweomer and thousands of warriors materializing from nowhere so moved Hir-li that his men were allowed to live.

"Well, Envoy, you're right enough," Brel said dryly. *"You're no general."*

"My apologies." Garin moaned. "I didn't realize how fast we'd come. I didn't realize that we were there ahead of you."

"You're cursed lucky we weren't held up by somewhat. They could have rallied against your force alone. To just charge like that, without finding out if we'd got into the pass yet—"

"I know, I know. Ah, ye gods! Ah, ye gods!"

Brel said nothing more, merely frowned into the campfire. In the gathering dark, they were sitting at a council fire of sorts, Brel, Garin, and Rhodry, while the dragon lazed nearby. She'd eaten all three of the dead horses and lay as swollen and drowsy as a snake who's swallowed a field mouse whole.

"Ah, well," Rhodry said at last. "It worked out in the event, Garro. They broke, they ran, we won."

"True, but—"

"No buts," Brel broke in. "In war, never allow yourself to worry about what might have been, good or bad. Our dragonmaster's right. We won, we only lost a few men, we've got prisoners and booty."

"My thanks," Garin said, "for forgiving my stupidity, I mean."

"Oh, I haven't done that. There's just no time to worry about it now."

Garin winced and concentrated on watching the fire.

"So, Dragonmaster," Brel went on, "the raven didn't even give you a fight of it?"

"She didn't," Rhodry said. "I don't mind admitting that I was afraid of what dweomer she might work, but when she saw us riding for her, she fled. We just chased her round in circles, mostly, until it was too late for her to warn her men."

"None of them had much stomach for a fight, did they?" Brel considered for a long moment. "Huh, well, I'm not going to judge the entire army by this one detachment. They might have had their reasons for being so demoralized."

"Just so. We can't count on this happening again. As for the raven, the dragon's right. She's terrified of Arzosah."

On the morrow, Brel sent the badly wounded men and the roped-together prisoners back to Lin Serr in the care of the lightly wounded, then reorganized his squads and marched on south. Rhodry returned to his scout duty, riding Arzosah high above the line of march. After her feast of dead horse, she was in a splendid mood, swirling and swooping with great flaps of her wings, calling back the occasional jest about what she was going to do with the raven when she found her.

"Roast her, slice her, eat her all up!" Arzosah chanted. "You build me a fire, Dragonmaster, and we'll have a fine fowl for the table."

"Roast her yourself," he called back. "Can't you breathe fire?"

Arzosah snorted, an explosion of sound.

"Of course not! What a silly tale that is! Why, if we could breathe fire, we'd burn our mouths. We'd bake our teeth and turn them brittle. Disgusting thought, really!"

They swooped toward the dwarven army, which was at that point marching through a shallow valley. As Arzosah overshot them and began to circle toward the west, Rhodry happened to glance at the southern end of that valley, where the road climbed to a narrow pass between the flanks of two hills. Across the pass hung a vast shimmering curtain of mist.

"Stop!" Rhodry shrieked. "Arzosah, turn back, turn back!"

She obeyed immediately, but turning in midair when you're flying fast is not such an easy thing to do. As she dipped down, Rhodry was thinking out strategy. Obviously, when the dwarves saw the mist, they'd halt. Should they then all try to march through that veil to face Alshandra? The army carried plenty of cold steel, after all, to work her harm, provided they were armed and ready for the fight. When Arzosah straightened out her flight and headed back toward the army, Rhodry realized that the dwarves weren't stopping, that they were marching straight on into the pass as if they saw nothing there—realized that they must have seen nothing. This mist hung thin and lavender-pale, not thick and billowing like the others, and it must have been invisible to anyone without elven blood or dweomer sight.

Yelling and cursing, Rhodry hung perilously far over Arzosah's neck and screamed at Brel to halt as the dragon glided downward. Too late. The front ranks jogged forward into the mist; moving at their solid dwarven pace, the rest of the squads followed.

"After them!" Rhodry yelled.

"Are you daft?"

"Do what I say! Follow them!"

With a shriek for the folly of it, Arzosah dived and swooped through the gate of mist into another country. Rhodry found himself flying over a broad brown plain, swirling with dust as the dwarven army below disintegrated into a shouting, spinning confusion. The sky hung low, as copper as the dust, while a great roil of clouds or perhaps smoke masked a bloody sun, huge and hanging low in the west.

"Horrible!" Arzosah moaned. "Absolutely horrible!"

"I see Brel over there trying to restore order at the edge. Land near him."

Whining and griping, she settled to earth in a spew of copper-colored dust. Rhodry slid down and ran to the warleader, who was alternately bellowing orders and blowing on a silver horn. Garin caught Rhodry's arm.

"What in the name of every god has happened to us?" the envoy snarled.

"It's some trap of Alshandra's. I couldn't warn you in time. You didn't see it? It was a mist, like, but purple, and hanging over the road."

"Not a thing. One moment we were hup-hupping up the pass, the next we were marching out here. Wait. For a bit, there, as we were marching, I thought the light was growing dim, somehow, but I thought I was just tired. Oh, ye gods!"

In a remarkably short time, Brel restored order. The men found their squads, the squads found their companies, the companies drew up in proper order, the carters followed suit. Brel smiled, walking up and down the ranks as he spoke to them in Dwarvish.

"He's basically just congratulating them for coming to themselves so quickly," Garin whispered to Rhodry. "And they deserve the praise, I must say. I—ye gods. Who's that?"

"Evandar!" Rhodry snapped. "I might have known."

Grinning in utter self-satisfaction, Evandar came strolling up to join them while the dwarven axmen gawked and swore. The Guardian was wearing the most peculiar lot of armor that Rhodry had ever seen. On his head, he had a high silver helm, crested with spikes of the same metal, while the visor, made of gold, sported a dragonish snout. His breastplate, silver again, grew more spikes, but under it he wore naught more than a tunic, judging by his sleeveless arms, guarded only by a pair of black leather vambraces. His legs, too, were bare except for high black boots, also spiked in such a way that it was a wonder he could walk without tripping. He did wear a short affair of silver plate and chains to protect his manhood, though Rhodry doubted if anyone could have sat down in such a thing. He carried a sword, enormously long and curved, with bites taken out of the blade here and there and jewels in the hilt.

The dwarven army burst out laughing. Rhodry trotted forward and grabbed Evandar's arm before he could turn them into something foul.

"May I ask why they greet me so rudely?" Evandar snarled.

"You look a proper sight, that's why. Here, you're not planning on joining the war in that—that—those—things, are you?"

With his lower lip stuck out, Evandar surveyed his costume.

"I thought it was rather grand," he said at last.

"Very grand. Splendid. But you can't fight in it."

"Oh, very well." All at once Evandar laughed. "I accept your guidance."

When the Guardian waved one hand in the air, his form shimmered and wavered, then solidified again to reveal him clothed in proper brigga, shirt, padding, and mail, with a broadsword in his hand as well, though all the metal portions were made of silver and some sort of black enamel work rather than steel.

"How's this?" Evandar said.

"Much better. Now, would you mind explaining?" Rhodry gestured with his arm at the plain. "Where are we?"

"In my own country at the battle plain, where we may find the mother of all roads. It would take our good axmen here a long time to march to Cengarn, and they could well be ambushed on the road again, so I'm taking a hand. I can join them up with Gwerbret Drwmyc and his men in but a few minutes, off to the south of Cengarn. They can march together."

Garin stepped forward and bowed.

"For that, good sir, you have my profound thanks," the envoy said. "And will you be fighting with us from now?"

"I can't, alas, not just yet. I'll rejoin you as soon as I can, but let us not forget Alshandra."

"True spoken," Rhodry said. "You're the only one who can defeat her. Am I right about that?"

"I wouldn't *know*, precisely, since I do not know every being that exists in every world of the vast and uncharted universe." Evandar paused for a grin. "But if I can find her, and if I can trap her and make her stand to face me, then—and these are several ifs of great import, mind—then I can no doubt put an end to her meddling."

"I'll pray the gods assist you," Garin said, bowing.

"The gods have very little to do with me or mine, alas. But before I go off to hunt, I'll finish the muster. One thing at a time, Dalla always says."

"Finish it?" Rhodry said.

"Prince Daralanteriel's bringing us archers. I'm about to give them a bit of a surprise and shorten their journey considerably. Come with me, Rhodry. First, let me send the men of Lin Serr off on their way, and then you come with me to fetch the prince. There's room on Arzosah's back for the likes of me."

"What?" the dragon roared. "Carry you on my back? You slimy, foul, abominable, greasy, loathsome—"

"Enough!" Rhodry held up the ring. "Carry him you will."

She moaned, flopping her head back to implore the sky, but in the end, of course, after the dwarves had been sent on their way, she carried them both as they flew through Evandar's country above the west-running mother of all roads.

Some days before, Gwerbret Drwmyc *had led his army of vassals and allies out of Dun Trebyc and started the long march north to Cengarn.* With close to twelve hundred men, a herd of extra horses, a line of provision carts, servants, and suchlike, the army could only travel some fifteen miles a day. They'd just reached Tryv Hael and picked up another five hundred riders, along with their provisions, when the dwarves joined them as well. Since he was riding at the rear of the march, guarding the supplies and breathing dust as befitted a silver dagger, Yraen only heard of these newest—and strangest —allies through the camp gossip.

"I'd heard tales of the Mountain People," Renydd said, "but I didn't know they were true."

"I've met some of them," Yraen said. "They're good men to have on your side. Not so good to have against you. How many are there?"

"Close to seven hundred, my Lord Erddyr tells me. They're camped near the gwerbret's personal guard."

Since Yraen didn't realize that Garin, whom he knew, was among the dwarven axmen, he didn't bother seeking the dwarves out. Enough men were gawking at the contingent as it was. When the army set out again on the morrow, the axmen marched in the van, while Yraen resumed his place at the rear.

• • •

On dragonback, Rhodry and Evandar flew over a misty country, where water tendrils twined silver round hummocks of green. On those they saw gardens, growing beside huts, or boats drawn up on sandy shores, but never a living soul, whether corporeal or not. Arzosah seemed to know the way. She flew fast and straight until they reached another cloud-gate, hanging white over a slow river. With a curl of her wings, the dragon ducked down, swooped through, and emerged into twilight over the Westlands. In the last of the sunlight, the grass stretched out, a green unbroken sea. Far ahead, like an islet of light, campfires gleamed.

"That'll be the muster," Evandar called out. "Take us there."

Yet in the end, they walked to the elven camp. When Arzosah flew over the herd of horses tethered out to graze, and fortunately she was flying fairly high still, the horses smelled her and panicked. Rearing and neighing, plunging and kicking, they pulled at their tethers in a frantic effort to escape. Dragons may be rare, but horses know a meat eater when they smell one. Evandar burst out laughing, but Rhodry leaned forward and screamed orders.

"Land over there! By the stream and well downwind!"

Arzosah settled to the grass a good half-mile away.

"You stay here until I call," Rhodry said. "Evandar, you and I have a walk ahead of us. Now this is a nasty little complication. How can I travel with the army? She'll panic every horse who gets a nose full of her scent."

"I'll think on it. There must be some enchantment I can work."

In the twilight, they hiked through the grass, rustling tall around them. By the time they reached the camp, the archers had recaptured those few horses which had got free and settled down the rest, but no one seemed inclined to forgive the cause of the trouble. Rhodry found himself surrounded by a pack of angry warriors, all shouting in Elvish at once. He shouted back while Evandar laughed, making things worse, until Calonderiel shoved his way through the mob.

"I should have known it would be you," Calonderiel snarled.

"Where in the name of the Dark Sun herself did you find a dragon? More to the point, why did you find a dragon? And what in hell are you doing bringing it out here?"

"Ye gods, I haven't seen you in years, and this is all the welcome I get?"

Calonderiel laughed, throwing one arm round Rhodry's shoulders.

"I've managed to forget my manners, sure enough. Here, let me guess. There's dweomer mixed up in this."

"More than either of us have ever seen before, and considering some of the things we've seen, that's a good bit." Rhodry glanced at Evandar. "Care to explain further?"

"I never explain. But I will announce that I've come to speed your way to the muster for Cengarn. First, though, allow me to solve the problem of the horses."

"Good," Rhodry said. "So you've thought of something."

Evandar laughed with a toss of his head, a gesture much like a horse tossing its mane, flung his arms into the air, too, as if he were a stallion, pawing the air with a laugh that turned to a whinny, and a toss of his head that did ripple his mane as his body seemed to unfold or stretch or swell—Rhodry never did quite see it happen, but all at once Evandar disappeared, and a golden stallion with a silver mane and tail pranced before them. With a snort and a flick of his tail, the stallion galloped away, turning into the herd, trotting and prancing, pausing to touch his nose to another's here or rub companionably along a neck there. The men stood entranced and watched without a word as the stallion worked his way across the field, moving farther and farther away as the horse guards shouted and pointed, and the herd began to whicker and stamp.

"What in the name of all that's holy?" Calonderiel whispered.

"I doubt me," Rhodry said, "that any of our gods have aught to do with this."

"What?"

"He's a Guardian. Do you remember, years ago, the autumn that Oldana died? Well, he's the Guardian I told you about then."

"I do remember. And the mad spirit wanted your silver ring."

"Just that. She's the cause of all this trouble."

The herd fell quiet and returned to their grazing. In his elven form, Evandar came jogging back to them. He paused, not in the least out of breath, and grinned at Rhodry.

"Call her back," he said. "It's perfectly safe."

Before Calonderiel could order him to wait, Rhodry held up the ring and yelled for Arzosah. In a flap of black wings, she came gliding over the camp and settled nearby. A few horses raised their heads and whickered a greeting; the rest ignored her. Calonderiel laughed in a burst of nerves.

"There you are," Evandar said. "Doubtless you have the only horses in the entire world who consider a dragon as harmless as a stable cat." He swung round and glared at Arzosah. "But you must never kill and eat one. Do you hear me, Arzosah Sothy Lorezohaz?"

"I do, you miserable pink worm, I hear you perfectly well."

"Good. Any that die in battle are yours. Never ever kill one yourself. It will break the dweomer."

"I could figure that out," she snarled. "Just because I was stupid enough to let you ensorcel me doesn't mean I have no wits at all."

They glared at each other until she looked away, muttering to herself.

"You'll have to do the same for Drwmyc's horses," Rhodry said. "Once we catch up to him, I mean."

"You speak true. We'd best be on our way. I've got a battle of my own brewing."

"Now wait a moment," Calonderiel broke in. "We can't travel at night."

"Oh, yes we can." Rhodry flashed him a grin. "Or rather, it won't be night where we're going."

Calonderiel looked at the dragon, then out to the herd, back to the dragon again.

"Well, I'm not inclined to argue with one of the Guardians," he said at last. "Where's Prince Dar? We'll get the men packed up and ready for the road."

"Good," Evandar said. "My plan is this. I'll take you into the

290

lands of men, then sneak on ahead and settle things with Drwmyc's horses *before* we bring the dragon among them."

"Splendid." Rhodry flashed him a grin. "Now that we know— oh, by every god in the sky!"

Calonderiel and Evandar were both looking at him, waiting no doubt for him to explain, but all at once he began to laugh his mad berserker's chortle, howling and choking and laughing some more until Arzosah swung her head round and hissed.

"My apologies," Rhodry gasped out. "But I've just realized why you had the omen about the dragon, Evandar. She's a weapon in herself, all right, a knife at the Horsekin's throat."

Arzosah understood first, rumbling and snorting in laughter, and one at a time the men joined in, while their enchanted horses grazed at peace, with barely a flick of their tails for the dragon in their midst.

As impatient as the combined army of men and dwarves was to reach Cengarn, horses are horses, and theirs needed to graze every morning. The men would water them, then let the stock feed for an hour or so while they rolled up their bedrolls and got their supplies stowed in the carts. That particular morning, when he cut his mount out of the herd, Yraen found himself wondering if someone had been prowling round the stock. The animals seemed restless, though not particularly frightened. When he asked one of the night guards, the lad confirmed his guess.

"There was an odd thing, just before the sun rose. I thought I saw a man walking out in the herd, but then I looked again, and I couldn't see a cursed thing. So I went out, like, just to see what I could see, and I thought I saw a stallion, a golden stallion with a silver mane and tail. So I rub my eyes, and by the gods, he's gone! I'm dreaming, I tell myself, but now I wonder."

"Maybe it was Epona's husband, come to cheer them up a bit."

They shared a laugh, and Yraen thought no more of it.

It was but a little while later that the men standing guard on the south-running road started to shout an alarum—dust rising, men on horseback coming! With no time to saddle up and arm properly, the men ran to the southern edge of the camp, formed into a shouting, cursing line, and realized that the contingent approaching was coming at an easy walk.

"More allies, maybe," Erddyr said. "That would be a pleasant thing."

Allies it turned out to be, over five hundred men of the Westfolk, archers all, with Prince Daralanteriel at their head, and best of all, they'd brought provisions and extra mounts. Since Dar knew him from their time together in Cengarn, Yraen introduced the prince to Gwerbret Drwmyc, then stood to one side of the circle of lords and half-listened to the exchange of ritual courtesies. He felt as if his blood would curdle with envy as he watched Dar, so much a warrior, such a good-looking man even if he wasn't quite human, with his raven-dark hair and deep-set gray eyes, slit like a cat's to reveal pupils of darker lavender, and with his straight stance and arrogant toss to his head, so much a prince, as well. Carra's husband. Yraen turned away and hoped that the prince's life never depended upon him in the coming war.

At the far edge of the camp, someone shouted a yelp of surprise like a kicked hound's bark. Other men took up the cry and began pointing at something. At first, all Yraen saw was the shadow, a birdlike shape winging over the farmlands; finally it occurred to him to look up. He thought it a shape-changer at first, in the form of some peculiar bird, but as it circled, dropping lower, he realized the truth from its huge size.

"A dragon! Oh, by the black ass of the Lord of Hell, Rhodry did it!" Yraen tossed back his head and howled triumph. "He truly went and did it!"

"What?" It was Lord Erddyr, who'd wandered his way. "What are you saying, man?"

"Well, your lordship, Rhodry went off hunting for a dragon, you see, and by the look of that, I'd say he found one."

Open-mouthed, Erddyr swung round just as the enormous creature landed out in the road. Dust plumed, then settled to reveal

Rhodry indeed, sliding down from the dragon's neck. With him was a man that Yraen recognized from years earlier, though it took him a moment to remember the name.

"That's Evandar, my lord," he said to Erddyr, "and he's the greatest dweomerman in the world, as far I know, anyway."

Erddyr made a strangled sort of noise, but no words came. The camp fell utterly silent, the men staring but never moving, never saying a word, never breathing, it seemed. A few had drawn their swords, but they held them loose in flaccid hands. The Westfolk archers merely smiled, watching the men's reactions more than the dragon. With Evandar in tow, Rhodry came strolling up, grinning in his usual daft way, and bowed to Lord Erddyr.

"It gladdens my heart to see you again, my lord." Rhodry glanced at Yraen. "You bastard! How did you get out of Cengarn?"

Yraen swung a pulled punch at him and hit him in the arm.

"A silver dagger's luck, and a little help from dweomer. I never thought I'd see you alive again."

"Your luck's not that good, to get rid of me so easily."

They shared a grin; then Rhodry turned to the noble-born, hurrying up to stand safely behind Lord Erddyr.

"My lords, Your Grace. We've brought you archers, Evandar and me, by dweomer as much as treaty bond."

Gwerbret Drwmyc stepped forward. "My good sir, I thank you from the bottom of my heart." He bowed in Evandar's direction. "Is there aught we can do for you in return?"

"Just carry on. Defeat the Horsekin, rescue the princess, save Cengarn. All that will please me more than I can ever say."

"Well, we'll do our best."

All at once, Evandar winced, tossed his head, bit his lip, and started to turn away, only to stumble. Rhodry grabbed his arm and steadied him.

"The iron. I've got to get away. Fare thee well, Rori."

Evandar took one step forward and disappeared with a flash of silver light. The noble-born stared open-mouthed for a long time, while Yraen shook his head and swore.

293

"Very well, Silver Dagger." The gwerbret turned to Rhodry. "You're going to explain all this, and you're going to do it now."

Evandar could remember a time when he had worn no form at all, but he couldn't, as he thought about it, remember how it had felt to be formless. He did know that life had seemed far more precarious then than it did now, that with no pattern to contain his consciousness, he might have ceased to exist at any moment. On the other hand, it also seemed to him that he'd been able to see farther in those days, farther and in all directions at once as he and his kind moved among the stars or upon the higher planes. Now he had eyes, or images of eyes, to channel his seeing, just as Alshandra had a discrete body, or the image of a body, that she could hide behind and within other images. He would have found her at once, back in the time when neither of them wore forms. Now he would have to hunt.

He stood upon a hilltop in his familiar country, the Lands, as they were known, and looked down at the green meadows, divided in one direction by the boundary forest and in the other, crosswise, direction by the silver river. He had created the entire landscape, so large that even from his height he couldn't see the edges of it. It stretched on into mist and a horizon where, or so he suspected, other lands had sprung up following the pattern of his own, wild lands with no lord to rule them. What if Alshandra had taken shelter there and made those lands her own?

Evandar took off his semblance of Deverry armor and heaped it on the hillside, then stripped off his semblance of clothes, too. As soon as he turned his attention away from them, they dissolved in a shimmer of mist. Naked, he crouched down and stretched out his arms. No tedious process of imaging for him—in an instant, he became a red hawk, crouched upon the ground. He shook his wings, bunched, leapt into the air, and flew. With a screech, the hawk circled the hillside once, then set out, flying fast and hard, for the horizon and whatever might lie under the distant mists.

· · ·

On the day after Rhodry and the dragon joined them, the army finally reached Cengarn. Some five miles south of the city, Gwerbret Drwmyc halted his army on the north-running road for the noon meal. While the men tended their horses, his grace and his vassals met in council, pacing back and forth in a cow pasture.

"They look worried," Yraen remarked.

"They should be," Rhodry said. "It's not such an easy thing, relieving a siege this size. We can't just ride in and push them off in a single day."

"Well, true. It's going to be a nasty little scrap."

"By now I'm sure they know we're coming."

"We kept a good watch out for scouts."

"Can you swing a sword and knock a raven from the sky?" Rhodry was grinning. "She's the only scout who matters."

Involuntarily, Yraen glanced up. Nothing moved against the blue, but for all he knew, the raven had flown over and left them long before.

Rather than risk a fight with tired horses, the lords decided to camp where they stood that afternoon. They did send out patrols to stand a roving guard against a possible attack, while Rhodry and the dragon circled above, watching for the raven shape-changer. Yraen, along with Renydd and five other men from Lord Erddyr's warband, rode one of the first patrols. They walked their horses north for about a mile, then cut to the west across pastureland, not that there was so much as a goat left in it.

"What the farmers didn't take to the dun," Yraen said, "the Horsekin have eaten by now."

"I'd wager it," Renydd said. "Huh—look over there. A cowherd's hut, I'd guess, and still standing."

More to give themselves a goal than for any real reason, they rode over to the circular hut, made of secondhand planks and dirty thatch. As they came close, they could smell the rot of a corpse. The horses tossed their heads and danced.

"I suppose we should go see how long ago he was killed," Renydd remarked. "It'd give us some idea of the kind of patrols they ride, maybe."

"Might just be a cow," Yraen said.

"Huh! No such luck, I'll wager. The rest of you stay mounted and on guard. Yraen and I will dismount and have a look."

Sure enough, it was a man they found in the hut, stripped naked and staked to the dirt floor, hand and foot, with iron spikes. Rot had swelled him, insects covered him, but still they could see how he'd been opened up and his organs cut out to be placed to either side. Retching and gagging, Yraen and Renydd fled back to the patrol. If he'd eaten more recently, Yraen decided, he would have heaved, but as it was, he managed to control himself.

"Ye gods," Renydd whispered. "Who would do that to some— some peasant, by the gods! He meant naught to them."

"True spoken. Well, we'd better get on with our patrol, if this is the kind of men we're facing."

Toward evening, Yraen found himself summoned to the council, which had gathered round a rough map of the city someone had drawn in a patch of dirt. As best he could remember, Yraen drew in the positions of the Horsekin's earthworks.

"They seem to have protected their eastern camp the most," Drwmyc remarked.

"They have, Your Grace. Jill thinks that their leaders are camped up on that east ridge. There's a lot of tents and banners there, anyway."

"If things go badly," Erddyr put in, "they could retreat straight into the hills."

"True spoken, my lord," Yraen said. "But these men don't look like they retreat much."

Drwmyc grunted once under his breath and went back to studying the map while the other lords crowded round. Since no one remembered to dismiss him, Yraen heard the rest of the council. The plan was simple: they would let the slower-moving carts, extra horses, and servants follow after the army, which would march straight for Cengarn. If they were met on the road, or if they lost badly in front of the town, they could fall back to a safer position with their supply train intact. If they could win and hold a position on the plain to the south and west of Cengarn, the supply train would catch up with them soon enough.

When the council broke up, Yraen walked through the camp and finally found Rhodry off at the edge of things. He was sitting at a small fire while the dragon slept nearby, though she opened one eye when Yraen approached. He sat down next to Rhodry and told him what he'd overheard.

"Sounds like a good plan to me," Rhodry said. "I wish I was riding with the army, though, instead of up in the sky."

"You would. Think we can win?"

Rhodry merely shrugged. There was, Yraen supposed, nothing more to be said than that.

On the morrow morning, riding armed and ready for war, the army reached the siege. Rhodry and the dragon left first, flying so high that they seemed only a bird's size in the sky. The horsemen jogged up the south road, traveling through burnt-out farms and past the occasional ruined village, until they crested a low rise and saw below them the broad plain leading up to the city. Yraen was expecting that the gwerbret would hold the army back behind this ridge to hide its size from the enemy, but Drwmyc waved them on. As they poured over the ridge and down, Yraen saw why—the Horsekin were armed and mounted and waiting in a rough semicircle round the southern flank of their camp. Rhodry had been right about the raven, and there was nothing left to hide.

Some hundred yards in front of the Horsekin line, a lone rider sat on his horse and held up a staff, wound with ribands. A herald. Drwmyc sent a herald of his own out to meet him, but he kept his men moving. They swept downhill and poured out onto the plain to the south and west, forming up in a rough semicircle of their own, elven archers at the left, the northwest point, dwarven axmen at the southeast, the right. Both sides had laid claim to a position now. When the battle came, and Yraen had no doubt that parley would fail, each side would try to force the other back, either into their camp or into a full rout.

In the midst of the two lines, the heralds met. In the bright and gusty noon, they parleyed for a long time, far longer than heralds usually did, or so it seemed. The Deverry army at last got a clear sight of what they were facing—massive men, heavily armored with solid breastplates worked into their chain mail; massive horses, caparisoned in studded leather. Long arms, long slashing sabers— they'd have the reach, all right, when the fighting started.

Yraen soothed his nervous horse and looked up at the town. From his position, near the middle of the crescent but well back, he could see the dun crowning the cliff, and a tiny pennant, defiant in the wind. The entire town would know their relief had arrived by now. Carra would be at a window up in the broch, he supposed, praying for her alien husband's safety. He looked up and down the line, found Prince Daralanteriel, riding with the gwerbret. The archers, then, would have Calonderiel in command while the prince, like the gwerbret, kept himself safe for as long as possible. Yraen only wished he could hate Dar; he tried, but the hatred was a thing of words only, running in his mind: Carra's husband.

At last, the two heralds bowed to each other and turned their horses, kicking them to a fast trot as they rode back to their respective commanders. All up and down the allies' line, men gathered themselves, loosening swords, pulling javelins, waiting for the signal to charge. The Horsekin drew their sabers with a flash of silver light, but they, too, waited, watching for the heralds in case they should ride out again. The silence lay as deep as water over the plain. Yraen could guess that the Horsekin had delivered the same demand as before: turn over Princess Carra's dead body. His guess was confirmed by a sudden howl of rage that came from someone near the gwerbret. Yraen turned to look and saw Prince Daralanteriel swinging his horse toward the enemy as if he would charge them alone. A lord grabbed his highness's reins just in time and hauled him back.

The moment hung a moment more, the silence, the waiting in the hot bright sun. Drwmyc raised his hand and signaled; his captain raised a horn and blew. With a howl, the Deverry line sprang forward. Javelins flew and winked in an arching shower of death as the Horsekin line charged to meet them, a slower charge of burdened horses, kicked to a fast trot. Caught toward the rear on high ground, Yraen had a chance to see the battle develop.

Off to the left, the Westfolk loosed a level flight of hunting arrows. Pierced through their caparisons, the first rank of horses reared and screamed, stumbling and falling. The second rank of the Horsekin charge tried to pull up and failed. More horses went down, kicking and rolling upon their riders as the arrows hissed forward again. The Horsekin cavalry was forced to pull to the southeast and tighten their line, allowing the Deverry men to surround what became a sloppy wedge. Yet as he jogged his horse downhill, searching for a way into the actual fighting, Yraen could see men falling as the heavy cavalry slammed into the Deverry line. Longer reach, longer weapons, heavy horses, armored themselves—they told badly when the charges became, as they always did, a thing of single combats, wheeling and dancing for position on the field.

The weight of their horses' slow charge pulled a couple of the Horsekin riders straight through the Deverry line. Riding hard, Yraen galloped for a man on a black coming straight for him. As Yraen wheeled his horse, he got a glimpse of blue and purple tattoos on the chin and jaw below an iron helmet with a long nasal bar. They swung, parried, trading blow for blow while he swore and yelled and Yraen stayed silent, flicking away the enemy's saber with his heavier broadsword until, in frustration, the man tried a hard side slash that left his right unguarded. Yraen caught the strike on his shield and slashed in to catch him solidly on the right arm. Blood welled through his mail as the bone snapped. Grunting in pain, he dropped the saber and tried to turn his horse. Yraen hesitated for the briefest of moments—normally he would have slashed at the mount, but the caparison baffled him. Instead, he risked a reach and a stab, caught the Horsekin warrior on the back, but his blade slid off heavy mail, turned so easily that he went sick with dread. He pulled back and let the man go, not out of fear for his own life, but for the battle, for the war.

Yraen glanced round and tried for an overview of the Deverry line. They were being pushed back. He knew it more by instinct than by sight as he paused his blowing horse. He rose in the stirrups and looked round, but in the dust and chaos he could get no clear view of the battle. All he could tell was that the center of the line had fallen back and now made a desperate sort of stand close to the rise of hill behind them.

"Ah, shit!"

Yraen sat back, kicked his horse to a lope, and headed for the fighting. Again, instinct more than sight made him glance up at the sky. Like a winged stone, the dragon dropping down. He felt rather than heard himself laugh and let his horse first slow to a walk, then amble to a stop, while he watched the dragon dive with her wings swept back straight for the thick of the Horsekin line. Yraen could imagine her roaring, but he heard nothing over the battle noise and the sudden whinnies of terrified horses. She leveled off, skimming over the cavalry with huge beats of her wings, while below her the enemy horses went mad.

Kicking, neighing, bucking, rearing, shrieking with that ghastly sound a horse only makes in agony—the Horsekin line broke, turned into a whirlpool of yelling riders and frenzied horses. Yraen had no time to wonder why his horse—why all the Deverry horses—treated the dragon with complete indifference. Screaming war cries, the Deverry line reformed and charged, slamming into the flank of chaos, as Arzosah flew upward, swung round in a turn, and dived again. As Yraen trotted forward, looking for a gap through which he could reach the front line, he could see Horsekin riders thrown, Horsekin lying trampled or desperately trying to get to their feet and run while Deverry men cut them down with the slash of a sword. Alien horns called out, sounding a retreat. The Horsekin who could control their horses turned and fled, charging for the gaps in their earthworks, where foot soldiers waited with spears to cover their retreat.

Deverry riders followed, slashing, harrying, killing where they could. Yraen rode down one unmounted cavalryman and killed him with a blow across the back of the neck before the Horsekin could turn and fight. He charged past the corpse, realized he'd gone too far, and pulled his horse's head round fast, peeling off to the east as the earthwork rose in front of him. He got a quick impression of a fringe of long spears as he swung past, then circled back to the safety of his own line.

The west and south of the field was theirs. On silver horns, the captains were sounding the signal to hold and stand as the Horsekin fled behind their circling earthworks to the north and east. Since Yraen could see the gwerbret's banner planted over it, he could guess that Drwmyc's warband had captured the half-finished ditch and mound to the southwest, lying some distance from the base of the steep cliffs that rose up to the dun. Yraen let his horse pick its way across the battleground, littered with the dead and wounded, and stared up at the sky. At last, he saw the dragon, flying fast and straight toward her own lines from the north. She circled round Cengarn once, then flew on to land behind the Deverry army. As she settled to the ground, a roar of cheers greeted her, and in answer, she rose for a brief moment to her hind feet, as if in a bow.

Since both Jill and Dallandra could scry out Yraen, the two dweomermasters had been keeping track of the relieving army's progress and knew, therefore, approximately when it would arrive at the siege. Before the battle started, they went up to the roof of the main broch and watched, waiting to transform into bird form if they needed to. Neither the raven nor Alshandra appeared.

"Odd," Dallandra said. "You'd think Alshandra would be here to inspire her men if naught else."

"True spoken. Perhaps the raven went to fetch her."

Below them, men crowded the walls of both town and dun to watch the battle. Until the dragon's swoop brought the relieving army the victory, Jill watched with a growing sense of dread. She knew enough about war craft to realize that without the dragon's aid, the relievers would have lost, and badly. As the Horsekin line broke, and their mounts began bolting and panicking, the men on the walls cheered and screeched in victory. Jill found herself shaking her head over and over in a long no.

"Oh, ye gods," Jill said. "We'll drive them off this time, if we're lucky, but the next?"

"What do you mean? The next?"

"The Horsekin know where Deverry is now, and they think a goddess has promised the country to them. They may well lose this siege, but what about when they come back? This war will look like a little skirmish. If Drwmyc and his men crush this lot, they might not return for years, but return they will."

For a moment, she was afraid that Dallandra would faint, she turned so pale and weak. Jill caught her arm in a strong grip.

"I'll be all right," Dallandra whispered. "It's just that here I was thinking we were saved, and there's not but worse trouble ahead."

"Well, it may not be for years and years. For all I know, neither of us will live to see it."

"Especially if they can't break this siege."

And, Jill supposed, it might well be that the relieving army would yet fail. Even though the Horsekin had ceded the western half of Cengarn's valley, their position to the east was still strong, especially if Alshandra arrived to help them defend it. She glanced up and saw the dragon circling the dun. On her back rode a man, a tiny figure at this distance, but she could guess it was Rhodry. When she flung up her arm in a wave, she could just make out him waving back. She laughed and waved again as the pair flew off.

"Well," Jill said to Dallandra, "that's why Evandar had the omen of the dragon."

"So it would seem."

"What's wrong?"

"I just had the strangest feeling round my heart, watching them. For Rhodry's sake, I mean, not ours. The beast will bring Cengarn naught but good."

"But Rhodry harm?"

Dallandra tried to speak, her lips half-parted as she shook her head. "I don't know," she said at last. "The omens aren't clear enough to speak. Harm and yet not harm. I just don't know."

They left the roof and hurried down to the great hall, where everyone was talking and shaking their heads over the wondrous creature they'd just seen.

Evandar in hawk form flew over the Lands, past the forest and the beacon tree, over the silver river, above the semblances of cities and the long green meadows. As he flew he called out, a harsh cry from the hawk's mouth, yet it was still her name. She would have to come to her name as long as she was in his dominion or in the lands that had once been Shaetano's, and when she did not come, he could assume that she'd taken herself away from them. He flew on farther, faster, heading for the misty horizon that he'd seen from the hill. Never did it come closer, not that horizons do come closer in our world, but in Evandar's lands there had been a time, when he was first creating them, that the horizon had marked an end that could be reached.

Below him, the mist lay with an edge like silver ferns, covering what had once been the horizon of the Lands. Through it he could see nothing. With a tuck of wings he dove, swooping through the mist, leveling just under its covering in a gray light hanging over a gray country, where huge boulders pushed up through thin soil, and dust blew in little scurries to match the mist. Yet here and there, he saw patches of green, lichen on a rock here, thin grass there. Little eyes gleamed in cracks and crannies; he heard little snarls and scrabblings. On and on it stretched, the gray and the broken rock. He began to circle back, knowing that Alshandra would never endure such a place.

His circling brought him to a dead tree, the black and stripped remains of a pine or some such straight-growing sort. Sitting with his back propped against it was an old man, dressed in shabby brown clothes; his skin, or his image of it, at least, was brown as well. He was paring an apple with a bent old knife; every now and then he would cut off a slice and eat it, but it seemed that he would never come to the end of the fruit, because the slice and the peel would grow back as soon as he'd done with them. Evandar's curiosity won a brief battle. He circled again and landed on a boulder nearby. The old man considered him for a moment with merry black eyes, then offered him a slice of apple. Evandar shivered his feathers and changed into elven form, then took the fruit. Never had he tasted a thing so sweet or so fresh.

"Hah," the old man said. "Well, now, you're a surprise."

"You're one yourself, good sir. May I ask what you're doing in this wretched place?"

"Doing what I can to make it less so. And what about you?"

"I'm looking for my wife. Sometimes she flies as a nighthawk, sometimes she walks as one of the Westfolk, but her name is Alshandra, and she's quite mad."

"Hah. Can't say I've seen her. I've seen no one since I came into this country. Except for you, of course."

"If you care to get out of here, watch the way I fly. There's a green land in that direction, with a river of silver and some meadows that I am, I'll admit, rather proud of. Come take our hospitality, if you'd like."

"Very kind of you, and perhaps, one of these days, I might do so."

Evandar stretched out his arms, shook himself all over, and changed into the hawk. He leapt from the rock and flew, heading back to the Lands, so intent upon finding Alshandra that he never gave another thought to the old man or wondered who he might be.

All day, with the elven archers and the dragon on guard, the relieving army worked furiously to dig itself into its new position behind some hasty ditches of its own. Once the supply train caught up with them, they barricaded the rear of the camp further with the carts. It was late in the evening before the men had time to talk among themselves, and then Yraen found out that their victory was in some ways a defeat.

"Well, look at their position now," Rhodry said. "As snug as a bear in its den, they are, with the hills round their back to the north and the ditches in front of them. They still block the city gates, all three of them, north, east, and south. What are we going to do? Haul ourselves up and down the western cliffs in baskets?"

Yraen peered through the gathering dark. Against the stars, he could see the rise of the city, sailing like a ship over the exhausted armies below. Carra's in there, he thought. And her blasted husband's out here. He felt sick, realizing how fiercely he was wanting Dar to die in the coming battle. No honor left. Just a cursed silver dagger, aren't you? Not a prince anymore at all. You couldn't have her anyway. She's carrying a royal child.

"Are you listening to me?" Rhodry snapped.

"What? My apologies. Just thinking."

"That's a bad thing for a fighting man to do."

Yraen smiled at the familiar jest.

"I was talking about our situation," Rhodry went on. "It's like a siege inside a siege. Well, if the bastards have water in their camp, anyway."

"I'm sure they dug a spring or two just in case this happened. From what I've seen of them, they don't leave one cursed thing to chance."

"Well, there we are, then. What worries me are those hills." Rhodry made a wide sweep with his arm. "I wish I'd paid more attention to them, like, before the war started. They could retreat through them for all I care, but what I'm wondering is, can they get enough men out that way to fall on us from behind?"

"Circle round, you mean? Good question."

And one, it turned out, that the noble-born had been wondering over themselves. It wasn't long before Lord Erddyr came through the camp, calling for volunteers to do a little night scouting. Rhodry stepped forward immediately. With his half-elven sight, he could see well in darkness, especially since the moon was half-full.

"And from a height I should be able to get the lay of the land for you, my lords."

"True spoken, Silver Dagger," Erddyr said. "Can that, er, beast of yours fly at night?"

"Well enough for a simple task like this."

Yet in the event, there was a limit to what Rhodry could discover. When he returned from a pass over the northern hills, he drew out the general shape of the land for the council of lords, but from his height, he hadn't been able to distinguish important details, such as whether the ground lay broken or smooth, or how thick the forest cover grew.

"We'll have to send scouts after all," Erddyr said. "At least you've given them an idea of what they'll be facing."

"I'll go on foot," Rhodry started to say. "I—"

"You'll do naught of the sort! You're the only man here who can ride that thing, and it proved its worth today."

"She, my lord. Not an it, but she."

"As you wish." Erddyr's smile was a bit glazed. "But you're staying here anyway."

"I'll go," Yraen said. "I've some idea of the country round here."

"Good," Erddyr said. "I'll find a few others, too. But listen, lad. Just get a quick idea of the lay of the land, how many wretched trees we've got to deal with, things like that. Don't risk too much. It's only the first night, and for all we know, we're in for a long stand-off of it."

By then, the wheel of stars marked out midnight. Yraen took his sword off his belt, because it might clank and give him away, though he kept his dagger, and he left his mail behind for the same reason. He rubbed ashes from a cold fire over his face and hands to darken them, then set out from the easternmost edge of the Deverry camp. With the sharp bulk of the ridge, fringed with tents, so clear against the stars, he had a good idea of where he was and where he was going. Since the woods here on the flat had been coppiced and the ground gleaned for every possible stick of dead wood, he could stay hidden and silent among the trees. He angled off to the south, following the line of the ridge but a good safe distance away, until he reached the flank of the low hill into which the actual ridge rose.

There he hesitated. He could see by the sudden immensity of shadow that about halfway up the hill the woods turned shrubby again. He could move there without being seen, but staying silent was another matter. He climbed the hill to the edge of the tended woods, found a low stone wall to mark the difference, and walked along it for a ways back in the direction of the Horsekin camp. He could see that with so much ground cover, the enemy wasn't going to be able to bring any kind of cavalry force out of their camp in this direction. But how far did the camp extend? He paused, considering. By sticking to the wall and keeping low, he would be impossible to see, and the footing was still good. It would do no harm to go on for a ways more.

Yet something stopped him, a feeling, a sudden sensation that the danger had just magnified itself. He dropped and crouched behind the wall, then began to move, hunkered down awkwardly, back in the direction he'd come. All at once, he heard them, crashing through the woods, men running downhill and toward him. He got up and ran, angling through the woods away from the wall, dodging through the dark shapes of trees in the lighter darkness of a starry night. He could hear them coming, didn't dare risk a look back, dodged off at an angle, heard them follow precisely. He could see ahead to the flat, he was coming clear at last, when something thrown struck him in the back.

Nothing bladed, just a weight, but it smacked the air from his lungs and made him stumble, gasping and tripping. From behind, he heard a shout and then a laugh of victory as he went down to his knees. He staggered to his feet, tried to run, wondered if the men chasing him could see in the dark like Rhodry, but the hands that grabbed his arm didn't belong to some man of the Westfolk. He twisted free, but another Horsekin clutched his shirt, and the first smacked him hard across the head with the haft of a spear. Yraen fell, and this time he lay still, gasping into the grass, feeling blood run down the side of his face, while his captors chattered above him in a language he'd never heard.

They waited, briefly, then hauled him up, one on either arm, and began to half-drag him up the hill while he staggered and tried to keep up. At the top of the ridge, another Horsekin waited with a lantern. He held it high in one hand and pointed to his long thin nose with the other, grinning as he sniffed the air with little noises.

Yraen understood; they'd smelled him out, not seen him, nor even needed to see or hear a scout to find one. The lantern light seemed to burn into his eyes and make him sick to his stomach as his captors dragged him along through the tents to a little clearing among them.

Other Horsekin came running, chortling, talking fast. His captors threw him onto his back in the dirt; one kicked him in the stomach for good measure. The man with the lantern called out, glancing round him as if looking for someone. When a Horsekin walked into the lantern light carrying a long spear, they all laughed.

"Wait!" A human man, vaguely familiar, stepped forward. "I claim this man's death. He helped kill my brother."

Dazed and bleeding, Yraen could only stare at him. Brother? Of course! He looked much like Lord Matyc, the same moonlight-pale hair, the same gray eyes, the same narrow face so tightly controlled that it might have been carved from stone. Yraen's captors stared puzzled at the fellow, as if they hadn't understood a word of what he'd said, but the guard carrying the long spear fell back as another Horsekin made his way through the circle. This one wore a long gold-threaded surcoat over his tunic and boots; a welter of charms glittered in his hair. Yraen could guess him an officer.

"I'll defer to you, Tren," he growled, then spoke in his own language.

All the Horsekin began babbling at once while Tren crossed his arms over his chest and glared at Yraen. Yet Yraen found it hard to believe that the lord hated him; the stance, the glare were as real as some pose a bard adopts while he sings a ballad. They seemed, however, to convince the Horsekin leader, who shouted his men into silence.

"Well, then," the leader remarked in an oddly conversational tone, "if he helped trap your brother, he's yours. Kill him now, any way you want."

"Rakzan Hir-li, I choose the way of my own people."

The rakzan bowed in a passable imitation of Deverry courtesy and stepped aside.

Tren drew his dagger and strode forward. With a wrench of his body, Yraen managed to get kneeling; he would have preferred to die on his feet, but there was no help for that now. Tren knelt just behind and to the left of him, grabbed his hair, and jerked his head back. Yraen concentrated on the pain and stared up at the night sky. Beyond the flaring torchlight, he could see the moon and a few glimmering stars. It pleased him that his last sight of the world would be the stars. Tren pulled him back to brace his body against his own chest.

"I'm sorry," Tren whispered. "But it's better this way. The way they treat their prisoners . . ."

Yraen remembered the staked cowherd and smiled. The dagger swung and bit. A red fire of pain sprang up and fell over him like a winding sheet. His last thought was Carra's name, but his lips refused to form the word before the darkness claimed him.

Tren wiped his dagger on the dead prisoner's shirt, then thrust the body away, letting it flop into the dirt. He rose to find himself face to face with Hir-li, who had taken the dead man's belt from the guards.

"Very cleanly done," the rakzan said. "You have a nice hand for these things, Lord Tren. Here. You'll want this."

Tren took the proffered silver dagger, hefting it in one hand.

"My thanks. This is how I knew who he was. Our spy told me about two silver daggers. One set up the fight, she said. The other did the killing."

"I see." Hir-li nodded, swallowing the lie. "Well, you have half your revenge, then, and a trophy."

Tren, however, kept the silver dagger not more than a scant hour. He was sitting in his tent, examining it by lamplight, wondering who the poor bastard was that he'd slain to spare him the long spear, and wondering as well why he'd done so, when Raena's maidservant shoved back the tent flap.

"Her Holiness summons you." She pointed one finger at the dagger. "Bring that."

Tren found her alone in the tent. Dressed only in a linen tunic, she was pacing back and forth in the silvery moon glow, her hair spread out round her shoulders, and it seemed that the long black mane had come alive, swirling and snapping in some private breeze. When she saw the dagger, she smiled, grabbed it in both hands, and held it up to catch the dweomer light. He knelt, thinking that the Goddess was upon her, but her voice sounded human enough, giggling like a lass who's been given a courting gift.

"Name your price for this, my lord."

"Take it as a gift to you and our Goddess both."

She laughed and rubbed the flat of the blade over her breasts, the edge so near her nipples that he winced. She saw the gesture and smiled as she lay the dagger down on a wooden chest.

"My thanks, then," she said, "and a pretty gift it is. I only wish I'd seen him die. Do you know who that was?"

Tren debated.

"I don't," he said at last. "That he was a silver dagger was enough reason for me to hate him."

"He was Rhodry Maelwaedd's friend. I'm sure he had a great deal to do with your brother's death."

Tren laughed himself, one short bark that he'd all unwittingly told Hir-li the truth.

"I shall treasure this blade," Raena went on. "I shall savor it, I shall brood over it, I shall work dweomer with it, and someday I shall have revenge with it."

"No doubt." Tren rose with a bow in her direction. "I have every faith that Her Highness will be successful."

"Do you? Good." She reached out and caught his arm. "There's blood all over your sleeve, Tren."

"So there is, Your Holiness. My apologies, but slitting a man's throat is a messy job."

"No need to apologize." She looked up with a soft smile, her eyes suddenly bright. "Don't be in such a hurry to leave me, my lord. You shall have a reward for this."

"Tonight, Your Holiness, my place is with my men. What if there's a night attack on the camp?"

"There won't be. The Goddess would have warned me."

He considered excuses, realized how fast her gleeful mood could turn to rage, then took her by the shoulders and kissed her on the mouth. With a little sob, she rubbed herself against him.

"My heart aches to say this, Silver Dagger," Erddyr said, *"but if Yraen's not here by now, he's not coming back. The same goes for the others."*

"None of them have come back?"

"None. It bodes ill."

Rhodry nodded, staring at the lightening sky.

"One more reason for blood." Rhodry drew his silver dagger and held it up to catch the dawn. "Yraen, you'll be avenged. I promise you that."

He tipped back his head and began to laugh, felt the laugh bubbling and shrieking out of his mouth while men turned to stare, and the dragon swung her head round and hissed. Lord Erddyr earned the admiration of every man in the camp by grabbing Rhodry by the shoulders and shaking him when he had a dagger in his hand and the fit upon him.

"Stop it! Stop it, man! That's an order!"

Rhodry felt the laughter leave him. For a moment, he stood trembling in Erddyr's hands and wondered who this red-faced lord might be. Then the name came back; he shook free and let out his breath in a long sigh.

"My apologies, my lord."

"You're forgiven." Erddyr wiped his forehead with the side of his hand. "You'd best go draw your rations. The sun's getting itself up in the blasted sky and all that."

"So it is. Think they'll attack today?"

"Who knows? I wouldn't if I were them. But ye gods, they're not even human. Who knows what they'll do?"

"Just so, my lord. Well, then. I think me we'd best decide what we want them to do, and make them do it. We'd best settle this affair soon, if you don't mind me saying so."

"I know that, we all do. The countryside's been stripped bare for this war as it is. Once these supplies are gone, well, there we are. But if they decide to sit on their behinds back of those earthworks, I don't know what we're going to do about it."

"Drive them out, my lord."

"What? Are you daft? How—" All at once, Erddyr grinned. "How, indeed? Send a ferret into the hole to drive the rats out, eh?"

"Just that, my lord."

Both men turned to look at Arzosah, stretching luxuriously in the morning sun.

"I'll just go have a bit of a talk with the gwerbret," Erddyr said. "Come with me, Silver Dagger. We'll just work out the details, like."

Although Tren was expecting a full council of war that morning, none was ever called. The Keepers of Discipline hurried through a suddenly crowded and undersupplied camp to estimate the amount of food left, while the captains themselves were pressed into service to keep order at the three small wells. Tren wondered how long it would be before they ran dry. The stream that flowed from Cengarn's walls now lay just outside their camp, and the good-sized river to the west might as well have been on the moon for all the good it would do them.

A couple of hours after sunrise, Rakzan Hir-li had Tren summoned. With a squad of guards trailing at a discreet distance in case of a Deverry attack from some unexpected direction, they walked up the east ridge and climbed the flank of the hill.

"We cannot stay here like this long," Hir-li remarked. "We Horsekin cannot endure it."

The general swept his arm in the direction of the camp, a jumble of tents and horses—mostly horses, it seemed, tied on short tethers in every available space.

"Endure what, my lord?" Tren said. "Thirst?"

"Nah, nah, nah, this shoving together, this crowd, this mob, this feeling of cattle all crammed into a pen. We live on the plains, we ride free on the plains. Only slaves live in packs, smelling each other's stink."

Tren was tempted to sarcasm. Instead, he mugged a thoughtful look.

"Well, my lord," he said at last, "maybe we should attack then. Once we retake the ground to the west—"

"Do you truly think we can, with that creature overhead?"

"Imph, well."

"I suspected that they would enlist bowmen. Those are a difficulty, but we could, in the end, ride them down. But if we cannot ride—"

Tren nodded, looking out over the Deverry army. Yesterday's battle and the subsequent panic had lost the Horsekin a fair number of warriors, mostly trampled by their own mounts, but still the Deverry men were outnumbered. With the dragon on their side, numbers didn't matter.

"I asked you to walk with me aways for some reason," Hir-li said. "You are favored by the priestess, are you not?"

"I suppose you could call it that."

"All men here would call it that."

An odd hesitancy in the warleader's voice caused Tren to swing round to face him. Hir-li was staring at the ground in a way that would have meant embarrassment in a human being.

"One wonders if her holiness has honored you by revealing how she means to defeat the dragon," Hir-li said. "Surely she must have a plan."

"She does, my lord. I thought she would have told you, or I would have mentioned it."

"Blessed be she for whom we fight and die, that she has inspired her priestess!" Hir-li looked up with a smile that showed fang. "And blessed be the sacred raven as well! Er, could you tell me, perhaps, what she told you?"

"Of course, not that she told me everything. I do know that the man who rides upon the dragon is the same man who killed my brother. I understand, now, why the Goddess gave me that longbow."

"Indeed, indeed." Hir-li grinned again. "Did her holiness happen to tell you when she would strike against the creature?"

"Soon, I suppose, but she didn't tell me much. Perhaps, my lord, you should summon her and ask her outright."

"It is not for me to summon a priestess, Lord Tren. It is for me, it is for all of us, to wait for her holy words." The warleader stared down into the demoralized camp. "I only pray that we won't have to wait long."

Simply because she knew Jill's brusque manner, Dallandra took on the job of bearing bad news. She found Carra up in the women's hall, sitting alone at the window and leaning onto the sill to crane her neck for a glimpse of the relieving army. Her thin underdress stretched tight over her swelling pregnancy. It's a fine world I've lured Elessi into, Dallandra thought. I hope to all the gods she isn't born in the middle of a siege. Carra glanced her way, then sat up properly, smiling.

"Good morning, Dalla. Have you any news?"

Dallandra hesitated, searching for phrases. Carra's smile melted away.

"What's happened to Dar?"

"Naught, naught. My apologies! I must look ghastly grim."

"You do, and I thought, well, maybe you'd scried out Dar, and . . ." Carra let her voice trail off.

"I've bad news, sure enough, but not about your husband. It's Yraen. He died scouting last night."

Carra made a painful sound, half a grunt, half a sob, and turned her face away.

"I know I shouldn't care," she whispered. "He was only a silver dagger, and just my guard, and princesses aren't supposed to care, but I do. Oh, Yraen!"

She dropped her face to her hands and sobbed, while Dallandra patted her shoulder to comfort her.

Evandar returned to the high hill overlooking the lands to find his armor and clothing gone. When he raised his hand, the astral stuff gathered and clung, and with the light he wove himself new, the leather trousers and long tunic of a man of the Westfolk, the chain mail and pot helm of a Deverry man. Once he was properly dressed again for war, he paced back and forth on the hill crest and considered where Alshandra might be.

"Well," he said aloud, "she's not in my Lands, and she's not in the Lands that lie a-borning. She never liked to fly high into the lands of golden light above us, though now and again she did fly low into the silver light beneath us. Into the silver light, therefore, shall I travel, but in this form, I think, not as the hawk, who has no hands."

He stepped off the hillside onto the air in the way an ordinary man might step off a stair onto the ground. As if a stairway stretched ahead of him, as well, he walked downward, thinking of Deverry with every step, until the light round him turned a strange silvery-blue. When he looked down, his own Lands had disappeared, and the rolling hills round Cengarn lay in their stead, these all a rusty-red from the auras of the grasses and trees. To Cengarn, he decided, he would go, in case Alshandra was lurking nearby in the hopes of troubling the unborn soul of their daughter, whose new body lay growing in Carra's womb.

Close to noon, the Deverry army saddled up. The carters harnessed up their teams and drove the carts out, loaded with everyone's gear as well as the general supplies, to clear the field of battle. Just as the army mounted, word passed along that the cavalry in the enemy camp was mounting in answer, while their spearmen were forming shield walls at the gaps in the earthworks.

"Shield walls, eh?" Erddyr said. "That doesn't sound like the cavalry will be coming out to meet our challenge. More of a precaution, them arming."

"Just so, my lord," Rhodry said. "Well, we're harnessed and ready to go. We'll see how long they can hide."

After a few words with Arzosah, Rhodry mounted, and they flew out to the south, circling to gain height and position off where the raven couldn't see. By the time they circled back, so high that Cengarn seemed only the size of a village, the Deverry army had mounted and trotted out to take up its position on the southern flat, about a hundred yards away from and opposite the earthworks and spearmen guarding the Horsekin camp. Arzosah flew round to the north so that she could dive from the rear.

"Now!" Rhodry yelled.

With a roar of laughter, the dragon tucked her wings and plunged, plummeting down toward the camp and roaring over and over. Such was the rush of air around him that Rhodry could do little more than cling to her harness with both hands as he bent low over her neck, but he could hear the whinnying and yelling below. As she leveled off and began to climb, he could look down and see the Horsekin camp erupting in a swirl of panicked cavalry.

"Again!" he yelled. "Try to drive them toward their own spearmen."

She rumbled in a long laugh and turned, dipping a wing and soaring into position while Rhodry clung for his life. As she leveled out, though, he caught a glimpse of a bird—the raven, he assumed—flying fast toward them from the west. Arzosah had seen her, too, judging from her sudden hiss.

"Hurry!" he called out. "One more pass before she gets here!"

Arzosah roared and dropped, down and down in a rush of wind that tore at Rhodry's clothes and tried to grab him from her back. He clung to the straps, his hands stinging and aching from the effort. Just as he felt that he was bound to be torn off and sent falling, she leveled with a huge roar, answered from below by the screams of horses and riders alike. Rhodry risked sitting up and leaning to the side to look down. Horses were plunging through one of the gaps, trampling the spearmen as they surrendered to an orgy of herd fear no matter how hard their riders yelled and beat at them with quirts and the flat of blades. Rhodry started to laugh, then swore as something sped by his face.

"Arrow!" he screamed. "They've got archers! Climb!"

"Just one," she yelled back. "I saw him. But I'm climbing."

With a few huge beats of her wings, she flew up well out of range of any bow on earth. As she turned, he got the barest glimpse of a man with a longbow, a tiny figure, smaller than a toy from his height, standing on the east ridge behind the tents with pennants. The rest of the camp, down in the lowlands, had broken into complete chaos, horses running and bucking, thrown riders scrambling up and running after them, infantry racing this way and that. The sound of yelling and neighing drifted up like the crash of waves on a distant shore. Beyond the earthworks, the Deverry army sprang to the attack as Horsekin charged out the gaps for want of anywhere else to go.

"Once more," Rhodry called. "We'll have them on the run good and proper, then."

"This is grand sport, Dragonmaster!"

Arzosah flew round to the north, turned once more, and suddenly roared in rage, gliding on silent wings, cocking her head this way and that. Rhodry heard a sound, a high squalling note, a piping gone sour that he recognized all too well. He rose in his stirrups as best he could and looked frantically round, but whoever or whatever was playing upon the whistle had turned invisible. The sound seemed to be coming from a point in the empty air off to the west, and it was to the west that Arzosah turned, snapping her huge jaws, roaring again with a flap of wings to gain height.

"Dive!" Rhodry yelled. "Make your dive! It can wait, whatever it is!"

The piping screech hung loud in the air, as if a huge invisible bird cried out as it flew away, always west and away from the battle. Hissing in blind rage, Arzosah followed the five sour notes. Rhodry turned back and realized that he couldn't even see the battlefield, it lay so far behind.

"Arzosah Sothy Lorezohaz!" He tossed back his head and intoned her name, called it out again, felt the name boiling out of him as if he spoke it with his entire body. "Ar Zo Sah Soth Ee Lore Ez O Haz!"

She moaned and fluttered, losing height, then flapping in a frenzy of wings to steady herself.

"The whistle, Master! They made it from my dead mate's bones!"

"Arzosah Sothy Lorezohaz! Turn back! I command you on this ring and your true name!"

She moaned again in a grief that tore his heart, then dipped one wing and turned, flying slowly as the whistle sounded again and again, louder, frantic, imploring.

"Vengeance!" the dragon screamed. "They killed him, then profaned him!"

"Back to the battle! You can get revenge there!"

She hesitated, fluttering her wings to hold her place.

"Arzosah Sothy Lorezohaz!"

With a roar, she flew, leaping forward, it seemed, as her enormous wings thwacked against the air. The whistle played in vain, repeating its ugly call, growing fainter and fainter until they left the sound behind at last and swept down over the battlefield. She roared, and the Horsekin cavalry broke once more, their mounts rearing then plunging free of their riders' control to race away from the huge beast chasing them. In her rage, Arzosah flew low, snapping at the enemy horses, growling and swinging her head back and forth. In a futile jab, the spearmen tried to hurl their spears—far too long for such an attack—and bring her down.

"The archer!" Rhodry yelled. "Climb!"

With one last roar, she did, angling her wings and flying hard. An arrow sped past below them, then another, falling back harmlessly as they swept over the east ridge.

"Another dive?" she called back.

"One more, truly."

Since she'd overshot the encampment and the battle both, she circled in a lazy turn, resting in a glide for a moment, then flapped and flew. All at once, she screamed, and Rhodry looked up to swear and yell.

"Turn!"

She was trying, dipping and flapping in a panic as bad as the one she'd caused below, but the white mist billowed up all round them and closed over them like a hand grasping a jewel. Whimper-

318

ing and trembling, Arzosah slowed her flight, gliding more than flapping, while Rhodry could only swear helplessly. He fumbled at his belt and pulled the bronze knife, glowing golden and sending long darts and glints of light from its point every time he moved his hand. Ahead, the day had turned silvery blue as the fog thinned out. With one last flap, Arzosah burst free and turned, circling over what seemed to be Cengarn but in a world gone mad.

Under the blue light, all the world glowed but the town itself, its houses dead black lumps behind a rise of dead black stone. All round the walls, though, ovoids of bright-colored light ran and scurried, while the battle raged as a war of lights, red and yellow and white, but mostly red, shot here and there with a living black, pulsing and surging all over the field. The circling hills glowed dull red and brown under the silvery, blue-shot sky where the sun hung as an enormous hole of light. Arzosah moaned and circled, gliding on currents of air made visible as long crystalline threads.

"Oh, ye gods," Rhodry whispered. "I think me we're in for it good and proper."

Floating over the town, just above the dun, in fact, hung Alshandra, with her golden hair streaming loose over her shoulders. She towered huge, fully as tall as the dragon was long, and she was carrying a bow. She smiled as she reached to her quiver and drew an arrow, smiled as she turned, keeping Rhodry and the dragon always in her sight.

"Evandar!" Rhodry didn't even know why he was calling. "Evandar!"

Alshandra laughed with a toss of her head and nocked the arrow to her bow, raised it slowly as she turned.

"Dodge!" Rhodry yelled.

Arzosah flapped and leapt up in an eddy of crystals, shimmering behind her in the bluish air. The enormous arrow sped a few bare feet below them. Alshandra howled in rage and drew another as the dragon's wings beat slower again.

"I'm tired," Arzosah moaned. "So tired, Dragonmaster."

"You'll be dead if you don't start flying. Get away from the town! Head south!"

With a shriek, Arzosah dipped low beneath another arrow's path, then took off, flying steadily, if slowly, toward the south. Howling in rage, Alshandra followed, running through the empty air. When Rhodry glanced back, he saw that she'd dropped the bow. An enormous great-ax gleamed in her hands, and she was gaining on them.

"Evandar!" In a last desperation Rhodry called again. "Evandar!"

On a wave of laughter, a berserk chortling to match Rhodry's own, Evandar burst into the blue light, swooping and plunging through the air with a broadsword in one hand and an oval shield in the other. Rhodry heard Alshandra scream in rage and terror as the vast figure of the Guardian swept past them. Ahead, shimmering in the blue light, hung another mist gate. Without waiting for an order, Arzosah flapped hard and flew straight for it. Just as they passed through, Rhodry glanced back to see Alshandra fleeing the battle. She shot straight upward like a diver returning to the surface of a lake and disappeared through a crack in the silver sky.

With a vast convulsion of light that left him dizzy, Rhodry and the dragon burst out into sunlight, normal blessed sunlight and clean air. Below them lay the fallow fields just south of Cengarn, all green and silent in the golden light of a late afternoon. Rhodry wept in a quick burst of tears, quickly over.

"Turn back," he called out. "You can land behind the battle and rest, and I'll find a horse and ride into the fight."

But by the time they returned, the battle was over. The Horsekin had retreated back into their protected camp, but the balance of numbers, once in their favor, had been very much tipped to the Deverry side.

When he heard Rhodry's call, a wave of thought billowing through the etheric plane, Evandar was already close to Cengarn. In a burst of images, he sped forward, following the anguish in the calls, until he saw the city, black against the living auras of the men and horses round it, those bright-colored lights that had puzzled Rhodry earlier.

He also saw Alshandra gaining on her prey as the exhausted dragon flapped desperately toward the south. With a howl of laughter, Evandar dropped down to hover between her and the dragon. At last, he thought. At last, I have her!

Shrieking, Alshandra leapt up, bursting through the semblance of sky that marked the boundary between the planes. For a brief moment, Evandar stood stunned, his useless sword in his hand; then he dropped the weapons and leapt after. He broke through the silver and found himself back in the Lands, hovering in midair in the pale sunlight. Slowly, he turned in a circle, saw at last the tiny form of the nighthawk, flying off toward the horizon. He started to transform, then hesitated, still in his elven shape. He'd been assuming, he realized, that she would stand and fight once he caught up with her. Apparently, she was going to keep running from him instead.

"You're never going to catch her," he said aloud. "If you fly after her up here, she'll drop back down to the blue light. If you chase her there, she'll pop up somewhere else, always working harm wherever she goes. This is a pretty little nastiness, I must say."

Evandar settled back to the green hillcrest. He knew that he needed to think and find some scheme, but there was the question of Time. It was moving, he supposed, back in the world of men. Dallandra always talked about Time moving, anyway, either fast or slow, dragging or flying, depending upon what she might be doing at the moment. Although he was never quite sure what she meant by such talk, he did know that events had a way of getting done with and situations had a way of changing, down in that world, whether you wanted them to or not. He had best move fast. If he could. Thinking of Dallandra made him worry, too. Where had she been during that battle? He decided that he'd best go and see.

When Alshandra's dweomer had transported Rhodry and Arzosah onto the etheric plane, Dallandra had seen it happen, but she'd been in no position to come to his aid. At the battle's start, Jill had rushed to the women's hall to stand guard over Carra, leaving Dallandra to take her turn watching over the town. Dallandra hurried up to the

roof of the main broch and looked out, making sure that the Horse-kin weren't attacking the walls—no one had been able to tell what the thrust of this battle was, in the first confusion of battle noise and sounding horns. When she saw the dragon dive and realized that the fight lay between the two armies, she stayed up on the roof rather than rushing off to the gates. As a precaution, she renewed the astral seals that lay over the town.

Sure enough, once the battle was well joined below, the raven mazrak appeared, flying round and round the dun. Every now and then, she flew directly over Dallandra and low, too, as if daring her to follow. Dallandra held her place and waited. She had no intention of donning her own bird form only to be lured away, leaving the dun open to magical attacks. The raven called out, a harsh cry of sheer frustration, then flew up high and darted off, disappearing into the glare of the sun.

"We're not going to get off that easy," Dallandra muttered to herself.

Although she kept glancing at the battle below, her real watch lay on the sky. She paced back and forth, wondering how the raven would mount her attack. Since her attempt to lure Dallandra away physically had failed, it was likely that she would retreat to some safe spot where she could go into a trance and approach the dun from the etheric. The seals would turn her back, of course—unless Al-shandra appeared and wiped them away. Dallandra knew perfectly well that neither she nor Jill had the power to set a seal that the Guardian couldn't destroy. She spent a few more minutes watching the battle until she could be sure that the Horsekin were in too much danger of their own to storm the city, then left the roof and hurried to her chamber.

Dallandra lay down on her bed, crossed her arms over her chest, and steadied her breathing. She closed her eyes, then transferred up to the etheric and her body of light, which she built in the elven manner as a tall silver flame, burning round the soul within, though still joined to her entranced body below with a silver cord. In this form, she could float through the ceiling of her chamber and travel out onto the etheric plane. She drifted onto the roof and realized that the golden dome had vanished, that the seals were shattered and gone.

Borne on a wave of fear, Dallandra rose up above the dun. All round her the battle raged in a towering fire of red auras and the misty clouds of life-force drifting from spilled blood. Overhead, she could just distinguish Alshandra as a small figure hovering next to an ordinary-looking body of light, a stylized human female molded of the blue light. Together they were drifting toward the dun. Setting the seals would do no more than delay them for a moment. In something like panic, Dallandra rose up high above the city. She'd never been trained to fight upon the etheric, could do no more than defend herself from attack, and she doubted whether her shields would hold against the Guardian's power. Wildfolk rushed to flock round her in a glowing flux of crystalline forms, darting this way and that, expanding as they tried to protect her, contracting again in fear.

At that moment, Rhodry and the dragon burst through into the etheric plane, wrapped in Alshandra's dweomer mist that allowed them to travel it physically. With a howl of triumph, the Guardian swept down, growing huge as she settled into position over the dun. Against Alshandra, Dallandra was powerless, but the human mazrak was another matter. She hovered nearby, her semblances of arms raised high above her head, ready to call down power from the astral and feed her make-believe goddess. With the Wildfolk rushing after, Dallandra charged her.

"You! Hold and stand in the name of the Light!"

The woman shrieked and fled. Dallandra followed, gained on her, sent the Wildfolk ahead to slow her down. They swarmed round her body of light like bees round a flower, darting this way and that, blinding her. Swearing and cursing, the woman batted at them with her incorporeal hands. Never once did she draw a sigil or a pentagram; never once did she chant a banishing. Dallandra could guess that she quite simply didn't know the proper symbols and lore.

"Stand in the name of the Light!"

With one last cry, the woman twirled round and dropped, sliding down her silver cord, absorbing it as she fled, until suddenly she disappeared. She'd returned to her body and escaped.

Dallandra spun round and rushed back to the dun, but by the time she reached it, there was no sign of Rhodry, the dragon, or Alshandra. For some minutes, she hovered on the etheric, looking round, keeping a watch. The fighting had ended some time before. Out on the battle plain a mist, pale gold to the etheric sight, drifted in long tendrils and streamers; many men had died or lay wounded and bleeding. She could see two lines of silvery-blue mist as well, the water veils that hung over the streams near the dun. They, too, were exhalations of force, but unlike the ghastly mists of blood-energy, these were pure and natural, mere elemental water on its own plane. Not, of course, that the water veils weren't dangerous to dweomerworkers—their raw force could tear a body of light or etheric double to shreds.

Glancing down, Dallandra realized that Jill was standing on the roof, renewing the seals. Dallandra returned to her own body, following the silver cord until she hovered in her familiar chamber and over the body lying corpse-still on the bed. She slipped back in, heard a rushy sort of click, and opened her eyes. Sunset light filled the room and glowed golden. She let out her breath in a long sigh and sat up, exhausted, her hands trembling as she pushed her hair back from her sweaty face.

When she rose, she nearly fell. She sat on the edge of the bed and stared at the sunlight falling in long shafts through the room while she gathered strength. All at once, she knew that Evandar had entered her chamber by the touch of his mind upon hers. She got to her feet just as he materialized, standing in the curve of her chamber's wall.

"Oh, thank every god!"

She rushed to him and threw herself into his arms, while he laughed and ran his fingers through her tangled hair. Although he felt solid, still he seemed cool against her and less than tangible, as he always did in the material world. When he kissed her, though, his mouth felt warm and real.

"I've missed you so much," she stammered. "Just so much."

"I know, my love, I know. I would have come to you sooner, but, ye gods, with all the iron outside the walls and a fair bit within, I can't bear it for long."

"Ah." For a moment she nearly wept. "I thought you'd deserted me."

"Never! Never, my love, never that. Did you truly think I would?"

"Well, I tried to call to you, but I never felt I'd reached you. I forgot about the iron."

"I never can forget how the pain burns."

"How can you come at all, then? The town and dun must stink of the stuff."

"They do. For a while I can put the pain aside, but only for a while before it wears me down."

"By sheer will, you mean? Not some dweomer spell?"

"By will alone and by love for you." He kissed her again. "I can't stay with you long, but I had to see how you fared."

"Well, none of us fare well, truly." She managed a wry grin. "But with the relieving army here, I've got hope again."

"As well you should. If I could stay and fight alongside them, I would, but I can't. All my will would have to go into fighting the iron instead, and I'd have no more dweomer than some stinking servant. I learned that at Rinbaladelan, you see. In the midst of the last battle, with iron all round me, I couldn't do much more than draw a bow like an ordinary archer."

"I understand, and truly, I don't suppose that one more archer would mean anything. The real war's with Alshandra. She's the key to everything. Can't you make her stop this?" Dallandra felt her voice shake. "Can't you imprison her?"

"I've been trying, up in my own country, searching and hunting, but always she flees from me. If I can't catch her, there's naught I can do. She's a fair bit stronger than I thought, alas."

Dallandra reached up and laid her hands on either side of his face.

"Will you be safe? Oh, ye gods, if I lost you—"

Evandar smiled, caught her wrists gently, and kissed her hands.

"I'm still the stronger," he said. "That's why she won't face me. Ah, Alshandra! Must I declare myself helpless to catch you? Must I? I think so. My country is her country, my love, and there we both reign. Not just me, but both of us."

"But if you can't stop her, who can?"

"Who, indeed? I do not like this sensation I feel. I wish to stop her; I cannot. Is it anger I feel? This hasn't ever happened before, my love. It's not like when Rinbaladelan fell." He paused, thinking something through. "Then I was overwhelmed. This is seeing a thing, reaching out for it, and finding it beyond your reach."

"It's called frustration."

"Ah. Well, I don't like it, not one whit."

He gave her a last kiss, then stepped back and disappeared. For a long time, Dallandra stood in the middle of her chamber, saw nothing, heard nothing but the sound of her heart, knocking against her ribs, it seemed, pounding out "ruin, ruin, ruin" over and over.

After she set the sigils over the astral dome, Jill returned to her chamber. Soon the gwerbret would insist on her presence at his council of war; she was debating whether she had time to look for Dallandra before it started when someone opened the door, and Dalla stepped in, standing with one hand on the open door, the other on the jamb as if she would have fallen without the support. Jill's first thought was that her friend had been stricken ill or even stabbed.

"Dalla!" Jill got up, nearly knocking the chair over. "What is it?"

"Ill news, ill news, the worst news in the world. There's naught Evandar can do about Alshandra. He's tried and failed."

Jill grabbed her by one arm and led her into the room.

"By the hells, Dalla, sit down! You look ready to faint."

"Maybe so. Don't you see what this means? She's clever enough to keep away from Evandar, up on the inner planes, and so we can't defeat her either here or there."

Spent and pale, Dallandra sank into the offered chair, then merely stared at the floor, her hands clasped between her legs.

"Dalla, Dalla—I understand matters of war, better than I want to, truly. Don't be so afraid! The relievers will win through on the morrow, Alshandra or no."

"I know that. But the real war won't be over. I mean Alshandra's war. She's not going to stop attacking Carra just because her army's gone. She and that mazrak of hers will follow us. It won't matter where we go, they'll follow. And she'll keep raising armies if she can, too, and more and more men will die. I can't stand it. Oh, ye gods, what have I done? I never should have meddled with Evandar's people, never!"

"Hush!" Jill got up and laid a firm hand on her shoulder. "It's not your blame, but hers. What were you to do? Abandon an entire race to extinction? If Alshandra weren't raving mad, everything would have been for the best. You've done naught but what's honorable and right, and you've done it the best you could."

Dallandra said nothing for a long time; then at last she looked up.

"My thanks, and truly, I know in my heart that I had to do it. But my war still won't be over on the morrow. She'll still hound us, forever if she has to. And she'll raise more armies, too, and keep ravaging the countryside."

Jill started to mouth some reassuring platitude or lie, then stopped. All at once, in her mind, the omens came together and wove their perfect knot. At that moment, she saw what must be done, and that she was the only person in Deverry who could do it.

"Jill!" Dallandra snapped. "What's wrong? You look like death."

"Do I? It's just from realizing the truth in what you're saying. She won't give up, will she? As long as she's strong enough to keep fighting, she'll wreak endless harm."

"Exactly. And I don't know what to do to stop her."

"But I do. We'll have to plan it out just so."

·   ·   ·

Since Labanna insisted that the princess sleep in the women's hall rather than her own chamber, the only place in the dun where Carra could be private at night was in her bed. By drawing the hangings all round and pretending to sleep, she could sit up cross-legged with her back against the headboard and think in the stuffy dark. That evening, worn out by watching the battle rage, she retired particularly early and shut herself up.

The battle, however, followed her. She heard voices out in the sleeping quarters and saw a light bloom through the crack in the hangings, which suddenly parted to reveal Dallandra, carrying a punched tin candle lantern. Even in that dappled light, Carra could see how grim the dweomermaster's eyes were, how tight and set her mouth.

"Your Highness, I've got a very important thing to ask you. If you truly don't want to do this, say me nay, and there'll be no shame in it, because it's a very dangerous thing. Do you understand?"

"I do." Carra felt her heart start knocking against her ribs. "But what—"

"Jill has a plan to trap Alshandra and put an end to her scheming. But we need bait. If you draw her attention, then perhaps we can lure her out where Jill can work on her. I want you to come up to the rooftop with me and stand out where Alshandra can see you. I'll be right there, because Alshandra hates me, too, and Jill will be —well, she'll be nearby, though you won't be able to see her."

Carra's mouth seemed to have turned to wood, all dry and unmoving. Finally, she forced her tongue and lips to form words.

"Very well. Of course. Let me get a shawl and my clogs."

"Splendid! And take along those bits of iron Jill gave you as well."

They hurried up the staircase to the last landing. Among the sacks of stones and arrows, Jill lay on her back, hands crossed over her chest, so still, so pale, that Carra at first thought her dead. Near her head knelt Jahdo, terrified in the candlelight.

"She's just in a trance," Dallandra whispered. "Don't worry."

Climbing up the ladder to the roof was difficult, but with Dallandra up above to help, Carra managed to scrabble out. For a moment, she stood in the cool night air and looked up at the stars, spread so close and bright above the town and dun. She'd been a virtual prisoner for so long that her fear vanished for a brief moment in this wider view. Dallandra dragged over a wooden stool and had her sit.

"Jahdo brought this up for you." The dweomermaster set the lantern down nearby. "Now, you sit here in the light, and we'll see what happens."

The fear returned like the smack of a heavy hand across her face. She nodded, crossing her arms over her stomach as if her all-too-human flesh could protect the unborn child within.

Up on the etheric, Jill hovered over the dun, riding the billows of the blue light in her simple etheric double as she looked down at Carra and Dalla below, the one's aura a timid pale ovoid, the other's a golden flame, both gleaming like gems in the pool of light from the candle flame. Wildfolk swarmed round the pair, as well, all bright shapes and flickering there on their home plane of existence. That night, they seemed far larger than normal, all puffed up and sharp with anger that someone should try to harm their Dallandra and young Carra as well.

Round Carra's neck gleamed a faint line of purplish light from the Gel da'Thae talismans Jahdo had given her, another protection, as were the lumps of iron set under her chair and tucked into her kirtle. If all went well, they would serve. If Jill failed, nothing on earth would protect the princess.

Jill widened her sight and looked out over the Horsekin camp, a seething mass of blood-red auras, shot here and there with black to mark the sinking vitality of some dying man. The relieving army looked much the same, an outer ring of boiling red to mark their rage and battle lust. Somewhere out there was Rhodry, and she felt a pang of real regret that she'd never see him again, even if he lived through his battle. She regretted, too, lying to Dallandra about this night's work, but there had, after all, been no time to argue. She thrust such sentimental thoughts aside and began to rise, circling like the falcon even though she wore a simple human form. She glided through the golden dome of her seals, rose even higher, until she hovered so far above that the glowing dome shone as small as a dropped coin.

At her height, the energy of the starry sky blazed in a silver web of light; her tiny form would be lost against its background, or so she could hope. For some moments she waited, calling on the Light that shines behind all the gods, the Light that she had served all her long life. In the silent way of the Light, she felt that she was less than alone though not accompanied. It was enough. She drew upon the strength of the Light and first imagined, then shaped out of the etheric substance, three spears of silver blue.

Down below her, a mist began to form. Only a white vortex at first, it grew into a woman's shape, huge, floating in the air to one side of the dun towers, then suddenly solidified—so dense and de-tailed that Jill knew Alshandra must be visible to those on the material plane. Very distantly, she heard a sound like a wind in trees and could guess that it came from the armies, one cheering, the other screaming defiance. Slowly, the Guardian drifted earthward in a tight spiral with Carra at its center.

Jill held her position until Alshandra pounced, sweeping down toward the tiny dome below. Jill plunged after, keeping a good dis-tance between them, but the tormented spirit never looked up. Straight as a stone she dropped, clubbing a fist into the seals at the zenith. The dome shook once, then vanished in a spray of gold light.

Jill dropped, stooping like the falcon straight down after. She could see Dallandra on her feet and using both arms to draw wards, which Alshandra flicked away as fast as the dweomermaster could make them.

"Alshandra!" Jill sent a wave of thought to the Guardian. "You fool! We've trapped you."

She hurled the first spear straight and true. Alshandra shrieked aloud and flung herself skyward as the shaft ripped through her astral body. Yet even as the spear dissipated and vanished, the wound healed over. Here on the etheric plane, Alshandra's dweomer would always be the stronger. Jill dodged back, heading east and away from the dun. The Horsekin had to see their goddess, had to see what was about to happen.

"Follow me if you dare!"

She hurled the second spear, which burned into the Guardian's legs. Screaming in rage, Alshandra darted after Jill. Swinging, swooping, first high, then gliding low over the Horsekin camp, Jill led her on, threatened her with the spear, and worst weapon of all, mocked her. Alshandra followed, chasing her to the south.

"You have no soul, you clumsy spirit! You can't catch me. You can't guess what we're going to do. You can't do anything but rage and spit, can you?"

Snarling, Alshandra flung herself forward, huge hands grasping at the spear. Jill dodged up high, then risked a quick glance round. Not far behind her rose the silver water veil, a mist of elemental force, from the stream that ran south through the portcullis in Cengarn's walls. It was a puny thing from a shallow trickle of water, but farther south it joined up with the stream that ran west of Cengarn. Together they formed a proper river.

When she feinted with the spear, Alshandra lunged toward her again. Jill threw herself up and back; still the Guardian rushed after. Jill swooped away barely in time and danced south again, always south and west. Below, the Horsekin were clamoring and shouting. Some had rushed to the earthworks to keep their goddess in sight; others were scurrying up the side of the east ridge and beyond. Splendid, Jill thought. You'll see somewhat tonight that you'll never forget. As she dodged to the south, heading for the joining of the two streams, Alshandra leapt at her and swung a huge hand, clipping Jill hard with her outstretched fingers, which were, of course, an enormous bludgeon of etheric force.

Jill flew into the air and tumbled this way and that, at last righting herself over the Deverry army. When she glanced down, she could see the silver cord that bound her to her body growing thin and pale. Alshandra swooped in from the side. Jill dropped, then flung herself back southward just as the Guardian charged. She could see the water veil from the two streams now, a high wall of raging force springing up high above the river. She flew up a little higher,

331

forcing Alshandra to follow, then risked a glance back. They'd angled away from the Horsekin camp, but at least the men up on the east ridge and the earthworks would see the end of this battle.

From a bare few yards away, Jill hurled the last spear directly at her face. Howling and tearing with both hands, Alshandra hovered for a moment, pulling the dissolving form out of her etheric substance, then thrust herself forward so fast that Jill's dodge came too late—just as she'd always known it would. In a kind of mock pain, she felt huge hands close round her almost throat.

"You puny little shrew!" The Guardian's thoughts hissed like water dancing on hot iron. "Who's more clever now?"

Jill grabbed Alshandra's wrists with her hands and writhed, twisting, summoning the last of her strength.

"Who indeed?"

She wrenched them both into the streaming water veil. Shrieking, Alshandra dropped her and tried to flee, but too late. The roil of elemental force tore at her form, wrenched great handfuls of her hair from her head, stripped the etheric substance out of her spirit's mold, and swirled it away. She bobbed and screamed, growing tattered first, then faint, but still the relentless etheric stream broke over and drowned her, shrank her to the flopping image of a tiny child, ill-formed and barely human. One last huge scream rang out across two worlds; then the river swept her away. Reborn she doubtless would be, but never would she come to life again as Alshandra the Guardian.

All at once, Jill felt herself bobbing up into the sky as huge patches of her own etheric double tore free and fell away. She looked down and saw the silver cord dangling, broken.

"It is over," she called out. "It is finished."

With the last of her living consciousness, she could hear three great knocks boom in answer, three thunderclaps rolling through the sky. In the streaming silver mist, a golden light began to shine, and it was a light that shone as sound, too, deafening her to the thunder, deafening her to the river's rush and the cheers and the howls far below in the land of the living. The light swept over her like a river and lifted her high and clear out of the water veil. All round her the light turned as hard as jewels, until it seemed she stood in a hall of light. When she looked at herself, she found she still had her memory of a body. Though it was a flickering thing, and pale, it seemed to her that, for this brief moment, she was young again. As well, she seemed to perceive through eyes and ears like a living woman would have.

In front of her, his hands stretched out to greet her, stood Nevyn, but as he'd looked in his youth, with his thick shock of untidy dark hair and joyous blue eyes.

"You waited?" Jill whispered. "You waited for me all these years?"

"Did you think I wouldn't?" He was smiling. "Did you truly think I wouldn't?"

Her hands grasped his. As he drew her close, the Light rose to wrap them round.

Carra had seen Alshandra appear, dropping out of a night sky like a hawk stooping to the kill. Too frightened to scream, she turned stone-still, as paralyzed as the rabbit that might have been the hawk's prey. All round the dun and town shouting went up, the hai! hai! hai! of the Horsekin, the howling curses of the relieving army. Dallandra stepped smoothly in between Carra and the plunging Guardian, then began to chant in Elvish, weaving her hands back and forth in peculiar patterns. For a moment, Alshandra hovered just above the roof, her feet close to touching the slates. The shouting rose like a sea, washing Dallandra's chants away.

All at once, Alshandra screamed and threw her head back in agony. She flung herself into the air, snatching at something that Carra couldn't see, swatting out with her huge hands. She darted away south and east, flying through the air, weaving and dipping as if she were trying to catch some invisible insect. Carra leapt to her feet and turned to watch.

"Stay right here." Dallandra grabbed her arm.

"Of course. But what—"

"It's Jill, of course."

Carra nodded and stood half-tranced, watching every swing and flurry of the Guardian's battle with her invisible opponent. Farther and farther away they danced—well over the city walls by now, swooping and springing up, floating this way and that over the Horsekin camp, which were shouting their false goddess's name as if to encourage her. The Guardian's figure turned tiny, but Carra could follow her path by the magical glow round her. Suddenly, Dallandra gasped, one dark sob.

"The stream! Oh, by the gods! Jill!"

"What? Dalla—"

Dallandra grabbed her arm again and swung her round toward the trapdoor.

"Get down and get inside. Hurry! Get inside and get Jahdo and go down to the great hall, down away from the roof."

"But Jill—"

"Is past our help." Dalla began to weep. "I should have known! Ah, ye gods! I should have known." She choked back the tears. "Carra, get inside!"

Stunned speechless, Carra climbed down the ladder into the darkness of the landing below. The lantern swinging in her teeth, Dallandra followed, then handed the light over once Carra was standing safely on the floor.

"My lady!" Jahdo wailed. "Somewhat's wrong! Look, look at Jill!"

Her body lay twisted round into a heap, her face drained of blood, her mouth slack open like an idiot's.

"She's dead." Dallandra tried to gentle her voice but failed. "Get out of here! Jahdo, take the lantern. Get the princess down to the great hall, and do it now!"

Jahdo grabbed the lantern in one hand and Carra's wrist in the other. As he tugged her toward the stairs, Carra looked back to see Dallandra pulling off her clothes as if she'd gone mad. It was all too much, suddenly. Sobbing aloud, Carra let the boy guide her down the long spiral to the safety below.

· · ·

That particular night, Rhodry had been billeted straight south of the city with Lord Erddyr's men, who were helping hold the investiture on the far side of the stream. When the shouting started in the Horsekin camp, he was on his feet and running, drawing his sword as he raced for the edge of the encampment. Around him, the warband grabbed for armor in a flood of oaths. All at once someone screamed, "Look up! Look up there!" Rhodry did and saw Alshandra, hovering just over the highest tower in Cengarn's dun, a tiny figure from this distance. She glowed silver with her magical light, as if she were a star sailing free in the earthly sky, sailing, then swooping and dipping, heading south and west, straight for the river.

"Ah, by the black hairy ass of the Lord of Hell!"

Donning armor suddenly seemed like the most futile thing in the world. His feet a little apart, he tipped back his head and watched Alshandra's peculiar flight, dodging some invisible threat there, swooping down on some invisible thing here, yet always heading south, then turning west as she passed directly overhead. Rhodry spun round and saw her heading straight for the river formed by the joining of the two streams. Closer and closer, seeming larger and larger she flew, hesitated once, and plunged forward—directly over the water.

All at once she shrieked, an enormous howl of pain that every man or Horsekin on the southern side of Cengarn could hear. Her enormous woman's form hung steady over the stream, then began to bob and swirl, began to tear apart and shatter. Even with his elven sight, Rhodry could see nothing more than Alshandra, howling and writhing, caught in some invisible web, but he knew that she had to be dying. The Horsekin shouting turned puzzled, then broke into a thousand cries of confusion and fear. The investing ring of Deverry men yelled and howled in triumph as Alshandra's tattered form began to shrink and ebb away.

Booming through the night came the three great knocks. Those Rhodry had heard before, the sign of the Great Ones, pronouncing a doom. He threw back his head and shrieked with berserk laughter as the last remnant of Alshandra's earthly body winked out like a blown candle. The sound of terror rose from the Horsekin camp like the trail of smoke.

"Master!" Arzosah's voice cut through the noise. "Master! The raven!"

Rhodry came to himself and ran to her. No time for harness —he set his foot upon her bowed neck and let her lift him up, then wedged himself between two scales of her crest at her shoulder. She crouched and flung herself into the air like a slung stone. Rhodry threw his left arm round one scale and gripped it tight. Her wings beat hard and steadily as she spiraled up over the camp and Cengarn's walls. Everywhere in the camps, and down in the town, lights bloomed as men blew fires into life or lit torches and rushed outside to stare up at the sky. The streets of the town began to fill as the trapped folk began to cheer for the dragon and her rider.

Arzosah circled once, dipping her wings as if to acknowledge the cheers, then headed for the dun. Rhodry could see, against the background of the starry sky, the dim shapes of two enormous birds, the beaky raven and a sleeker shape, glowing a faint gray as she flapped and dodged. There was no doubt that the raven was winning the battle, gaining height and diving down to stab at its prey with a vicious beak.

"This is going to be sweet," Arzosah called back.

The dragon went into a glide, raised her head, and roared as she plunged straight for the raven. Squawking and shrieking, the raven turned and flew, her wings pumping the air as she fled. Arzosah flapped once, gained—then suddenly the raven disappeared, slipping into another world and safety. Rhodry swore under his breath with every foul oath he knew, while Arzosah slowed her flight and turned back in a huge circle. Down below, the Horsekin were wailing and keening as if they saw their deaths riding for them in the night sky.

"Camp or dun?" Arzosah called. "The air belongs to us now, since the bitch Alshandra is dead."

"To the dun!"

Arzosah circled the main broch and landed gracefully upon the roof in a scatter of stones and arrows until her front talons clutched the low wall round the edge and held her steady. Rhodry grabbed at her crest, slipped, and tumbled inelegantly onto the slates.

As he picked himself up, he heard someone weeping and laughing together in long choking litany. He glanced round and saw Dallandra, wearing only a tunic, crouched at the far side of the roof. When he ran to her, she rose and flung herself into his arms.

"Rhodry, oh, by the Goddess, Rhodry!"

"It is at that. Dalla, hush, hush! It's over, for the night at least. Hush, hush."

Something wet ran down his arm. Her shoulder was bleeding through her tunic.

"You're wounded!"

"It's but a scratch, a gift from the raven. She's got a vicious beak on her."

"That was you I saw? Where's Jill?"

She went stone-still in his arms, leaning back to look up at him, her face streaked with dirt and tears. Rhodry felt his arms tighten round her of their own will.

"Dalla—"

"She's dead." Her voice was a whisper. "Just now. She killed Alshandra, but she died with her. She turned herself into bait, Rhodry. She knew she'd die, too, and she didn't tell me. She just did it. Baited the trap and saved us all."

Voices came hurrying closer, voices and a shriek of mourning through the trapdoor below. Rhodry was suddenly aware of Arzosah, stepping off the wall and settling herself near him, filling half the roof as she did so. All round the dun swirled the distant keening of the Horsekin, mourning their dead goddess. Rhodry wondered why he wasn't keening himself, opened his mouth to speak, at least, to Dallandra and try to comfort her, found he could make no sound at all. Dalla herself had turned as hard as steel.

"Close the trap, Rhodry. Keep them off the roof! I've got to set the seals over the dome. If the raven comes back, the town's in danger."

"But that wound—"

337

"Curse the wound! You can help or you can hinder, but I'm doing the work I have to do."

Rhodry ran for the trapdoor, yelled a few words to those below, then shut it and knelt upon it to keep it shut. The dragon hunched, then leapt into a glide. With a flap of wings, she settled herself on one of the shorter brochs nearby to leave the main roof clear for Dallandra's workings. Rhodry crouched and watched as Dallandra paced round, muttering spells in the elven tongue, but he truly saw none of it. All he could think of was Jill, gone from him forever. He realized that he was shaking his head in time to Dallandra's chanting, mouthing no, no, no over and over until at last, just as she finished setting the last seal, he burst out keening. From far below, he heard the dragon roar in answer.

"Rhodry, go back to the camp." Dallandra knelt beside him. "There's naught you can do here, and they'll need you on the morrow."

He fell silent, rocked back on his heels to stare up at the cold and indifferent stars.

"Go," she whispered. "Go back to the army. Avenge her on the morrow."

Nodding agreement, he rose.

"I'll see you when we win through," he said. "Fare you well till then."

Yelling for order, swinging a long whip all round him, Rakzan Hir-li rode bareback through the Horsekin camp, his warhorse snorting and kicking as it forced itself through the mob. Torches flared, campfires burst into light as the soldiers raged round, howling and babbling, swirling like water through the tents. Carrying his unstrung longbow like a staff, Tren scrambled to the higher ground at the end of the east ridge, watched the chaos, and laughed. So. She had failed them all, just as she'd failed him earlier. Shoot a man on dragonback with a longbow. It could be a proverb, as he thought about it, a fine bardic image for utter futility. He looked at the bow in his hands, then with a snarl of rage raised one knee and broke the shaft over it.

338

With a scream of rage, he threw the useless pieces as hard as he could and watched them fall, unnoticed, into the mob below. He laughed again, a long choking snarl of it.

All at once, he remembered the high priestess. On her he could take some small revenge for the way he'd been tricked. He drew his sword to protect himself from the rioting troops and plunged back down into the mob. He whacked a path for himself with the flat of the blade, shoving servants and warriors aside, screeching orders at any man or Horsekin who'd listen, until he reached her tent. A mob swirled round that, too. He beat a few men back from the side of it, then slit the canvas with his sword and ducked through to the screams of maidservants. The sobbing girls were crouched in the middle of the tent, but Raena was gone. Tren ducked back out.

"She's flown," he called out. "Someone find Rakzan Hir-li! Someone tell him!"

Those few warriors who understood him screamed and scurried. Tren kept forcing a path until he could climb down from the captains' camp. Here and there, he saw the Keepers of Discipline, whipping and smacking what troops they could grab back into some semblance of order. The screaming was lessening, though he saw Horsekin weeping all round him. Fools! he thought.

Down on the flat, the chaos and rioting still raged. Just as he reached his warband's encampment, he saw a fire flare in tents some distance off. Yelling and smoke alike plumed to the sky. Ddary came rushing up and grabbed his arm. Other men mobbed them round.

"My lord, what's going on?"

"Panic and terror, Captain, panic and terror. I doubt me if there's any sort of guard on the northern side of the camp. A careful man could walk away, if he wanted."

"And would you hold that to our shame?"

"Never. But do it now and do it fast. The Keepers have a hold over their men's souls. They'll take charge quick enough."

His men began to grab weapons, to scoop up a blanket here, a sack of food there, and slip away, a few men one way, a few others, another. On the southern edge of the camp, the fires were spreading from tent to tent. Horsekin yelled and swore, rushed this way and that, some with buckets, some with blankets to beat out the flames, but most just running to be running, yelling to be yelling. Tren watched the fires leap toward the sky and laughed again.

"My lord!" Ddary grabbed his arm. "Come with us."

"Nah, nah, nah. My place is here. If the other gods favor me, I'll have one last chance at that cursed silver dagger before I die. I bargained my honor away for him, and I'll kill him yet."

"My lord, please!"

"Go! Ddary, I order you on the oath you swore me. Go and go now!"

Ddary wiped quick tears from his eyes, then turned and ran into the night. Tren stood and watched the fires for a few moments, then hurried back to the east ridge before anyone could come look for him and find his men gone. Little danger of that—the camp surged with a screaming mob as the panic spread itself like the flames. He could hear horses, too, whinnying in terror, and the sound of hooves. Some at least had pulled their tethers and fled. Their red surcoats stained with smoke and blood, the Keepers ran through, swinging their whips and shouting. Tren glanced up, saw smoke billowing into the sky to join the clouds. Clouds? He'd seen no clouds obscuring the stars when they'd been watching their goddess fight and die.

All at once, thunder boomed and cracked. The shouting in the camp changed to a shriek of prayer as suddenly rain came, pouring down cold in great sheets, dousing the flaming tents with a hiss as huge as the dragon's. Somewhere, the high priestess was working her dweomer. Men and Horsekin alike shouted in triumph and danced like mad things in the blessed rain. Tren was surprised at himself for being so disappointed. With a shrug, he began working his way to the east ridge, climbing up the muddy slope as carefully as he could in the sudden darkness.

He gained the ridge just as the rain lessened to a drizzle. In the captains' camp, Horsekin were trotting back and forth, but purposefully now, pulling things free of the muck, rounding up comrades, calling out to one another in normal voices. Inside Hir-li's tent, lanterns glimmered, and the shadows of Horsekin moved back and forth on the walls. As Tren approached, he could hear angry voices snarling back and forth. He ducked under the tent flap and slipped in.

Saber in hand, Hir-li stood at the far end, while in front of him rakzanir jabbered and shoved one another. The high priestess was not among them. For some moments, Tren stood unnoticed in the shadows while he tried to pick up the drift of the talk but failed. Finally, Hir-li saw him and bellowed out an order. The Horsekin captains fell still long enough for Tren to make his way through to the warleader's side; then they started their arguing again.

"What do you think of the vision, Lord Tren?" Hir-li bent his head and bellowed the question above the noise. "Some say it's but an illusion brought about by our goddess's enemies. If our priestess can bring down the rain, they say, surely Alshandra's power remains great."

"What does the warleader say?"

"That dweomer folk work their spells from their own power, not from the gods." Hir-li showed fang in what might have been a smile. "And now, what do you say?"

Tren considered, unwilling to end up spitted upon the warleader's saber if he argued the wrong side of a theological question.

"I wouldn't presume to interpret the vision," Tren said at last. "The high priestess is the only one who can do that."

When Hir-li swore and spit onto the carpet, Tren stepped back, ready to dodge a blow. The warleader grinned, all fangs now, and grabbed his arm.

"Come out the back, where it's quieter."

Half-dragged, Tren had no choice but to follow. He was glad enough, anyway, to get outside. Although the rain had stopped completely, the air was still fresh and clean. Light seeped through the canvas and gleamed on the charms braided into the warleader's mane.

"Where is the high priestess, my lord?" Tren said.

"No one knows. Her maidservants told me that there are things missing from her tent. She had a special cloth sack in which she could carry ritual implements when she became the sacred raven avatar. That sack is gone."

"Are the ritual things gone, too?"

"They are not." Hir-li let go Tren's arm. "Only a few clothes. That stupid silver dagger. Some jewels. Those are missing. I'd say she's deserted us, except—" He waved his hand at the sky. "She did send the rain."

"A last favor?"

"Do you think so?"

Tren rubbed his bruised arm, considered tact, then cursed that to the hells along with their false goddess and her priestess both.

"I think, Rakzan Hir-li, that whether the priestess is gone or no, there's not much left for us but death in battle."

Hir-li nodded, making the charms jingle and chime.

"I think the same, Lord Tren, but I see no reason to tell the other officers this. Instead, I will tell them that the priestess told you she'd return by dawn."

"Very well. But why lie?"

"Because, Lord Tren, I do not wish to die alone."

The Deverry army stood on alert, watching the Horsekin camp burn, until the unnatural rain burst from the sky. Soaked and grumbling about dweomer, noble-born and riders alike milled round the camp. When the rain stopped, someone managed to get enough fire going to light a couple of torches that had been in his tent and thus were still dry. By their flickering light, Drwmyc addressed the men, or as many as could hear him, anyway, as he stood on the back of a supply cart.

"Men, we have dweomer on our side, too. You've seen it fly over you, haven't you? None of us thought there was such a thing as a dragon, much less one who could talk, but here she is, on our side and fighting for Deverry and the High King. What in the name of all that's holy is one puny rainstorm compared to that?"

The men closest cheered him; the ones in the middle distance repeated what he'd said to the ones at the rear, who cheered in turn.

With a double guard set round the camp, the army went off to sleep as best they could before the fighting on the morrow.

Rhodry, however, walked behind their lines and found Arzosah, lying as if on guard in front of the tent he'd been issued. He should have been sharing it with Yraen. They should have been standing there together, wondering what Jill was going to say on the morrow when they gained the victory.

"What's wrong?" Arzosah rumbled. "You stink of sadness."

"What do you mean, what's wrong? Yraen's dead, Jill's dead. What more needs to be wrong?"

"You could be dead yourself. Or worse yet, so could I."

Rhodry managed a brief twitch of a smile and came over, reaching up to scratch the ridges above her eyes. She rumbled, letting her head droop low.

"My heart aches for you, losing your friends," she said at last. "It truly does."

"My thanks, then. I'll not be able to mourn them properly till they're avenged, though. This is no time for tears. I want blood."

She rumbled a little louder in approval. He walked round her head and scratched the other ridge. All at once, she swung her head up so fast that she nearly knocked him over. She sniffed the wind, peering through the darkness, then hissed. Trailing a faint silver light, Evandar came strolling up to them.

"I owe you thanks," Rhodry said, "for saving my life and Arzosah's as well."

"Most welcome." Evandar glanced at the dragon. "You've done well, you know. You've been a good if somewhat scaly little lass."

She growled, trembling with rage. In the light that hung round him, her eyes glittered more steel than copper.

"Peace, peace," Rhodry broke in fast. "How do you fare, Evandar? Alshandra's gone. Do you mourn her?"

"Why should I? She infuriated me."

"Well, true, but didn't you love her once?"

"Oh." Evandar considered for a long moment. "I hadn't thought of that. Since I don't feel particularly mournful, I couldn't have loved her much."

"Hah!" Arzosah snarled. "I doubt me if you've ever loved anyone but yourself."

"Indeed? And I suppose you did?"

"Have I not mourned my mate, all these long years? Isn't it love that makes me drive these stinking Horsekin to their deaths like cattle to the slaughterer's pen? That's true love, not milksop sniveling."

Evandar growled like a dragon himself.

"Enough!" Rhodry said. "We have a thing or two to talk about. That whistle. I carried it once, so I remember it well. What did you mean, they made it from his bones?"

"That sound! We dragons know, we dragons hear. It cries in his voice still."

"It looked like a finger bone," Rhodry said. "But it was too long for a human bone or elven either."

"From the tip of his wing, then." She threw back her head and snarled. "It drew me like a lure."

"And is that why they wanted the thing so badly?" Evandar put in. "I'll wager it was. Alshandra knew I'd drawn the dragon into this, and she wanted the whistle to use against her."

"If she weren't dead already, I'd kill her," Arzosah growled.

"But she is, she is."

"And Jill with her." Rhodry heard his voice hang small and still in the night air.

For a long moment, Evandar considered, his head cocked to one side, the smile gone.

"Oh, stop it!" Rhodry spun on his heel and looked away, out over the silent camp.

"My heart aches for you," Evandar said. "My apologies."

Rhodry let out his breath in a long sigh.

"I'll have vengeance on the morrow."

"So we all will," Evandar said. "Here. Do you want to know who killed Yraen?"

"With all my heart and soul."

"Very well, then. That I can do for you."

Rhodry turned back to find Evandar staring at the sky, still dark with the unnatural clouds.

"Ah, I see it," Evandar whispered. "The man that killed Yraen is the man that has the longbow. He's a blond fellow, tall and rather slender, with a face as sharp as a knife."

"Oh, is he now?" Rhodry felt a smile growing beyond his power to stop it. "Then maybe I'll see if I can blunt it for him on the morrow. If I can find him, if the gods are willing."

"Then I'll wish you the best of luck." Evandar shivered like a man who feels a cold draft down his neck. "The iron is starting to ache my bones. Fare thee well, Rori, till tomorrow."

With a shimmer like moonlight on water, Evandar disappeared.

For the rest of that night, they laid Jill's body out on an improvised bier in the great hall. Though there were no flowers to be had, a weeping Lady Labanna put candles all round to light her way to the Otherlands. Jahdo sat crouched in the curve of the wall and watched while Dallandra, her wounded arm bound, chanted an elven prayer over her friend's corpse. Carra was sobbing so hard that she couldn't stand, while the other women cried silently nearby. A few at a time, the men came through to pay their respects and to drink a toast in her honor. Gwerbret Cadmar himself came last and stopped to say a word to the boy.

"There, there, Jahdo, the siege will be over on the morrow. We'll find a place for you here in the dun, the stables or suchlike."

"My thanks, Your Grace. You do truly be kind, to think of me now."

The gwerbret laid a comforting hand on Jahdo's head, then hobbled off, leaning on his stick. *I'll never see my Mam and Da again now,* Jahdo thought, and thinking that, he began to weep himself. Dallandra finished her prayer and came over, holding out her hand.

"Come say farewell, Jahdo, and then we'll all go upstairs. You can sleep in my chamber tonight. We'll put a mattress on the floor."

"My thanks, my lady." He scrambled to his feet and felt his head sway. "I'm so tired."

He had to summon courage to look at the body, but when he did, he was glad he'd done it. This wasn't Jill, not this frail old woman, this broken thing of bones and skin. He turned away and buried his face against Dallandra, who put her arm round his shoulders and led him away.

"Truly, she's gone, isn't she?" Dalla said. "She's gone back to the Light, Jahdo, where we'll all go in the end, every one of us, to dwell in the Otherlands with the Light."

Although he didn't understand what she meant, the tone of her voice soothed him like music. That night, he slept as if all battles were done, but before dawn, the sound of silver horns woke him.

With no one to banish them, the unnatural clouds lingered, lowering over dun and camp. In light as gray as steel, Rhodry unrolled Arzosah's harness, then considered her as she crouched, waiting. All round them, the camp was coming awake, as the men gobbled down a hasty meal and began to arm.

"I wonder," Rhodry said. "When the riders from the dun sally, you're going to terrify their horses. They've never even got a good look at you."

"A good smell of me, you mean." Arzosah yawned.

"Doesn't matter which. What does matter is Evandar's dweomer, and he's never cast it on them. I've been thinking. As soon as they start to sally from the dun, you'd best leave the battle."

"Good. I'm tired."

"But I'll have a horse here waiting. I want that archer."

Lord Erddyr gladly gave Rhodry a warhorse, a sturdy-looking roan with a deep chest, who'd lost his rider in yesterday's fighting. As Rhodry saddled it up, he could feel his berserker's grin biting into his face. At last, he would be able to fight the kind of battle he knew rather than some misty thing of dweomer. Ah, Jill, Jill, he thought to himself, I wish to every god we could celebrate this victory together when the night comes! All at once, it occurred to him that just maybe they might, though in some great hall in the Otherlands. He laughed, making the roan toss up its head and dance a few steps.

"You've never carried a berserker before, have you, lad?" Rhodry patted its neck to soothe it. "Well, you won't hear me over the battle noise."

He left the roan in the charge of a carter, then returned to Arzosah. They took to the air just as the gwerbret drew up his men and led them out of camp. The dragon circled, making a lazy turn over the dun and town. Far below and tiny with the distance, Cadmar's warband stood beside their horses at the south gate, ready to join the battle once the Horsekin had been cleared away. Behind them, in a disorganized mass, stood the town militia, ready to loot and dispatch the Horsekin wounded. Rhodry figured they'd earned every coin or trinket they could find. Arzosah passed over and flew on, swinging round over the northern hills, fluttering a moment, then starting her long glide down.

When she reached the Horsekin camp, she roared a signal for the battle to begin. In terror, the cavalry, already mounted, leapt forward and lunged for the gaps in the earthworks. Since the riders were urging them to run, the horses stayed sane this time, bursting out like arrows from a bow into the Deverry line. Dust plumed up as the two lines met in a howl of war cries, tearing the air. Arzosah leveled, then flew upward again, flapping hard and swinging toward the west. Over the river where Jill had died, she pivoted round and came at the Horsekin cavalry broadside. This time, panic broke out like the fires of the night before. Caught by the press of battle, the heavy chargers could neither run nor turn. Instead they reared, kicking and bucking, while the Deverry riders pressed forward on steady mounts.

Arzosah roared, dipping down, down, dangerously down. Rhodry could see the faces of the Horsekin warriors that scattered away from her, smell the acrid sweat of terrified horses as she skimmed the army. He felt a jolt, heard a shriek. Suddenly she swooped up, flapping hard to gain height, because in her claws she held a Horsekin warleader. Dressed in cloth of gold buckled over his armor, he screamed and writhed in her talons as they gained height, hundreds of yards now above the Horsekin line. His finery shredded and billowed round him while she rumbled in laughter.

"For my mate!" she hissed.

And dropped him. With a long shriek, he fell, spinning down and down, to land among his own men like a stone from a catapult. Rhodry heard the cavalry shriek in pure horror when he struck. Although he twisted round to look back, Arzosah was flying away from the battlefield, and he could see nothing.

"They're sallying," she called out. "I'll land now."

Rhodry twisted back and looked toward the dun. The gates were swinging open and Cadmar's warband was racing out, four abreast. The dragon flew south until they found the carts and servants, waiting a safe distance away. Rhodry slid down from her back and ran to his new mount, the waiting roan.

"Watch out for that blasted archer!" Arzosah bellowed.

"I will." He set his foot in the stirrup and mounted. "I know what a longbow can do."

As they trotted that last mile back to the battlefield, Rhodry saw black smoke plume into the sky. So, they'd gained the Horsekin camp and fired it once again, had they? Fearing he'd be too late, he drew his sword and smacked the roan to a run, but when they burst over the last rise, he saw below him a battlefield in chaos. He pulled up to let the roan catch its breath while he oriented himself. Although the main thrust of the cavalry had been smashed and routed, all over the muddy field riders paired off or mobbed each other in clots of three and four. Horses were slipping and falling, their riders falling again over the corpses and the wounded, or struggling to their feet covered in bloody muck to search for a loose horse.

Out on the center of the field, the infantry was making a stand, drawn up in ragged squares, three shields deep on a side. Around these hedges of spears, the Deverry riders milled, half-helpless. Every now and then, a rider would charge in, only to pull off at the last moment from the steel-tipped pikes. Behind the field, the enemy camp burned, but badly, as the fire set in haste by the men sallying smoldered in wet canvas and soaked wood. Black smoke poured out to mingle with dust and hang in flat sheets over the battle.

Shouting broke out on the left. The dwarven axmen were attacking the largest square. In dead silence, they moved forward, axes swinging low, slicing like scythes below the line of shields. Since the spearmen had set their weapons at a high angle for horsemen, they began to lose their wall as they scrabbled to change position. The waiting horsemen could charge, slamming into the break from the side while the dwarves went on cutting from in front. At first, Rhodry couldn't find the Westfolk archers; then he realized that they'd dismounted and gone to their longbows. Up like deadly rain, the arrows flashed in the murky light and fell among the spearmen. Yelling and cursing, they swung their shields up to catch the shafts. The dwarves kept coming, and the Deverry men charged again. The curses turned to screaming as the shield wall broke.

Rhodry started down, letting the roan pick its way through the dead and dying while he rose in the stirrups, searching for the enemy archer. All round him, little eddies of mounted combat swirled; infantrymen ran for their lives while horsemen charged after, cutting them down with no mercy. Rhodry dodged and swore and kept clear, swinging round the fighting with no shame. He'd risked his life to bring them the dragon, and the dragon had brought them the victory. Now, for reward, he wanted vengeance.

He headed toward the east ridge, looking—always looking—for the archer even as he came to feel the search hopeless. Evandar had told him only a sketch of words; he'd never seen the man himself. What he couldn't know, of course, was that the archer was looking for him, his futile bow laid aside. For that reason alone, they met. As he rode toward the trampled, smoldering remains of tents below the eastern hills, Rhodry saw a human rider in Deverry gear, mounted on a gray, trotting straight for him. Thinking him an ally, he paused the roan. His shield still hung at the saddle-peak.

"Silver Dagger?" the fellow called out.

"I am, at that. Who's looking for me?"

For an answer, the rider charged straight for him. Caught off-guard, Rhodry flung up his sword in a clumsy parry that caught the other's strike by luck alone. The roan danced and swung away barely in time to avoid the gray, who would have otherwise slammed straight into its flank. Swearing, Rhodry twisted in the saddle. A strike from the rear glanced off his mail but left a streak of pain behind. As he pulled his horse's head round to face the enemy, Rhodry began to laugh. His enemy flinched in the saddle, a gesture that made his horse begin to back. With a curse of his own, the enemy threw his weight forward, halting the horse but leaving him off-balance.

Laughter flowed of its own will as Rhodry risked a lean and a stab at his sword arm. The enemy caught it on his blade and pushed the thrust away, then circled the blade over and slashed. With no shield, Rhodry could only parry, a solid block, this time, that hung their blades together in a lock of brute force. Rhodry saw his face, lean and pale and as sharp as a knife blade, gray eyes as well. He howled and forced the man's sword down, slipped his own free, and struck, a circling slantwise blow that caught him high on the chest, hard enough to make him grunt and sway. With a lean and a knee, he swung the gray round and left Rhodry no target but his shield. A red spiral twined on a blue ground.

"Brin Mawrvelin!" Rhodry gasped.

"It is, Silver Dagger." He was panting for breath himself. "I'm Matyc's brother."

Rhodry shrilled with laughter that he could no more have controlled than he could have stopped the sun in its course, but it seemed that Lord Tren heard it as mockery. With a bark of rage, he spurred the gray straight forward. As the roan danced to the side and past, Rhodry twisted and struck at his shield arm from behind the shield. Tren swore and let the shield dangle, then fall. He leaned and swung the gray round with his weight and his knees just as Rhodry struck again. This cut missed, and once more they faced other, Tren dead pale and swaying. His arm hung useless at a wrong angle.

With a dangerous lean, Rhodry ducked under Tren's weak stab and slapped the sword blade hard across the lord's mouth. He reeled back in the saddle. On the backhand, Rhodry smacked the gray hard on the neck. When the horse reared, Tren tumbled off into the mud of the battlefield. Chortling under his breath, Rhodry dismounted and ran to him. In the slippery welter, Tren was trying to get up. He leaned on the broken arm, cried out, choked on the blood from his broken mouth, and fell back again. Rhodry wrapped both hands round his sword hilt and raised it high.

"Yraen!" he cried out, then plunged the point into Tren's neck.

Laughter overwhelmed him. He pulled the sword free and stood beside the corpse, howling and swaying, until he saw, far above him, a raven, far too large to be an ordinary bird.

"Come down!" Rhodry shrieked. "Come down, my lady raven! Come down, and we'll have a fight of it on my ground."

With a long cry, she flew off, heading north into the hills. Rhodry felt the berserker fit leave him. For a moment, he stood panting for breath; then he wept in a brief scatter of tears. Without another glance at Tren's body, he mounted the roan and rode off, back to a dying battle, still screaming behind him.

When the battle began that morning, and all the men in the dun had gone down to the gates to wait for their chance to sally, Lady Labanna gathered all the women round her in the great hall, where they would wait, or so she announced, for the outcome. For some while, Carra dutifully sat in a chair near the lady's own and waited with Lightning lying at her feet. Every servant and wounded man in the dun eventually drifted in to join them; as the hall filled up, it grew hot and the air heavy with the smell of the barely washed. News came only rarely, when one of the men up on the dun wall thought to climb down and relay to the lady what little he could see. Standing in the doorway, Jahdo did report the dragon's flight over the dun, and briefly, everyone cheered. More waiting, no news; Carra decided to use her condition to her advantage.

"My lady, I feel so faint," she whispered. "May I go to my chamber and lie down?"

"Certainly, child! Ocradda, will you help Her Highness?"

Up in her chamber, Carra listened at the door until she could be sure that Ocradda had gone back downstairs, then crept out and hurried up to the roof. Passing through the landing where she'd seen Jill lying dead was no easy task, but remembering that Jill would have wanted her to be strong kept her climbing. Panting for breath and slightly dizzy from the climb, she hauled herself onto the roof among the heaped stones and bundled arrows, while Lightning whined below at the foot of the ladder he couldn't climb.

"I'll be right down. I daren't stay here long."

Carra walked to the southern edge of the dun and looked out, peering through the smokey air, only to find that she could see little and interpret less. Far below, like pieces on the board of some mad game, clots of men rode back and forth, met and swayed. She could pick out the shield squares, hear the drift of faint shouting, watch the smoke spread from the ruined camp. It seemed clear enough that Cengarn's allies were winning through, but somehow she'd never considered that they would do otherwise. What mattered to her now was one thing only: would Dar live, would he reach her, would she ever see him again? She walked round the roof, fetched up eventually at the northern edge, and realized that by standing just right and holding her head at the proper angle, she could see the north gate.

A ragged contingent of militia seemed to be waiting there. As she watched, she saw the gate swing open, and the pack trotted out, heading for the ruined camp. All at once, she realized that the lord and his men must have sallied from the south gate earlier, that the scavengers would never have left till the battle had gone their way. Yet, no matter where she stood on the roof, the south gate stayed stubbornly hidden behind hillside and house.

"Carra!" It was Dallandra, climbing onto the roof. "Ye gods, you little idiot! What are you doing up here?"

"Trying to see. Oh, please, Dalla, don't be so vexed with me. I get so sick of it, shut up like a prize sow!"

"I can sympathize, but you've forgotten the raven mazrak, haven't you?"

Carra went sick and cold. She had, at that. Scowling up at the sky, Dalla stood in the center of the roof and turned, looking all the way round the horizon.

"Well, no sign of her," the dweomermaster said at last. "She may have fled. With Alshandra gone, she can't have much power or magic left. I swear it, she didn't know one thing about what she was doing!"

"What do you mean? How can you work magic if you don't know how?"

"A very good question indeed, Your Highness. I don't pretend to understand it, but I think that our raven was drawing all her power from her false goddess, rather as if she were a waterspout leading rainwater down to a barrel."

Dallandra walked over to join Carra, then looked up again, studying the sky.

"There!" At last she pointed. "Look to the north! Can you see that bird up there?"

Carra could just distinguish a speck, moving with the same motion as a bird flying fast and hard.

"Is that her? How can you tell?"

"Elven eyes are a fair bit better than human ones. Poor Carra! You're about to learn many a strange thing about your husband's people."

"Will you stop calling me 'poor Carra'! I get so sick of that, too, everyone pitying me."

"Then stop acting so piteous. You bring it on yourself."

Carra felt her cheeks burning with a blush. The truth in Dalla's words was like a slap across the face. Rather than answer, she walked a few steps toward the south and stared out. Far down below on the winding streets, a warrior was coming, trotting beside his foaming horse to spare it his weight as they climbed the last hill to the dun. His helm hung at the saddle-peak, and she could see his raven-dark hair. On his back he carried a slung bow.

"Dar! Dar!"

He heard, looked up, laughed, and waved. Dallandra forgotten, Carra dashed for the ladder and went down so fast and clumsily that she nearly missed a rung, but she caught herself in time. With Lightning bounding after, she hurried down the staircase, spiraling round and round, bursting into the great hall, dashing past the startled women and out of the broch just as Dar raced into the ward, his near-foundered horse trailing behind. By then, both of them were so out of breath that they could only cling to each other and gasp, laughing when they had the air, staring into each other's eyes when they didn't.

"You're alive," she gasped at last. "Thank the Goddess!"

"Very much alive." He bent his head and kissed her. "And so are you."

As they clung together, as she nestled into his arms, she realized at last what Jill and Dallandra had been trying to tell her, that she'd been in perhaps the worst danger of all. Around them the ward filled with servants, shouting and laughing, calling out to one another about the victory. Dar only held her the tighter and laughed, a crow of triumph, while she clung to him and laughed as well.

With the fighting done, Rhodry turned the roan over to one of Erddyr's men and walked into the Horsekin camp. It was a mad gesture, and he knew it, but he wanted to find Yraen's body. The camp lay strewn, blood-soaked wreckage. In places, sheltered by an overhang or wagon, the fires still flickered among canvas and cloth; in others, smoke wisped above black slabs and tangles. Over everything hung stench—wool, hair, flesh, all charred and stinking wet from the unnatural rain of the night before. Corpses, both human and Horsekin, lay in pools of bloodstained mud. Here and there, dying horses staggered, trying to find their way home, or lay collapsed on the ground, struggling to rise.

Some yards in, Rhodry came to a blackened tent crumpled over a smoldering wagon. Half-smothered in the soaked canvas lay a man, moaning and struggling to free himself—a Horsekin slave, judging by his iron anklet. Rhodry knelt down and pulled him free, turned him over, and looked into a face that was more a boy's than a man's, a blond lad, his narrow face covered with blood from a cut over one eye, his chest crushed by the blow of some heavy weapon. He looked so familiar that Rhodry found himself searching for his name. The lad tried to speak, then gulped for air and died. Rhodry laid him down, closed his eyes, and knelt for a moment, trying to remember where he'd seen him before. At length, he realized that the slave merely reminded him of someone he used to know, Amyr, a man who'd ridden in his warband, back in the days when he'd ruled as gwerbret, back before the secret of his elven blood had deposed him. And where had Amyr died? He couldn't remember— in some battle or another—along with plenty of other men who'd sworn to him, no doubt, men whose names he'd forgotten at this lapse of time.

With a shake of his head, Rhodry got up. Above, the sky was clearing fast; a few white thunderheads piled and scudded, their towering palaces of cloud touched and turned golden by the late sun. He watched them for a moment, a promise of some paradise, forever unreachable, then walked on, hunting back and forth among the wreckage and the dead. The farther uphill he went, the less burnt the tents and the easier the hunting; he drew his sword and kept alert, because there were likely to be stragglers, hiding out and desperate. All at once, he heard someone call his name and turned to find Evandar, still dressed in his illusion of armor.

"The gwerbret's asking for you," Evandar said. "He's at the south gate."

Rhodry swore with every foul oath he could muster.

"What's so wrong?" Evandar stepped back out of reach. "What are you looking for, anyway?"

"Yraen's body." Rhodry paused to run filthy hands through filthy hair. "You can call me daft for it, but I want to know how he died, and I want him properly buried."

Evandar sighed, leaning on a spear, whether real or an illusion, Rhodry couldn't tell.

"Do you know where he is?" Rhodry snapped. "I never know what you've seen or not."

"He's dead."

"I mean his body."

"Why do you care?"

"I don't know." Rhodry felt himself tremble, turned half away and rubbed his eyes hard on the back of his sleeve. "I don't even know."

"But it means much to you. Well, then. You go to the gwerbret. I'll see what I can do."

Before Rhodry could answer, he disappeared. Rhodry stood for a moment, looking round, wondering if he dared trust Evandar. Whether he did or not, there was no disobeying a direct order from the gwerbret. With one last shake of his head, he headed for the south gate.

Gwerbret Cadmar was sitting on the wet ground, his back to a broken wagon, with Drwmyc of Dun Trebyc kneeling on one knee beside him. Rhodry dropped to both knees before the lords.

"You called for me, Your Grace?"

"I did," Cadmar said. "You've earned your hire ten times over, Silver Dagger, by fetching that beast. I wanted to thank you personally."

"His Grace is most generous to an outcast man."

"His Grace knows what's fitting and due. At the victory feast, Silver Dagger, you'll sit at my table."

Rhodry felt his eyes fill with tears beyond all his power to stop them. He could only shake his head and stammer until the gwerbret dismissed him out of sympathy.

By then, the sun was sinking low in the sky. Although men searched for any friends they knew to be left behind on the battlefield, everyone was too exhausted, and too many lords and captains were dead, for the army to mount an organized hunt for wounded. Rhodry helped one man with a broken arm inside the city walls, then wandered up to the dun, his mad search for Yraen forgotten as the battle fever deserted him. All through the ward lay wounded men, dying men, dumped there by comrades who could do nothing more for them. Over by the main well, the chirurgeons had set up a surgery of sorts, using the back of a wagon to lay the wounded on while servants rushed round, bringing kettles of water and helping tear bandages from whatever cloth they could commandeer. Off to one side, Dallandra was measuring out herbs by the handful and brewing them up in the vessels that servants brought her. In this chaos, she would have not a moment for a word with him.

Rhodry was about to go into the main broch and scrounge something to eat when he heard a boy's voice calling his name. For a moment, Rhodry didn't recognize the ragged child, his dirty face streaked with fresh tears, who came running across the ward. The boy stopped and stepped back as fast as if Rhodry had slapped him.

"It's Jahdo, Rhodry," the lad said, gulping for breath. "Is it that you've forgotten me?"

"What? I haven't at that, lad. I wouldn't say I'm truly myself now, that's all. Where's your master?"

"You haven't heard? He were slain. They did attack us, and he did go down to the walls to curse them, but the man with the longbow did kill him. He were a bard, a true bard, but the archer did slay him all the same."

"Oh, did he now?" Rhodry could hear his voice, cold, steady, a thing of pure hate. "Well, the archer's dead, lad. I killed him myself, and not all that long ago."

Jahdo stopped crying. He started to grin, then let the expression fade into bewilderment, and finally turned away, trying to wipe his eyes but only smearing the dirt on his face with a dirtier sleeve.

"What's so wrong?" Rhodry said.

"I know not. Truly it does gladden my heart that Meer be avenged. He were Gel da'Thae, and vengeance will make him sing, when they come to tell him in the Deathworld. Surely someone will tonight, there be so many men dead."

"That's true enough, and the war not over yet."

"Not over?"

"Well, lad, we have to harry the routed Horsekin. We don't want them coming right back, do we now? We'll be leaving in a couple of days."

"Oh. Rhodry, may I come with you?"

"What?"

"I could be your page, like, and learn to fight. It be needful that I find some kind of place."

"But lad, you'll never make a warrior. You could be killed."

"Well, I do doubt that ever will I see my home again anyway, not with Meer gone, and me naught in everyone's eyes."

"No man knows what another's Wyrd has in store for him. Your tale's a sad one, but there's naught I can do to—hold a moment. Jill told me once that she'd promised Meer you'd get home."

"But she be dead, too, in the saving of us all.", Silent tears welled and ran. "And Meer be dead, and here I have naught and am naught, not like at home. This be a harsh place, Deverry, whether or no you do cut off people's heads like the Slavers did. And so I thought, it be needful for me to learn to be harsh, too."

"Hush, lad! For her sake and Meer's both, I'll honor her promise. I'll see what we can do about getting you home once the war's over."

Jahdo grinned and stammered thanks in a joy that was the first clean thing Rhodry had seen all that long day.

"How many men have we lost?" Garin said.

"Seventy-some dead outright," Brel Avro said. "We'll lose a few of the wounded before morning, I'll wager."

Garin swore under his breath, but only feebly. His legs were melting under him, it seemed, and his heart knocked against his lungs. He sat down hard on the floor and rested his head on his knees. With a grunt, the warleader knelt beside him.

"Are you hurt?"

"No. Just weary."

"So we all are, so we all are."

They were sitting in the common room of the underground inn, which Brel had commandeered for a hospital and command post both. It held, just barely, all the wounded dwarves in its chambers and hallways. On a table near the hearth, by the leaping light of fire and torches, the chirurgeon they'd brought with them was still stitching wounds, whistling tunelessly under his breath as he did so. Garin felt like screaming at him to shut up.

"Drink this." Brel shoved a tiny glass stoup of herbed liquor under Garin's nose. "It'll bring the blood back to your head."

Garin took the stoup and tried a cautious sip—bitter, fiery, but invigorating. The scent knifed into his nose and made him remember other times he'd drunk in this inn.

"I wonder if Rori lived through the fight," Garin said.

"Good question. He's a berserker, after all."

Garin nodded, gulping down another mouthful of pale fire.

"Well, Cengarn's free," Brel went on. "And we've fulfilled our obligation, but I'll tell you something, Envoy. If our gwerbret rides after the murdering scum, I say we join him."

Garin tossed off the last of the liquor and saluted him with the empty stoup.

"So do I." He wiped his mouth and mustaches on the back of his hand. "I'll tell him that, too. We'll be meeting in council tonight. Here, help me up. I'd best go attend upon his grace. By the Thunderer! I don't even know if he's still alive."

Once he was on his feet, Garin could keep moving, though the liquor and the aftermath of the day's battle made the firelight dance round him in golden waves. Outside, it was cooling off, and blessedly dim with twilight. The streets, though, were still crammed with livestock and refugees, prudently waiting for dawn to leave the shelter of the walls. The stench of dung and urine hung thick in the air as Garin dodged cows and children, sidestepped camps and cooking fires. Every now and then, he stepped over a wounded man, too, who'd managed to drag himself inside the walls.

Cadmar's ward was mobbed. Wounded men, wounded horses, servants rushing back and forth, soldiers searching for friends, women weeping—the dwarf could barely push himself through and reach the door of the great hall. Inside, packed into the torchlight, the men who could still stand stood round or perched on tables, swilling ale, gobbling chunks of cold meat. The elven archers huddled together, drinking more than eating, across the hall by open windows. No one, men or Westfolk, seemed to be talking much.

Garin slipped in and kept to the wall, inching round the curve until he could see the table of honor and count up the noble-born. The two gwerbrets still lived, relatively unscathed, but then, no one would have let them lead charges. Prince Daralanteriel stood next to Cadmar's chair, his face smeared with dirt and cold fury as he clasped a silver goblet so tightly in one hand that Garin feared it might smash. Calonderiel sat next to Tieryn Magryn. This lord, that lord—many accounted for, Lord Erddyr with his head bandaged and blood streaking his beard, the child-lord, as Garin thought of Gwandyc, looking wide-eyed and pale, but no sign of Comerr and Nomyr.

All at once, Garin broke out grinning. Sitting at the end of the table, speaking to no one, was Rhodry, with a young lad in a dirty shirt standing behind him like a page. Garin started over, dodging through clusters of people until the gwerbret noticed him.

"Here!" Cadmar hauled himself to his feet. "Let the envoy through! Someone find him a chair."

Garin took the chair, but he waved away mead—he didn't fancy pouring it down on top of the medicinal.

"Rori!" he called down. "It gladdens my heart to see you!"

Rhodry smiled and waved.

"Our berserker's a friend of yours, Envoy?" Cadmar said.

"He is, Your Grace. It gladdens my heart to see you and so many of your lords alive, too. Uh, is Tieryn Comerr—?"

"Dead? He is, and Lord Nomyr and young Peddyn, too, which aches my heart. Our prince here's lost his lieutenant, Jennantar, as well."

"Your Highness." Garin bobbed his head in the prince's direction. "My heart sorrows for you."

Daralanteriel started to speak, then thought better of it, frowning hard into his goblet.

"He'll be avenged," Calonderiel said flatly. "They all will. And what of your people, Envoy? I saw them in the middle of hard fighting."

"We've lost a fair number, truly. But then, every warband gathered here today has lost far too highly for the peace of anyone's heart."

"Well said, Envoy." Calonderiel nodded in his direction. "Well said, indeed."

Every man within earshot raised goblet or tankard in grim salute.

That night, the army slept anywhere it could, whether in dun walls or out of them. With Jahdo in tow, Rhodry left the town and picked his way through the dead and dying until he found Arzosah, who'd made herself a camp off to the west and far away from the carnage. A stream ran through the western plain, and the dragon had settled herself in a copse of trees beside it. When Rhodry found her, she lay inert, so drowsy that he knew she must have fed well. He decided against asking her upon what. The boy, who was carrying a lantern, held it up to wash her in its dappled light.

"Oh, she be so grand," Jahdo whispered. "Never have I seen her so close, just did I see her fly, like, over the town."

At that, Arzosah raised a drowsy head and opened one eye. Jahdo stifled a shriek.

"What's this?" the dragon rumbled. "Another dwarf?"

"Nah, nah, nah," Rhodry said. "A child, and he's under my protection. By the power of your name, I enjoin you to treat him as a friend and protect him if ever need be."

Arzosah yawned with a long whining sigh.

"Another burden! May the god of dragons help me! First this wretched dragonmaster, and now his cub!"

"Arzosah—" Rhodry held up the ring.

"I hear you! Of course, I'll have to obey you. I promise, I promise. He shall be as my own little hatchling would be."

"How do dragons treat their hatchlings?"

"My, you're clever! But have no fear. A hatchling is our greatest treasure." She swung her head and squinted at Jahdo. "What's your name, lad?"

"Jahdo, my lady." He swallowed heavily. "Truly, you be the most beautiful thing that ever I did see, in my whole life."

Arzosah rumbled.

"At least he has nice manners. Very well, Jahdo. You may count yourself a dragon friend. Now please, Dragonmaster, won't you take these wretched straps off me? I'm so tired."

With Jahdo's help, Rhodry undid her harness and let her shake it off. The boy had brought his tattered blankets from the dun, and Rhodry found his bedroll in the general clutter of gear. They both just barely had the strength to spread them out, and as soon as Rhodry lay down, boots, sword belt, and all, he fell asleep.

With the morning, the men and lords alike found the life to cull the battlefield. The warbands began rescuing what wounded men had survived till dawn, killing those Horsekin who'd done the same, and looting the dead, enemy and friend alike. Rhodry sent Jahdo back into Cengarn with a message for Garin, asking the envoy to find the boy some food and clothes as a personal favor. Once the lad was on his way, Rhodry harnessed up a grumbling Arzosah.

"I don't want to fly today," she snarled. "My wings ache."

"My heart bleeds. I'm not taking any chances. I've seen these Horsekin fight now. For all I know, they're hale and hateful enough to regroup for another fight. No one's keeping a decent watch, as far as I can tell."

"Oh, very well, but I'll wager they're not. They're not demons, you know, only made of flesh and blood, just like poor, weary dragons are."

In the event, Arzosah was proved right. They found the remnant of the routed army camped, if you could call the straggling disorder they found a camp, some ten miles away. Rhodry had to marvel that they'd managed to retreat so far. As far as he could tell in their brief circle round the encampment, the Horsekin force numbered in the high hundreds, but they had far fewer horses—and fewer still remained after Arzosah risked one low pass over the herd. Screaming and cursing, the Horsekin rushed out a volley of futile spears, then contented themselves with trying to round up their fleeing stock.

362

"They'll get used to me, sooner or later," Arzosah called back over the beating of her wings. "We'd best not play this trick too often."

"Just so. Let's get back to Cengarn. Land up at the gwerbret's dun."

By the time they returned, the town was emptying out. In long weary lines, farmers trudged out the gates, driving their remaining cattle before them, carrying children on their shoulders and cages of chickens in their hands. They would find their houses burnt and their fields ravaged, but in their carts they had their ploughs and seed corn, more precious than gold here in the aftermath of siege. We came in time, Rhodry thought. They won't starve, and they won't be speared and butchered. When tears sprang to his eyes, he was shocked at himself, that he, a noble-born man no matter how far he'd fallen in the world, would be so proud of saving the lives of farmers, crude peasants all of them. But despite his bemused surprise, he felt like singing when he saw them heading home.

Arzosah landed on the roof of one of the lower brochs. Rhodry unharnessed her, then tied his gear and the harness into a neat bundle.

"Carry this down with you, will you?"

"I will. I'll find a nice spot for us to camp. Would anyone mind if I ate some more of those dead horses, Master? I hate to see them going to waste."

"I don't see why you shouldn't. But don't eat any of the men, not human, not dwarven, not elven—not even the Horsekin. I don't want everyone running to me and crying sacrilege."

"Oh, very well, if you say so."

"I do say so. And when you've done eating, you stay at our camp and go to sleep." Rhodry held up the ring and caught the sunlight upon the metal. "Wait for me there."

"I will, I will. What are you going to do?"

"I don't know. Walk round a bit. See where my new page has got to. Find some ale and drink myself blind."

"Here, you're still heartsick over Jill's death!"

"Just so. Did you think I wouldn't be?"

The dragon rustled her wings in a shrug, then seized the gear in her talons, bunched, and leapt into the air. For a moment, he watched her glide, heading for the battlefield and its rich harvest of horse meat, then climbed through the trapdoor and hurried downstairs through the silent tower and out to the ward.

Its doors flung wide in triumph, Cadmar's main broch stood silent and empty. Rhodry found a page hurrying out and discovered why. To celebrate the victory, there would be a feast that night, but out in the meadows to the south of town, the only area that could accommodate the entire army. The servants and whatever town folk could be pressed into service had already rolled out the barrels of ale and carried down the various sacks of provisions. Except for the guards at the gates, the warbands had gone off for the grimmer task of helping bury the dead. Rhodry stood looking up at the towers and wished that Yraen were alive.

From inside the great hall, a harp trilled in a minor key, as if the bard were practicing a mourning song, but when he went to the doorway, Rhodry saw Evandar, his armor gone, sitting cross-legged on the table of honor up by the dragon hearth. The lap harp he played stood long and narrow in the trapezoidal elven style, all inlaid with mother-of-pearl in a pattern of seahorses and seaweeds. Drawn by the music, Rhodry joined him, but Evandar never looked up, merely frowned over his song as it began to take shape, a melody so filled with hiraedd that Rhodry's eyes filled with tears. Evandar glanced up, saw him, and let the song die in a scatter of random notes.

"No need to stop for my sake." Rhodry wiped his eyes on his sleeve.

"It's Jill that makes you so sad, then?"

"It is, and Yraen, and every good man killed here."

Evandar nodded, looked at the harp for a moment, then picked it up and tossed it into the air. Rhodry yelped, but long before it reached the stone floor the harp disappeared, as if it had fallen through some invisible window. Evandar climbed down from the table and stretched like a cat.

364

"Ill news, Rori. I never did find Yraen. He's somewhere in the old siege camp, I suppose, buried under the other dead in a trench. I'm sorry. I wanted to set your mind at rest."

"You have my thanks." Rhodry sighed sharply and looked away. "You were right yesterday. It doesn't much matter. He's dead. Where he lies won't change that."

"It aches my heart to see you so sad."

"Truly? I didn't think you cared much for the likes of us."

"Only for you and Dalla. The rest come and go like birds, here in the spring, gone in the fall of the year. I can never tell one from the other."

"Ah. Well, I suppose we'd look that way to you."

Evandar nodded, glancing round the great hall with a peculiar expression on his face, as if he were judging it and finding it somehow lacking.

"What are you doing?" Rhodry said.

"Making plans." Evandar flashed him a grin, then wandered over to the hearth. He ran one hand over the carving and peered at the designs. "This is a fine bit of carving, wouldn't you say?"

"It is, I suppose."

"Imph." Evandar had his tongue stuck out of the corner of his mouth while he examined the tiny bands of interlace down the dragon's body. "These delicate bits here. Did the masons cut them with a chisel?"

"How would I know?"

"I wonder how many masons it took to do this? Do you know?"

"I don't. Ye gods, who cares? Will you stop worrying at that blasted stone?"

Evandar straightened up and blinked at him.

"Oh well, lots of time later, I suppose."

"For what?"

"Studying this hearth. By the by, what about Jill's books?"

"What about them?"

"She borrowed some of them from a man I know down Bardek way."

"Then you'd best take them back to him. We should fetch them out of her chamber right now. You don't want the servants tearing out pages to light fires and suchlike."

If the ward had seemed empty, Jill's familiar chamber felt so cold and dead that he wondered if her very possessions somehow knew that their mistress would never come home again. When he and Evandar stepped in, silence seemed to slap them in the face, even though her narrow bed stood unmade, just as if she'd use it again, and a book lay open on the table, where it would catch the light from the window, just as if she were coming back to read it. Her packs and sacks of herbs and other medicines sat in the curve of the wall. She'd probably planned on using them to tend the wounded after the siege was lifted. Rhodry ran one hand over her pillow and felt his throat clench.

"There's a lot of those books," Evandar said. "Dalla will want most of them. I'll just take these three back to Meranaldan."

"Meranaldan? That's an elven name! You said he lived in Bardek."

"I said he lived down Bardek way, which is a very different thing." Evandar began picking up the books, one at a time, and slung them into the air to disappear just as the harp had. "It's a riddle."

Then there was, Rhodry supposed, no arguing with him. He went to the window and leaned onto the sill to look down to the distant cobbles.

"What about the things in this chest?" Evandar said. "Do you think any of them have dweomer?"

"I wouldn't know if they did. You could ask Dalla."

Far below, a dog was trotting across the ward. Rhodry watched until it disappeared round the corner of the stables. Behind him, he heard Evandar sigh, then walk over to join him.

"I don't understand sorrow, Rori, but I can see yours. It's interesting, truly. Dalla taught me to understand joy, and I think you're going to teach me sorrow. You and Dalla loved each other once, didn't you?"

Rhodry spun round to find Evandar smiling, someone who possessed more dweomer than any human being ever could muster, someone who could, for all Rhodry knew, make him disappear as completely and utterly as the books had.

"I wouldn't call it love, and I doubt if she would either. Does it trouble your heart?"

"Not at all, not at all. That's not the sorrow I meant. I was just thinking that you and she were two sides of a pair, sorrow and joy."

"I don't understand."

"Well, is loving you going to bring me aught but sorrow?"

All at once, Rhodry remembered the kiss he'd been given so long ago. He thought of stepping back, but he was caught against the window.

"It's never brought anyone much but sorrow," Rhodry said. "Why should you be any different?"

"No reason in the world, truly."

Rhodry started to speak, thought better of it, then twisted away from the narrow space and strode out into the middle of the room.

"Are you going to look through that chest?" Evandar said from behind him. "I'd imagine you'd want something of Jill's, just to keep, like."

"I don't." He took a step toward the door. "If you find anything dweomer in there, do what you think fit with it. You'd know better than I."

Rhodry was unaware of the other man moving, but all at once he felt hands upon his shoulders—cool hands that were more like glass than flesh, but the touch of another being had its comfort, alien or not. He froze, feeling tears rising in his throat.

"It's not like I still loved Jill," he said, more to himself than to Evandar. "It just seems that my whole life's gone with her. The life I had before, or who I was before. Ah, ye gods, I don't know what I mean."

The hands stroked along his shoulders, held him a little tighter. Rhodry turned, knocked them away, found himself looking straight into Evandar's eyes, as turquoise as a summer sea, and as alien.

"I don't understand that, either," Evandar said. "But maybe Dalla will."

"Maybe so. It doesn't much matter now."

"Why not?"

"Will you stop?"

Evandar laughed and made him a mocking sort of bow.

"What will you do now, then?"

"Go with the army after the Horsekin. They need me to scout. If we don't harry them to our borders, who knows what they'll do?"

"True enough, but Cadmar doesn't need a dragon to find his enemies."

"So? It's the shape-changer I'm after. I've sworn vengeance on that bitch, for Yraen and Jill and Meer as well."

Evandar sighed and looked away, and it seemed that he was, if not sad, then at least miming sadness.

"Very well, then. I'll see you again when I do."

With a flicker of light, like a glint of sun on moving water, Evandar disappeared. Rhodry stood for a moment, staring at the place where he'd been, then swore under his breath. He strode out of the chamber and hurried down the staircase to the comfort of things he understood, even if those things were war and death.

Dallandra had spent the previous night working with the chirurgeons. All of them had driven themselves to work by lantern light until a few hours before dawn, when it became clear that they would only do more harm than help if they didn't get some sleep. She dragged herself to her chamber and bed only to dream of wounds, broken bone, all white and shattered, cut flesh, bruised flesh, red blood, and blackening gore. After a few hours of this she woke, went down to work some more, then finally, near noon, crawled back to her bed and slept without dreaming. She woke again late in the day to the stink of old blood; she'd forgotten to wash.

Feeling as if she'd gag, she got up, found an inadequate pitcher of water, bent her head over the basin, and poured the whole thing over, then dabbled the worst of the blood from her hands in the resulting mess. She staggered down to the women's hall, only to find it empty, went down to the great hall but found no one but Jahdo.

Freshly bathed and combed, the lad was wearing clean clothes, a shirt of obvious dwarven craftsmanship, a pair of trousers of the same, both the right length but far too wide for him. He had them belted with a strip of leather, tied in a knot for want of a buckle.

"What's this?" she said, laughing. "Have you been adopted by the Mountain Folk?"

"I've not, my lady, but Rhodry, he did take me on as his page, and then he did send me to Garin, who did give me these things."

"Good, good." She glanced round. "Where is everyone?"

"At the victory feast, my lady. It do be late in the day. Rhodry sent me here to see if I could find you."

"Ah. Well, you have. Can you haul a couple of buckets of water up to my chamber for me?"

"I will, my lady, and gladly."

After a cold wash and a change of clothes, she felt nearly alive again, but she lingered in her chamber. She was tempted to leave Cengarn, to step through a gate into Evandar's country and leave the wounded and dying, the stinking streets and the ravaged countryside all far behind her. Yet if she left, what would happen to Carra and the baby? The raven mazrak still flew free, as far as any one knew. Was she still a threat?

"Evandar, Evandar," she said aloud. "I miss you."

"And you're never far from my thoughts, either, my love."

All at once he appeared, leaning comfortably against the wall near the window. He was dressed in his green tunic and leather trousers, and he had a red rose tucked behind one ear. When she ran to him, he threw his arms round her, but he felt barely substantial, as if she clung to a creature of glass, all smooth and cold. The rose gave off the richest perfume she'd ever smelled, so sweet and strong that she knew it had never grown upon the earth.

"It's been a hellish time," he remarked. "I'm glad I've seen this."

"What?" She pulled away. "How can you say that?"

"It's all been very interesting. I never quite understood before when you spoke of death."

"Oh. I see. Well, there's been enough of that and more to come, truly."

"True." Evandar held her close, stroking her hair. "It aches your heart so badly, my love. I wish you could find some comfort for it."

"You're comfort enough, but I know you can't stay here long."

"Won't you come away with me, back to our country, just for a little while?"

"How long will your little while be as Cengarn measures Time? Days? Years?"

Evandar smiled with a rueful twist of his cherry-colored mouth.

"Well, so it might be if we grew distracted and lingered. Very well. I've things I must attend to, but you'll see me again soon. But here, I've no objection to Rhodry, you know, none at all."

With that he vanished, leaving the cool touch of his hands on hers like a scent. Dallandra raised her hands to her face to drink it in, then wept. She would just manage to force the tears under control when some image or memory would rise of the slaughter behind her—a wounded man dying even as she tried to staunch his wounds, the heap of corpses thrown outside the dun gates to wait for burial, the look on a man's face when she told him his friend would lose a leg—and she would weep again. She rose from the chair, paced across the room, sobbing in frustration as much as grief, strode back and forth, until she heard someone walk up to the doorway and spun round, hoping for Evandar, finding Rhodry instead, clean and shaven and wearing a new linen shirt with Cengarn's blazon upon it.

"You've not come out to the feasting," he said. "Here, what's so wrong?"

"What's wrong?" She found herself screaming at him. "What do you mean? So many men dead and dying, and you ask me what's wrong? Ye gods! How death-besotted are you people?"

In three quick strides, he crossed the room. He grabbed her wrists and pulled her close.

"Hush, hush," he whispered. "You're so weary you're half-mad, Dalla."

She looked up into his eyes and felt her rage leave her.

"Maybe so." She twisted away from him. "I do know I can't bear the feasting. I just can't."

"The worst is over. The bard's done all his declamations, the gwerbrets have had their speeches, and the real drinking's started."

At that she managed to smile, but mostly because he wanted her to. It would be very easy, she realized, to fall into his arms and bed at that moment, just for the comfort of it, especially when she remembered Evandar's odd little remark. Irritably, she turned and walked a few steps away. The room was growing dim with twilight. On her little table stood a pair of candles, stuck to a piece of broken plate with drops of wax. She waved her hand and lit them in a flare light and a dance of long shadows.

"Do you want me to go away?" Rhodry said.

"Do you want to stay?"

He shrugged and went to sit on the windowsill, perching there much as Jill had always done. She could see past him to the evening sky, darkening as the first stars appeared.

"Dalla, will you answer me one question?"

"About what?"

"Dweomer, I suppose you'd call it."

"Well, if it's not a forbidden thing to answer, I will."

"Fair enough. Let me think."

For a long time he stared at the floor, while the shadows grew in the room round the pool of candlelight.

"Jill said she'd answer if I ever had the guts to ask," he said at last. "When a man dies, is that the end of him?" He turned to look at her. "Or does he live again, in some other life?"

She was too surprised to answer at first. He waited patiently.

"Well, *he* won't live again, exactly, but his soul will take on another body and another life."

"Huh. I'd come to think that it must be true, but I wanted to know, you see."

It occurred to her that it was probably grief driving him to ask.

"It's not like Jill herself will ever return," Dallandra went on, "but another person with somewhat of Jill about her. Although they

371

say, truly, that the greater your dweomer grows, the more you become your soul, not just some mask for it, and then, or so they say, you do come back again in some true sense."

"I'm not sure I understand all of that."

"I don't suppose you need to."

"Probably not." Rhodry smiled, just faintly. "But if you know that the men killed here today will live again, why are you so distraught?"

"Didn't they suffer as they died? And won't their kin and clans suffer because they've lost them? Besides, it won't be them come back, not in any real sense. The men they were are gone. It's like a seed, a grain of wheat, say. The seed bursts and dies, a stalk of wheat grows, and there'll be another seed—but the first one's gone forever."

"I see. In a way. Ah, well, the bards will sing of them, not by name, truly, but they'll sing of this battle down the long years, and so we'll all live a little while past our dying."

She could find nothing to say to that, and weeping again seemed too great a luxury to allow herself. He looked out the window, where the stars glittered in the vast drift of the Snowy Road, sat studying the sky for a long time, so long that she began to wonder what he might be thinking, and how much he'd understood. Finally, he got up, walking over to face her.

"You never answered me," he said. "Do you want me to go?"

She had one brief struggle with her dignity.

"I don't," she said. "I'd rather you stayed the night."

He smiled, then slipped his arms round her waist to draw her close and kiss her.

After the feasting and the assigning of praise, after the bard songs and the salutes with the last of Cadmar's mead, the army stumbled to its tents late. Jahdo had fallen asleep under one of the tables, but woke when the men began to leave. He crawled out and trotted through the crowd, looking for Rhodry, but he was tired enough to give up fast. When he carried his lantern back to their camp, he found Arzosah still awake, preening her claws with her enormous tongue.

"Ah, there you are, little hatchling," she remarked. "Where's our master?"

"I couldn't find him. He did tell me that he were going up to the dun to look for Dallandra, but he never did come back."

"Ah." The dragon made the thundering sound that did her for laughter. "Well, then, I wouldn't worry about him."

"Be you sure he did not fall into some danger?"

"Very sure. You'll understand when you're older."

"Here! You do sound just like my mam!"

"Didn't I tell the master that you'd be as a hatchling to me? Now go wash that sticky stuff off your face with stream water and then get to bed. We'll be having a long morning of it."

"Oh, I doubt me that the army will be a-marching at dawn. They did have a fearsome lot to drink."

Arzosah laughed again.

"No doubt, no doubt. But they'll be mustering and suchlike, and the master will need you to pack up his gear. So off to bed you go."

When Rhodry woke in the morning, he found Dallandra up and dressed, kneeling on the floor and sorting out packets of medicinals. He lay in bed and merely watched her for a while, the delicate way her hands moved at her work, the confident way she glanced at this herb or that. All at once, she turned her head and smiled at him.

"How long have you been awake?" she said.

"Not very." He stifled a yawn. "Dalla, do you love me?"

"Not truly. Do you want me to?"

"I don't. I just don't fancy breaking your heart."

"Good, but I wouldn't worry about it." She paused, sitting back on her heels. "Do you want me to come down to the muster and kiss you farewell and suchlike when the army rides out?"

"I'd just as soon you didn't."

She looked so relieved that he knew they understood each other very well.

When he went downstairs, Rhodry stopped at the kitchen hut and bullied a serving lass into giving him a loaf of yesterday's bread, then left Cengarn. Out on the battlefield, all the men and Horsekin had been buried, but ravens still wheeled and dipped over dead horses. He could see Arzosah moving among them and glutting herself while the ravens shrieked in rage for their interrupted meal.

Jahdo sat waiting for him at their camp. Rhodry handed the boy a chunk of bread, then sat down opposite him to eat.

"When will the army be marching?" Jahdo asked.

"Some time today, most like. I've been thinking. It'd be best if you stayed here, to help Dalla, like. You can learn a little herbcraft and help her guard the princess."

"Oh, please, I don't want to stay behind like a lass."

Rhodry grinned.

"Nicely spoken, but this is going to be a forced march all the way. We'll be driving them and harrying them, and there's too many ways you could get killed. I can't keep Jill's promise if that happens, can I now?"

Jahdo wept, two thin trails of tears, hastily stifled. He stared down at his chunk of bread for a long time.

"Sometimes the best thing a man can do is naught," Rhodry said. "I learned that lesson myself, riding this war. It'll be best if you learn it now, early like, and don't wait as long as I have."

"Well." The boy looked up at last. "If you do order me, naught is all I can do about that. But please, be it truly needful for me to stay?"

"It is. If I thought your Wyrd was war, I'd bring you along. But it's not, lad. I've no idea what your Wyrd will be, but I know it's not riding in a warband. Stay with Dalla."

"I will, then. But I do hope you come back, Rhodry."

"So do I." He smiled in a weary sort of way. "So do I."

Jahdo wasn't the only person in the dun ordered to stay behind against his will. Later that morning, when Rhodry joined the lords and warleaders, he found them sorting out the unwounded men, most for the pursuing army, but some for the fort guard. With the raven mazrak on the loose, Cengarn would need one. For all anyone knew, she'd flown off to muster more Horsekin for yet another attack. Calonderiel counted up his archers and delegated a hundred of them to remain behind and guard the walls.

"And you, my prince," he said to Daralanteriel, "are staying behind to captain them."

"Now here!" Dar snarled. "If you think I'm going to hide in a stone tent like a woman—"

"You're going to stay in the stone tents like a sensible man. Have you already forgotten that the point of this war is killing your wife?"

Dar started to argue, thought better of it with his mouth still open.

"Guard her well, and you'll assure the victory," Calonderiel went on. "Am I right, Rhodry?"

"You are at that," Rhodry chimed in. "Dar, don't be a fool. They need you here, not haring round the countryside."

"Well and good, then," the prince said. "Stay I will, but if any man says one word to my shame—"

"I'll knock some sense into him myself," Calonderiel said. "And you know that's no idle threat."

That afternoon, Rhodry and Arzosah flew out first and found the remnants of the Horsekin army crawling north, some fifteen miles away, then circled back to lead Cengarn's men after. The grim pursuit went on for months, until as the old chronicle remarks, "the last of the savages still alive fled back into the high mountains, where, or so we may hope, they perished in the winter snows."

But during all those weeks of slaughter, Rhodry saw no sign of the enemy shape-changer, neither in bird nor woman form.

FUTURE
The Westlands, 1117

❖

CAUDA DRACONIS

*In most of the lands of our map, this figure
mingles evil with good, and good with evil,
so that it does mitigate both the joys and the
sorrows of our lives. If it fall into the Land
of Silver, that is to say, the land of kin and
clan, then does it bring a fortunate end to
such affairs, though the caster must always
bear in mind that no matter of blood ties
will remain unvexed for long.*

—The Omenbook of Gwarn,
Loremaster

A LATE MORNING SUN laid pale light over grass that grew brown under naked trees. When Rhodry went to the stream to drink, he found the water cold enough to sting. Swearing, he washed his face, tossing his head in a scatter of drops. Samaen had been and gone, he supposed, not that he could know for sure without a priest to tell the days. In his heart, though, he felt winter. Calonderiel strolled over to join him.

"Autumn's here, sure enough," the warleader said. "I'm glad the gwerbret's called an end to this chase."

"So am I. Will you be heading south today?"

"I will. Gwerbret Cadmar's heading back to Cengarn, of course, and his allies with him. What about you? Are you riding home? Your father's going to be waiting at the winter camps."

"Will he? I'd like to see him again, truly. No doubt Arzosah would be glad of it, if I gave her leave to go."

"No doubt. I'm sick of hearing that wyrm grumble and whine, I tell you. You can have one of my horses for the ride home, of course."

Rhodry sighed, running damp hands through his hair to shove it clear of his face. He'd never told Calonderiel about Angmar and Haen Marn, nor did he want to now. Cal would only voice his own doubts. The island might never return; he might never see Angmar

378

again; he might waste the rest of his life, haunting the Northlands, waiting in vain, when he could return to his people and live in honor and comfort, out in the peace of the grasslands.

"Well, there's Jahdo," Rhodry said. "I took the lad into my charge, you know, and made him a promise."

"True. You could bring him west with you. We'll take him home in the spring."

"I suppose."

"Ye gods, you're bound and determined to stay in Cengarn, aren't you?" All at once Calonderiel grinned. "Wait a moment! Am I right in thinking Dallandra has somewhat to do with this?"

"You're not."

"Hah! When Dar brings his lady back to us, ride with him, will you? Bring Dalla home, too."

Rhodry looked away. Across the stream lay a long meadow, and beyond it the hills rose, brown and sere. A blue mist hung in the chilly air, while far away he could see the high mountains rise, their peaks gleaming white.

"I don't know, Cal, I just don't know. Who knows what a man's Wyrd will bring him? Spring's a long way away yet."

"So it is. Well, then, I'll hope I see you again and leave it at that."

Rhodry had one more farewell to make. He and Garin sat together to share a meager breakfast of stale flatbread and moldy cheese. Neither spoke until they were done eating.

"Well, Rori," the envoy said, "looks like neither of us will be going down to the Halls of the Dead just yet."

"So it does. But one of these days, I'll be coming back to Lin Serr, on my way to Haen Marn if naught else."

"Good. I'll hold you to that."

They shook hands on it.

Round noon, the army split up. Cadmar's forces, including one silver dagger and a dragon, and the dwarven axmen headed out east by different roads to return to their respective cities, while Calonderiel led his men south.

The gwerbret and his men had a long ride of it. The rain came day after day, washing them with an aching cold, sickening the men and horses both, turning the roads to mud. Although rain was the usual fare in the Northlands this time of year, Rhodry couldn't help wondering if the raven woman lay behind the storms. He'd seen dweomerworkers call the weather before, and taking a petty revenge would be like her.

The weather, though, was the least of their troubles. By then, the provisions they'd brought with them were mostly exhausted. The Horsekin had already stripped most of the food from the countryside, forcing Cadmar to ride home by a roundabout route to scavenge what he could. Everywhere they stopped, they met starvation. Although the Horsekin had killed most of the farmers they'd plundered, here and there a few who'd escaped huddled in shacks built on the ruins of their steadings. On the road they met starvation, too. Men leading cows so thin their ribs showed, women carrying children in the same condition, a whole family here, a broken one there, desperately heading south in the hope that some friend or kinsman had been spared and could take them in—the army passed them all, riding so hungry itself that it could do nothing for them.

During the day, Rhodry and the dragon would hunt, but she found little enough game, and Rhodry didn't care to test the power of the ring by ordering her to share the kills. At night, they would join the other men in camp. It seemed that every day, some man or another had died either from fever or an old wound. They lost horses, too, until a good quarter of the army was walking home, not riding. When the rain finally stopped, what firewood they found lay soaked on freezing ground. The gwerbret walked among his men that night and talked to as many as he could.

"It's not much farther now, lads, not much farther at all. A few more days and we'll be home with a good fire and Cengarn's stores to feed us."

Everyone tried to smile and agree, but those few days loomed as large as one of the Hells.

That night, Rhodry dreamed of the raven woman, or rather, she invaded his sleep again. He was dreaming of Lin Serr and of walking down a long tunnel, shimmering blue in phosphorescent light upon marble. Ahead stood a round opening, glowing golden, and in the dream he heard a voice saying, "The Halls of the Dead." He hesitated, wondering if he should go forward, when he saw her, striding toward him down the hallway from the direction in which he'd come. His first thought was to run into the golden light, but his courage saved him. He stood his ground and waited till she stood in front of him and smiled.

"What a coward you are," Rhodry said. "Coming only in dreams. You can't have much faith in your wretched dweomer."

Her smile disappeared.

"Or don't you even have much power left, with Alshandra dead?" he went on. "A few farmwives' spells, I'll wager, and no more."

"Mock all you want, but leave that ugly beast of yours somewhere and come to me upon the ground. Then we'll be seeing which one of us the coward may be."

When he hesitated, she laughed, but it was such a nervous giggle that he realized how much she feared him—as much as he feared her.

"Look here at this." She held up a silver dagger. "Do you know who this did belong to? Your friend, Yraen. The man who did slit his throat gave me his dagger for a trinket."

"You're lying."

"I do not. It be mine, now, back in the day world, and I keep it with me always."

"You lie, bitch!"

"I do not, and I'll prove it. The dagger carries a little wyvern graved upon the blade, right up by the hilt. The thongs wrapping the hilt were made of pale buckskin once, but now they be all dark and stained."

Choked with grief, Rhodry could say nothing.

"I do tell the truth, don't I?" She tossed back her head and laughed. "I do have it, Rhodry Maelwaedd, and while I do keep it, I have the keeping of your friend's precious honor, too. Think on it! His silver dagger does belong to a woman and an enemy!"

Rhodry stepped forward, grabbing at her throat, but she was

gone, the hallway was gone—he was lying awake in a tangle of damp blankets and swearing at a dawn-streaked sky. Arzosah had swung her head round and was watching him.

"Did that woman come into your dreams again?"

"She did." Rhodry sat up, pushing the blankets away. "How did you know?"

"You were tossing and muttering in your sleep, that's how."

"It was a wretched thing. Ah, ye gods, it's hard to believe it's real. Maybe it's just the hunger and the cold."

"Don't be silly. She's a shape-changer and a sorcerer. Why shouldn't she come to you in dreams?"

"And a fine comfort you are."

"Better than you deserve. Tell me about it, Dragonmaster. I love this sort of lore."

Rhodry obliged, more to get it straight in his own mind than to please her, though the dragon listened in dead seriousness.

"By the scaly gods of the air," Arzosah said, "I'm glad you didn't run for that gold light you saw."

"Truly? Why?"

"Well, if you had, your soul would have been loose from your body, and that would have been a splendid mess! You'd have been fighting on her dweomer-ground. I'll wager you'd have lost, too, and ych! I would have been her slave as well as you. Ych, ych, ych, how disgusting!"

"Your sympathy warms my heart." Rhodry shook himself like a wet dog. "And the worst of it is, I still feel like she's watching me or suchlike."

"Quick! Mount up! She must be round here somewhere."

Since he slept dressed, of course, in that cold, all Rhodry had to do was pull on his boots and buckle on his sword belt. Arzosah bent her neck, carried him up, then took to the air while he was still wedging himself between the enormous scales where her crest met her spine. He clung to her and looked down, watching as she rose higher and began to circle. The army spun slowly under them, and the hills as well, dark under their cloak of pines.

"No sign of her yet!" Rhodry called.

"But I smell dweomer."

Arzosah swung round to the west and flew hard, rolling through the air while Rhodry clung for quite literally dear life. Far ahead, a black speck appeared. The dragon climbed, flying far higher than any bird, even a dweomer one, could easily go. Ahead, the speck resolved itself into the raven, gliding along the wind, flying slowly. Bit by bit, they overtook her, came close enough to see that in her claws she carried a bulging cloth sack. Arzosah curved her wings to steady herself, then stooped like a falcon and plunged.

The whistle in the wind gave them away. The raven twisted round, saw them, shrieked, and flew, cawing and flapping straight ahead to a sudden mist, billowing in a clear sky. Rhodry howled out oaths and curses in vain as she skittered through and disappeared. Roaring in rage, Arzosah flung herself at the same spot, but nothing happened—they were still flying over the Northlands and the pine-dark hills.

"May her womb rot green within her," Rhodry growled, "and the slime drip down to her knees."

"You should have been a bard, you curse so well! Let's go back. My wings ache with all this wretched damp. I do hope you let me eat a nice fat cow once we're all safe in the city, Dragonmaster. The gods all know I've earned one."

"I doubt if there's a nice fat cow anywhere near Cengarn. But you're right—let's get back to the army."

When they flew over the camp, they found the army gone, confident, no doubt, that Rhodry would catch up to them with no trouble. Following the track, they flew south and, indeed, found the army right away. They'd only ridden a few miles and called a halt to swarm round something they'd met in the road. As the dragon swooped down to join them, Rhodry recognized provision carts and men from the fort-guard at Cengarn.

"Saved!" he called out. "It looks like we'll be eating today after all!"

Sure enough, the town had sent what provisions it could spare, scant but better than the naught they'd had before. When Rhodry took a chunk of flatbread and another of cheese from one of the carters, he thought that he'd never smelled food as good.

"But here," he said to the man, "how did you know where we were?"

"The dweomermaster told us, of course. The lady of the Westfolk."

Rhodry laughed, but at himself. Of course. Dallandra would have been scrying them out, no doubt during their entire march, and she'd know exactly when they'd be returning.

On the day that Cadmar and his men finally rode home, Dallandra sent Jahdo down to join the welcome at the dun gates. Although the boy was fretting with excitement, she preferred to stay up in her chamber till the confusion and greetings were over. Much to her amusement, though, the other women in the dun were surprised at her.

"Oh, come now, Dalla," Carra said. "Don't you want to see Rhodry as soon as ever you can?"

Dallandra laughed, turning the girl red with embarrassment.

"It's not that sort of thing between us. Truly."

And yet, she had to admit that it was good to see him when, late that evening, he came to find her. She'd eaten alone, avoiding the feast in the great hall, then brought out one of Jill's books to study by dweomer light. Although Dallandra had never been the studious sort of dweomerworker before, ever since Jill's death she'd taken to poring over the books her friend had left behind. She was just considering an interesting passage about astral currents when she heard someone opening the door. She smiled, knowing before she looked up that it would be him.

"You're turning into a hermit like Jill," Rhodry said.

"The dweomer takes you that way, sooner or later. It gladdens my heart to see you safe and well, though."

"My thanks, and the same to you."

"Have you seen Jahdo? He's talked of naught else but your homecoming for days. And the dragon's, of course."

"Has he now? Well, he sat with me most of the evening. I sent him off to bed a while ago. He can keep Arzosah company tonight."

"Oh?" She raised a teasing eyebrow. "And why's that?"

He smiled, then strode over, putting his hands on her shoulders and bending down to kiss her. She rose, took a second kiss, and found herself slipping into his arms as easily as if he'd never left the dun. Later—much later—she would wonder at herself, that she could spend months and even years away from Rhodry Maelwaedd with never a thought about him, only to take him into her bed the moment he asked.

After that first night home, Rhodry and Arzosah made a camp outside Cengarn, to spare the dun's horses the sight of her and to spare Dallandra scandal. They found a cozy spot in a sheltered hollow near the base of the north cliff. Jahdo helped him build a proper fire pit with flat stones, and the town guard donated a tent from its stores. Rhodry took to spending much of his time there in the dragon's company. Every afternoon, some while before sunset, she would fly off to hunt deer, grumbling, usually, because he wouldn't allow her to steal a cow or two from the local farmers. Once she did bring back a bear, stinking of grease, who'd waited a little too long to retreat to his winter cave. Rhodry made her take that kill some distance away before she ate.

On an afternoon warm with false summer, Arzosah had just flown off, leaving Rhodry to sit alone in the sun, when he saw a man striding toward him across the meadow. He rose, watching while Evandar came strolling up, smiling as if the world couldn't please him more.

"I've just had a word with Dalla," Evandar announced. "She tells me that Carra will have the baby soon."

"That concerns you?"

"It does, most completely so." He let the smile fade. "As do you, of course."

"I'm well enough."

"Are you? Truly?"

"Truly."

Evandar considered, studying his face for so long that Rhodry finally turned and walked a few steps away.

"Oh, here," Evandar said. "I don't mean to distress you."

"You don't."

"Indeed?"

All at once, Evandar stood facing him again. Cengarn was gone. They stood on a grassy island in a sea of white mist. Nearby grew a clump of white birches, their slender branches nodding, their leaves all yellow with autumn. On the other side of the trees there seemed to be a stone well—Rhodry couldn't see it clearly through the opalescent haze.

"Evandar, take me back."

"Not just yet. It's pleasant here. Come sit down."

Before Rhodry could say a word, he found himself doing just that, sitting beside Evandar in the tall grass, as soft and green as spring growth. The seeming-elf lounged back on one elbow, his yellow hair gleaming in a dim sunlight that seemed to come from everywhere and nowhere.

"The town might need me," Rhodry said. "And Carra and the child, too, to defend them, like."

The mist, the island, the birches were all gone. They sat on the stubbly grass in front of Rhodry's tent near Cengarn. The sun was setting.

"My thanks," Rhodry said somewhat dryly.

"Most welcome. You're a hard man to argue with. Not an easy man to love, either."

For a long moment, they merely looked at each other in the fading light. Evandar sighed, turning away, clasping his arms round his knees in such a human gesture that Rhodry was oddly touched. Evandar wasn't the first man who'd been devoted to him, though he was perhaps the first to admit it. Rhodry found himself remembering Amyr again, and other men who'd ridden in his warband, and Gwin as well, his personal bodyguard, all those years ago when he'd been a noble lord and taken the devotion of other men for granted. Perhaps, he realized, he was remembering Gwin most of all.

"You look sad," Evandar remarked.

"I am. I was thinking of a man who died in my service. A long time ago, now."

"Did it ache your heart when he died?"

Rhodry hesitated, wondering if he dared admit the truth.

"It does now, remembering him."

"Even though it's been a long time?"

"Just so."

"But it didn't then?"

"Of course it did! Why are you asking me all this?"

Evandar considered for a moment. "I just wanted to make sure I understood it a-right."

"Understand what?"

"Grief. It's a very strange thing to me."

"I'll wager, my friend, that there's a cursed lot of things you don't understand."

"So Dalla always says. I thought I was the master of riddles, but I think me that I'm the barest apprentice, compared to this thing you call the world."

"Indeed? Well, one of my noble ancestors wrote a book, and in it he said that it was a grand thing to know you're ignorant, because only then can a man open his heart and learn."

"But your heart's as closed as a stone."

"And what's it to you?" Rhodry could hear himself snarling. "Why don't you go ask Dalla these cursed stupid questions?"

"I told you already. Dalla could never bring me sorrow. Even if I were never to see her again, I'd have joy, remembering her. But you're the one who can answer me the riddle of grief. Please, Rori? Tell me about this fellow, the one who makes you feel sad, remembering him."

At that moment, Evandar looked so much like a child, eager to hear some tale, that Rhodry gave in.

"There was a man I met once in the worst of circumstances," he said. "His name was Gwin, and he started out as my enemy, but in the end, he proved to be my friend, the truest friend I ever had, really. That was when I was lord of Aberwyn, and so I could give him a position in life, after he'd had none. He would have died for me, but thanks be to every god in the sky, he never had to. One winter he took ill, though. It was a wasting disease. The chirurgeon said he had stones in his stomach, and in the end, they killed him. But at least he died his own death, not one meant for me."

"Do you miss him still?"

"Nah, nah, nah, it was too long ago for that."

"Then why—"

"Will you hold your tongue? Or better yet—go away."

"Shan't. Didn't I give you the dweomer ring? You should gift me in return. It's only fair."

"Well, it could well be, but why do you want to hear this wretched tale? It's not much of a gift."

"It is to me. I'll wager it holds the answer to this riddle."

Rhodry sighed in sheer exasperation. Evandar smiled, a flash of charm like sun breaking through clouds.

"Please, Rori?"

"Oh, very well. My heart's still troubled because he loved me, and in my own way, I loved him as well, but I never said it, not once, not even when he was dying in my arms."

"So he never knew?"

"Just that."

"So you feel that you lied to him?"

"I do, blast you! And I lied twice, because I knew he was going, but I promised him we'd ride together in the spring, when he was well." He felt his voice break. "But I think he knew the truth of that. He smiled at me, you see, and died."

"That *is* sad. That I do understand."

"Splendid! Now will you go away?"

"Shan't."

"Oh, ye gods! What more do you want from me?"

Evandar considered, frowning.

"I want to know what Dalla feels like," he said at last, "when she sleeps all night in your arms."

Rhodry could find not a single word to say.

"She tells me that she loves you no more than you love her," Evandar went on. "But I love the pair of you. I want to understand."

His eyes seemed pools of loneliness. For the first time, Rhodry realized, he was seeing into Evandar's soul, and he found at last something human in that loneliness. After a moment, Evandar spoke again.

"It's because of her that I began to love you. I want to know what she knows. Afterwards, I'll go away, so I'll understand what sorrow is, and the missing of someone."

"It's not a thing most people want to know."

"But I do." Evandar turned to him and laid a hand on his arm.

Rhodry hesitated, on the verge of shaking it off. Evandar looked at him steadily, his mouth a melancholy twist. For Gwin's sake, Rhodry bent his head and kissed the sadness away. All round them the world turned sunny again, there on the island in the mist, and they lay down together in the soft grass.

As the time drew near for Elessario's birth, Ocradda, who presided over all the childbirths in the dun, took charge of Carra. She brought the actual midwife up from the town, though, a stout gray woman named Polla, whose ready smile put Carra right at ease from the moment she walked into the lass's bedchamber. Feeling very much in the way, Dallandra hovered in the curve of the wall while Polla had Carra lie down with her dresses hiked up. The midwife stared off into space while she ran gentle fingers over her patient's swollen middle.

"Well, now," Polla said at last. "It's in a good position, head down and ready, sure enough. I'll wager it drops soon."

She was proved right not two days later. Dallandra was walking out in the ward when Jahdo came racing up to her.

"Oh, my lady, my lady, they did send me into town to fetch Polla. Lady Ocradda says you'd best come upstairs."

Fearing trouble, Dallandra rushed into the broch and up the staircase, but she found Carra just beginning her labor. Her water had broken not long before, and now, dressed only in a thin shift, she crouched miserably on the birthing stool with Ocradda standing behind her, rubbing her shoulders and talking softly. When Dallandra came in, Carra looked up and groaned. Sweat beaded her forehead and upper lip.

"Does Dar know?" she gasped.

"Ye gods," Ocradda said, "I forgot all about the prince!"

"I'll go tell him, Carra," Dallandra said. "And then I'll be right back."

Finding Dar turned out to be no easy matter. Some said he'd gone riding, others that he was down in the town or out in the stables. Dallandra walked all over the dun before she finally found the prince with Rhodry as the pair of them walked in the south gate. Dar was carrying blue ribands, looped round one hand, a present for his lady.

"Your Highness," Dallandra said, "Carra's time has come upon her. She's upstairs with the women now."

Daralanteriel turned dead white. Rhodry caught his arm.

"Come have a tankard with me, Your Highness. It'll do to pass the time."

When Dallandra got back to the chamber, she found things moving along. Ocradda had summoned a servant lass to clamber onto a chest and tie a stout rope from a beam in the ceiling, so that Carra would have support. Under the pierced stool, she'd spread a heap of rags covered by a clean, new cloth. Carra now sat astride with her shift hitched up round her waist and her face as pale as the linen. Over on the bed lay wraps for the baby, and a kettle of wash water stayed warm by the fire in the hearth.

"Your husband's down in the great hall, waiting," Dallandra said. "He looks terrified, I must say."

"Good," Carra muttered. "I wish he had to do this, not me."

"I remember thinking the same thing," Polla said. "All five times. Now breathe, lass, nice and steady. That's right. Good deep breaths."

There was nothing else to do but wait and suffer with Carra through contraction after contraction. Sometimes Polla would have

390

her stand up to ease the pain, leaning into the midwife's strong arms for support; at others, taking a few steps back and forth seemed to help her. Mostly she clung to the heavy knotted rope while she sat on the high stool and wept. After what seemed a very long time, the chamber began to darken as the short winter day faded. Dallandra lit candle lanterns with a splint at the hearth, then set them round the chamber. Polla took one and put it close by the stool, so she could kneel beside Carra every now and then to check her progress. The pains grew worse and worse, closer and closer together.

"It's coming!" Polla called out. "Now, lass. Here's where you can push."

Moaning, leaning hard into the rope, Carra did just that. Dallandra and Ocradda hurried over, standing right nearby, muttering encouragement and watching the midwife. At last, the baby slipped out into Polla's waiting hands with a good strong howl of a cry.

"Oh, what a pity! A daughter," Polla said, sighing. "Ah, well, they can't all be sons, can they? She's a pretty creature, and no doubt the Goddess will favor you more next time."

Panting so hard that she was drooling, Carra seemed not to hear her. Clutching her rope, she leaned forward dangerously far to catch a glimpse of her child. Ocradda grabbed her shoulders to steady her. Polla took her little silver knife and slashed the umbilical cord.

"Hold her while I tie it off, herbwoman."

Dalla took the baby, all red and sticky, held her still while Polla did just that, then handed her to Carra. She grabbed her child, clasping her tight against her sweaty breasts, cooing to her and touching her face with an awe-struck finger. All at once, she winced and moaned again. Ocradda knelt down fast by the birthing stool and spread a big square of white cloth under it.

"Ah, good." Ocradda sighed. "Here's the afterbirth."

"Is it all there?" Polla said.

With great care, Ocradda looked through the liverish raw mass. "It is, truly."

"May the goddesses all be praised," the two women sang out in a chant. "Let us give them all thanks! May they be praised for the

391

life of this child! May they be praised for giving us back the life of its mother! In their hands they held her blood and her life. Now they have given her back to us."

"May they be praised," Dalla sang. "May they live forever!"

While the other women helped Carra into a clean nightgown, this one slit down the front, and helped her lie down, Dalla washed the baby in warm water. Although the infant lay quiet in her hands, she wasn't truly asleep. Every now and then, her big yellow eyes would open in the unfocused stare of the just-born; once Dalla saw a flicker of what might have been recognition.

"Elessi," she whispered. "Elessi, it's me, Dalla. You're home, my sweet. You've come home at last."

Again, and for the briefest of moments, the child seemed to recognize—not her words, certainly—but the sound of her voice. Dallandra wrapped her in a piece of blanket, thinned and softened with age, and brought her to Carra.

"Oh!" Carra reached out eager arms. "She's so beautiful!"

"Put her to suck, love," Polla said. "It'll help your pains."

Carra, however, seemed to have forgotten that such a thing as pain even existed. She cuddled the child close, helped her find a nipple, then merely stared, grinning all the while, as her newborn suckled.

Watching them made Dallandra's eyes fill with tears. Suddenly, and for the first time in hundreds of years, she remembered her own child, her little half-human son, whom she'd left behind with his dweomermaster of a father when she'd gone off to Evandar's country. She turned cold all over when she realized that she couldn't even remember her child's name. Aloda—well, it had started out with those syllables of her own father's name, but how exactly had they shaped the patronymic? Alodadaelanteriel? Perhaps. Most likely, in fact. But right away they'd given him a Deverry-sounding nickname, Loddlaen.

Dalla left the other women to fuss over Carra and the child and went down to the great hall. By a blazing fire in the dragon hearth, Dar paced back and forth, while Rhodry sat slumped on a bench at the table of honor to keep him company. Not far away, curled up in the straw with a couple of dogs, Jahdo lay asleep. In one corner, a servant stood polishing tankards. Otherwise, the vast hall lay empty.

"A daughter, and both are fine," Dallandra announced. "Dar, you can go up now."

Without a single word, the prince raced across the room and bounded up the stairs. The servant smiled in a rather sentimental way and brought Dalla over a tankard of ale.

"The other women will be wanting a bite to eat, I'll reckon. I'll just be in the kitchen hut, cutting up cold meat and suchlike, if you need me."

"My thanks." Dalla watched him go, then turned and spoke in Elvish. "I don't suppose you want to go see the child."

"I was never that much interested in my own, to tell you the truth," Rhodry answered in the same. "Not until they had teeth and a few words, anyway."

"I'd forgotten that you had children."

When she sat down next to him, Rhodry turned a little to face her. In the firelight, she could see the streak of silver gleaming in his hair.

"Four sons," he said. "Four legitimate sons, and a daughter, who wasn't. There may be others for all I know."

When she made a sour face at him, he laughed, but mercifully it was a normal mirth.

"Neither of us are the kin-bound sort," Dalla said. "You know, I left a child with Aderyn when I went into Evandar's country. Loddlaen, his name was. I wonder what his Wyrd brought him?"

The expression on Rhodry's face took her utterly aback. For a moment he stared, his mouth slack, then winced as if some old wound had stabbed him, and finally he looked away and stared into the fire.

"You know, don't you?" she said. "And it wasn't good."

He merely nodded and took a long swallow of his ale.

"Rori, tell me."

"Are you sure you want to know?"

Dallandra considered, watching the flames leap against the chimney wall.

"I don't," she said at last. "Not the details, at least. Did he die violently?"

"I'm afraid so. It blasted near broke Aderyn's heart."

"It would have. He's the one who loved the child."

He cocked his head to one side, seemed to be waiting for her to ask more, but she found that she had no words, not even to frame questions. For a long while, they sat together, watching the fire, and neither of them spoke until the other women came down, all talking and laughing, to eat the meal the servant set out for them.

Although the birth went well, there was trouble of a different sort in the morning. Dalla had just come into the great hall when Polla swept down upon her, Ocradda bobbing in her wake.

"You've got to come speak to Carra," the midwife snapped. "She won't keep Elessi in the swaddling bands."

"Indeed?"

"She says the child hates them. Utter nonsense. Babies need to feel secure, and besides, if she's not wrapped, she's likely to catch her death of cold. It's drafty, this time of year."

"And she insists on keeping the babe in bed with her, not in the cradle," Ocradda added.

"At least that way she'll be warm," Dalla said. "My dear friends, Carra's just following the elvish ways, her husband's ways."

That gave them pause, but for sake of peace, Dalla went with them to speak with Carra. She found Carra sitting up in bed, propped by pillows, and cuddling the sleeping baby. When Dallandra came over, Elessi opened her big yellow eyes, looked in the elven woman's direction with a vastly solemn stare, then shut them again. Carra wasted no time.

"I won't do it! She hates the bands, and she screams, and I won't wrap her."

"Very well then," Dalla said. "Her father's people don't wrap their babies, after all, and no harm seems to come to them."

"But Dalla!" Polla stepped forward. "Most babies need—"

"She isn't most babies!" Carra snapped.

"Just so," Dalla said.

Polla hesitated, considering her next move. All at once, Ocradda shrieked. Dalla spun round to find Evandar standing in the corner where the partition met the curve of the outer wall. Her hands clasped over her mouth, Ocradda stared in pure horror, but Carra merely watched, her eyes as solemn as the baby's.

"My apologies," Evandar said with a lazy grin. "I didn't mean to startle you so badly." He bowed to the servingwoman, then to the midwife. "Good dames, consider me the child's grandfather. In a way I am, as perhaps our Dalla will tell you in some detail, or perhaps not, as she chooses. But I very much wished to see Elessario in her new home."

"Well, here she is." Carra sat up straight, holding the baby in the crook of one arm, running the other hand through her own hair to smooth it back from her face. "She's very beautiful."

Evandar walked over to the bedside and looked at the child. With a large pink and toothless yawn, Elessi woke and turned her head his way. For a long time, they stared into one another's eyes. Even though the infant was too young to focus her sight properly, Dalla was suddenly sure that she recognized the soul who'd been her father back in her old home. The moment passed as the baby turned to snuggle her face into her new mother's breast.

"A beauty she is," Evandar agreed. "My thanks to you, Carra, for this birthing. Did you suffer much?"

Polla made a clicking noise with her tongue and stepped forward to intervene, but Dalla laid a hand on her arm and held her back.

"I did, truly, but it was worth it." Carra was smiling, utterly bemused by this strange creature. "Why do you ask?"

"I think me I owe you a fee, that's why, just as your people would pay to a wet nurse—or truly, that's much too cold, isn't it? Not a nurse's fee, but a fine present, a gift." Evandar smiled in a sudden delight that had an almost overpowering charm. "A gift. That's what you shall have, the finest gift I can give you."

"Now here." Carra laughed in answer to that smile. "I did it with no hope of reward, good sir!"

"Nonetheless, you shall have one. Now, here's a riddle for you. You shall have the gift as soon as I can fetch it for you, but you won't realize what it is or what you have for years and years."

All at once, suddenly and completely, he was gone. Shuddering, Polla and Ocradda turned toward Dalla, as if for comfort, but Carra laughed aloud, still caught by Evandar's warmth.

"Well, I've got a charming kinsman!" she said. "But Dalla, who is he? A dweomermaster, obviously, because he can come and go like that."

Dalla decided that half a lie would be far better than an unexplainable truth.

"He is at that, Carra. One of the greatest dweomermasters the Westlands has ever known."

"Oooh, how wonderful, then! But why did he say he owed me somewhat? Or wait, I know! He's seen some omen, hasn't he, about my Elessi's Wyrd?"

"He has, indeed, and truly, she's a very important little lass."

"Wonderful and twice wonderful." Carra looked at the child sleeping in the crook of her arm. "But I'd love you anyway, splendid Wyrd or no. I wonder what gift your grandfather has for me? Dalla, do you know?"

"I don't, and if I know Evandar, he'll never tell you, either. Once he sets a riddle, it's for the hearer to puzzle out without another clue from him."

"Well, he said I'd find out someday." Carra paused for a yawn. "If I remember that long."

Dalla gathered up the other women and herded them out then and there while the swaddling bands were still forgotten. She herself, however, learned the answer to the riddle later that night, when Evandar appeared in her chamber, crystalizing into the lamplight just as she was brushing out her hair. He sat down on her bed and lounged back on one elbow, smiling while he watched her.

"I wondered if you'd come back," she said. "Does the child please you?"

"She does, indeed, though I'd wish her ears were proper long ones. It doesn't matter much, truly."

"And what about that riddle? What gift are you planning to give her? Some of your gifts can be beastly dangerous, my love."

"So I'm finding out." Evandar looked sincerely rueful. "So I put a bit of thought into this one. But you have to swear you'll never tell her. I refuse to let her know the answer to the riddle unless she puzzles it out."

"Oh, very well, then. I swear I won't tell her or so much as hint at the answer."

"My thanks, then. I've done for her what I did for your Aderyn, given her the life of an elf—but this time I did it right. I didn't understand, then, about aging and the wheel of Time, but I've learned a fair bit now. She shall have youth as well, four hundred years, four hundred years, four hundred years and more."

"Ye gods! Then, my love, you've given her a splendid gift indeed, life to match her beloved Dar's."

Evandar laughed and tossed up one hand. A long spray of silver sparks gushed to the ceiling, then fell in a glittering shower. When it hit the floor, he was gone.

Another pair of beings were discussing Evandar's riddles that night. In their hollow by the cliff, Rhodry and Arzosah had a blazing fire burning, thanks to the townfolk who'd brought them wood. The dragon lay stretched out, curving her body into a crescent to catch the fire's heat, and Rhodry leaned comfortably against her belly to watch the flames dance.

"I can't live like this much longer," she grumbled. "Fires are all very well, but my back is cold, Rhodry Dragonmaster. I need my nice toasty cave, I do. Can't we go back there till the snows have been and gone?"

"And what would I eat and suchlike?"

"Huh. Now that, truly, is a problem." She heaved a vast sigh. "But a slave that dies of cold is of no use to its master."

Rhodry considered. He was quite sure that feeding a dragon through the winter would strain Cengarn's depleted stores. Better to let her fly off and feed herself. If he ordered and enjoined her to return in the spring, doubtless the dweomer of his ring would force her back.

"Well, it could be that I'll let you go home, if and only if we don't find any Horsekin riding the town's way. We'll scout round here for an eightnight, and then we'll decide."

"If I had the chance to kill Horsekin, I wouldn't want to leave. Blood and vengeance would keep me warm."

Rhodry got up, put more wood on the fire, then sat cross-legged by her head and facing her. She yawned, curling her enormous tongue cat-fashion, then laid her head on her paws and watched him with a glittery eye. More and more, he hated thinking that such a beautiful creature lived as a slave.

"I hear your old enemy appeared in town today," Rhodry said.

"Evandar, you mean? That oozing slug, that pink and hairy creature of slime and shame! I hate the very sound of his name, and he's cursed lucky he knows mine."

"Indeed? You know, there's somewhat I've always wanted to ask you. How did he learn it, anyway?"

Arzosah arched her neck in a rattle of scales.

"He tricked me, the fiend, that scum of three worlds!"

"Well, I figured that. I merely wondered how he could have bested someone as clever as you."

She relaxed, lowering her head and allowing him to scratch behind her eye-ridge.

"It was a riddling game," she said at last. "He offered me the ring for a prize, you see, if I won, and I could smell the dweomer on the silver. It intrigued me, wondering what the ring might do if I owned it. And he flattered me, saying that he wished to learn new riddles from a master of riddles, and everyone knew that Wyrmkind produced the greatest riddlemasters of all. Indeed, say I, and what prize will you want if I lose? Oh, come now, says he, there's no chance of that. Like a dolt, I thought no more about it."

"And you lost?"

"The contest? Not at all, not at all—that's how clever the swine was. First I asked a riddle, then he, and each time we answered the other, back and forth, all even, like, for hours and hours, while I could smell the dweomer like the best perfume in the world. Finally, he failed at one, or looking back on it, I'll wager the oozing slug pretended to fail. If I answered his next, then the ring would be mine."

She curled a paw and studied her talons for a long moment.

"And?" Rhodry said.

"By then I wanted that ring so badly it was like lust. It was hot, truly, so hot in the sun that I felt all watery. We were sitting on a rocky ledge, you see, very high up it was, and ever so lovely and warm. That must have been it, the sun and the dweomer-lust together." She looked up, her jet-black lips drawn back from her fangs. "So he asked his last riddle, and like a fool, I blurted out the answer before I could stop to think." ·

"The answer was your name?"

"It was." She tossed back her head and hissed like a thousand cats. "In a black, black night, two copper moons sail above a cavern filled with flashing blades, and this night can fly and hunt the forest glades, far and wide resounds its fame, what, oh what, is the black night's name? And I answered him! He laughed, Dragonmaster, he mocked me, there on the high ridge. I had one last moment of freedom, before he should say my name aloud, so I flicked a claw to knock him from the ridge and send him spinning down to his death, but he was gone, just gone, vanished by his slimy oozing excuse for dweomer. I leapt into the air and flew, for days I flew, this way and that, trying to smell out the ring and find him that way, but never could I sniff a trace of him."

Rhodry glanced at the silver band glittering on his finger.

"This should have been your prize."

"It should. He cheated me out of my name and my prize both. Which is why I say he's as lucky as a fiend can be, to know my name, or I'd have eaten him long before this."

"Tell me somewhat honestly." Rhodry held up his hand and flashed reflected light from the ring. "If this ring should be lost, would you be able to take your revenge on Evandar?"

"Alas, I could not, because he knows the name, and on his tongue the name alone has all the power that any being would need.

The ring was for you, because you're but an elf and a man both, and the name alone wouldn't have given you the power to enslave me."

"I see."

For a long time, Rhodry stared into the fire, wondering at himself for the strange idea that was forming in his mind.

"Master?" she said at last. "What's so wrong? You look sad."

"I was remembering a time long ago, when I served as a slave in a far-off country. A rich woman owned me, and though she was kind, I was still her slave."

"I never knew that. How did you get free?"

"My brother came and found me, then bought my freedom."

"Ah. It's a fine thing to have kin like that."

"It is, truly. I haven't seen him in years and years, but I hope he's well, wherever he may be."

He considered for a moment longer, then slipped the ring off to hold it up twixt thumb and forefinger. Puzzled, she raised her head and swung it his way, to watch him with both eyes.

"If this ring were lost," he said, "would you kill me?"

"Never, and I swear that upon the ring. I've come to respect you, Rhodry Dragonmaster, with all my heart. You would have made a fine dragon, I think, if your Wyrd had allowed it."

He laughed with a toss of his head.

"But if it were lost, you'd fly off, never to return?"

She hesitated, cocking her head, rustling her crest.

"Once I would have said yes and without thinking twice," she said. "But now I have the strangest feeling round my heart."

"Indeed? What?"

"A wondering if I'd go, because it would sadden me to be gone as much as it would please me to be free. Why are you asking me this? Is it just to torment me, slave as I am?"

"Never." Rhodry smiled briefly. "Here."

He tossed the ring straight up in the air as far as he could. Glittering, it flew up into the darkness, then tumbled back down into the pool of firelight. Arzosah swung her massive head its way and snapped—gulped and swallowed. The ring was gone.

"There, you have your prize at last. Go free, my well-loved

friend, if you want, or stay if you want. It's your choice now, not mine."

Arzosah clambered to her feet in a long glitter of body, shook herself twice, stretched her wings out and out, roofing over the fire and casting vast shadows, but all the while she stared at him. For a moment, she crouched on the edge of flight, started to speak, thought better of it, and shook her wings. Rhodry merely waited, smiling. All at once, she folded her wings back, turned round in a half-circle, and lay down again with her other side toward the fire.

"Well, my back does get so cold," she remarked. "You're a clever man."

"Am I now? Why?"

"I shan't answer that, because you know cursed well." She flopped her head onto her extended paws and sighed. "You called me well-loved. Is that true?"

"It is."

Arzosah rumbled for a moment, then swung her head his way.

"I'll fly with you a fair while more, then. Truly, Rhodry—nah nah nah, I shan't call you that anymore, because it's a name from the language of men. Rori you shall be, Rori Dragonfriend."

"My lady, never have I had a title that pleased me as much."

"Good. Now, here, I'll have to fly home before the first snow, but I promise you this: in the spring, I'll return. You have my sworn word on that."

And not for one moment did he doubt that she would keep it.

EPILOGUE
The Rhiddaer, 1117

POPULUS

A figure of most mixed import, which does color its character with those omens falling near it upon our map, but in general, it does signify good rather than evil, for when the people come together, there is feasting and merriment. In one thing only does it bode ill, matters of dweomer and secret things, for such have no part in the pleasures of public life. Thus, when it falls into the Land of Salt, this figure does bode evil most foul.

—The Omenbook of Gwarn,
Loremaster

CERR CAWNEN LAY LIKE a turquoise in the midst of a world of white. The high mountains to the north stood shrouded in clouds. In the rolling farmlands to the south, only the roofs and chimneys of the houses poked up, feathered with wood smoke, through the first heavy snow. The water meadows surrounding the town lay frozen in a lace of silver. Behind the stone ring of town walls, Loc Vaed stretched unfrozen, from its long green shallows out to blue deeper water and the central rock of Citadel, where the public buildings and the houses of the few wealthy families stood. The rest of the town huddled in the shallows: a jumble and welter of houses and shops all perched on pilings or crannogs, joined by little bridges to one another in the rough equivalent of city blocks, which in turn bristled with jetties and rickety stairs leading down to the stretches of open water between them. Fed by volcanic springs as it was, the lake would stay clear all winter, shrouded under mists and steam where the heat from the water hit the chilly air.

With the harvest in and safely stowed in Citadel's public granaries, the town had time for celebrations. Soon Admi, Chief Speaker of the town and head of the Council of Five, would be marrying off his daughter to the son of a merchant house. The two grand families would be throwing a public feast; they'd brought musicians in from every village around. Up on Citadel, another family was also considering plans, though these would be a fair bit less splendid.

"It were best we wait till the feasting be done," Dera said to her daughter. "We don't want your wedding to be lost, like."

"Oh here, Mam!" Niffa said with a laugh. "And who would be noticing the ratter's lass's wedding anyway?"

"We do have friends in this town. It be needful for us to set things up right, like, for the celebrating. At the dark time of the year, the folk will be glad of a nice occasion, they will."

Niffa smiled, surrendering. There never was any stopping Dera once she got an idea in her head.

"So now," Dera said. "I'll have your Da just stop by and tell Demet's da, like, of the plans."

"I can go tell Demet."

"Now hush! It be needful to do things right, and the fathers, they be the ones to discuss it, like, now that we've made the decisions." Dera paused for a wicked grin. "Men do like that, lass, the thinking that they've decided a thing. You remember that once you're married."

"Well and good, then, Mam."

Dera let her smile fade and turned away, looking into the hearth where a fire crackled to keep off the damp. In the last few months, she'd aged. The wrinkles round her blue eyes ran deep, now, and gray stained her yellow hair.

"It be our Jahdo you be thinking of, bain't?" Niffa said.

"It is. Ah, ye gods, I wonder if he still draws breath, wherever he may be."

"Mam, if he were to die, I'd know it. I swear I would."

Dera nodded agreement, then stared into the fire, as if she, too, could see the salamanders leaping and darting among the flames. At times, Niffa wondered if her mother really could see the Wildfolk as she could but denied it for some stubborn reason of her own. There was no doubt that people did laugh at you, if you blundered and let them know what you could see. Of course, when it was a death you foretold, the laughing stopped. Niffa had learned early to hold her tongue about such omens with everyone but her mother. With a vast sigh, Dera got up from the bench.

"I'll just go fetch your Da. At least we've got the wedding to look forward to."

Niffa took the chance to slip out, grabbing her hooded cloak from the row of nails by the door. The ratters lived in two rooms attached to the public granaries, theirs by a written right going back as far as anyone could remember, provided that they and their ferrets "did work with all due diligence" to trap and kill the rats come for the grain. To get out, Niffa had to squeeze down a narrow corridor, then climb down a ladder to the alley running between the granaries, squat stone buildings clinging halfway up Citadel's hill. Soon she would be leaving Citadel, going over to the crannog house where her betrothed lived with his family, the weavers. She would have to learn to spin, she supposed, and how to handle cloth instead of ferrets.

"I've got to marry someone."

She startled herself by speaking aloud, glanced round furtively, but there on the edge of twilight no one walked nearby. Every day that her wedding grew closer, her heart ached more and more. She loved Demet, she supposed, and she knew she was lucky to be allowed to marry a man she honestly did care for. I wish I could have gone with that Gel da'Thae bard instead of Jahdo, she thought. I wish I could see what lies off to the east, or to the south, or even off to the west, Gel da'Thae or no Gel da'Thae. Not that there was the slightest chance of her ever traveling, of course, not the slightest chance in the world.

Down at the shore stood a rickety wooden jetty, beaded with coracles. These little round boats belonged to everyone and no one; Niffa helped herself to the nearest. She laid her cloak on the thwart and rowed across the steamy lake to tie up at another jetty, then made a haphazard way to the actual shore, climbing from house to house and deck to deck until she gained solid ground. When she looked up, she could see lanterns bobbing up top the city wall. The town militia kept a perpetual guard, even in winter.

She climbed up a ladder to the catwalks and eventually found

Demet, her betrothed, over the east gate of the city. He was a blond lad, tall and on the beefy side, with a ready grin and pleasant blue eyes. He was grinning now, as he held his lantern up to see his visitor.

"And what be you doing, up on the walls? Going to join the militia?"

She laughed, laying a hand on his arm.

"I come with bad news, truly. Mam wants our wedding to wait till round the darkest day."

Demet swore, turning away and setting the lantern down in a niche on the wall proper.

"I did hope you'd be mine a bit sooner than that," he growled.

"And so did I."

He sighed, leaning on folded arms on the top of the wall. She could just reach to do the same. Out across the snowy dark, the moon was rising, full and pale against the winter stars.

"Here!" Demet said abruptly. "There be someone out there!"

Sure enough, when she followed his point she could see a figure, all wrapped in a cloak, judging from the silhouette, making a slow way through the snow toward the city. Demet hailed his sergeant, who came striding along to look.

"Well, now, it be needful to keep the gates shut, but whoever that may be, he'll freeze if he spends the night out there." The sergeant paused, chewing on his mustaches. "Well, now. I'm not sure what be best to do."

The guards consulted, arguing back and forth, calling down to an officer on the ground, while the figure walked closer and closer. Niffa suddenly felt a profound dread, a sick terror, as if she'd bitten into a piece of meat and tasted poison. Whoever that figure was, it meant nothing but harm to Cerr Cawnen. She wanted to cry out, to warn against opening the gate, to announce that better this creature freeze to death now and spare them all harm, but the words would not come, and who would be listening to the ratters' lass, anyway?

She pressed back against the wall as the officer in charge came bustling up the ladder, followed by Verrarc, the youngest member of the Council of Five. Bundled up in a cloak of the finest blue wool, trimmed with embroidered flowers round the hood, the councilman stood just about Demet's height, and he was as blond, too, though more slender. When he glanced Niffa's way with a polite nod, she shrank back and refused to look at him.

The officer grabbed the lantern and leaned over the wall just as the cloaked figure reached the gates.

"Who goes?" he bellowed.

"Oh, ye gods, have mercy!" It was a woman's voice, drifting up faint. "Let me in, I pray you. I've not eaten for days."

"Raena!" Verrarc called out. "It that really you?"

"It is, Verro. Oh please, have mercy!"

In a flood of orders, the councilman sent guards down to open the gates, then followed, smiling in the light of his lantern. Demet stayed with Niffa, who was waiting till the excitement died below to climb down. He glanced her way and rolled his eyes heavenward.

"So, her people must have turned her out," Demet said. "Sent her back to her lover, did they? I wonder if she'll be any more faithful to him than she was to her husband?"

Even though Niffa knew the story of Raena and Verrarc's old scandal as well as he did—after all, everyone in the town had talked of naught else, two years past—it took her a moment to figure out what he meant. The woman at the gates brought with her such a stink of bad omens that Niffa simply couldn't identify her with something as human as the councilman's adulterous love affair. Yet when she climbed down and saw the woman, she recognized her, even though Raena's long black hair was all matted and dirty, and she was no longer as fleshy as Niffa had been remembering. Thin and somehow shrunken, she clung to Verrarc's arm as he helped her hobble across the rough ground.

"She did have a bad time of it, then," Demet murmured, "if she did walk here from her people's farm up by Penli. That be a fair long journey."

Niffa stopped herself just in time from blurting out a sudden truth—that's not where she did come from, she's been elsewhere. She knew it even as she could never have said how she knew, just as she knew, in spite of herself, that letting Raena into Cerr Cawnen

408

was like clutching a rat to your breast. She looked up and found the moon, but as she watched, it sailed behind torn clouds and turned them to dirty fire.

And in the Lands, Evandar went to the silver river to free his brother from the oak, only to find tree and the soul within both gone. Where the oak had stood lay a raven's feather, blue-black and three feet long, left behind, no doubt, to mock him.

"So," he said aloud. "Our little friend has found herself a new god, has she? Now this will be a nuisance and a half!"

GLOSSARY

ABER (Deverrian) A river mouth, an estuary.

ALAR (Elvish) A group of elves, who may or may not be blood kin, who choose to travel together for some indefinite period of time.

ALARDAN (Elv.) The meeting of several alarli, usually the occasion for a drunken party.

ANGWIDD (Dev.) Unexplored, unknown.

ASTRAL The plane of existence directly "above" or "within" the etheric (q.v.). In other systems of magic, often referred to as the Akashic Record or the Treasure House of Images.

AURA The field of electromagnetic energy that permeates and emanates from every living being.

AVER (Dev.) A river.

BARA (Elv.) An enclitic that indicates that the preceding adjective in an elvish agglutinated word is the name of the element following the enclitic, as can+bara+melim = Rough River. (rough+name marker+river)

BEL (Dev.) The chief god of the Deverry pantheon.

BEL (Elv.) An enclitic, similar in function to bara, except that it indicates that a preceding verb is the name of the following element in the agglutinated term, as in Darabeldal, Flowing Lake.

BLUE LIGHT Another name for the etheric plane (q.v.).

BODY OF LIGHT An artificial thought-form (q.v.) constructed by a dweomermaster to allow him or her to travel through the inner planes of existence.

BRIGGA (Dev.) Loose wool trousers worn by men and boys.

BRIGHT COURT, DARK COURT I've chosen these terms for the traditional divide between the groups of Fair Folk, rather than using Seelie and Unseelie Court, names that are localized in our own world to Scotland.

BROCH (Dev.) A squat tower in which people live. Originally, in the homeland, these towers had one big fireplace in the center of the ground floor and a number of booths or tiny roomlets up the sides, but by the time of our narrative, this ancient style has given way to regular floors with hearths and chimneys on either side of the structure.

CADVRIDOC (Dev.) A warleader. Not a general in the modern sense, the cadvridoc is supposed to take the advice and counsel of the noble-born lords under him, but his is the right of final decision.

CAPTAIN (trans. of the Dev. *pendaely*) The second in command, after the lord himself, of a noble's warband. An interesting point is that the word *taely* (the root or unmutated form of *–daely*) can mean either a warband or a family depending on context.

CWM (Dev.) A valley.

DAL (Elv.) A lake.

DUN (Dev.) A fort.

DWEOMER (trans. of Dev. *dwunddaevad*) In its strict sense, a system of magic aimed at personal enlightenment through harmony with the natural universe in all its planes and manifestations; in the popular sense, magic, sorcery.

ELVES I have chosen this common name for the people the Deverrians call Elcyion Lacar (literally, the "bright spirits," or "Bright Fey"). They are also known as the Westfolk among men and dwarves, though the Dwarvish name for the race is Carx Taen. To the Gel da'Thae they are the Children of the Gods, Graekaebi Zo Uhmveo, while they call themselves, quite simply, Impar, the People.

ENSORCEL To produce an effect similar to hypnosis by direct manipulation of a person's aura. (True hypnosis manipulates the victim's consciousness only and thus is more easily resisted.)

ETHERIC The plane of existence directly "above" the physical. With its magnetic substance and currents, it holds physical matter in an invisible matrix and is the true source of what we call "life."

ETHERIC DOUBLE The true being of a person, the electromagnetic structure that holds the body together and that is the actual seat of consciousness.

GEIS, GEAS A taboo, usually a prohibition against doing something. Breaking geis results in ritual pollution and the disfavor if not active enmity of the gods. In societies that truly believe in geis, a person who breaks it usually dies fairly quickly, either of morbid depression or some unconsciously self-inflicted "accident," unless he or she makes ritual amends.

GEL DA'THAE Also known as the Horsekin, are a humanoid, naturally psychic race that lives to the north and west of Deverry proper. Their psychic talents manifest mostly as an enormous empathy with animals. To the elves they are the Meradan (lit. demons) or Hordes, because they destroyed the elven civilization of the far western mountains in ages past.

GEOMANCY A system of divination, codified during the late Middle Ages, involving the element of earth. The names of the figures used in this book having the following meanings: Albus, the White One; Cauda Draconis, the Dragon's Tail; Conjunctio, a Joining; Fortuna Minor, the Lesser Luck; Tristitia, Grief; Populus, the People.

GREAT ONES Spirits, once human but now disincarnate, who exist on an unknowably high plane of existence and who have dedicated themselves to the eventual enlightenment of all sentient beings. They are also known to the Buddhists as Boddhisattvas.

GWERBRET (Dev. The name derives from the Gaulish *vergobretes*.) The highest rank of nobility below the royal family itself. Gwerbrets (Dev. *gwerbretion*) function as the chief magistrates of their regions, and even kings hesitate to override their decisions because of their many ancient prerogatives.

HOB A male ferret. The females are called "jills," though for obvious reasons I've chosen not to use the term.

LWDD (Dev.) A blood-price; differs from wergild in that the amount of lwdd is negotiable in some circumstances, rather than being irrevocably set by law.

MAZRAK (Gel.) A shape-changer. A magician who can turn him or herself into animal form and back again at will.

MALOVER (Dev.) A full, formal court of law with both a priest of Bel and either a gwerbret or a tieryn in attendance.

MELIM (Elv.) A river.

MOR (Dev.) A sea, ocean.

PECL (Dev.) Far, distant.

RHAN (Dev.) A political unit of land; thus, gwerbretrhyn, tierynrhyn, the area under the control of a given gwerbret or tieryn. The size of the various rhans (Dev. rhannau) varies widely, depending on the vagaries of inheritance and the fortunes of war rather than some legal definition.

SCRYING The art of seeing distant people and places by magic.

SIGIL An abstract magical figure, usually representing either a particular spirit or a particular kind of energy or power. These figures, which look a lot like geometrical scribbles, are derived by various rules from secret magical diagrams.

TAER (Dev.) Land, country.

THOUGHT FORM An image or three-dimensional form that has been fashioned out of either etheric or astral substance, usually by the action of a trained mind. If enough trained minds work together to build the same thought form, it will exist independently for a period of time based on the amount of energy put into it. (Putting energy into such a form is known as *ensouling* the thought form.) Manifestations of gods or saints are usually thought forms picked up by the highly intuitive, such as children, or those with a touch of second sight. It is also possible for many untrained minds acting together to make fuzzy, ill-defined thought forms that can be picked up the same way, such as UFOs and sightings of the Devil.

TIERYN (Dev.) An intermediate rank of the noble-born, below a gwerbret but above an ordinary lord (Dev. *arcloedd*).

WYRD (trans. of Dev. *tingedd*) Fate, destiny; the inescapable problems carried over from a sentient being's last incarnation.

YNIS (Dev.) An island.

ABOUT THE AUTHOR

Katharine Kerr spent her childhood in a Great Lakes industrial city and her adolescence in a stereotypical corner of southern California, from whence she fled to the Bay Area just in time to join a number of the various Revolutions then in progress. Upon dropping out of dropping out, she got married and devoted herself to reading as many off-the-wall, obscure, and just plain peculiar books as she could get her hands on. As the logical result of such a life, she has now become a professional storyteller and an amateur skeptic, who regards all True Believers with a jaundiced eye, even those who true-believe in Science.

Kerr is the author of the Deverry series of historical fantasies: *Polar City Blues*; *Resurrection*; and the new trilogy, A *Time of War*, of which this is the second volume.